ANOM: LEGACY

by

Jason R. James

For my Mom and Dad,

with thanks for their

endless encouragement

and

boundless love.

PROLOGUE

Anna Jordan sat at the conference table, trying her best not to look bored. It was a losing battle. For the last fifteen minutes, John Theroux, the head of PR, had been droning on about advanced research into the field of genetic anomalies. It was mind-numbing—all of it. None of that was John's fault. The problem was the presentation itself. Each slide of the Power-Point was designed to induce boredom—to fill up time without ever saying anything important. It served as a preamble for their guests, a chance for them to drop their guard and gather their confidence. For Anna, it was the third time she'd sat through the presentation this week, and it was torture.

Across the conference table, Senator Franklin Ross from Texas wasn't faring any better. The old man's eyelids were half closed, and his chin rested heavily in his hand. The senator's aides, however, adopted a different demeanor. Ross was flanked by two men wearing near-identical gray suits. They both sat leaning over the table, feverishly taking notes on every word that escaped John's mouth. They didn't have a choice. It would fall to them to brief the senator on the details he'd missed in his stupor.

Anna had a different job. She sat at the table in her white blazer and blue silk blouse, her eyes fixed on the senator. She wore no jewelry and very little makeup. Her red hair was pulled back in a loose bun, and her delicate hands were folded, one over the other, on top of the table. It was a look achieved by careful design, intended to project authority.

"Which finally brings us to the Battle of Chicago," John said, pointing to the screen. "Reah Labs has analyzed over thirty independent media sources, and we can now say, with some degree of certainty, that the bronze man *was*, in fact, a genetic anomaly. We believe the first—"

"Cut all the horseshit!" Senator Ross sat forward in his chair, and now his eyes were fully open.

Anna forced a polite smile. "Thank you, John. I think that's all we need today. You're free to go."

"Yes, ma'am." John gathered his briefcase and nodded across the table at Ross. "Thank you for your time, Senator. If there's anything else you or your staff need..."

Ross didn't answer. John nodded again, this time at Anna, as he walked through the double

doors out of the conference room. Anna, however, kept her eyes fixed on Senator Ross. She
kept her hands folded on top of the table, and she
kept her thin smile chiseled on her face—all of it
perfectly practiced. She was waiting, her silence
a weapon.

The senator, on the other hand, looked agitated. He shifted his weight to one side of his
chair like he couldn't make himself comfortable, and he was unsure where to put his hands—
first on the table, then resting on the arms of his
chair, and finally one hand propped up under his
chin. She knew Ross had been waiting, too, and
now his patience was at an end.

The senator's aide on his left tried to speak.
"Senator Ross—"

"Shut up, Robert," Ross growled at the man,
shifting his weight in his chair again. "Pick up
your things and get out. Go on, the both of you."

Ross waited for the men to leave and the
doors to close behind them before he continued.
"You ready to tell me what I'm doing here, Miss
Jordan, or are you intent on wasting even more
of my time?"

"Senator Ross, I don't think—"

"'Cause I can tell you right now what I'm
doing here." Ross leaned back in his chair. "My
committee has been investigating your company for over a month now. Best I can tell,
either Reah Labs created that bronze man who
attacked Chicago, or at the very least, you knew

he was out there. Either way, you and your company are staring down the barrel, Miss Jordan, and you look to me like a woman in need of a favor."

Anna let the last word hang between them as she watched a smug grin spread across Ross's face. Like all men in power, the senator was proud of himself, even if the reason for that pride was inconsequential. In this case, Ross was gloating over his realization of the obvious. Anna would let him savor his moment—it was easier that way.

"Senator Ross," she started again, "we invited you here, but not because we're looking for any favors. We need a partner."

Ross laughed, slapping his hand down on the table. "Well, ain't you got some stones on you, Miss Jordan? I swear to God, you do. All right, then. Let me speak a little more plain. From where I'm sitting, your company's a sinking ship, and now you're asking me to climb up on board. That just ain't going to happen."

Anna opened the black portfolio in front of her and pulled out a paper. She slid it across the table to Ross.

The senator glanced down at the missive. "And what's this supposed to be?"

"It's a transcript of a secure communication between NORTHCOM and Colonel Edward McCann, the commanding officer at Fort Blaney." Anna pulled back the paper. "It shows that Colonel McCann disobeyed orders to observe and advise in Chicago. Instead, he ordered his men to directly intervene. What's worse, he ordered our genetic anomalies into combat, a role for which they were untrained and ill suited."

Ross chuckled. "You really expect anyone to believe this nonsense—that some no-name colonel went rogue and disobeyed a direct order from Northern Command? You really have no clue how our armed services work, do you Miss Jordan?"

"No, I suppose I don't, Senator Ross, but I can understand a man like you. So why don't we—what did you say before?—cut all the horseshit, and you give me a number? How much is it going to cost for you to believe that transcript?"

Ross rocked back in his chair again. "There are those stones I was talking about." He chuckled again. "All right, Miss Jordan, let's lay our cards down on the table, shall we? I know how much you're paying Johnson and how much you're paying Briggs, and they're only junior members on my committee. You're talking to the chairman, now. That means I get double."

"Of course you do, Senator." Anna smiled.

Anna rode up in the elevator alone with her thoughts. Her meeting with Senator Ross had gone even better than she expected. He had demanded twice as much money as she already paid to Johnson and Briggs, but in truth, Anna was willing to offer him four times as much—not that Ross needed to know that detail. She was just as happy letting the senator bask in another one of his victories. After all, he deserved it.

The elevator doors opened, and Anna stepped out. Across from her, a heavyset woman with a blonde bob smiled from behind a desk.

"Welcome back, Miss Jordan," the woman drawled in a thick southern accent. "You missed a pair of phone calls while you were out. The first one—"

Anna raised her hand. "I'm going to my office, Lois. I don't want any phone calls. I don't want any messages."

"But you need to—" Lois tried again.

Anna walked away without answering. She wasn't about to argue over phone calls with her secretary, for Christ's sake. She was the chief operating officer of the company, and if she wanted to be left alone for five minutes—or five hours, or five days—Lois would need to take down a message and hold it. Anna turned the corner, stepped inside her office, and slammed the door behind her harder than she intended. The meeting with Senator Ross was her third conference of the week, and Anna was exhausted.

The Battle of Chicago had proven to be a disaster for Reah Labs. It introduced the world to Anoms, but it came with a considerable price. In this case, a metal-skinned monster tried to raze the Willis Tower. Less than twenty-four hours after the battle, the President addressed a fearful nation. A week later, the Senate Select Committee on the Battle of Chicago was formed. Reah Labs was left scrambling in the aftermath, desperate to right their ship.

Anna stepped out of her high heels and walked around her desk to stare out the floor-to-ceiling window. She could see the familiar silhouette of the Willis Tower rising above the city to her right, and on her left, Lake Michigan stretched away to the horizon, reflecting the orange light of the setting sun.

She had never asked to become the public face of Reah Labs. It was just another part of her job—maybe the only part she truly resented. When Gwendolyn Thomas first offered her the position of Chief Operating Officer, Anna had jumped at the chance. It felt like a natural culmination—the opportunity of her dreams, really—but when Gwen outlined the role she would have to play in the public, Anna demurred. She had no interest in adding the pressures of public life to an already demanding job. It was the only time she ever truly argued with the Reah Labs CEO. She begged Gwen to find someone else, but Gwen's answer was simple: There *was* no one else.

Anna stepped away from the widow, lifting one of her hands to her mouth, ready to bite her fingernail. She stopped herself. Instead of biting down, she looked at the manicured pink nail, running her thumb back and forth over the smooth enamel. Biting her nails was a nervous habit from childhood, but Anna remembered she didn't do that anymore. She wasn't a child, and Anna Jordan didn't get nervous.

She understood the real problem with the Battle of Chicago was the timing of it all. If it had only occurred two weeks later, there would have been no Senate investigation necessary. Two more weeks, and Reah Labs could have played the hero. Two more weeks, and they would have launched Phase Three, a massive proposal to the U.S. government on the weaponization of genetic anomalies. It would have done for Reah Labs what the B-2 did for Northrop Grumman or what the Peacemaker did for Samuel Colt, but when the Red Moon took over the Willis Tower, Phase Three was rendered obsolete.

Maybe Gwen was right. She said Reah Labs would have been better served if the tower had just fallen. It was a terrible thought, and Anna felt instantly guilty for even entertaining it, but guilty or not, it didn't mean Gwen was wrong. Anna shook her head, trying to snap herself out of her own spiraling machinations. She just needed a break. She needed to clear her head. She needed...coffee.

Still on autopilot, Anna took the first dozen

steps towards the breakroom, staring down at her stocking feet padding over the carpeted floor, cycling through the endless to-do list in her head and wondering how any of it would possibly get done. Then a loud bang from the end of the hallway broke her concentration.

Anna looked up. The metal door to the emergency stairwell was kicked open, and two men wearing black SWAT uniforms poured into the hall. They wore Kevlar helmets, bulletproof vests, and gray-fogged goggles, and they each carried an MP5 submachine gun raised to their shoulder.

Anna knew they weren't cops. She could tell by the way they moved into the hallway. She had seen this before. These men were killers. Their uniforms were only a ruse; the white, block-lettered "POLICE" across their vests an expedient. They were Knights of the Crusade—fanatics—and they were there because of her.

Anna broke into a sprint down the hall, charging for the two men, desperate to close the distance. She could see their arms go tense, pulling their guns in tighter to their shoulders. They were taking aim.

Anna drew in her breath, and suddenly, everything around her went pitch black, plunged into absolute darkness. She dove forward, somersaulting over the carpet and landing at the feet of the two men. They opened fire.

Anna could hear the rapid percussion of gunfire somewhere over her head, but as she stared up at the ceiling, there was still no light.

If it were *only* darkness around her, Anna knew she would have seen the muzzle flashes over her head. The MP5s should have lit up the hallway like strobes in a nightclub, but they didn't, and Anna was the reason. As she held her breath, she twisted the visible light around the hallway, creating a void in space that was darker than pitched tar—oppressive and empty. They couldn't see, because she was literally holding back the visible light around them, stopping it from reaching their eyes.

Anna blinked and refocused, as she had been trained to do by the researchers at Reah Labs. Then, at least for her, the darkness around her transformed. Now she was seeing through the ultraviolet rays of the spectrum, and the two men standing over her were outlined in pale light. It was like looking at the negatives from a roll of film.

The two men emptied their weapons, but they had missed her. They dropped out their magazines to reload, but Anna knew more bullets wouldn't do them any good. She rose silently back to her feet, and all the danger she had felt running down the hallway—all of that fear —it slipped away. She drew a push dagger from the waistband of her skirt and wedged the small

14

triangular blade between her middle and ring fingers, sizing up the first man on her right. If this were another fight—if he could actually see her—Anna knew she would already be dead. But now, in the darkness, this was going to be easy.

Anna punched the dagger deep into the man's neck, twisting the blade, and a wet, gurgling sound came from his throat. She ripped it free, and a spray of hot blood splashed across her face.

The second man called out in the darkness, "Collins?"

Anna reached for the pistol strapped to the second man's hip. She pulled it free from its holster and pointed it at the center of the second man's face.

The man called out again, and Anna could hear the panic in his voice. "Collins?"

Anna let go of her breath, and all at once, the darkness dropped away. Light flooded the hallway. Now, she could see the man in his dark SWAT uniform in perfect detail, and the man could see her. He tried to swing around his MP5, but Anna pulled her trigger first. The second man jerked back into the wall and slid down, lifeless, a red smear trailing on the white plaster as he sank to the floor.

Anna flipped the safety on and tucked the pistol into the waistband of her skirt. Then she knelt over the second man and picked up his machine gun. She pulled back the charging handle, let it go, and started back toward the elevator.

"Miss Jordan! Miss Jordan!" Lois shrieked from behind her desk, waving her arms wildly in the air.

"Shut up, Lois!" Anna barked, "Get Gwen on the phone. Now!"

"Yes, Miss Jordan." Lois snatched up the phone and started to dial, but then, without warning, she hung up the receiver and rose calmly from her desk. The woman seemed entirely different to Anna than she had appeared only a moment before. The look of terror that had been etched on her face was smoothed away, both of her arms were resting at her sides instead of flailing over her head, and her shrill voice had dropped an octave and somehow lost its Southern drawl.

"You don't have to use the phone, love. I'm right here," Lois said.

Anna closed her eyes. She hated it whenever Gwen talked through one of her puppets, like she was doing now with Lois. It was one thing to control a person's actions—to move them about like pieces on a chessboard—but when she turned someone else into her personal walkie talkie, it set Anna's skin crawling.

"The Knights of the Crusade are here," Anna said, trying to imagine Gwen standing in front of her instead of Lois.

"I'm well aware. You should come upstairs and join me for a drink. Leave the machine gun with Lois," Lois said, smiling.

Anna held out the MP5.

"Thank you, Miss Jordan," Lois said, the natural tenor and drawl back in her voice.

Anna thought about using the elevator, but if there were other Knights in the building, it wasn't worth the risk. The last thing she needed to do was wait for an elevator only to have it arrive carrying a small platoon. Instead, she opted for the stairs.

Anna pulled the Beretta from behind her back and climbed the steps two at a time. On the landing between the two floors, she had to step over a twisted body wearing dark tactical gear. His partner, dressed in a similar Kevlar vest and helmet, laid sprawled on his back over the next flight of stairs, his throat slashed open with a jagged cut. She hurried past the bodies and stepped through the emergency door at the top of the stairs.

Anna looked over the reception area in front of Gwen's office and saw that it was empty, but a flash of movement in her periphery made her think again. She wheeled around, raising her gun, but by a miracle, she stopped herself from pulling the trigger. John Theroux was standing there with his back against the wall, a pair of office scissors poised above his head.

"Jesus, John." Anna lowered her gun.

"Sorry, love. Can't be too careful." John winked at her.

Anna didn't need the second tell. "Love,"

would have been more than enough. John Theroux would never dare call her that. This was Gwen trying to be funny.

"Well, here. Take this, *love*." Anna pushed the Beretta into John's empty hand. "I could've killed him you know."

John shrugged. "I have others."

Anna crossed the reception room to the double oak doors leading into Gwen's office, but before she could grab hold of the handle, the doors pulled open from the inside.

"Hi, Anna. Come in," a man's voice sang from the office.

Anna stepped through the open doors. On the other side, Noah Kincaid smiled sheepishly, looking down at his feet, and rubbing his thumb back and forth over a worn leather keychain. Noah was tall and thin, with a stretched face and a sharp Adam's apple. His hair was a mop of blonde, and a pair of white headphones hugged his ears. He wore a pair of dark blue jeans, black sneakers, and a red zip-up hoodie over a gray tee. It was a sloppy look that Gwendolyn Thomas wouldn't have tolerated from anyone else, but Noah was her bodyguard and her favorite, and she decreed a long time ago that he could wear whatever he liked.

Anna smiled at him. "Hi, Noah. Did you kill —"

"Yes," Noah answered, almost laughing, his eyes never looking up from his shoes. "I saw—I saw them coming, so I— I knew they were coming, and so I— I killed them both."

Anna took a deep breath and forced herself to finish the original question. "Did you kill the two men in the stairwell?"

It was still difficult—finishing her sentences when Noah had already interrupted with his answer—but it was important to Gwen, and Anna had committed herself to doing better.

Noah Kincaid was an Anom like Anna, only Noah's gift was time. His testing showed reliable predictive accuracy up to six seconds in advance. It was like he had started watching some movie six seconds before everyone else on the planet, and so he always knew what was coming next. It made him an effective bodyguard—in a fight, six seconds was a lifetime—but there were other challenges, like answering questions before they were asked.

Across the room, Gwendolyn Thomas sat behind her glass desk, her elbows resting on the arms of her chair and her fingertips steepled together. She was five years older than Anna, but certainly no one would guess their age difference by looking at Gwen. Her dark-brown hair fell pin-straight to her shoulders, and her pale blue eyes stared a thousand miles into the distance. Her skin was alabaster and flawless, as always, and now, sitting behind her desk, Anna thought she looked like grace and power in equal measure.

Anna crossed the room and sat down in one of the chairs facing the desk.

Gwen closed her eyes. "I offered you a drink, love. God knows you've earned it."

Anna shook her head. "Not now. How many Knights are still left in the building?"

"Four... No, three," Gwen smiled, correcting herself. "They're down to three, but that was only the first wave. They were feeling us out, I'm afraid. The second attack is starting now in the lobby. If you don't want any coffee, love, at least go to the sink and wash your face. You look a mess."

Anna crossed the room to the wet bar and turned on the faucet. She grabbed a handful of napkins and held them under the water. "How many people are you controlling?"

Gwen opened her eyes. "There are thirty Knights rushing into the lobby as we speak. Two more are climbing the east stairs. I have everyone else in the building under my control—a virtual army to keep us safe."

"And the Knights?" Anna asked, "Can you take control of any of them?"

Gwen frowned. "No, they've locked me out again. Each one of our invaders has been mentally spiked. It seems the Knights of the Crusade are learning from their past mistakes."

Anna leaned over the sink, suddenly light-headed.

"What's wrong?" Gwen chided from behind

her desk. "We both knew this day was coming. We've been operational in Chicago for six months now, and with all that's happened, it was only a matter of time. As much as we like to kid ourselves, the Knights aren't stupid."

"I know that." Anna dabbed the wet napkins across her face. "I just—I thought we'd have more time."

"And I thought we got more time than we deserved. We were careless at the end, Anna, partly out of necessity. We'll need to do better when we move out west. After we finish here, we can discuss our plans to—" Gwen's voice cut out.

Anna spun away from the sink to look at her. "What is it? What's wrong?"

Gwen's hands had come down. Now they were clutching the arms of her chair, and her face was ghost-white, somehow paler than usual.

"Gwen, what is it?" Anna tried again, hoping to steady her voice.

"He's here." Gwen stood up, walking around her desk. "They brought the Incubus—he's just entered the lobby with the Knights. They want to end it here."

"Are you sure it's him?" Anna felt a lead weight drop into her stomach. "Where is he now?"

Gwen ignored her. Instead, she turned to Noah. "Call up to the helicopter and tell them to get ready. We're leaving."

Anna grabbed Gwen by her arm, trying to get

her to focus. "Where is the Incubus *now*?"

Gwen pulled away. "Everyone in the lobby is dead, so I don't know where he is. On his way up here, I imagine." Gwen forced the smile back to her face. "So, are you coming, love?"

Outside of Gwen's office, John Theroux stood waiting, his Beretta in one hand and his scissors in the other, ready to attack anyone who came up the stairs; Gwen touched her hand to his cheek. "John, you're doing great, but now I need you to focus yourself on the elevators. Kill anyone who tries to enter this room. Do you understand me?"

"Yes, ma'am." John turned to face the elevators, taking his aim at the metal doors.

"Wait, let me get the gun back." Anna reached out for the Beretta, but Gwen grabbed her by the wrist.

"Let him have it. We won't need it," Gwen said.

Anna tried to twist away. "But if the Incubus reaches us—"

Gwen pulled Anna by the wrist again. "If he reaches us, then we're already dead. That's why we're running, love."

Noah was the first one up the stairs, kicking open the door at the top of the landing and stumbling outside onto the roof. Gwen and Anna both followed him. Outside, the sun was sinking below the horizon. The cold wind swirled past Anna's face, and for a second, it stole her breath. She could see the helicopter waiting on the other side of the building, its rotor blades slowly spinning in place but ramping up faster and faster. They were almost to safety. The three of them started together in a sprint across the roof.

Suddenly, Noah stopped. He turned and threw his arm across Gwen's shoulder, pushing her back into one of the exhaust vents, pinning her against the aluminum wall. In the same breath, he reached behind him, grabbed Anna by her arm, and dragged her down to her knees. A second later, a chunk of gravel kicked up in front of them on the roof.

"It's a sniper," Noah said.

Gwen looked back at the stairs, twisting under Noah's arm. "Fine, but we can't stay here, either. We can't, Noah."

Anna pressed her back against the exhaust vent and pushed herself up to her feet. They were only twenty yards away from the helicopter, but if a sniper had an angle on the roof, it may as well have been miles. "Maybe we can make a run for it?"

Noah shook his head.

Now Anna looked back at the door leading to the stairs, too. She knew that Gwen was right: They couldn't wait much longer. Run across the roof now, and the sniper would probably kill them. Wait for the Incubus, and there would be no doubt.

Anna took Gwen and Noah by their hands. "You stay with me and don't let go."

Anna drew in her breath, and as the darkness wrapped over them, she took off running for the helicopter, pulling Gwen and Noah behind her. She knew, in her head, there was still a risk they might die. The sniper could fire into the darkness and get lucky, but at least now they had a chance.

Another step and they reached their escape. Anna pulled Gwen and Noah inside the helicopter, and as she let go of her breath, the pitch-black air fell away. Then the helicopter lifted from the roof and climbed into the darkening sky.

CHAPTER 1

Jeremy Cross was falling. He could feel the air blistering past his face and the wind screaming in his ears. He was going to die.

Below him, he could see the bronze man, Titan, falling, too. He twisted through the air, flailing his arms. The metal man was going to die, just like Jeremy—and Titan wanted to live.

Then Titan hit the ground. Even across all that distance—even with the roar of the air pounding inside his ears—Jeremy could still hear the dull resonance of impact. He could see the splintered bricks and the crater of dark brown earth opening under him, and at the very center, he could see the broken body of Titan.

Jeremy knew he'd be next unless he found a way to stop himself—to zero out his gravity. Jeremy strained his fingers, reaching for the air around him, trying to hold himself in place. Only it didn't work, and now he was out of time.

Suddenly, Jeremy was standing upright on the ground, somehow still alive, facing the crater left by Titan. Jeremy walked to its edge and looked down. At the bottom, Titan was gone, and a different body had taken his place. It was Talon.

Talon looked just like Jeremy remembered him, with his dark hair and thin beard. He was smiling, because Talon was always smiling, but now he was lying face-up in the dirt, and pale pink blood streamed from both sides of his mouth. His blank eyes were staring up into the sky, and one of his legs had twisted sharply under his body. He wasn't moving. Jeremy knew he was dead.

Then he heard Talon's voice. It rose from the bottom of the crater, thin and gasping for air. "Help... me..."

Jeremy felt his stomach turn to water. Why was he just standing there? Talon needed help. Jeremy needed to get down into the crater. He needed to get Talon out. There was still time. He just needed to move, and he could still save him, but Jeremy held his place. It was like both of his feet had sunk into the ground, and now all he could do was stand there and watch.

Then Jeremy felt someone waiting behind him. He wheeled around, ready to fight, just as a bronze hand clamped around his throat, lifting him off his feet and hoisting him into the air. Jeremy fought for air, but it was no use. Titan's grip only tightened around his neck.

Jeremy wanted to raise his gravity. He wanted to fight back and break free. He wanted to rip off Titan's arm just like he had done before. He just needed to breathe, and he couldn't. He couldn't breathe. He couldn't—

Jeremy opened his eyes and fell to the floor, slamming against the cold tiles with a dull thud. He gasped for air and rolled onto his side.

"Lights," Jeremy coughed into the floor, and the sound cut off in his throat. He managed another heavy breath, filling his lungs the best he could. And another, slower this time. And another.

Finally, Jeremy rolled onto his back and tried again. "Lights."

This time, the computer recognized his voice, and the lights came on. Jeremy pushed himself up against the side of his bed, letting his head loll back onto the mattress. He rubbed his eyes, staring straight up at the ceiling.

"Time?"

The soft, electronic voice answered, "The time is three thirty-eight in the morning."

"Perfect."

Jeremy struggled to his feet and stumbled into the bathroom. The lights were always brighter in there, and he half-closed his eyes against the glare of the fluorescents. His head was killing him. It felt like someone was hammering a nail through his forehead, and with every breath he took, they somehow managed another swing.

Jeremy reached inside the shower stall and

cranked the water to hot. Then he turned away and slapped his hand down on the counter, feeling around for the small bottle of aspirin without looking. He picked it up and gave it a shake, hoping he was wrong. There was no sound—no rattle from inside. It was empty.

He threw the bottle against the wall and looked at himself in the mirror. "Bet you're loving this, aren't you, Dad?"

Jeremy turned on the faucet and slurped a handful of the water. Then he filled his hand again and splashed the water into his face, running it over the back of his head.

He focused on his reflection. "Good talk, Dad. Thanks for the advice."

He turned away and stepped into the shower and the cloud of steam.

Jeremy's dreams had started the week after Chicago. They were always different, but also eerily the same. Every night, he found himself back in the city. He was either standing on the observation deck of Willis Tower, or he was down inside the building, trying to stop the explosion, or he was waiting on the ground outside, watching it all happen without him. Talon was always there, too. Usually, he was already dead. Sometimes he was still dying. A couple of times, Jeremy was the one who actually broke him in half. In his dreams, he could feel himself punching Talon over and over again. Then he would grab him by the arms and squeeze until the bones in Talon's spine shattered. Other times, Titan was the one responsible for killing Talon. Jeremy would be forced to stand there, frozen in place, and he would watch it all happen.

The headaches started soon after the dreams. Jeremy would wake up in a cold sweat, or gasping for air, or falling to the ground—sometimes all three—and his skull would feel like it was being wedged apart from the inside out. After a week of migraines, he complained to Dr. Barnes. That's when he got the aspirin. When he finished the first bottle, he got another. Yesterday, he finished the third. He wasn't sure if the headaches were caused by the lack of sleep or something else. Honestly, he didn't care. After three straight months, he just wanted it to stop.

Jeremy sat on the edge of his bed and got dressed—blue compression shirt with black, military-issue pants and boots. It was as close as he got to a uniform. The clock on the video screen read four twelve in the morning. Now he would have to wait. The magnetic locks on his door wouldn't release until five. He learned that much the day after Chicago.

Jeremy rolled back his shoulders, edged off his bed, and laid out on his stomach on the floor. He put his knuckles down on the cold tile and started doing pushups. Anything was better than sitting alone with his thoughts. He learned that the day after Chicago, too.

Forty-five minutes later, a dull buzzing filled the room. Jeremy stood up, and the alarm intended to wake him up shut off automatically. He stepped to his door, and it slid open. From the other side of the Rec Room, Nyx's door opened a second later.

Just like Jeremy, Nyx was already dressed in her uniform—a dark purple compression shirt with black pants and boots. She wore a pair of leather fingerless gloves, and her dark hair was pulled back in a taut French braid. Apparently, she'd been up early, too.

Nyx was another Anom in the program. While Jeremy could manipulate the gravitational fields around his body, Nyx controlled something closer to pure energy. She could teleport around the battlefield in flashes of light or blast her enemies with bolts of energy fired from her hands. She was with Jeremy in Chicago when they faced off against Titan, and he knew she was the only reason more people didn't die. When Major Ellison's plan to rescue the hostages got shot to hell, Nyx was the one who decided to improvise. She teleported all the hostages to safety. She was the hero that day.

Now, she smiled at Jeremy from across the Rec Room. "What time for you?"

"Three thirty. You?"

"Closer to three... not that it's a competition." They walked together to the kitchen at the back of the Rec Room. Nyx moved to the counter, found a bowl, and poured in a packet of oatmeal.

Jeremy sat down on one of the stools and poured his own cereal into a bowl, splashing it with milk. "How are your hands?"

Nyx flexed her fingers. "Still sore. I'll have to go easier today. What about your head?"

Jeremy pushed his spoon through his cereal. "Same as yesterday."

Another door on the left wall slid open, and Jeremy and Nyx both turned to see Gauntlet step into the Rec Room. Just like every other day they had been together, Gauntlet's body was already wrapped in his blood-red armor, with heavy, black vambraces over his forearms, and his head was encased in his red helmet, his eyes hidden behind the obsidian black lenses. Jeremy could see the hilt of his broadsword rising over his shoulder.

Gauntlet was a warrior—strong, fast, and precise. As far as genetic powers, Jeremy couldn't explain anything more than that—Gauntlet was a fighter. In Chicago, he cut through an army and held off Titan when no one else could stand against him. Gauntlet had been willing to sacrifice everything that day, and for Jeremy, knowing that was enough.

Now, Gauntlet walked into the kitchen and sat down next to Jeremy, but as he perched on his stool, his armored helmet split vertically down its middle. Then it peeled away from his head, separating left and right, folding down over Gauntlet's shoulders like a pair of medieval pauldrons, exposing his face. Jeremy and Nyx both waited.

"Pass the cereal," Gauntlet said. "Please."

Jeremy had to smile. Even after all these months, the man under the armor was still a surprise. He was older than Jeremy, with auburn hair and deep-set brown eyes. Freckles were scattered across his nose. It was a face that was somehow too normal. Jeremy had seen for himself what Gauntlet was capable of in a fight. Looking now at the man's face, it was hard to believe.

Jeremy pushed the box of cereal across the kitchen island. It still felt awkward, meeting like this every morning for "family breakfast." That's what Jeremy called it.

It was a routine that started the first day after Chicago. Even then, it wasn't planned. They had just found each other early the next morning. They needed to be together, needed to sit with someone else who was there. It happened again on the second day, the three of them finding each other in the kitchen before the morning briefing. They met again the day after that. Three months later, and it was still routine.

It wasn't exactly a friendship—Jeremy understood that much. Rather, it was something else, a bond forged from common experience. That didn't make it any less real, or any less valuable. They needed each other.

Gauntlet poured his cereal into a bowl. Jeremy looked down at his own breakfast. The rings were fat and bloated with milk. He hadn't been hungry before, but he was less hungry now.

Jeremy let go of his spoon. "Are you both sure you want to do this?"

Nyx pulled her oatmeal from the microwave and walked to the island. "Yes. Why? Do you not?"

"I didn't say that. It's just—"

Nyx sat down. "It's been three months, G. We have every right to see him."

"I know that," Jeremy answered.

The math was easy to understand. Four of them had gone into the Willis Tower. Only three had walked away. The fourth member of their team, Talon, was carried out on a stretcher. He was the one who was ordered to engage Titan—the one who had to stand toe to toe with the bronze man. He had been outmatched from the start.

For a while, they weren't sure Talon would even make it. Jeremy remembered the list of injuries: a fractured skull, crushed hand, broken ribs, a collapsed lung, a ruptured spleen, and a shattered spinal column. It was a miracle he was alive at all.

For the first month, Major Ellison would keep them up to date with a single sentence: "Talon remains in critical condition." Eventually, even those reports stopped. That's when they figured out, if nothing else, Talon would live.

Jeremy pushed his bowl of cereal away. "All right. So, we ask to see Talon. What do we do if they tell us no?"

Nyx shook her head. "They won't. They can't. It's been three months."

An electronic ping sounded from the elevator, and the double steel doors slid open as Major Stuart Ellison stepped into the Rec Room. He was dressed in his gray camouflage with his sleeves rolled up to his biceps. His straw-brown hair was cut high and tight, and his soft face was fresh-shaven—the model soldier, always. He carried his tablet under one arm, and he walked directly to the conference table and pulled out his chair.

"Let's get started," he said, never looking over at the kitchen.

Behind Ellison, Lara Miller walked toward the table. She wore a navy pencil skirt and matching jacket over her white blouse. Her blonde hair was pulled back in a loose bun, and today she wore her glasses.

Lara served as a bridge between the two worlds—the Army and the Anoms. She was an employee of Reah Labs, charged with coordinating civilian researchers on the base, but she was also the company's liaison to the Army. Almost everyone at Fort Blaney referred to her by her code name, Mirror—an apt enough description considering her abilities. Jeremy was the lone exception. Before Chicago, he insisted on calling her Lara. It felt so important at the time. Now, he didn't know what to call her. They had barely spoken since the event.

Behind Lara, Agent Dubov wheeled himself out of the elevator and into the Rec Room. Jeremy bristled at the very sight of the man. Dubov was confined to a wheelchair, missing both his legs below the knee, and in place of his hands, he brandished a pair of silver hooks. He was pale and bald—even missing his eyebrows—and his face consisted of only sharp angles—his defined cheekbones and thin nose leading down to a pointed chin.

Dubov was supposed to belong to the CIA, but Jeremy had his doubts. He first appeared at their morning briefings a week after Chicago, introduced by Ellison as a "special consultant". Not long after, he was also sitting next to Lara during her individual debriefing sessions, but the man would never speak. That's what Jeremy hated most about him. He would sit and watch, and every so often, you would hear the soft metallic click of his claws tapping together, like he was strumming his fingers.

Now, Dubov maneuvered his chair to the other side of Ellison just as Jeremy and Nyx took their seats. Gauntlet, as always, remained standing.

"There were no developments overnight," Ellison started, reading from his tablet. "The groups we've identified as recruiting Anoms—the Ryoku, Kamen Molotochek, the Knights of the Crusade, and a half-dozen smaller fringe militias are all reporting back as normal chatter. No imminent threats reported. As for the Red Moon, communications are dark. Looks like they're still recovering from their setback in Chicago—"

"Sure they are." Jeremy leaned back in his chair, almost laughing.

Ellison glared back across the table, but as quick as the anger flashed over him, it was gone—replaced by something much colder.

"Advanced training exercises are canceled again today," Ellison continued, "In fact, looking at the numbers, we're taking you all back to individual research training, starting with baseline testing."

Now, Jeremy laughed out loud. "Three months after Chicago, and you're still wasting our time with this bullshit. We should be training for our next fight, and you know it."

Ellison didn't answer. He fixed his eyes on Jeremy and held his tongue, but whatever patience he could muster was spent. Jeremy could see the raw emotions rippling over the major's face, and he didn't care—he simply didn't care if Ellison exploded with his threats and bile. He knew what the man really thought of Anoms—what he thought of Jeremy most of all—and pretending any different was pointless.

Lara shook her head. "Jeremy, don't do this."

"He knows what he's doing." Jeremy turned away from the table to look at Nyx. "Hell, we all know what he's doing. He's setting us up to fail—again. Just like Chicago."

Lara still shook her head. "That's not true. We're all working for the same thing."

Ellison didn't answer.

Then Nyx found her voice. "We don't care about the training. I'm sorry, Major, but we don't. If you want baseline testing, we can do that, but it's been three months. We want to see Talon before we do anything else. We're not asking this time. You can't keep us away from him after three months."

"I actually wasn't finished with my briefing," Ellison answered, and now a slow smile spread over his face. "It seems there's one last item I need to cover. Your friend, Talon, has been transferred out of Fort Blaney. He'll continue his recovery at another Reah Labs facility."

Nyx paled. "What? When? Why would you move him?"

"It happened last night," Ellison said. "We wanted to avoid the distraction."

Then Jeremy fixed his eyes on Lara. "Last night, huh? How do you like that? It's almost like the Major knew what we were going to ask him."

Ellison still smiled, but Lara looked down at her hands folded on top of the table. For the moment, none of them spoke, and the only sound was the faint metallic click of Dubov tapping his claws, one against the other.

Finally, Ellison pushed back from the table and rose to his feet. "So, we should start the day."

CHAPTER 2

Ellison looked down at his own watch. It was just before six forty-five in the morning. He was still early. It had taken less time than he'd expected to quell the Anoms' unrest. He thought, at first, there would be more pushback when he told them about Talon's transfer. He was wrong. They resigned themselves with barely a word, and now all three of the Anoms were locked behind closed doors, engaged in individual research training.

If they had taken a stand—if they had cared enough to challenge him and refused to cooperate in their training—maybe Ellison would have found something there to admire. They hadn't, and now it was one more reason why he was certain the Anoms would fail, with or without him.

On the field of battle, devotion to the unit —the bond between brothers-in-arms—could prove invaluable. It allowed the individual to go beyond his own capacity. It was power, but power absent of discipline was lost in chaos. Loyalty may have been the fire, but discipline was the steel. Ellison was convinced the Anoms possessed neither.

Mirror told him last night about their plan to see Talon. She had gleaned the information from her debriefing with Nyx, but even before Mirror's confirmation, Ellison suspected something like it was brewing. He had seen the seeds of sedition before, first at the Citadel and again in Afghanistan. It was always ugly—always the work of cowards, idiots, or both—men who felt backed into a corner. When they were only asking to see Talon it was one thing, even though it promised nothing more than distraction. *Demanding* to see Talon, at the threat of refusing orders... That was something else. It would prove the first step down the road to insurrection, and Ellison preferred to stop that trek before it could get started. The only surprise was how quickly the Anoms gave up.

Ellison turned to Mirror in the hallway. "Go to the infirmary and start your rounds. I'll need a full status report on each subject when you're done. Then I want to meet with all Reah Labs staff in the afternoon to get a debriefing on the morning training sessions. I'll expect full reports from each team."

"That's not a problem," Mirror said, avoiding Ellison's eye, "but I'm still not sure what just happened. I told you they would ask to see Talon. Why aren't we letting them? It might actually do *him* some good, too—remind him what he's working for."

"That's not your decision," Ellison answered.

Lara shook her head. "I know that. That's not what I'm saying. I just... I don't understand."

"And you don't need to understand," Ellison said, "I made the decision for the good of my team, and it was backed by Colonel McCann. Now, is there anything else, or can you start your evaluations?"

Mirror went rigid, raising her hand in mock salute. "No, sir." Then she walked away toward the elevator. Ellison watched her go. Behind him, he could hear the metallic click of Dubov tapping his hooks.

"What do you think of her, Major?" Dubov asked, his voice almost whistling between his teeth.

Ellison waited for the elevator doors to close before he answered. "I think Agent Mirror is still recovering after Chicago. I think she's under considerable stress, just like the rest of us."

Dubov clicked his tongue, and it sounded eerily like his tapping hooks. "Maybe she is, but then again, maybe she's not." Dubov turned away in his chair. "It's difficult for any of us to evaluate a person when we're... Well, when you're as close as the two of you seem to be. Don't you think so, Major?"

Ellison could feel the muscles in his neck tighten. He understood Dubov's implication perfectly—just as the man intended—but why bring up his sleeping with Mirror now? Was it some kind of veiled threat on Ellison's career? To what end? A warning for the major to keep in line? Or, if not a threat, then why mention it at all?

Ellison thought about wrapping his hands around Dubov's throat and throttling him in his wheelchair. A satisfying fantasy, maybe, but an impossible answer. Dubov was under the authority of Agent Hayden, and that made him untouchable, at least for now.

Instead, Ellison choked back his own pride. "Agent Mirror is the least of my concerns."

"Maybe she is. Maybe she's not."

Ellison turned and walked away. He wouldn't waste any more of his time trying to placate Dubov. He had real duties that required his attention, starting with his morning briefing with Colonel McCann. Ellison turned the corner, stepped directly to the Colonel's door, and knocked.

McCann barked from the other side. "Come in."

Ellison opened the door and saw McCann sitting behind his desk. A layer of white papers and manila folders covered the desktop like the first snowfall of winter. They were all strewn about, facing in different directions without any purpose or order—a reflection of the colonel himself over these last months.

Ellison had noticed the change in McCann almost immediately—the strain in the old man's eyes, the tightness in his voice, his patience with the men growing thinner by the day—and at first, Ellison tried to ignore it. He had hoped it was a momentary lapse, but now, three months later, there were no signs of improvement.

The part of McCann that made him a soldier—the character he honed to a razor's edge—had been dulled. Instead, that essential piece of the colonel's character had been replaced by a politician's paranoia, always looking ahead and planning the next turn in his career.

Ellison could see that now. What was worse, the men could see it, too. They could see how desperate McCann was to tighten his grip over his command, but soldiers rarely respond to desperation. The tighter McCann held, the further Fort Blaney slipped away from his grasp. Ellison understood that the men—his men—would never follow a politician. They needed a soldier.

Chicago had taken its toll on McCann. It should have been heralded as a complete success—the first field application of genetic anomaly warfare. It should have been celebrated for saving the Willis Tower and countless lives in the process. It should have been the old man's crowning victory. It was none of those things.

As soon as the fight spilled out of the tower and onto the street, the narrative had to change. The world watched as a bronze man killed soldiers and Chicago police on live television. In the aftermath, people were afraid, angry, and confused. They wanted answers, and the first answer was obvious. Someone needed to own the Battle of Chicago—someone would have to fall on their sword—and blood, just like shit, ran downhill. The old man realized as much. He understood that his military career would soon be over, and he was afraid.

McCann leaned back in his chair, raising his black Army mug to his lips. "Good morning, Stuart. How did things go?"

Ellison stepped forward and folded his hands behind his back, adopting the posture of parade rest. He was about to launch into his morning report, but before he could begin, a familiar voice spoke from behind him.

"Tell us all about it, Major. How many rebels did you get to execute this morning?"

Ellison refused to turn around. He didn't need to. The thin, Irish voice behind him was unmistakable. Hayden stepped past the Major and pulled out one of the chairs in front of the colonel's desk. He sat down, leaned back, and crossed his legs at the ankles, fishing inside his jacket pocket for his cigarettes.

Ellison could feel the bile rising in his own throat. He hated everything about the man seated next to him—his stringy blonde hair, his wrinkled suits, and his incessant smoking. Most of all, Ellison despised Hayden for his air of superiority—the way he carried himself around the base, as if he were watching everyone else play some elaborate game. Hayden was supposed to be an outsider, an observer—a nobody. At least that was the lie Ellison told himself before he learned the darker truth, because in practice, Hayden was none of those things. Instead, he was the only power that actually mattered at Fort Blaney, pulling the strings of Reah Labs and the Army alike, but Hayden was also a small man, and Ellison knew he deserved better.

Hayden flipped open his lighter and touched the flame to the end of his cigarette. "Go ahead, Stuart. Tell us all about it."

Ellison choked down his bile; he wouldn't let himself be baited. "This morning went as we expected. They asked to see Talon. We told them he was transferred. They seemed to accept that answer."

McCann arched his eyebrows. "So the remaining Anoms are in testing now?"

"Yes, sir."

Hayden clapped his hands with mock applause. "Major Ellison, our hero."

"And the rest of your report?" McCann asked.

"There's nothing else worth reporting, sir. Normal chatter from our watch list, but nothing specific. Still nothing from the Red Moon. It was a quiet night."

"That's not what I heard." Hayden smiled, his top lip curling over the stray tooth sticking out from the others. "All that information right at your fingertips, and you still manage to miss something important. I suppose that's the Army for you. Isn't that right, Major?"

Ellison bristled. "I pulled the overnight reports myself. There's nothing—"

"Tell your team to search Ryoku communications for the Chinese phrase 'Pòmén.' I assume they can handle that much," Hayden said.

Ellison's jaw tightened. "And what the hell is Pòmén?"

Hayden pulled the cigarette from his mouth and blew out a thin line of smoke. "From what I understand, it's the name of the Ryoku's newest Anom recruit. Translates to 'broken gate' or 'broken door'—some bullshit like that. Maybe he can turn his pinky finger into a skeleton key."

"But the Ryoku are Japanese..." Ellison said.

Hayden laughed. "Is that so? Well, I wonder why they're speaking another language then, Major, because if the Ryoku were expanding their reach into China, that seems like the kind of thing your men should already know?"

Colonel McCann sat forward in his chair. "Have Captain Reyes look into it. Whoever this Broken Gate is, we need to know, and the sooner the better."

"Yes, sir," Ellison answered.

"Now, is there anything else?" McCann shuffled through the papers on his desk, looking for something, but only vaguely glancing at each of the missives. "Any word about the Senate investigation into Chicago?"

Ellison shook his head. The question itself was simple enough, but the anxiety woven between the words was unmistakable. Only three months ago, McCann would have marched into the Command Center himself to get to the bottom of the Ryoku and the Broken Gate, and he would have told the politicians in DC to go to hell with their investigation. Not anymore. Now, he hid behind his desk, and he looked old.

Ellison found his voice. "No, sir, there's nothing new from the Select Committee on Chicago. They reconvene on Wednesday."

"Good." McCann rose from his seat. "Then I think that's everything for this morning, Major. You're dismissed."

Ellison raised his hand in salute. McCann answered with the same. Then Ellison turned on his heels and stepped out of the room, walking for the elevator. He would need to talk to Captain Reyes in the Command Center. If they really missed the Ryoku recruiting a new Anom from China, someone would have to answer for it, but for now, that could wait. Ellison was expected in the infirmary.

When the silver doors of the elevator slid open again, Dr. Barnes was waiting on the other side.

Ellison offered a quick nod as he stepped out. "Doctor."

"Nice of you to join us today, Major. Where would you like to start?" Barnes groused.

Doctor Barnes was an old man with white hair, deep-set wrinkles across his face, and dark circles under his eyes. There was nothing warm or inviting about the man, but he was efficient, and for Ellison, that was enough.

Ellison scanned across the infirmary. "Where's Agent Mirror?"

"This way," Barnes said, holding out his hand to the first door on the right. Both men stepped into the room together.

Inside, the lights were dimmed low. Mirror sat in a desk chair, staring at an interior window, but on the other side of the glass, the room was pitch black. Her right hand was reaching down, resting on top of a bronze canister laying atop a steel medical table.

She was talking as they entered the room, her voice soft and distant. "...and what was the village like? What's the very first thing you can remember?"

Ellison looked again at the canister on the table and realized his mistake. It wasn't a canister at all. It was the broken half arm of Titan. Ellison looked closer, and he could see the upturned hand at one end of the arm. The other end stopped at a jagged break where G-Force had ripped it clean from the rest of the bronze man's body. Ellison leaned over the table and he could see Titan's fingers twitching.

Dr. Barnes closed the door behind them, and Mirror reached over with her free hand to toggle a switch, cutting the microphone.

"You're using the deprivation room?" Ellison asked.

Mirror still stared through the black window. "I think it helps him focus."

Ellison stepped closer to the glass, his vision adjusting to the darkness. "He doesn't have eyes, Mirror. He doesn't have ears. Why are you—"

"He doesn't have eyes, but he can see," Lara answered. "Trust me, Major. I've *seen* what he can see. The darkness helps him."

"Helps with what?" Ellison questioned.

"He's in pain, Major, and we can't help him. He's also angry—at all of us for bringing him here, at the Red Moon for leaving him here, and at the world for no reason at all."

"I don't care about him being angry. Can we use him or not?" Ellison asked.

"Maybe, eventually. I honestly don't know." Mirror shook her head.

Ellison folded his hands behind his back. "I want to see him. Turn on the lights."

Mirror pressed a button, and from the other side of the glass window, the lights came on full. Then Ellison could see the prisoner lying on his back. Titan was immense, nearly seven feet tall, and his skin looked like burnished bronze. Nylon straps stretched across his body at the shoulders and waist, holding him down on the bed at the center of the room. He was missing his left arm at the shoulder, his right arm was gone at the elbow, and one of his legs was cut off at the knee. As the lights came on, he turned away his face.

Suddenly, there was a metallic bang from somewhere behind Ellison. He turned and looked. It was the missing half of Titan's arm. The hand was now clenched into a fist, and it was banging down against the steel table.

Ellison stepped back. "And you think that's him, still controlling his arm?"

"You tell me." Mirror pressed the button again, and the room on the other side of the window went black. The banging stopped on the table, and the clenched fist of the severed arm fell open.

Ellison turned back to Mirror. "And what about Talon? I need his report, too."

Mirror let go of Titan's broken arm and stood up. "I haven't seen him yet. I was waiting for you. You're better at lying to people's faces."

Ellison forced a smile. "Then after you."

They walked across the hallway into the first room on the left. Talon was waiting for them, sitting up in his bed. Ellison thought the Anom's face still looked swollen, even three months after the incident, but it had been so bruised and beaten in those first weeks after Chicago that it was hard to remember what it looked like before. Other than that, Talon appeared to be fine, except for his missing hand. It had been mangled during the fight with Titan, and Dr. Barnes was unable to save it. He'd amputated below the elbow.

Mirror was the first to speak. "How are you feeling today?"

"I'm good. I got more energy today, so I'm feeling good." Talon offered a thin smile. "I mean, I've still been better, but you know—"

Ellison raised his hand. "Let me see your hand—the construct you've been working on, I mean."

Talon's smile fell away. "Yes, sir."

Talon raised his arm, the one with the missing hand, holding it out to Major Ellison, and a cloud of green smoke started swirling over his skin, forming where his hand should have been. It twisted back on itself, getting thicker, until the smoke ignited into green flames. Then, suddenly, the flames transformed into a crystalline construct.

Ellison shook his head. The idea was for Talon to create a new hand—something he could actually use in a fight. The end result fell far short. The construct was roughly the same size as a missing hand and arm, but the shape was all wrong—a tapered cylinder with tendrils twisting out in every direction from its end. It reminded Ellison more of an overgrown houseplant than a crystalline prosthetic.

"That's still worthless," Ellison said, turning

for the door.

"It's not worthless!" Mirror snapped, and the steel in her voice was enough to stop Ellison where he stood. Slowly, he turned back to face her.

Ellison knew Mirror had been stretched to her breaking point—after Chicago, they were all pushed to their limits—but with this last outburst, she was treading into dangerous waters.

Mirror must have sensed the danger, too, because when she spoke again, her voice was softer. "It's not worthless, Major. It's better—much better. You know that learning a new construct takes time."

Ellison straightened. "All right. Then I suppose he has more time. We'll evaluate him again in a week."

Talon shook his arm, and the crystalline houseplant evaporated into smoke. "Thank you. I'll keep working on it, Major, every chance I get. I promise."

"I should hope so." Ellison turned away and stepped out of the room.

He still needed to meet with Captain Reyes in the Command Center. He would order him to start another analysis of the overnight intercepts. If they truly missed something from the Ryoku the first time, they sure as hell wouldn't miss it again.

Ellison was halfway back to the elevator when Mirror caught him in the hallway.

"I'll be honest, Major, I still don't get your decision," she said. "Why can't they see each other? They're begging, and I know it would help Talon, too." Lara pointed behind her back to Talon's room. "If you think this is helping your team, you need to reconsider!"

Ellison's patience was at an end; he wheeled back on Mirror. "I told you I made my decision, and as far as *helping my team*, it's clear you have no concept of what we're trying to do here. You have no regard for the discipline it takes to be a soldier."

"The hell I don't—" Mirror tried to interrupt him, but Ellison wouldn't allow it.

He raised his voice even louder. "Do you remember what Talon was like before Chicago, Agent Mirror? Lazy. Insolent. Inept. You think it's some accident *he's* the one lying in that bed? We failed that boy, and the broken kid in that room, that's the result. Now, by some miracle, he gets a second chance, and you want to coddle him right back to where he was. I won't allow it."

"Fine!" Mirror shouted back at Ellison. "But you don't understand, either. You have no idea what you're doing to any of them—emotionally, psychologically! No one gave you that right!"

Ellison stood his ground without answering. He had been careful from the beginning to keep this part of his life divided. It was the only way he knew how to preserve his relationship with Mirror and still function as the Executive Officer at Fort Blaney, but now, in her anger, Mirror had finally blurred that line. She was yelling at the man she slept with, not the colonel's XO. It would fall to Ellison to remind her.

He lowered his voice. "I've made my decision. All I need to hear from you now is a 'Yes, sir,' and then you can finish your job."

Mirror stood silent, and Ellison thought she might scream at him again; instead, she raised her chin and answered in a clear voice, "Yes, sir."

"That's better," Ellison said.

Mirror turned away sharply and walked back inside Talon's room, closing the door behind her. Ellison stood still, watching her go, and found himself admiring her restraint. It would have been easy to slam the door like a child, but even in her anger, Mirror found the capacity to think before she acted. It was a trait they had in common. As for her anger, Ellison could weather that storm, too—a momentary inconvenience for a longer-lasting victory: Agent Dubov had been proven wrong.

Dubov had thought that Ellison was a man blinded by his own infatuation. Now it was clear that nothing could be further from the truth. Ellison saw Mirror perfectly for who and what she was—a beautiful instrument and a pleasant enough distraction—and this was his proof: Even in her anger, she did exactly what Ellison expected. Just like everyone else at Fort Blaney, she obeyed.

CHAPTER 3

Jeremy turned his shoulders and threw a right cross into the center of the punching shield. As it landed, the shield drove back and away from his body, recoiling into the hydraulic piston that held it in place. Then the metal frame, welded to the piston and bolted to the floor, shuddered, the steel joints groaning under the stress—but it held. The next instant, the hydraulic arm was pushing the shield back into place. Jeremy turned his shoulders to punch again.

"Fifty! That's fifty. Hold up, G," Dr. John Langer called out from behind his computer station.

Jeremy dropped his hands and rolled back his shoulders. If he really just hit fifty strikes, he would have to take Langer at his word. It felt more like two hundred.

John Langer leaned forward to stare at his monitor. The squat researcher was wearing a green flannel shirt, his khaki pants, and a white lab coat with a brown coffee stain on the lapel.

JASON R. JAMES

His dark hair was a mess, and a scraggly beard covered the lower half of his face.

Langer reached for his mouse without looking, still fixated on the monitor. "Just let me run a post-test calibration. Make it official. Aaa-aaaand... Done!" Langer leaned back in his chair, spinning around. "You, my friend, just landed fifty strikes at plus fourteen gravity. It was beautiful—literally, beautiful. Swear to God, I could kiss you right now."

Jeremy laughed softly. "No offense, Doc, but I'd make you shave first."

Langer waved his hand. "Yeah, yeah. Story of my life."

Jeremy smiled; he couldn't help it. Langer's enthusiasm for the work was contagious, but the truth was, Jeremy wanted exactly the opposite. He wanted to be angry—he *was* angry.

He meant what he had said to Major Ellison. Individual research training was a waste of time. It was busy work—one big science experiment in a controlled environment—that did nothing to prepare them for the realities they were going to face. Chicago was just one example.

Three months ago, they were tossed into the deep end unprepared—and it cost them Talon. It probably should have cost them more. They got lucky, but Chicago was just the beginning. Jeremy knew the next trial was coming, and they were no more ready to face it now than they had been three months ago.

Jeremy picked up his water bottle and towel, taking a drink and wiping his face. It had been a long day. Langer had started his training with gravitational field variances—making Jeremy stand perfectly still at the center of the room and asking him to manipulate the gravitational fields around his body. It was the standing still that made it so difficult. Jeremy was always better when he was moving—when he could focus on *doing* something. Even so, Langer seemed pleased with the results. Jeremy created a constant field of plus eight gravity around his body—roughly the same gravitational density as iron. He tried to kick it up to a plus ten, but after a couple of minutes he got lightheaded, and the field dropped.

Next, Langer switched the tests to look at gravitational resonance. Jeremy liked this better, but not by much. Langer would have him generate a gravity field, and then Jeremy would drop the field, take a breath, and pick the field back up before it could dissipate completely. It felt like filling a balloon with air without pinching shut the neck—a constant game of catch up. He topped out this morning with a field of plus twenty-four. Even Langer was impressed by that.

After resonance training, it was time for lunch. They gave Jeremy thirty minutes. Then it was right back to training. In the afternoon, they started with the punching shield—fifty strikes at zero gravity, working their way up to plus fourteen.

Jeremy took another drink and wiped his towel across the back of his neck, trying to soak up the sweat. That's when his fingers grazed against his scar.

It was a thin, raised mark just at the base of his hairline, the only evidence of the implant he received on his first day at Blaney. Since his arrival, he had asked everyone about the microchip implanted inside his neck—Langer, Ellison, even Colonel McCann. All of them were ready with the same answer: It was harmless—only used for GPS and real-time telemetry. Nothing to worry about. But Jeremy knew the truth. The chip inside his neck was packed with enough explosives to rupture his brainstem. It was a fail-safe in case he ever needed to be put down.

Langer looked back at his computer screen. "So, what do you want to do now, G? We can try you at plus sixteen. See how that goes?"

Jeremy sat down in a chair by the wall. "Here's an idea. Why don't you grab a scalpel and cut Reah's C-4 microchip out of the back of my neck? Maybe that's something we could try? A fun little training exercise."

Langer leaned back in his chair and laughed, but the sound was all nerves—the kind of laugh a child makes when he's caught stealing candy. Jeremy liked the doctor well-enough, and he knew talking about the chip made Langer uncomfortable, but right now he didn't care. It was his neck —his life—they were treating as disposable.

Langer raised both of his hands in mock surrender. "I already told you, I can neither confirm nor deny the presence of explosives in your brain."

"Come on, Doc!"

"What?" Langer pleaded. "What do you want me to say here? That chip is there for your protection. I already told you that."

"Yeah? How is killing me going to save me?"

"What do you want me to say here, G? You know the truth, but what? You need me to say it out loud for you?" Langer pushed himself away from his desk. "All right. You win. *Your* chip, inside of *your* neck, isn't there for *your* protection. The chip we have in Gauntlet's neck, *that's* for your protection. And the chip we have in Nyx, *that's* for your protection. And all the chips, including yours, that's for *my* protection, okay? What more do you want from me?"

Jeremy leaned his head against the wall. "It's not right, Doc. It's not right, and you know it. It's not human."

"Yeah, but *you're* not human," Langer said.

The words fell over Jeremy like ice water, stealing away his breath. He looked back at Langer.

"I didn't mean it like that, G." Langer held out his hand, trying to backtrack. "I meant to say, 'technically.' *Technically* speaking—genetically, that is—you're *not* a human. Your DNA is something else. I mean, we have a whole other name for it, right? Genetic anomaly, right? You know that."

"Yeah, I know it." Jeremy stood up. "Let's just get back to work."

Before Langer could answer, the door to the lab opened; Lara was standing on the other side. "Excuse me, Dr. Langer. G-Force, it's time for your debriefing."

Jeremy picked up his towel and mopped it across his face again. "I still have another hour in here, at least."

"No." Lara shook her head. "Major Ellison ordered extended debriefings today, and your time is up."

"Right." Jeremy picked up his water bottle and started for the door.

Dr. Langer called after him, "Hey! We all good, G?"

Jeremy turned back. "Yeah, we're good Doc. Don't sweat it."

Jeremy followed Lara out the door. He couldn't look at her, and he didn't trust himself to speak, but as they stepped into the elevator and it started to descend, Jeremy needed to know the truth.

"So, did you tell the major we wanted to see Talon?"

Lara stared straight ahead. "You know I can't answer that."

"You're the reason he got transferred, right?"

"I can't answer that either," Lara said.

The doors opened, and Jeremy stepped out first. He already knew where they were going. He turned the corner and stepped into the debriefing room. The room itself had changed significantly in the three months since Chicago. The beige carpet was gone, replaced by the white tile floor that filled the other rooms at Blaney. The houseplants were gone too. So were the paintings and the lamps. Only the wood-paneled walls and leather chairs remained, but they did little to balance the cold, sterile feeling of the room.

Dubov was already inside, waiting for Jeremy, his hooked hands folded in his lap. Jeremy sat down in the chair across from him. Lara took the empty seat next to Dubov. Together they formed a triangle, Jeremy facing the other two, but now, reading their faces, he doubted any of them wanted to be there. It was one more obligation—an expectation to be met without any real purpose.

Lara reached inside her bag and removed the red pinewood derby car she had taken from Jeremy's room when he first signed on to join Reah Labs. She was supposed to use the car to read Jeremy's thoughts and memories, but it had never worked. Now, she placed the car on the arm of her chair. Just like in every other debriefing, Jeremy guessed she would try to read him again.

She reached back into her bag, pulled out her tablet, and began. "As always, there are no recording devices allowed in this room, but I will be taking notes. Let's begin. G-Force, I want you to—"

"I don't want him here." Jeremy set his jaw and stared at Dubov.

Lara forced a smile. "We've already been over this. Agent Dubov isn't here because of you. He's monitoring me. Reah Labs wants to evaluate *my* process—"

"Then evaluate it with someone else," Jeremy said.

Lara looked down at her hands. "They need to know why I can't read you. It's become a concern."

"You can't read Gauntlet, either," Jeremy countered.

"I know, but we think that's a function of his armor," Lara answered

Jeremy sat back in his chair. "And I thought you already had my problem solved, too. You said I was spiked."

Lara shook her head. "But that's not how it works. No mental spikes can last for three months. Even our most powerful psychic Anoms can't do that. Whatever's going on with you, it must be something else." Lara forced a smile and folded her hands in her lap—she was changing the subject. "So, let's start with how you're feeling today."

"I feel fine," Jeremy chafed at the question—more of the same drivel that couldn't help anyone. Why would it matter how he was feeling? It would be easier if she just got to the point.

"This morning, as you started training, you asked Dr. Langer for more aspirin," Lara said.

"I told you I feel fine."

"Your sleep patterns are still off," Lara continued.

Jeremy looked away at the wall, forcing a smile but fighting to keep his voice even. "If you're gonna keep answering your own questions, do I really need to be here?"

Lara laid her hand on top of the derby car. "I can sense that you're angry."

Jeremy laughed. "If you need psychic powers for that, I think we're in lot more trouble than I realized."

"Don't blame me because you're so obvious," Lara said. "You're allowed to be angry. It doesn't scare me. I've seen lots of people angry. Why don't you tell me how we ruined your life this week? My guess is it's about a lot more than just Talon."

Jeremy rose out of his seat, walking behind the chair and leaning over to dig his fingers into the leather. "We know what you're trying to do. How you're cutting us off from each other. You're trying to make us better weapons, right?"

"That's just not true," Lara started. "You know that we tried—"

"I *know* that I've written my mom twice since Chicago, and I know she would've written back by now. So where are my letters? Why haven't I heard from my mom? Why haven't I heard anything from Kate? You can't just rip us away from our lives."

Lara cradled the derby car in both of her hands. "It's more complicated than that, G-Force, and you know it. You came here to keep them safe. You came here after you almost got killed in a shopping mall. This is a secure, government research facility. We can't just drop a postcard whenever you get the urge—"

"All right, then prove it," Jeremy said, raising his voice. "If I'm really a person—if I'm supposed to be more than some biological weapon to you —tell me why you tried to stop me in Chicago. Right now, on the record. Tell me you weren't just sitting there, doing the math in your head, figuring out what it would cost to lose another one of your weapons. Tell me you actually worried about losing Jeremy Cross instead of G-Force."

"Don't do this. Not today," Lara answered.

"Why? Are we not supposed to talk like this in front of Captain Hook over here?" Jeremy looked over at Dubov. The skeletal man kept quiet in his chair, his face a blank, his claws tapping gently in his lap. "You afraid you're gonna get a bad grade on your 'process'?"

"I shouldn't have said anything to you in Chicago—" Lara started.

"But you did. You told me to stop. Remember?" Jeremy pushed back from the empty chair. "You told me to stop because you knew Titan was going to kill me. He *should've* killed me. So, what happened, Agent Mirror? Was your conscience just too slow to save Talon?"

Lara turned away. "That's not fair..."

Jeremy shook his head. "No, it's not fair. Doesn't mean I'm wrong."

Lara gathered her breath and kept her voice. "No, it doesn't mean you're wrong. I know that I've made mistakes. Is that what you need to hear? So have you. So have all of us, but that's not why we're here, is it? To replay our mistakes? To punish each other? Sit down so we can talk. Please."

Jeremy walked around the chair and sat down. He had said all that he needed to say— even more than he intended. Keeping on his feet now would only be petulant. If Lara wanted to waste more of their time talking, she had the right. He could listen to her just as well sitting down.

Lara looked down at her hands. "You mentioned your mother before. Have you been thinking about her recently?"

"No," Jeremy lied.

"It's been three months since you've seen her," Lara said. "Are you worried about her?"

"I don't feel guilty about leaving, if that's

what you're asking."

Lara looked down at the derby car in her hands. "I never brought up guilt, but is that what you're feeling? You think your mom would resent you for being here?"

Jeremy laughed. "My mom didn't want me crossing the street, okay? That's not what this is. And besides, you can't even read me like that. You said so."

"I can read the big emotions," Lara confessed, "and right now, guilt is the only thing I feel coming off of you. You make it look like anger on the outside, but it's guilt. I was there when you left, remember? She begged you not to come here, and now it's been three months. You feel guilty, and angry, and...scared? What are you afraid of?"

"I don't feel any of those things."

Lara set the car down on the arm of the chair. "You're afraid for your mom. Is that why it's so important for you to see Talon again? You need to make sure he's all right, because if *you* end up like Talon—or if you end up worse—what happens to your mom then?"

"What happens to my mom?" Jeremy rolled his eyes and laughed, but the sound was cold and mocking. "She already solved that mystery. When I'm gone, my mom has nobody." Jeremy pinched his fingers to the bridge of his nose. "She told me that one about a month after my dad died. She said we needed to take a road trip out to St. Louis. A little family-bonding time, she called it. In reality, it was thirteen hours stuck in the car, just me and her." Jeremy laughed again. "I think we spent more time staring out the damn windshield than we did talking to each other, but that was the *one thing* she needed to get off her chest. She said she needed me to hear her say it. She told me that when I go off to college, she'd be left with no one. So, you tell me, Mirror, you think I need to feel guilty about that?"

Lara sat forward in her chair. "Why St. Louis?"

"She said we were going to check out Washington University. Imagine that one. On the way to look at a college, and she's telling me don't go away to school." Jeremy looked away. "She didn't want me going to St. Louis. She didn't want me going anywhere. We only went because she missed my dad. St. Louis is where they met." Jeremy shook his head. "We didn't even make it onto campus. We just drove around the city for hours, and she showed me their first apartment. She showed me where she used to wait tables, and the park where my dad proposed. My mom was lonely, and now she's alone."

"But your parents never lived in St. Louis," a thin voice spoke, and it took Jeremy a second to realize its source. It was Dubov, his hairless face jutting forward from his neck and shoulders like a buzzard looking over fresh roadkill.

"What?" Jeremy's face twisted in confusion.

Dubov pushed the joystick on his wheelchair,

rolling it forward. "I said your parents never lived in St. Louis. There's no mention in their file."

Jeremy shrugged his shoulders. "Well, I don't have the water bill to prove it, but that was the story—unless you know something I don't."

Dubov smiled, his wan skin wrinkling around his cheeks and jaw. Then another sound escaped him—a short sound like clicking in the back of his throat; it was laughter.

"That's very good. So they lived together in St. Louis." Dubov turned his chair away from the others and started rolling for the door. "That's very good. We're done now."

Lara rose to her feet. "Agent Dubov, I still have more time."

"No." Dubov waved his hook in the air and looked over his shoulder. "I said we're done."

Jeremy rose to his feet and walked for the door.

"G-Force, wait. Please." Lara called after him.

Jeremy turned around in the open doorway. "What? What is it?"

Lara smiled—a look that was pleasant enough—but Jeremy could also see the strain at the edges of her lips and around her eyes as she struggled to maintain her composure. "I'm not against you. I thought you already knew that, but if I need to say it again, I will. We're not your enemy."

Jeremy let the words sink into silence before

he finally answered, "Okay. Then I guess you're not against us."

"What happened, G?" Lara sank down into her chair, and everything about her looked and sounded tired, like she had been running the same race ever since Chicago, and Jeremy never bothered to notice. She fought to keep her smile. "It wasn't like this before," she said. "At least not with us. What changed after Chicago?"

Jeremy shifted his weight, fixing his eyes on Lara. "Three months ago, you wouldn't have said anything to Ellison, and Talon would still be here. You want to know what changed after Chicago? You did. You switched sides."

CHAPTER 4

Lara walked down the hallway only looking up every seventh or eighth step. The rest of her attention was held by the tablet she cradled in her arm as she reviewed her notes from the day. It was her last chance to get everything straight in her own head.

She knew from the start that it would prove to be a long day. In fact, she had been dreading it since the night before, when she first told Ellison about the Anoms' plan to ask to see Talon. Lara remembered how Ellison's eyes went wide at the report, just like a kid on Christmas morning. Then he was up, out of his chair, pacing around the room—a bundle of raw nerves too excited to keep still. Of course, he feigned the proper amount of indignation. He wondered out loud how they could muster the gall to question his judgment, but the reasoning for Ellison's anger was spurious at best. Lara understood that for the major, this was nothing more than a new game—a chance to affirm his authority over the Anoms—and he wouldn't let the opportunity pass him by.

Ellison's inevitable overreaction was the main reason Lara debated telling him about it at all. The night before, when she first saw the idea forming inside the mind of Nyx, Lara knew it spelled trouble. The fact that Nyx's desire to see Talon was motivated by her strong feelings of anger and guilt over what happened in Chicago only made things worse. It transformed a simple request into a cause worth fighting for, and Lara couldn't know for certain how far the Anoms were willing to go. She wished she could just ignore it altogether and let things play out, but then again, she had responsibilities of her own.

Even so, the realities of the day had proven worse than she anticipated. It started with Ellison dressing her down in the hallway of the infirmary and followed with Nyx railing against her for betraying her trust in their debriefing session. Then G-Force practically accused her of causing Talon's injuries through her own indifference. At least Gauntlet was still refusing to answer *any* of her questions, his stoic silence a blessing in disguise.

Lara looked up from her tablet. She was standing in front of Major Ellison's door, her last stop for the night. She knocked, but before Ellison could answer, she reached for the handle and let herself in. Ellison stood up quickly from his chair at the table in the center of the room. It was obvious to Lara he wasn't expecting her, or if he was, perhaps she had underestimated the major's self-confidence. Ellison's outer shirt was draped over the back of his chair. So were his pants. He stood in front of Lara wearing nothing more than his white tee shirt and a pair of pale-blue boxers.

Lara closed the door behind her, but didn't speak—she wasn't about to ruin the awkward-ness of the moment by talking. In all their time together, she had never used her powers on Ellison before, and she had no plans for that to change. But there were moments, like now, when his thoughts were transparent. Ellison de-manded respect and prized his authority above all else. Watching him squirm to achieve either one now while standing in his underwear was a sweeter revenge than Lara could've hoped.

Ellison cleared his throat. "I wasn't sure you would be here tonight."

"Neither was I."

The truth of it was, there was no one else at Fort Blaney who could take Ellison's place. Lara would never allow herself to sleep with one of the Anoms. She needed their complete con-fidence for her work to be successful, and she would never jeopardize that for a good night's sleep. As for the civilian researchers, they all had a penchant for gossip, and that found a way of interfering with her work, too—Lara had learned that much from experience. None of the enlisted men could offer her the privacy she needed with all of them living in communal barracks. Hayden and Dubov were too vile to even consider, and McCann was too honorable to ever allow for the indiscretion. That only left her with the major.

Lara hated herself for coming back to Ellison's room, but the only alternative would have been worse. She touched the locket hanging from around her neck. In training, they had called it her anchor. It was a link to her identity —a talisman of memory—and she despised it. Spending the night with Ellison was her chance to escape. She could set the locket aside, and with it, she could take off the memories and emotions of everyone else. She could sleep, and then if nightmares came, at least they would be her own. Her pride seemed a fair price to pay for a night of peace.

"If you're waiting for an apology, it's not going to happen. You were out of your depth this morning, and you needed a reminder," Ellison said.

"And you enjoyed reminding me," Lara answered.

"I can't afford to treat you different out there from anyone else—not if I expect to do my job," Ellison barked. "There are already enough rumors flying around this base."

"And you're worried about appearances,"

Lara pressed.

She crossed the room to the table, pulled out one of the chairs, and sat down. She thought about challenging Ellison again—preying on his insecurity. She knew that if she wanted to, with the right push, she could escalate their sharp words now into something closer to a real fight.

Maybe she would demand an apology from him, or raise her voice. She could tell the Major how his insistence on being right made him look weak, or she could conjure a few tears and really test his resolve. But ultimately, Lara chose none of the above. She simply didn't care enough to start a fight, and she had no interest in seeing one through to its end.

The relationship between them was born from familiarity and valued only for its convenience. She chose Ellison because of the freedom offered to the XO of the base, and the reliability of his character. After all, the major was nothing if not routine. She had expected nothing more from Ellison from the very beginning, and it would be unfair now to pretend that she did.

Instead, she offered him a thin smile—a token of reconciliation.

It was all the encouragement Ellison needed. Whatever awkwardness or embarrassment he may have felt before, it evaporated. He was back in control now, advancing towards Lara, reaching for her hand, a lopsided grin plastered across his face.

Lara pulled away before he could touch her. "I need to give you my full report first. It's about G-Force."

Ellison changed again. Now, his jaw tightened, and his smile fell away. He sat down heavily in the chair across from Lara. "And what does your boyfriend want now?"

Lara rolled her eyes. "He's a child, Stuart, with a harmless crush."

"What does he want?" Ellison growled.

Lara looked down at her tablet. "He was asking about his mom and his friend Kate in our debriefing session. He wants to know why they haven't answered his letters. I think it's time we told him the truth."

Ellison leaned back in his chair. "And what truth is that supposed to be?"

"We need to tell him they're both dead. He has a right to know. Now that he's specifically asking for them—"

Ellison lowered his chair back to the ground and put his elbows on the table, folding his hands. "You're the one who decided to keep it a secret in the first place. You said he was too unstable to hear that kind of news. In fact, you said it would place our entire program in jeopardy. That was your report, wasn't it?"

Lara remembered sitting in the command center when Colonel McCann told her about the deaths of Emily Cross and Katherine Marino. The colonel sat across the table from her, with Agent Hayden rocking back in his chair on the colonel's right. Major Ellison was seated on Lara's left. According to the medical reports, Emily had suffered a massive heart attack just a couple of days after G-Force left for Fort Blaney. Less than a week later, Kate Marino ODed on some pills. Lara was told the news the day after Chicago.

McCann looked at her from across the table. "Well?"

That was it. With one word, all the responsibility for what came next fell to Lara. She tried to think through the different scenarios—to play out how things might unfold when G-Force was told the news that his mom and best friend were both dead.

With almost anyone else, it would have been an easy assessment; she could simply read their thoughts and report back exactly how they would react to hearing this kind of news. But G-Force was different. Lara could only read his broadest emotions, and at the time, in the aftermath of Chicago, those emotions were ready to explode.

What made it worse was the inescapable fact that G-Force was legitimately dangerous. Lara had just watched him rip a metal man limb from limb, so what would he do when he heard about his mom and Kate? If G-Force lost control—if he used his powers in a rage—someone would get hurt.

But there was more. Lara also worried about herself. She knew that if they told G-Force about his mom and Kate, he would inevitably turn to her for support. He would need Lara to be his emotional strength, and she couldn't be that person for him— not after Chicago.

She had gotten too close, and it had almost cost them dearly. She had told him to let Titan escape. If he had actually listened to her—if G-Force had turned his back and walked away—the cost in lives would have been catastrophic. Lara wouldn't risk making that same mistake again. She needed to disengage from Jeremy Cross, for both of their sakes.

Colonel McCann shifted his weight in his chair. "Agent Mirror—"

"I don't think we should tell him," Lara said, her words suddenly tumbling out. "We don't know how he'll react. It would put the entire program at risk."

Ellison stood up from the table in his room, walked to the sink, and filled a glass with water. "So now you're reversing your position? You want us to tell G-Force everything?"

Lara nodded. "I do. He deserves the truth."

Ellison forced a smile. "Then I'll take your recommendation to the colonel first thing in the morning. If he signs off, we can tell your boyfriend whatever you want." Ellison turned around and dumped the rest of his water into the sink before looking back at Lara. "Is there anything else?"

She shook her head. "No."

"Are you staying the night?"

Lara smiled. "Is that an invitation?" She already knew the answer. Ellison reached for her again, but Lara pulled away. "If you want me to stay, I'll need a minute."

She rose from her chair and walked to the bathroom, closing the door behind her.

The next morning, Lara sat at the conference table in the Rec Room, seated across from G-Force and Nyx. The two Anoms sat rigid, their eyes fixed straight ahead, focused on the wall behind her. Lara thought they both looked angry, but also tired of being angry, like they were carrying a weight they couldn't put down. Gauntlet stood off to one side of the table, as usual, his face hidden behind his blood-red helmet, but Lara imagined he looked just as sour as the other two.

Next to her, Ellison sat droning on through the morning briefing. "...most groups came back as normal chatter. We flagged a communication from the Ryoku early this morning regarding one of their new recruits named 'Pòmén.' We cycled back through the last two weeks, and that name pops up maybe a dozen more times. We don't have anything specific yet, but we're looking into it. Hopefully, we'll know something more by tomorrow. As for the Red Moon, things are still quiet..."

Lara looked down at her hands folded in her lap. She was finding it hard to pay attention, too distracted by her own thoughts. Ellison had broken the news to her in the elevator as they descended to the Rec Room: Colonel McCann had approved her request. She was ordered to tell G-Force about his mom and Kate immediately after the briefing.

A ripple of nausea churned in her stomach. How do you start that kind of conversation? How many words would she even get out before he figured out the rest on his own? Then Lara realized the words wouldn't matter at all. As soon as she opened her mouth, Emily Cross and Katherine Marino would be dead. It didn't matter that they died weeks ago. This would be the moment he lost them both.

Lara looked up from her hands, and the room around her was silent. G-Force and Nyx were both staring at her from across the table.

"I said, 'You have news that needs to be shared,'" Ellison repeated.

Lara fumbled. "Wait—you said we would speak in private after the briefing."

"I said you would speak *at the end* of the briefing," Ellison corrected her.

This wasn't what she intended. It certainly wasn't how she imagined it. Lara assumed they would take G-Force aside into the debriefing room and speak to him alone. Not like this. Not like it was just another point of business in their daily routine. Not putting him on display for the others.

Lara pushed her chair back from the table.

"Major, I think we should take a minute—"

"We're not going to draw this out. The last item is for G-Force." Ellison placed his hands flat on top of the table.

"Major, wait." Lara kept her voice low and prayed that Ellison would listen.

He didn't. "Three months ago, G-Force, your mother suffered a massive heart attack and died in her sleep. A week later, we learned that your friend, Katherine Marino, died from a drug overdose. We would have said something earlier, but Katherine Marino's death just cleared our security checks, and we were advised to tell you of both at the same time. All of us at Fort Blaney are very sorry for your loss."

It was done. The words couldn't be unsaid. Whatever she might have done to soften the blow, or protect him, it was too late. Ellison stole that chance away, and she hated him for it, but her own anger felt so small in the moment, and she felt guilty for even giving it life. This time was for Jeremy.

She looked across the table at him and waited—bracing herself for the inevitable. She watched as he hunched forward in his chair, his eyes focused on the tabletop and both of his hands closed into fists. She could see his knuckles turning white as he tried to somehow close his hands even tighter, but then there was no other reaction. No cries of anguish or screams of anger. No pounding fists or cursed words. Just painful quiet. Lara realized she was holding her breath. She looked around the room, and the others all looked the same—even Ellison—every one of them coiled like a spring.

Finally, Ellison spoke. "All of our morning training sessions have been canceled out of respect. Afternoon debriefings will proceed as scheduled. That's all for now." Ellison stood up from his chair and walked toward the elevator, but Lara couldn't leave.

"Jeremy..." she said.

"Don't," he answered, and the word was only a breath—less than a whisper—empty of all emotion. There was no anger behind it. No weight of grief. No stain of remorse. It was cold and sterile and finite. He didn't even look up as he spoke. Then Lara understood. Whoever he had been before Chicago—whoever Lara thought she knew—that Jeremy Cross had died, too. This was someone else.

Lara rose silently from the table and followed Ellison out of the room.

CHAPTER 5

Jeremy sat at the conference table staring down at the wood grain, tracing the lines back and forth with his eyes. He had been there, alone, for an hour—maybe longer. Jeremy couldn't say for sure, because everything around him felt slow and heavy. His arms, his head, his thoughts, even his own breathing—it all felt like he was running through wet sand.

He was also tired. The more he tried to focus his eyes on the wood grain, the harder it was to keep them open. His vision would blur, and the darker lines of the table would run together into drab, oaken brown. Then he would see their faces—his mom and Kate—flashing up from the bottom of his memory. He would see his mom curled up under her blanket with one of her books, and Kate smiling, waiting for him outside his house.

That's when Jeremy would open his eyes wider. He would force himself to refocus on the grain of the table. It was the best he could do to choke the memories back down, because his mom wasn't reading a book at home and he knew Kate would never smile again. If he let himself think about either one, he would only have to remind himself that they were dead, and the wound would rip open again.

"We should talk," a voice growled from behind him, but Jeremy knew who it was without looking up from the table—Gauntlet.

Jeremy shook his head. "I'm not talking to you, or Nyx, or anyone else. I'm sure as hell not talking to Mirror. I'm done."

Gauntlet walked around the table and sat down in the chair across from Jeremy. "I only need five minutes."

Jeremy pushed back from the table and turned away. He remembered all the stories he'd had to endure after his dad died—countless men and women sharing their own personal tragedies, but all of them building to the same bullshit conclusion: you're not in this alone. As if somehow a shared experience was enough to drag you out of grief. That's how Jeremy knew they were all lying. If they had really understood what he was feeling in that moment—if they'd had any idea—they would have known just how insulting their "help" really was.

But this was different. Gauntlet wasn't some long-lost friend of his father's, or a distant cousin he had never met before. Gauntlet was there in Chicago—he stood face to face with Titan, too—and now he was asking Jeremy to listen. And Gauntlet never asked for anything. Five minutes was the least he deserved.

Jeremy turned to face him. "Talk then."

"What did you mean when you said you were done?"

Jeremy scoffed. "I mean I'm done wasting my time here. I agreed to all this to keep my mom and Katie safe. I stayed because I thought we were going to help people. Seems like I was wrong on both counts, so I'm done."

"And you think they're going to let you walk away?" Gauntlet rubbed his hand across the back of his neck, and then he slapped his hand down flat on the table, holding it in place until finally, Jeremy looked down. Gauntlet lifted his palm to the side, and under his hand, lying on top of the table, Jeremy could see Gauntlet's microchip, no bigger than a grain of rice.

"There's a reason they call it a leash," Gauntlet said.

"How did you—" Jeremy started to ask.

"I'll answer all of your questions, but not here." Gauntlet closed his hand over the chip; he picked it up from the table and rubbed it again across the back of his neck. "You need to come with me."

Without saying another word, Jeremy rose from his chair and followed Gauntlet out of the Rec Room and into his personal quarters. Inside, Gauntlet's room looked like the mirror image of Jeremy's own, with a bed on one side and a desk and video screen on the opposite wall.

As soon as the door closed behind them, Jeremy started again with his question. "How did you get the microchip—"

"My armor dug it out from my neck as soon as they injected me with it." Gauntlet pulled out his desk chair and turned back to face Jeremy. "Now I just carry it around. It makes everyone feel safer."

"And you can help me, too? Or your armor can? It can do the same thing for me?" Jeremy asked.

Gauntlet shook his head. "What is it you think I can do, G-Force? What are my powers?"

It was a fair question and should have been easy. After all, Jeremy had seen him in action. He knew Gauntlet was a skilled fighter—he had proven that much in Chicago—and he seemed to have an entire medieval arsenal available at his fingertips, everything from a sword and shield to a wrist-mounted crossbow and a pair of battle-axes. But was any of that really a *power*? For that matter, was Gauntlet even an Anom?

Jeremy shrugged. "You wear that suit."

"That's right," Gauntlet answered. "And now it's time for you to understand how I got it, and why I'm here, and how I'm going to help you."

As he finished speaking, Gauntlet's helmet separated along the centerline, folding down over both of his shoulders. He pulled the broadsword from his back and set it down on top of his desk, and before Jeremy could fully understand what was happening, Gauntlet raised both of his arms over his head and punched down with his fists toward the floor. All at once, the armor began pouring off Gauntlet's body, falling away from his skin like dark sheets of blood. It splashed to the floor and ran away in a thousand directions at once like mercury, swirling past Jeremy's feet in tiny, crimson eddies. Then it started to climb. The red armor rose on itself, scaling upwards into the air, building walls where none had been before around Jeremy and Gauntlet until finally, it closed over both of their heads, surrounding them in a blood-red cell

Across from Jeremy, Gauntlet stood practically naked, with only the metal halves of his helmet folded down over his shoulders and the black vambraces around his wrists and forearms. The rest of him was bare. Jeremy could see that Gauntlet's arms, legs, and torso were just as pale and freckled as his face—no surprise there—and even though he still seemed tall, Jeremy thought the man behind the armor looked painfully thin—almost frail. Jeremy had wondered before how much work the suit was doing to supplement Gauntlet's strength and agility. Looking at the naked man standing in front of him now, the answer was obvious. The suit was doing everything.

Gauntlet reached for the bed, pulling off his comforter and wrapping it around his body. He sat down heavily in the desk chair behind him, almost collapsing, hacking and coughing so much that it rattled his slight frame under the blanket. Somehow, to Jeremy, the man looked even paler now, almost ashen.

"You all right?" Jeremy started forward

Gauntlet raised his hand, waving him off as the last of his coughing subsided. Finally, he managed a full breath and nodded. "It's the armor. Atrophy. I just need a minute."

Gauntlet reached out with his hand, touching his fingers against the red wall of the cell, and the liquid armor answered. It spiraled around his fingertips, wrapping over his whole hand up to his wrist. Then Gauntlet closed his eyes and breathed deeply.

Jeremy reached out and poked his own finger against another wall. Nothing happened. It didn't cover his hand like Gauntlet's. It didn't even feel wet. It was dry and flexible, pushing away from his finger and then snapping back into place like the mesh of a trampoline.

"What is it?" Jeremy asked.

"It's a biomechanical, semi-viscous graphene. They called it Exocorium. Trust me, you've never heard of it."

Jeremy sat down on the edge of the bed, looking up at the red armor stretching over their heads. "So why wrap us up in this bubble? What's the point?"

Gauntlet opened his eyes. "The point is, I need to talk to you alone. This way, in here, I know that we are. So let's start at the beginning..."

CHAPTER 6

"My name is Michael Reilly."

It was strange for Gauntlet to say his name out loud—almost as strange hearing it, like he was talking about a ghost.

Across from him, G-Force raised both of his eyebrows, and the corner of his mouth curled up in a smile. Gauntlet wondered if there had ever been a time when he had looked so clueless. He decided there wasn't.

"Why are you telling me this now?" G-Force asked.

Gauntlet nodded; it was a good question. "I'm telling you now because you want to escape Fort Blaney and Reah Labs. So do I, but the only way we leave here alive is if we're together. That means I need you to trust me, and trust starts with honesty. Then you can decide for yourself."

As he spoke, Gauntlet could see Jeremy's face start to change—his eyebrows came down and his smile faded. He was listening.

"By the time I was twenty-three, I was living out of a homeless shelter." Gauntlet caught himself smiling at the memory. "It's funny. When you say it out loud, it sounds worse than it really was. At the time, it just felt normal—how things had to be. Then spring of that first year I met Domingo, and that was my real beginning. Everything else—everything that happened before Dom—that was all just prologue."

Gauntlet remembered the first time he saw the old man—back before he was ever Gauntlet—a thousand years ago when he was still just Michael Reilly. He had been sitting on top of his bed in the shelter, reading through a Physics textbook he picked up from the shelter library when Domingo walked into the room.

Domingo was old, with deep-set wrinkles around his eyes and cheeks, each one folding his dark-tanned skin into a thin crease. His hair was feathery white, and he had a full, white mustache filling the space above his upper lip. He wore gold, wire-rimmed glasses over his eyes, and he was smiling, showing his big, white teeth.

He sat down on the bed across from Michael. "Billy said that about you." Domingo pointed at the book. "He said you liked to read."

Michael closed the book and set it aside. "Yeah, well, Billy talks too much."

Domingo smiled. "Yeah. That's true, too. Billy loves to talk, but he don't lie. You're just who he said you were."

"What is it you want, old man?"

"Yeah, you got an edge, too. That's good. You need that part, too." Domingo rubbed his hand over his mouth and mustache, sliding it down across the whiskers of his chin and throat. "What I want is to help you. I want to teach you a trade. I'm going to show you how to play chess, and how to win money doing it. My name's Domingo, but everybody 'round here calls me Saint Dom. You heard of me?"

Michael shook his head.

Domingo smiled. "Well, you just did."

Gauntlet shook himself free of the memory; he was back in the present, talking to G-Force. He leaned forward in his chair. "Dom made his money playing chess—catching speed games in the park. He would hustle tourists who didn't mind paying him for the show. In the park and in the shelter, everyone knew him as one of the greats. He grew up in Washington Square learning chess from the legends. Then he took his game over to Union. He made good money, too, but for Dom it was never enough. Most chess guys, they treat their game like it's their business, but Dom always wanted a franchise.

"So he offered me a deal. He'd front me the money to start my own game, and I would pay him back thirty percent of what I earned. Then, just like he promised, he taught me how to play. First, he showed me how to win a game honest, and once I could do that often enough, he taught me how to cheat and not get caught. The very last thing he taught me were the rules of the game, and for Dom, there was only one."

Michael sat at one of the chess tables in Union Square Park. It was early spring, a few months after he'd first met Saint Dom. The sun was bright overhead, and there were pink buds starting on the trees, but the air was still cold, and when the wind blew, it was biting.

Domingo sat across from him at the chessboard. The old man was wrapped in a gray knit sweater with an unraveled hole at one of his elbows, and he wore a shapeless blue driving cap. He sat at an angle to the board, his legs crossed at the knees and his hand covering his mouth. He was staring down at the chess pieces, taking his time. They weren't playing speed chess today—that was saved for practice. This was a real game, slow and deliberate, because Saint Dom was teaching.

He reached down and picked up his bishop, letting it hang for a second in the air, and finally, he made his move. Dom leaned back on the bench, still staring at the board.

"So, Mikey, you ready for tomorrow? You ready to start the real game?"

"I already told you that I've been ready, old-timer," Michael laughed.

Domingo ran his hand down his whiskered chin and neck. "So I guess you better know all the rules, then."

"I know the rules."

"You think I'm talking about this bullshit?" Dom swiped his hand over the chess board, knocking the pieces to the ground. "I'm not talking about this—not this little bullshit game. I'm talking about this." He waved his finger in a circle over his head. "I'm talking about the big game. You don't know the real rules yet, because I haven't taught you."

Michael sat up straighter on the bench. "All right, Dom. Then teach."

The old man held up his finger. "There's just one rule you got to follow, and it's simple and easy, and sometimes it's impossible: you never run away from this table. You understand me? Never—not if you want respect."

Domingo looked at Michael, his eyes hard. "You take somebody's money at this table because you win, that's fine. They're paying you for your skill. You earned it. If you take somebody's money at this table because you cheat, that's fine, too—they're paying you for your smarts. But if you take somebody's money and you run—then you're stealing. You see that difference?"

Dom leaned back, rubbing his hand back and forth over his neck. "My whole life, I only ran out of a game twice. One time because I was desperate, and once because I was scared. I regretted it both times. That's the thing, Mikey." Domingo's eyes went back to the chessboard, passing over the ruined game and the scattered pieces. "You run out on this game, you *always regret it."*

"By the end of my first summer, I was earning good money," Gauntlet said. "But that's when I met Piper, and everything changed."

"And who is that?" G-Force asked. "Just another homeless chess player?"

Gauntlet smirked. "No. Not even close, but she could've been. She was smart enough for it. But Piper wasn't homeless, and she didn't care about making money at a chess game. That kind of worry was beneath her."

"Why?"

Gauntlet leaned forward in his chair. "You know how they say the same game of chess has never been played twice because of all the possibilities? I don't know if that's true or not. Doesn't feel like it because when you play long enough you start to see patterns. People repeat themselves...but that's not Piper. She was the fork in the road you never saw coming."

Michael remembered the day perfectly. It was a Friday. By early afternoon, the city was already a furnace and the park was crowded. He remembered sitting at the table, sweating through his shirt, but he didn't mind. Days like this drove people outside, and the more people in the park meant more money. That was always a good thing.

Michael scanned the crowd, looking for his next player—someone looking to waste their time and who could afford to do it at the chessboard. Then, out of nowhere, a woman stepped from the crowd and began walking straight towards him. She sat down without an invitation, as if she had scheduled an appointment.

The woman had long, dark hair and pale skin. Her eyes were hidden behind a pair of oversized sunglasses, and she wore a white and blue patterned sundress with flip-flops. Michael never would have picked her out as one of his players. She didn't fit the type.

Dom had always taught him to avoid the pretty players—they were too distracting, he said—but maybe a small distraction on a hot summer day would be all right. The woman was half a dozen years older than Michael, too, but that wasn't a problem, either. He liked playing against the older players. They typically had more money to lose, and that made them careless.

The real problem, as far as Michael was concerned, was the woman's attitude as she approached. She was cloaked in confidence, and somehow that confidence felt all wrong. Everyone else who sat down at his table knew they were about to get hustled, and that absolute assurance would show up in one of two ways. Either they would put on a false bravado—talking a big game as they took their seats—or they would sit down nervous, fumbling through a quick introduction and then chattering about nothing through the rest of the game so they could hurry up and lose. This woman had done neither. She sat down without a word like she was meeting an old friend for coffee.

Dom always said that if something felt wrong, it probably was. He should get up and walk away before the game could even start, and Michael was ready to do just that. He was halfway through some excuse about taking a break to use the bathroom when the woman took out a twenty-dollar bill and laid it on the table.

She lifted her sunglasses on top of her head, showing her ice-blue eyes. "I imagine you'd let me win the first couple of games before you took me for real money on the third. I'd rather we start playing to win from the start."

Then Michael was on his feet, turning to leave.

"It's not a con," the woman said. "My afternoon meeting was canceled, I'm bored, and I've seen you here before. I really just want someone to talk to. You can talk while we play, right?"

Michael sank back down on the bench. "Yeah, we can talk while we play. If that's what you want?" It still didn't feel right, but twenty guaranteed dollars was hard to ignore. Michael set up the board.

The game between them took longer than it should have. The woman was a better player than he'd expected, and Dom had been right—beauty was a distraction. Even worse was the conversation, itself. Most talk at the chessboard was trash—quick jabs traded back and forth to rattle the other player—but this conversation was real. Somehow, it felt closer to confession. The woman was laying out her thoughts on religion and social class and art and economics, and she was asking Michael to do the same. The more he listened, the more he wanted her to keep talking. Finally, most of the board was clear, and Michael had mate in three moves. She must have known it, too, because that's when the woman tipped over her king and rose to her feet.

"I enjoyed that," she said. "I was worried that with the way you were fumbling all over yourself to get away from me, you'd be just another handsome face, but you're something more than that, aren't you?" She smiled. "And now I'd like to take you to lunch."

She extended her hand, but Michael threw up his arms in mock surrender and shook his head. "I really can't."

The woman lowered her sunglasses back over her eyes. "I understand. This is your job. So, tell me how much more you'd make sitting here in the next hour?"

Michael shrugged. "I don't know. It's a nice day. Pretty busy out. It's hard to say."

"I'll pay you sixty dollars for your time. That's on top of the twenty I already paid you for the game."

Michael agreed. It was a chance to get out of the heat, and it was another hour they could spend talking, but the lunch went even longer than he'd expected. By the time he returned to his game, it was almost four. He didn't care. The eighty dollars in his pocket was nice, and the distraction was worth it, but when it was all over and Piper left, he tried not think about her.

Only the next day, she came back. It was late in the afternoon, and she sat down, just like before, at Michael's table, putting her twenty dollars on the board. They played one game. Then she took Michael out to an early dinner and paid him a hundred bucks for his time. It was after midnight when they finally said goodbye.

On the third day, Piper showed up again. It was almost dark. This time there was no chess played between them. She sat down at his table, and for the first time since they'd met, Michael thought she looked nervous. Her hands kept fidgeting—first folded together, then laid flat on top of the table, and then folded again.

Finally, she came out with it. "I would like to keep seeing you. I think you're smart, and I think you're handsome, but I don't want to pay for your company. I'm not looking for an escort."

Michael shook his head. "That's not what this is."

"Good," Piper said. "So let's plan on dinner tomorrow night. In my apartment?"

She slid a note across the table, and written in pen was her address: 157 West 57th Street, Apt. 61B. Michael took the paper, folded it in half, and tucked it inside his pocket. The next night, they met for dinner. Two months later, and Michael moved into the apartment for good.

"Dom always said that chess was like life. In the beginning, you only see potential—nothing but an open board filled with possibilities. Then you live a little, and you transition into the middlegame. That's when your life catches up to you. Now you've made some choices. You've probably made some mistakes. You've done things that can never be undone, and that's when you reach the endgame.

"Dom would say the endgame was all about faith. He would say most people, by that point, think everything's been decided. They're beaten, and now they're just counting down the moves to the end. But Dom would say the endgame is the only time you see a miracle.

"Piper was my mine."

Gauntlet lowered his eyes. He knew that he needed to say more—he needed to explain everything, and he was barely scratching the surface—but before he could start, the armor around him began to change. The walls, floor, and ceiling of the blood-red cell trembled violently, but that wasn't exactly the truth, either. Gauntlet couldn't *feel* the armor shaking at all. It was the *armor* communicating to *him*; the *armor* detecting micro-vibrations rippling through the steel walls and floors of Fort Blaney, trembling through the Exocorium and into Gauntlet's fingertips; the *armor* letting him know that the elevator to the Rec Room was descending.

Gauntlet stood up, and the armor around his hand twined farther up his arm, covering his shoulder and running across his chest. The red walls peeled away, dissolving back to the floor, and the Exocorium pooled over Gauntlet's feet, climbing up his legs, covering his waist and wrapping around his back. Then the blood-red cell was gone, and only Gauntlet remained in his armor.

He lifted his sword from the desk and slid it into place over his shoulder. Finally, his helmet folded up, sealing around his head. As soon as the metal clicked shut, Gauntlet could feel his whole body relax. His arms, shoulders, and back felt lighter. He could see more. He could hear more. He could feel again, and breathe again. It all felt normal.

He looked down at G-Force. "There's more I need to tell you—and I will—but we're about to be interrupted. For now, I need you to trust me, and I need you to wait."

G-Force nodded.

Gauntlet turned away and started for the door. "Then we should go. They're here."

CHAPTER 7

Ellison stood at perfect attention in front of Colonel McCann's desk, his eyes fixed straight ahead, staring at the back wall. His formality was a defense. Anything less, and Ellison's anger would have seeped through the cracks in his façade. He wouldn't afford them that pleasure.

McCann sat behind his desk, staring down at an opened folder, holding his black Army mug just under his lips. To Ellison's right, Agent Dubov sat in his wheelchair, his two hooks folded in his lap, and Agent Hayden leaned against the back wall, his arms across his chest, staring down at the floor. They were all silent—all waiting. That's when Ellison understood his inclusion was nothing more than a courtesy.

"I don't think it's a good idea, sir," Ellison finally said.

McCann closed the folder on top of his desk and lowered his mug. "You don't have to think it's a good idea, Stuart, because it's an order. You just need to follow it."

"Sir, if the CIA wants to use one of our assets, don't you think I should be involved in planning the operation?" Ellison asked.

Hayden laughed, unfolding his arms. "It's not like anyone called dibs, Major. The Anoms are here as independent contractors. They don't belong to you, or the Army. As for planning *my* operation, if it were up to me, I never would have told you in the first place."

Ellison went rigid, and for the first time he looked down at the colonel. "With all due respect, sir, as your XO I have authority over the operations on this base. That includes all personnel—Army, independent contractor, or CIA. As long as we're standing in Fort Blaney—"

"With all due respect?" Hayden laughed again, mimicking the words from Ellison. He walked around and sat on the edge of the colonel's desk, staring up at the major, daring him to meet his eye. "I can tell you exactly what to do with all your respect, Major. I'd be happy to."

Ellison seethed inside, his jaw clenching tight. He wanted to scream back into the face of Hayden—to tell him what *he* could do with his independent contractors and secret operations. He wanted to slam his fist into Hayden's smug, smirking face, but none of that was Ellison's place. If Hayden was overreaching, it was up to McCann to hammer him back into place.

Ellison squared his shoulders. "Colonel McCann, sir, with all due respect—"

"Jesus, Stuart." McCann leaned forward, propping both of his elbows up on his desk and holding his head in his hands. "I gave you an order. Just do what I said."

Ellison's stomach dropped, but there was nothing more to say. McCann had made up his mind. Instead, he swallowed his vitriol and offered a terse, "Yes, sir."

Hayden motioned towards the door. "After you, Major."

Ellison turned on his heels and left the office. He walked quickly into the elevator at the end of the hall without looking back. Hayden and Dubov followed close behind him.

As they started to descend, Hayden rocked back on his heels, reaching inside his coat pocket for his cigarettes. "You weren't wrong back there, Major, but you still lost your argument. I wonder why that is?"

Ellison wouldn't take the bait. He already knew why he'd lost. It all fell back on McCann and the colonel's weakness. He was a shell of the officer Ellison once knew, but even *that* man— the man before Chicago—had been weaker than Ellison realized.

Ellison looked down at the floor. "Colonel McCann gave an order."

"Yes, he did, and what does that order say about the colonel?" Hayden asked.

The elevator doors opened, and Ellison stepped out into the Rec Room. Hayden and

Dubov both followed him. The room itself was empty, dark, and quiet. It was surprising, but only because Ellison had never been in the room alone. The Anoms were always expecting him, and they made sure to be waiting. This was different.

He walked behind the long conference table and leaned both of his hands against the back of a chair, dropping his head. He didn't want to be here. When he had canceled training in the morning, it wasn't done on a whim. Ellison recognized that the Anoms needed a break from his demands. Honestly, he was just as desperate for a break from them. The loss suffered by G-Force provided a convenient excuse. He would have avoided them all for the rest of the day, but it wasn't his choice.

Hayden sat down at the table next to Ellison, leaning back in his chair. "So, Major, are you going to call in your assets, or should I do it for you?"

Ellison scowled at Hayden, but before he could answer the other man's quip, a door on the left side of the room opened. Gauntlet and G-Force stepped out.

Hayden drummed his hands down on the table in rapid succession. "There he is. Just the man I wanted to see."

G-Force stepped out into the center of the room, his jaw set. "That's funny. I was hoping to not see any of you for the rest of the day. I thought you said we were done, Major."

"The CIA is putting together a team for a special operation. Mission specifics are need-to-know," Ellison said.

"Well, I guess I need to know," G-Force answered, "because I'm not going with any of you unless I know what you're asking."

"Then it's a good thing you're not invited." Hayden rose to his feet, slapping his hand one last time on the tabletop as a smirk stretched across his face. "I said I was looking for a man, not a boy. We want the big one." He pointed at Gauntlet.

G-Force balled up his fists. "And I told you, we're not going anywhere."

Hayden laughed. "Oh, sweet boy, I don't think you understand how big a mistake you're making."

G-Force started forward, but Gauntlet grabbed him by the arm. G-Force turned, and Gauntlet said something to him in a low voice. Ellison couldn't make out the words, but whatever he said, it seemed to satisfy G-Force for the moment. The younger man nodded, and then he opened his hands and relaxed his shoulders.

"I'm ready," Gauntlet growled from behind his helmet.

"I thought so," Hayden said, "and you can tell your friend not to worry. We'll bring you back good as new—nothing like what happened to your man in Chicago."

Hayden turned away and walked to the elevator. Dubov and Ellison both followed. Finally, Gauntlet stepped inside with them. The doors closed, and the elevator started to climb.

CHAPTER 8

Ellison sat straight up in the bed, slapping his hand blindly down on the nightstand. The shrill ring from the base phone roused him from a dead sleep, and now his brain was swimming in the twilight—acting on autopilot rather than conscious choice.

The phone rang again in the blackened room, and Ellison swatted his hand across the nightstand. This time he hit the receiver, but it was too late. Mirror woke up next to him. She pushed herself up on her elbow, clutching at the sheets around her. In the dark, Ellison couldn't see her face, but he could hear her breathing—quick, ragged gasps. She was panicked.

"Where am I?" she screamed.

Ellison grabbed the phone and raised it to his ear. "Hold on." He reached out with his other hand and curled his fingers around Mirror's shoulder. Almost immediately, he could hear her breathing slow down. The muscles under his hand softened and relaxed. She was coming out of her episode.

Most nights, Mirror would sleep like a corpse next to him, barely moving. Then she would wake herself up at some ungodly hour, dress, and leave before Ellison ever rolled out of bed. But on rare occasions, like tonight, something would shatter that routine. On those nights, Mirror would wake up disoriented and afraid. That's when she relied on Ellison. She had told him the best thing he could do was provide physical contact, even if it was just a hand on her shoulder. Then she could focus herself—find her bearings.

Mirror took another slow breath. "I'm okay. I'm—I'm going into the bathroom." Ellison knew she wouldn't go back to sleep. She never did. Instead, she slinked out from under the sheets and walked through the darkened room to the bathroom, closing the door behind her before she turned on the light.

Ellison turned his attention back to the phone. "This is the major."

"Yes, sir," the voice of Captain Reyes answered. "Sorry to wake you, sir, but we have a hit in the command center. It's registered priority one."

"I'll be right there," Ellison said.

He turned on the lights and dressed quickly. These were the moments he lived for—the reason he still cherished his role as Executive Officer even with McCann's other failings. Ellison was a man of action—a soldier first and always—ready to answer the call of battle, and now, standing on the precipice of that moment, the feeling was intoxicating.

He called through the closed door of the bathroom, "I'm leaving," and he didn't wait for an answer.

A priority-one event—if that's truly what this was—meant a clear threat to American security. Maybe it was the Red Moon, ready to test them again after Chicago with another attack. Maybe it was someone else. It didn't matter. If it came to a fight, Ellison would gladly lead his men onto the field of battle.

The doors of the Command Center opened, and Ellison walked inside. Captain Reyes stood up, raising his hand in quick salute. The four men around the conference table did the same.

"As you were," Ellison barked. "Show me what you've got, Captain."

"Yes, sir." Reyes reached for a stack of loose papers on his desk, handing them to the major. The topmost page showed a black-and-white image of a man in a dark suit and sunglasses. He was wearing a black t-shirt under his jacket, and his dark hair was tied back in a bun.

Reyes began his report. "We pulled these images from closed circuit security cameras at Hong Kong International Airport. We think that first man is Kaito Yoshida. Our facial recognition returned a ninety-three percent match, and even with the poor quality of the image, we're fairly confident."

It was even better than Ellison could've hoped. Kaito Yoshida was one of the most wanted men on the planet, and the purported head of the Ryoku terror group operating out of East Asia. It was believed by many that he orchestrated the Rainbow Bridge collapse in Tokyo—according to some reports, he brought it down with his own hands—and now, Ellison had him. Careers were made on less.

"So, you found the Shogun," a thin Irish voice said over Ellison's shoulder. "Mind if I take a look?"

Ellison turned around, bristling to see Hayden standing so close, but he knew better than to recoil his hand; instead, he handed over the picture. "What are you doing here?"

Hayden sat down at the conference table still looking at the image. "Don't worry yourself about it, Major. I'm not going to steal your moment. I'm just curious is all."

"That's not what I meant," Ellison said, and he could feel his face flush red. "I thought you were running an operation."

"Oh, I was, or rather I was going to before I sent Dubov in my place. I realized I'm much more valuable staying right here." Hayden reached inside his jacket pocket, fishing for his cigarettes. "By all means, Captain, continue with your briefing."

Reyes looked at Ellison. "Sir?"

Ellison nodded.

"Yes, sir. As I was saying, we tracked Yoshida entering the airport at thirteen-thirty local time with three associates."

Ellison looked at the next page he was holding. It was another picture from the airport, a wider shot. This time Yoshida was flanked on both sides. Two men wearing suits walked on his right, and a woman wearing light-colored pants, high heels, and a dark top stood on his left.

The two men in suits looked as if they could be opposites. The one standing closer to Yoshida had a slight frame. He was short with light hair, and he wore a pair of rectangular glasses. It was hard for Ellison to pick up all the details of the man's face through the grainy picture, but looking at him now, he thought he looked nervous—something about the man's thin lips and down-turned eyes.

The other man, walking on the right, couldn't have been more different—he was massive, built like an industrial refrigerator with a neck almost thicker than his head and buzzed black hair. The way he kept his eyes fixed straight ahead and held his arms slightly out from his body reminded Ellison of a bull.

As for the woman, just like Yoshida, she wore a pair of dark sunglasses. Her hair was pulled back in a high ponytail, and she trailed a small rolling suitcase behind her. Of the four of them, she was the only one who looked up at the camera, smiling, as if she knew her picture was being taken.

Reyes continued, "We only hit on facial recognition for one other—the woman."

"Who is she?" Ellison asked.

"We don't have much. No real name. No history. Just an alias—Kumiho. She's rumored to be a top lieutenant in the Ryoku."

Ellison handed the pages back to Reyes. "And what about Pòmén? Could one of those other two be the Broken Gate?"

Reyes shook his head. "There's no way of knowing that, sir."

Hayden laughed, tossing the photograph of Yoshida on top of the table. "Just like Army intelligence. Always willing to talk even when they've got nothing worth saying. Maybe, instead, you can tell us some of the things you *do* know."

"Yes, sir," Reyes answered. "We've confirmed that all four individuals boarded a flight from Hong Kong to San Francisco. They're current ETA is eleven hundred hours local time."

"San Francisco, you said?" Hayden leaned back in his chair, folding his hands behind his head. "Well, isn't that just perfect? It seems as if we've been looking at the wrong things, Major."

Ellison picked up the picture of Yoshida from the table. "What do you mean?"

"You really don't get it, do you? We all

thought Pòmén was a person—some Anom they were supposed to be recruiting—but it's the name of their mission." Hayden arched his eyebrows. "You know any famous gates lying around San Francisco, Major? Or maybe you can think of some other reason why a man who tears down bridges would want to visit?"

Ellison paled as he wheeled back on Reyes. "Wake up the colonel. Get him down here now. Put Fort Blaney on yellow alert. We're going to need briefing reports, and airport surveillance —"

"Everyone hold where you are!" Hayden raised his voice, and it was the loudest Ellison had ever heard him. He fished one of his cigarettes free from the pack, pulling it out with his lips, and everyone else in the Command Center —even Ellison—waited as he lit the end, took a long drag, and exhaled a thin line of smoke. "You said their plane won't land until eleven a.m. Pacific Time, isn't that right?"

Reyes nodded.

Hayden continued, "Well, that gives us all time to catch our breath and have a little conversation, doesn't it?"

Ellison squared his shoulders to Hayden. "There's nothing to have a conversation about. This is a priority-one event, and I have a responsibility—"

"I know what the protocols are, Stuart, better than you do." Hayden looked down at the orange ember of his cigarette burning between his fingers. "But then I want you to ask yourself if you still think those protocols are going to work here. And I want you to ask yourself what kind of effort it's going to take to stop a man like Kaito Yoshida. And the last thing I want you to ask yourself is this: Do you still believe Colonel McCann has the guts to make that call?"

Ellison didn't answer.

Hayden dragged again on his cigarette. "Because if you ask my opinion, Stuart, if you take this up to the colonel, it's already dead in the water, and I think you know it." Hayden put out his cigarette on the tabletop. "Maybe, instead, we hand this one off to the CIA—plan another special operation with the Anoms. We could get all the same resources to do the job, and none of the handwringing or headache."

Ellison shook his head. "It's a priority-one event. It requires a military response."

"But what if it wasn't a priority one? What if it was something much simpler? We could call it an interrogation." Hayden smiled. "That's the only way we get to San Francisco, Stuart, by leaving McCann in the dark, and you know it."

Ellison turned away from Hayden. He hated the suggestion of circumventing McCann's authority—even if the old man was slipping, he deserved better than having Ellison run an operation behind his back—but he also knew that

Hayden was right. The only way they could stop Yoshida would be to cut out McCann entirely. It was a line he could only cross once.

Ellison drew in his breath and turned back to Hayden. "If I allow this to happen, I want it to be my team in the field—my men with the Anoms—and I want command over the operation. That's the only way this works."

Hayden stood up from his chair, slapping his hand down on Ellison's shoulder. "You can have whatever you want, Major, as long as we get Yoshida."

CHAPTER 9

Jeremy sat on the concrete floor of the hangar, his back against the wall and his knees pulled up to his chest. Outside, through the double sliding doors, he could see fields of black asphalt broken up by lengths of rusted chain-link fence, and a line of pale-green weeds growing wherever the two met. The mid-morning sky was washed-out blue. It might've been the perfect California day—it looked as much—but Jeremy wanted to be anywhere else. Just eight hours ago, he was.

It was five-thirty in the morning, and they were gathered around the table in the Rec Room. Nyx sat next to Jeremy, her dark hair pulled back in a low ponytail. Gauntlet was still absent.

Across the table, Major Ellison and Lara sat in their usual seats, but instead of Agent Dubov, Hayden took his place, sitting on the other side of Ellison.

Hayden was the first to speak. "So, who wants to take a field trip?"

Ellison broke in before either Jeremy or Nyx could answer. "The CIA has requested our support in a special operation. We received intelligence last night that a high-value target is arriving in San Francisco. We're going to assist in detaining that target for transport and interrogation."

"Why the CIA?" Nyx asked. "Why isn't the Army doing this?"

Hayden lowered his chair to the floor. "The Army's in the business of reacting to a problem when it's already too late. In the CIA, we prefer to handle our business before the real trouble starts."

Ellison continued, "Our target is planning an attack on San Francisco. We also think he may be an Anom. We're assisting the CIA in order to save lives. That should be reason enough."

Then Ellison spent the next twenty minutes briefing them on the details of the operation. A passenger jet would land on the northernmost runway at San Francisco International Airport. Jeremy, Nyx, and a small strike team led by Ellison would ride out in a baggage car to meet the plane while it was still on the runway. Once they were in position, Jeremy would rip through the tail of the fuselage, and Nyx would flash herself and the rest of the strike team into the cockpit. The plan was to meet somewhere in the middle of the plane, hopefully with their target in custody. Meanwhile, a secondary team supported by Blackhawk helicopters would secure the perimeter and prepare for evac.

When Ellison had finished talking, Hayden pushed himself back from the table. "Just a quick snatch-and-grab. Who knows? You might even like it. A little more surgical than you're used to."

Now, back in San Francisco, Jeremy banged his head against the metal wall of the hanger. Sitting around a table on the other side of the country, everything had a way of sounding painfully simple—just a quick little snatch-and-grab, Hayden said—but Chicago was supposed to be easy, too. Then you get boots on the ground, blood on your hands, and suddenly everything goes sideways. You're left improvising, and every decision only compounds on itself, carrying you farther away from where you intended to go like a riptide in the ocean.

Jeremy banged his head against the hangar again. The dull thrumming inside his ears was getting louder—it sounded like the heavy, even percussion of a Blackhawk's rotor blades—until finally it was the only thing he could hear. He still stared at the washed-out sky through the open hangar doors, but now it felt like it was all around him. He was falling, and all he could see was the pale-blue sky and the bronze man falling below him.

Jeremy slammed his head against the metal wall a third time. Then the thumping in his ears stopped, and Titan was gone. He needed to focus on the task at hand. He looked away from the open hangar doors and down at the concrete floor next to him. There, on the ground, four playing cards were arranged in a square, two on the top and two on the bottom, each one printed with a different portrait. Jeremy used his index finger to slide the top cards down even with the bottom two. Now they made a straight line. On the far left, the ace of spades was printed with a picture of Kaito Yoshida—the Shogun. He was their primary target.

Jeremy closed his eyes, and he was back at Fort Blaney, sitting around the conference table.

"Why do you think the target's an Anom?" Nyx folded her arms across her chest.

Hayden's thin lips curled into a smile as he dug inside his jacket pocket. "Oh, we're fairly certain he is."

Hayden tossed the playing card face up on the table—the ace of spades—with Kaito Yoshida's picture embossed on the front. Nyx snatched it off the table almost as soon as it fell. She was so quick Jeremy couldn't even register the picture in his mind.

Nyx stood up out of her seat, holding the card in front of Hayden's face. "Are you joking about this?"

"No, I don't think I am," Hayden answered, the smile slipping off his face.

"You have us going after Kai? With a small strike team?" Nyx laughed and threw the picture down on top of the table. She turned to Lara. "Did you know about this?"

Lara shook her head. "If I had, I would have said something to you. Not sprung it on you like this."

Jeremy, meanwhile, felt lost. He didn't recognize the name Kai, and the man in the picture was unfamiliar. Whoever it was, Nyx wasn't happy to see him. She paced behind her chair, refusing to look across the table, and Jeremy didn't know if she was too angry or too afraid to look at Ellison.

Whatever Nyx was feeling, Lara's reaction seemed to be the same. Across the table, she looked suddenly pale and withdrawn. The only difference between the two women was that Lara couldn't pull her eyes away from the picture. She sat, staring down at the face emblazoned on the playing card as if she were waiting for it to come to life—afraid that maybe it just might.

Apparently, Ellison was confused, too; he glanced back and forth between Lara and Nyx before he finally spoke. "Kaito Yoshida—the man on that card —is the leader of the Ryoku terror—"

"Kai Yoshida is a killer." Nyx grabbed the back of her chair, fixing her eyes on Ellison. "He's going to kill us, every member of your small strike team, and half the people in that airport, and he's going to make it look easy, because that's what he was trained to do —right here at Blaney."

"What do you mean, 'right here at Blaney'? You're saying we trained him?" Ellison asked.

"That's exactly what she said, Major," Hayden answered, but he kept his eyes on Nyx. "Most of us here have a history with the Shogun."

"Is that what we're calling it now? History?" Nyx spit out her words. "Is history what killed Forcefield on Kai's way out the door? You remember him, don't you Agent Hayden? He killed Dr. Sutter, too. You remember him? You want me to keep going? He killed —"

"He killed a lot of people," Hayden finished for her. "I know that, same as you. And now he's back, so what do you want me to say? You can sit this one out because you know him? Because you're scared? That's not the business we're in."

Jeremy hunched forward in his chair, rubbing his hand back and forth across the back of his neck, feeling for his scar. "But in a way, that's better. Isn't it? The fact that we know him makes it easier. If this guy trained at Fort Blaney, we can just blow out his brainstem and be done with it. I mean, that's the point of these things, right?"

Hayden reached inside his jacket for his cigarettes. "That's a brilliant idea—truly. Just think of all the lives we could've saved if we had had a brain like yours back then. Makes me wonder what the rest of us were even doing."

"Kaito's not on a leash." Lara reached across the table for the playing card, turning it so that it was facing her right-side up. "Back then it never occurred to us. We didn't imagine... The microchipping started after Kaito. In fact, he's the reason."

"And the reason you called in the Army?" Ellison asked.

"Yoshida was a turning point for all of us." Hayden flicked open his lighter and touched the flame to the end of his cigarette. "It was the first time we saw what a single, highly-skilled, very motivated Anom could actually accomplish. He changed our research, our mission… He changed everything."

"So, how do we stop him now?" Jeremy asked.

Lara pushed the card back into the middle of the table. "When he was here, Kaito Yoshida was a Class Five Physic. He can change the state of inorganic matter with very few, if any, limitations—from solid, to liquid, to gas, and back again. He can turn the ground under your feet to quicksand, change an armored Humvee to vapor, or condense the air in the sky and drop two tons of solid nitrogen on top of your head. He makes Titan look like a teddy bear."

A black boot stepped down on the concrete floor of the hangar, landing over the playing card that bore the likeness of Yoshida. Jeremy looked up. Nyx stood over him, staring down with her hands on her hips. She wore her black pants and deep-purple compression shirt along with her black fingerless gloves. Her dark hair was pulled back into a tight French braid. She looked ready.

"What the hell are you doing?" she asked, her eyes moving from Jeremy to the playing cards lined up next to him.

"I'm studying their faces. I don't want to miss anyone on the plane."

"You don't need to remember their faces. They're going to be the only ones trying to kill us. Pretty hard to miss." Nyx looked down at both of her hands, turning her palms over, stretching out her fingers and closing them again.

"Your hands still hurting?"

"I'm fine," she answered.

Jeremy laughed. "You haven't been fine since Chicago."

Nyx faked a smile and spread out her fingers in front of Jeremy's face, wiggling them back and forth as if she were playing a piano. "Doc told me it's all in my head, remember?"

"Doesn't mean you're okay," Jeremy said.

"I'm okay enough." Nyx leaned her back against the hangar wall and slid down to the floor, sitting next to Jeremy. "And what about you? How's the head?"

Now it was Jeremy's turn to force a smile. "I'm guessing it feels about the same as your hands—not exactly right, but good enough not to matter."

Nyx picked up the Kaito playing card from the ground, holding it in front of her face.

"You two were friends?" Jeremy asked.

Nyx shook her head. "We were in the same circumstance at the same time. I'm not sure that's enough to be friends. I guess we'll find that out if he kills me."

She handed the card to Jeremy. He looked at the picture again. Yoshida wore a pair of dark sunglasses, and his long hair was pulled back. He didn't look dangerous, but Jeremy knew better.

"I'm not going to be late this time, Nyx." Jeremy dropped the playing card to the ground. "I can promise you that much."

"Don't do that," Nyx said, a sudden edge in her voice.

Jeremy looked up. "Don't do what?"

"Don't pretend like you would've made the difference in Chicago. I was there, too, remember? I was ten feet away, and I still couldn't save Talon. Gauntlet was there, too. Talon couldn't even save himself. So, if you say one more word about Chicago, I swear I might blast your pretty-boy face into next Tuesday. It's insulting to the rest of us."

Jeremy turned his shoulders to face her. "You don't think we could've done more?"

"Of course we could've done more!" Nyx snapped at him. "We should've saved him. You don't think I go to sleep telling myself that every night—playing out all the different what-if's in my head? How I should've flashed him away when I realized he was in trouble. Or maybe I could've flashed him away in midair before he hit that pillar and shattered his back. But every morning I wake up and none of it matters. Talon's still hurt, because sometimes that's just what happens. Sometimes you can do everything right, and people still get hurt."

"I know that..." Jeremy started to answer.

"But you don't sound like you know it!" Nyx

shouted back. "What do you think's going to happen, G? We're about to step in it, and people are going to get hurt, or worse." She looked down at her hands, opening her fingers. "Better that it's us."

Jeremy looked at the playing cards scattered across the ground and reached for the picture of Yoshida. "Better that it's him."

Nyx smiled. "Maybe—if that's what it takes."

Jeremy pushed the card away. He didn't want to think about the price the day might exact from them. He would rather focus on mission briefings and those damn playing cards, and then he could pretend Ellison's plan was enough to keep them safe. Anything else would send him spiraling back to Chicago. Jeremy had already lost so much—Talon, and Kate, and his mom and dad. He didn't want to imagine the next name on that list, as if thought itself could manifest into reality, but now Nyx had left him with no other choice. She threw back that curtain, thin as it was, and there was nowhere else to look.

CHAPTER 10

"This is why I hate flying," the Texan drawled, shifting his weight in the cramped airplane seat. Kaito Yoshida found himself nodding at the sentiment. This was why he hated flying, too.

Kaito had been sitting next to the Texan since takeoff from Hong Kong. It was a twelve-hour flight, and the Texan had been talking for eleven of those hours. He was a big man—tall with a pot belly. At one point, only a couple of hours into the flight, he had slapped his hand against his stomach and declared, "I ain't got a six pack. This here's a keg." Then he laughed raucously at his own joke.

The Texan had blonde hair mixed with gray —a moustache and full beard. He wore brown leather boots, and a big, silver belt buckle mostly hidden by the fold of his gut. Kaito thought the only thing missing from the cowboy was a tattoo across his forehead reading "USA."

Now the Texan pushed his heavy body back

against his seat, fighting for more leg room, and he swirled the last of his whiskey around in the bottom of his plastic cup. "You see, Kay-Doe, when you jam a hundred human beings into a steel tube, you're just invitin' trouble. But when you keep 'em locked up together for twelve hours straight and throw in a screaming baby, well, you're lucky if someone doesn't get killed. Only thing to do about it is drink. Am I right?"

From several rows in front of them, a baby screamed again.

The Texan slugged the last of his whiskey down his gullet and then elbowed Kaito in the arm, as if to emphasize his point. Kaito closed his eyes. He reminded himself that it wouldn't be much longer now. They were almost to San Francisco.

Just then, a small chime sounded from Kaito's wrist. He opened his eyes and looked down at the altimeter he wore in place of his wristwatch. They had finally passed below thirteen thousand feet in their descent. Kaito squeezed the silver button on the side of the altimeter to silence the alarm, and then unbuckled his lap belt.

The Texan leaned across the chair. "I don't think you can do that right now, Kay-Doe. Captain's got that sign lit up."

Kaito ignored the man. He stood up, opened the overhead bin, and pulled out his black duffle, setting the bag down on his empty seat. He unzipped the top and took out the red harness, slipping it over his arms and clipping the strap across his waist.

"Sir, I'm going to need you to return to your seat," a woman's voice ordered from the aisle.

Kaito looked up and found himself face to face with one of the flight attendants. She wore a smart navy-blue skirt with a white blouse, and her dark hair was styled in a short pixie cut. She was smiling, but twelve hours into their flight, and the look was tired and forced.

"I'm not going to do that." Kaito clipped the harness strap across his chest, pulling it tight.

The flight attendant's smile fell away. "Sir, you need to sit dow—"

Her last word died in the air as a large hand covered in dark gray fur closed around her throat, choking her to silence. Kaito could see long, black claws, each one curved over like a karambit, digging into the woman's skin, sending streams of bright red trickling down her neck and staining her white blouse.

Kaito still looked in the flight attendant's eyes. She had been frustrated with him before. Then she was angry. Now she was terrified. Kaito cocked his head to the left to look behind her. Kumiho stood in the aisle, pressed against the woman's back—it was *her* hand holding the flight attendant in place.

The rest of Kumiho looked as she always did —the same way she appeared in the Hong Kong airport, and the same way she looked for the entire twelve hours of their flight. Her long black hair was pulled back in a tight ponytail, high on the back of her head, but there was no smile on her face—no snarl, either. If anything, she looked bored. Her whole appearance reminded Kaito of the way his parents looked on Sundays in their church—a pair of blank slates only there for the sake of routine. The only change at all—or at least the only change that Kaito could see—were the claws curving down from the ends of Kumiho's fingers, and the matted gray fur covering her hand and forearm.

Kaito was impressed. He had seen Kumiho transition before, changing her shape from the slight femme fatale into the broad, hulking beast—a hybrid Anom who resembled something very close to the werewolves in old horror films. But it had always been all or nothing with her. She was either all Kumiho or all monster. Kaito had no idea she could transform herself one limb at a time, and he was struck by the restraint such a gradual metamorphosis would require. He had known her for three years, and frankly, he was surprised she had enough steel to hold herself back.

"New trick?" Kaito asked.

"New to you," she answered.

Kaito smiled. He would have to compliment her on her self-control later. As for now, he gave a nod, and Kumiho lifted the flight attendant off the ground by her throat. She spun her around, and slammed her down, prone in the aisle.

"What the hell, Kay-Doe?" the Texan lurched forward from his seat, trying to stand up, but he forgot about his seatbelt. Kaito punched out his fist, and a black orb the size of a bowling ball formed in mid-air above the Texan. It fell straight down, landing square on the man's fat gut, and the Texan doubled over in his seat. Then he puked. Whiskey and wet pretzels sprayed across the airplane's floor.

Someone screamed at the front of the airplane's cabin, and a man with broad shoulders wearing a navy polo stepped into the aisle. From his thick arms and bristled haircut, Kaito pegged him as ex-military—possibly an Air Marshal. The man started running down the aisle, undoubtedly racing back to help.

Kaito punched forward with his hand, and in the middle of the air, twenty feet away, a black cylinder that looked like cut onyx appeared out of nothing. It flew forward, travelling at the same velocity as Kaito's clenched fist, and it connected with the man's jaw. There was a sudden explosion of broken teeth flying into the seats around them like popcorn exploding from a bag. Then both the man in the polo and the black cylinder fell to the ground. There were more screams, but no one else stood up from their seats.

Kaito reached into his duffle bag and pulled out a second harness, handing it to Kumiho.

Then he turned and started for the back of the plane. In front of him, Janus and Shān already stood in the aisle.

In another time and place, the two men might have seemed comical. Janus, with his feathery white hair, was only a wisp of a man. Shān was his opposite, tall and broad, and built like a block of marble. Both men already wore their harnesses.

As Kaito reached the two men, he held out one of the straps hanging from his waist, offering it to Janus. On the end was a metal carabiner. Janus clipped the strap into place, and in turn, he held out his own carabiner to Kaito. Yoshida locked it in.

"Have you activated your cells in California?" Janus looked up nervously from the strap buckled to his harness. "I don't feel like swimming five miles to shore."

"My men will be waiting for us in boats," Kaito assured him. "I told you I've planned for everything."

Kumiho joined them at the back of the plane. She held out her carabiner, and just like before, Kaito clipped it to a ring on his own harness. The whole process was repeated again until all four of them were bound together by the nylon straps —an inseparable ring.

"Now, let's try to enjoy this part. It should be fun." Kaito raised both of his hands over his head, touching his fingers to the ceiling of the airplane's cabin, and he closed his eyes. All at once, the heavy white plastic of the ceiling started to melt away under his touch, slipping over his fingers and running down his hands and wrists like hot wax.

The effect spread across the ceiling of the plane and moved to the walls on either side of the cabin, the heavy white plastic shedding from the metal airframe like sheets of water sloughing off a windowpane.

Kaito could hear screams all around him—loud voices lost in panicked cries. He could hear the metallic clicks of seatbelts releasing on either side of the aisle, and the sounds of people scrambling out of their seats, climbing over the rows in front of them or behind, doing anything in their power to get away from the dripping plastic, but there was nowhere for them to go.

Kaito opened his eyes. He watched as the metal airframe warped and folded around his hands, the silver aluminum dripping down into the cabin.

A woman screamed behind them, "Please don't—"

But her voice was lost in a roar of rushing air. Kaito's body jerked back like a thousand hands were pulling on him at once, throwing him out into the wind, and the cold, and the nothingness of the sky. He was falling.

Kaito could feel the air cutting across his face, sucking at his jacket, stealing the wind out of his lungs. Then, all at once, he was surrounded by water. He wasn't falling through the sky anymore. He was sinking instead into a clear pool. This effect only lasted for a second. Then the water tore away from his body, and Kaito and the others were dropping again through the empty sky.

It wasn't the ocean they hit—not yet. Kaito knew, even for all his powers, there was no way he could survive a fall like that. Instead, the water around them was his own doing, formed from the air. It only lasted for a second before it was ripped apart by gravity and the wind, but it was still enough to slow them down.

Kaito formed the water again. The four of them connected by the nylon straps were surrounded by another globe of water, slowing them down in the middle of the air—sinking instead of falling—if only for a second. Then he did it again and again, controlling their descent.

Kaito looked down. Far below them, the pieces of the airplane were still in freefall toward the Pacific, torn in half where Kaito had turned the airframe to liquid. He watched as it hit the water, exploding into two clouds of shrapnel against the gray Pacific.

He told himself it was a sacrifice of necessity —a choice he would gladly make again. The passengers on the plane had given their lives as martyrs to a cause they would never understand. If needed, Kaito would do no less himself. They were all soldiers now in the same war, whether they knew it or not, and sacrifice such as theirs was required.

CHAPTER 11

Jeremy could hear Ellison's voice roaring across the hangar. "Everyone on me!"

Nyx and Jeremy rose to their feet and turned to look at the major. They could see him walking quickly between the other soldiers, heading straight for them, his jaw set and his face red.

Nyx crossed her arms over her chest. "What happened?"

"Flight 834 is down," Ellison growled between his teeth.

Nyx's eyes went wide. "What? How?"

"How do you think?" Ellison answered. "We were tracking the plane five miles off the coast when it dropped off our radar. Coast Guard is scrambling now. What do you think they're going to find?"

Nyx shook her head. "Kai didn't fly out of Hong Kong just to blow up a plane, and he sure as hell didn't kill himself, if that's what you're thinking, Major."

Ellison folded his hands behind his back and stared down at Nyx. "I'm not saying Yoshida's dead—far from it—but he's out in the wind, which makes him twice as dangerous." Ellison raised his voice so everyone in the hangar could hear him. "As far as we're concerned, the threat posed by Kaito Yoshida and the Ryoku is still imminent. I want everyone to maintain ready status until further notice."

Two hours later, Jeremy was lying flat on his back on the cement floor, his hands folded on top of his chest and his eyes closed. He wasn't asleep—he wasn't even tired—but there was little else to do. The only alternative was pacing in endless circles around the hangar. That was Nyx's choice. She had spent the last two hours walking in an endless loop. At first, Jeremy had tried to walk with her—he thought she might want to talk, but after the second circuit, when Nyx still hadn't spoken a word, Jeremy gave up. That's when he bailed and found his place on the floor.

Now, stretched out on the concrete, it wasn't exactly comfortable, but at least it was cool against his back, and there were worse ways to spend an afternoon—like following Ellison through the forest to play another round of capture the flag, or sitting in a laboratory suffering through Individual Research Training with John Langer.

"You should wake up," Nyx said, and she

kicked the bottom of Jeremy's boot.

Jeremy kept his eyes shut. "Why would I want to do that?"

"Because Ellison ordered us to stay ready," Nyx said.

Jeremy pushed himself up on his elbow. "Yoshida already blew up a plane. Even if he's still alive, maybe that's enough terrorism for one day, don't you think?"

Nyx shook her head. "You don't know Kai."

Before Jeremy could answer, a new voice called out from behind them, "Hey there! Excuse me. You're the Anoms, right?"

Jeremy twisted around, and saw one of the soldiers walking towards them, a tall man with a shaved head. He was smiling.

"Don't think we've actually met," the soldier continued. "I'm Sergeant Stevenson, part of the second unit."

Jeremy climbed to his feet. "Right. I'm G-Force." He held out his hand.

Stevenson laughed. "Yeah, that's the same stupid name they told us in the briefing." He looked at Nyx. "And what are we supposed to call you?"

Nyx put her hands on her hips. "Call me none of your business."

Stevenson laughed again. "Come on, that's not true, is it? After all, you're the reason we're here, right—genetic anomalies, I mean."

"What do you need from us, Sergeant?" Nyx

growled.

Stevenson smiled. "Me and my men were just talking, and we realized we've never seen what any of you people can do in person. We thought you could put on a show for us—something like a demonstration."

Jeremy felt his stomach turn heavy and drop. He couldn't get a clear read on Sergeant Stevenson when he walked over, but now the man was painfully obvious—he was just another bored asshole looking to fill his time. Maybe the men in his unit sent him over here on a dare, or maybe Stevenson dreamt up this genius plan on his own. It didn't matter. To Nyx's credit, she saw through him from the start.

Nyx dropped her arms, her hands balled into fists at her side. "You should go back to your men, Sergeant."

"What are you so angry about?" Stevenson chided. "We're just having some fun here, aren't we? Give us a quick show and we'll leave you alone."

Nyx shifted her weight from one foot to the other. "You want a show, Sergeant? G-Force can control gravitational fields. They covered that in your briefing, right? It means he can crush your skull like a grape. I bet he'd pop that tiny head of yours right off your shoulders."

Stevenson laughed. "And what about you, beautiful? What do you get to squeeze?"

Then Jeremy had heard enough. He stepped

between Nyx and Stevenson. "Walk away, Sergeant."

"Or what?" Stevenson's hand moved to the Beretta holstered on his hip. "You're gonna crush my head like a grape? You think I'd ever let that happen?"

A crack like thunder rippled through the hangar. Stevenson looked down at the floor, and a jagged fissure in the cement ran straight between his legs. He traced the line back with his eyes, following the break in the concrete to its origin at Jeremy's feet. It was one of a hundred cracks, all of them spider-webbing out across the shattered floor from where Jeremy stood. Stevenson went pale.

"You really think that gun can stop me?" Jeremy asked.

The soldiers on the other side of the hangar scrambled to their feet, yelling for Stevenson to fall back. Jeremy could hear the panic in their voices. Stevenson must have felt it, too. The ashen-faced sergeant listened to the men. He edged away from Jeremy and Nyx, his hand still on his pistol, until finally he deemed himself at a safe distance. Then Stevenson turned and walked quickly back to the other soldiers.

"What the hell was that?" Nyx hissed under her breath, still staring at the soldiers across the hangar. "I'm not some damsel in distress. I don't need you defending my honor."

"That's not what I was doing. That's not—"

Jeremy stopped himself. "Wait a minute, are you seriously angry at *me*? Because of something that guy said?" Jeremy pointed to the crowd of soldiers.

"I need you to fight with me, not for me. There's a difference," Nyx snapped, keeping her voice low. "I don't need you to save me."

"That's bullshit!" Jeremy said. "What was I supposed to do? Just stand here?"

"Don't do it again," Nyx said.

Jeremy looked at her. He had seen Nyx angry with him before. She had a way of setting her jaw, and then her eyes would half-close and thin lines would wrinkle her forehead. This look was something different—somehow softer. It was still anger, but it was bleeding into guilt.

"You mean with Yoshida, right?" Jeremy asked. "You don't want me squaring up with the Shogun if it means saving your life?"

"Just… don't do it again," Nyx repeated.

Before Jeremy could answer, a new sound filled the hangar. It was the roar of helicopter rotors as two Blackhawks touched down outside. Then Ellison was running through the open hangar doors, waving his arms over his head and signaling everyone to load into the choppers.

Jeremy tucked his radio receiver into his ear, and he could hear Ellison shouting over the other noise. "—go! We are go! Unit one, load up on my left! Unit two on the right! G-Force, to the left! Nyx on the right! We are go! I repeat, we are go!"

Jeremy ran out of the hangar with everyone else and scrambled into the Blackhawk. He took the first empty seat, but even before he could strap himself in, the helicopter was lifting off the tarmac into the San Francisco sky.

Ellison's voice screamed again through Jeremy's receiver. "We have contact with multiple Ryoku gunmen on the Golden Gate Bridge. Yoshida is confirmed to be with them. Local police are in the area, but we're taking lead—"

A new voice cut over the radio. "Just where they said they were going. Good thing we were waiting at the airport."

Jeremy thought it sounded like Sergeant Stevenson, but he couldn't be sure. He looked around to see for himself, but there was no sign of the sergeant in the Blackhawk. Ellison and Nyx were missing, too. All three must have loaded in the other helicopter.

"What's our plan, Major?" It was Nyx's voice over the radio.

"We're deploying at both ends of the bridge. Unit one to the north and unit two to the south. We fast-rope in and engage and neutralize the hostiles. Nyx and G-Force will push through to the center of the bridge. Find Yoshida. He's our finish line. Screw that up, and nothing else matters."

Silence came back over the radio, and the only noise Jeremy could hear was the roar of the

Blackhawk. The helicopter banked to the left, and out of the open cargo door Jeremy could see the rising burnt-orange towers of the Golden Gate Bridge. The Blackhawk was over the water.

Jeremy watched as the soldiers did final checks of their gear—pulling down goggles, racking the charging handles on their M4's, or touching their fingertips to various pockets. They were nervous; so was he.

Jeremy had practiced fast-rope insertions often enough at Fort Blaney, so he knew what was coming next. The soldiers would slide down a rope suspended from the helicopter one at a time, taking up defensive positions around the insertion point until the last man was clear. Then they would advance together on their target. Jeremy's role was the only one that was different. He would be the first man out the door, and he didn't get the benefit of a rope. They had practiced that, too, but practice and real life were almost always different.

The Blackhawk turned left again, and Jeremy's open door was pointed straight down the road leading across the Golden Gate Bridge. He could see cars jammed from one end of the bridge to the other, none of them moving. They were stuck behind a barricade of other vehicles, intentionally turned in on themselves to block the road, and Jeremy could see a crowd of men gathered behind the barricade. They had rifles—machine guns—all trained on the Blackhawk.

A voice screamed in his ear over the receiver. "Go, go, go! Now, now, now!"

CHAPTER 12

Jeremy stepped out of the Blackhawk, and for a second, he was falling. His first instinct was to zero-out his gravity and float softly to the ground, but that wasn't the plan—that wouldn't help anybody. Instead, he raised his gravity and slammed into the street like a literal ton of bricks, crushing the asphalt under him and leaving a shallow crater in the road.

Then Jeremy pushed out against the gravity field around him, forcing it higher, using it as a shield for the Blackhawk helicopter and the men fast-roping down behind him. Jeremy could feel the pressure of the gravity field pushing against his body. It was a sensation like sinking into warm mud, and it was painfully quiet inside the field. The roar of the Blackhawk, the percussion of the machine guns, and the shouts of the men all sounded far away. Jeremy's hands started shaking. He pushed harder against the gravity field, but he felt the ground sway unsteady under his feet.

"Unit one clear!" a voice shouted over his receiver.

Jeremy made one last push against the gravity field. Then he dove to his right behind a car and let the field drop. All at once, the noise of the world came rushing back, filling the space around him. So did the fresh air. Jeremy drank it in, trying not to shake.

Nyx flashed out of her seat in the Blackhawk in a flare of purple light. The two soldiers on either side of her were gone too. In that same instant, all three of them reappeared, standing in the road, facing a crowd of armed men taking cover behind abandoned cars.

Then, for a whole second, nothing seemed to happen. Nyx had teleported out of the Blackhawk so fast that everyone else was still trying to react, but the lull only lasted for that second. Then the men behind the cars switched their aim, swinging down their machine guns to point at this new threat on the ground, and they opened fire.

The two soldiers Nyx brought with her sprinted out to the flanks, diving for cover— just like they were trained to do—answering the armed men with gunfire of their own, but Nyx held her ground. She punched out with both of her hands at once, and two bolts of energy shot forward, slamming against one of the cars the Ryoku were using as a barricade. The side doors of the beige sedan crumpled as the energy bolts struck home, and the whole car rocked back before settling into place. Nyx didn't have time to hit it again.

She flashed away, back inside the helicopter. The other soldiers were on their feet now, shuffling forward to the rope suspended from the Blackhawk. Some of them would fast-rope down to the roadway. Nyx would take care of the rest. She grabbed two more soldiers by the backs of their collars and flashed down to the street again.

As soon as their feet touched the ground, the soldiers with her were moving—rifles raised and firing as they ran for cover—but Nyx felt her stomach twist and the stale taste of vomit rise in her throat. One of her knees buckled, and she dropped to the pavement, reaching out with her right hand to steady herself on the ground.

Teleporting always came with waves of nausea—it was something about screwing with her equilibrium—and the quick turnaround was taking its toll. Up and down; back and forth. It felt like Nyx was spinning circles in place.

She spit on the ground, trying not to puke, and punched out with her left hand. Another energy bolt shot towards the barricade of cars. It hit a black SUV, and the windshield shattered in a spray of glass.

Nyx flashed up to the Blackhawk again. Only one soldier was left inside. It was Major Ellison.

Nyx grabbed him by his shoulders and flashed down to the pavement. Then Nyx punched out twice—a right followed by a left—and two thin energy bolts shot forward. They both struck the beige sedan again, but this time the car barely moved. Nyx was exhausted.

Ellison ran to his right, raising his rifle to fire off a spray of bullets at the Ryoku. Nyx followed behind him, moving as fast as she could, and they both tumbled over a concrete barrier at the side of the road. Nyx landed harder than expected, dropping onto her stomach and chest and knocking the last of her wind from her lungs.

"You good, freak show?" a voice asked from above her.

Nyx looked up. Sergeant Stevenson was kneeling next to her, his M4 tucked against his shoulder, trained on the barricade of cars. Before she could answer, Stevenson pulled the trigger and a three-round burst popped from his rifle. He fired again. And again. Stevenson dropped out his magazine, reached for another on his belt, and slammed it home.

He looked down at Nyx. "I said, you good?"

She nodded.

Stevenson fired his rifle again and scurried forward, staying low behind the concrete barrier until he was crouched next to Ellison.

Nyx could hear the Major's voice over her receiver. "Blackhawks one and two, get eyes on the bridge. I want you to find Yoshida."

Another voice answered. "Copy that. Black-hawk one is gaining altitude and circling now. Over."

A different voice broke over the receiver. "Major, this is Blackhawk two. I've spotted an adult male on foot approaching the south tower. Looks like he might be your man. Over."

Ellison turned back to look at Nyx, pressing his hand against the contact mic around his throat. "G-Force and Nyx, you are free to engage. I repeat, engage Yoshida!"

Jeremy heard Ellison over his receiver, "Engage Yoshida!"

All at once, the noise around him faded out as if Jeremy had raised his gravity field—only he hadn't. This was something else, and now his head felt like it was splitting open. Jeremy knew Ellison's order was coming. It was the whole reason he was here in the first place. If the Ryoku were just a bunch of guys with machine guns, they would have left him back at Fort Blaney. He was here to answer Yoshida, but that didn't mean he wanted the job.

Jeremy tried to catch his breath. Suddenly, he was hyperventilating. He reached behind him, touching his hand to the grill of the sedan he was using as cover, trying to steady himself. He could do this. He took a deeper breath. He *knew* he could do this.

Jeremy closed his eyes, raised his gravity, and

his fingers crunched through the plastic of the grill, pushing his arm forward, until he found the engine block. Jeremy raised his gravity even more. He closed his hand over the metal of the engine, and he could feel it twisting and oozing between his fingers like stale Play-Doh.

Jeremy rose to his feet, spinning his body as if he were throwing a hammer for the track team, and the car dragged behind him. He spun again, and this time the car wrenched off the ground. He let go.

For a second, the gray sedan seemed to hang in the air, floating in a silent arc toward the huddle of Ryoku gunmen. Then it fell, slamming down on top of another car, and the dull crunch of crushing metal mixed with the sound of shattering glass. The Ryoku gunmen dove to the ground behind their makeshift barricade, covering their heads, but Jeremy was already running. As soon as he let go of the car, he charged after it, using it as cover as it tumbled through the air, and when the sedan fell on top of the other car, Jeremy leapt.

He zeroed out his gravity and jumped over the sedan. He passed above the Ryoku gunmen. He cleared three more rows of stalled cars before he finally landed back on the road.

Now he was well past the barricade, but Jeremy could still hear the men shouting behind him—there was another burst of gunfire. He thought about turning back. He could charge at the Ryoku gunmen from behind, split their attention, and take them out one at a time—it would have been easy—but that wasn't *his* objective.

Instead, he started running in the opposite direction. He had to reach Yoshida. That was the only thing that mattered. The Blackhawk pilot said a man was approaching the south tower.

Jeremy scanned his eyes across the bridge, but he couldn't see anyone walking. A quick movement on his right caught his attention. Jeremy glanced over. It was a woman looking out the passenger window of her SUV. She was watching him from only a foot away, her face pale and taut. She looked afraid.

Then, for the first time, Jeremy really looked at the cars lining the bridge. Some were empty—they belonged to the lucky few who ran off the bridge before the Ryoku could force them back into their cars—but other vehicles held men and women, whole families, and they all looked scared. The Golden Gate Bridge may have been the Ryoku's target, but these were the people who would be their victims.

"G-Force, you have incoming from the north." The voice over his receiver sounded like the pilot of the Blackhawk.

Jeremy looked up, and then he could see the man, too. He recognized the face from one of the pictures they pasted on the playing cards. This man was the King of Clubs—the King, not the

Ace—so Kaito Yoshida was somewhere else. This man was nothing more than his lackey.

The King of Clubs stepped in front of a white box truck, and Jeremy thought the similarities between the two were fitting. The man in front of him looked like a walking refrigerator—a bull dressed in a black suit. He marched forward between the rows of cars with his arms outstretched to his sides.

Jeremy stepped closer. "I'm not here for you, but I can be."

The big man didn't answer. He stood his ground and rolled his head from side to side, and Jeremy could hear the bones popping in his neck.

Then there was nothing more to say. Jeremy ran forward, drew in his breath, and raised his gravity. He threw a left hook to the side of the big man's head. It landed, solid, just along the man's jawline in front of his ear, with the same weight as a cinderblock. It should've knocked him out cold, but the other man didn't move. His head didn't even snap to the side.

Jeremy threw the hook, and when his hand connected, it stopped in place. It was like punching his fist against a wall, and it *felt* like hitting concrete—the white-hot pain raced from Jeremy's knuckles up the length of his arm. He raised his gravity more and fired a right cross into the center of the big man's face. This time, as the punch landed, it felt like Jeremy broke his hand. He punched again—a left hook down to the body. He punched again—a right uppercut tucked under the big man's chin. And again—a left jab to the man's eye socket.

Each time it felt like Jeremy was hammering his fists into a steel plate, but the man didn't move. He wasn't bleeding or staggering back. In fact, he was smiling, his thin lips stretching wider with every punch.

Jeremy lowered his hands, dropped the gravity field, and tried to catch his breath. That's when the big man finally hit back—a straight punch to the face. Jeremy saw it coming, but he was too slow to do anything about it. Jeremy felt his nose crushed under the man's heavy hand. Both his eyes welled with tears, and he staggered back as his nose began to fill with blood.

Then the big man spun on his heels, faster than Jeremy thought possible for someone his size, and he threw a back kick aimed at Jeremy's chest. Jeremy tried to raise his gravity field—tried to block it—but there was simply no time.

The kick landed and sent Jeremy sprawling off his feet, flailing through the air. He fell back in the roadway, and for a second, he couldn't breathe—and with the tears in his eyes, he couldn't see, either. He could only taste the warm, metallic blood pooling inside his mouth. Jeremy forced himself up onto all fours and spit. Wet blood spattered across the asphalt. He wiped his mouth with the back of his hand and reached for the car next to him, pulling himself up to his feet.

He had to find the big man again. He had to know which direction the next attack was coming from. He had to raise his gravity field before he could get knocked down again, or worse. Jeremy blinked his eyes against the light, and when he opened them again, he could see the massive figure standing exactly where he was before, in front of the box truck, with his arms down at his sides; he was waiting.

Nyx edged herself higher on the concrete barrier, craning her neck to peer over the top, exposing as little of her face as possible. From where she was hiding, twenty yards away, she could see three cars, a couple of dark SUVs, and a light-blue mini-van blocking the road. They were lined up in a makeshift blockade, and behind it, she could see the Ryoku soldiers moving on the other side of the cars.

Just then, as if to prove they were still a threat, one of the Ryoku gunmen raised his AK-47 over the hood of a black SUV and squeezed the trigger. Nyx dropped down below the wall as the machine gun erupted with a spray of bullets. Sergeant Stevenson, still kneeling next to her, raised his own weapon over the concrete barrier and answered, emptying his magazine. More gunfire erupted from the Ryoku, and another soldier answered with his M4—this one from the other side of the road.

Nyx raised her eyes above the concrete wall again. Now she looked well-past the blockade, her eyes traveling over the bridge. In the distance, she could see the white top of a charter bus stuck in the traffic jam. Another burst of gunfire came from the Ryoku, and Nyx ducked behind the wall.

"Are you going or what?" a heavy hand slapped down on her shoulder.

Nyx turned to look.

It was Stevenson; he dropped the magazine from his M4 and reached for a new one. "You go on three, all right, freak show?"

Stevenson slammed his magazine into place and edged in front of Nyx. "Here we go. One... two... three!"

Stevenson jumped up, unloading his M4 into the barricade of cars, and Nyx scrambled to her feet. She spotted the white roof of the bus again and closed her eyes. Then she felt like her body was filled with electricity from the tips of her fingernails to the bottoms of her heels—every muscle buzzing alive with sharp, numbing pain—and even though her eyes were closed, she could see the flash of light in front of her.

Nyx opened her eyes and found herself kneeling on top of the roof of the charter bus. The Ryoku gunmen, crouching behind their barricade, were a hundred yards behind her. In front was the Golden Gate Bridge and somewhere, far in the distance, was Kaito Yoshida.

Nyx jumped down from the bus, and in mid-air she flashed herself to the roadway. This time the wave of nausea followed her—she could feel her stomach tighten—but she ignored it. This was no time to get sick. She started running up the bridge, weaving between the jammed cars.

Nyx knew it would be faster to pick another target and flash again, jumping across the bridge a hundred yards at a time, but she couldn't risk it. She would need all her strength—all that energy—to face Kaito, and even then, she understood, it might not be enough.

All at once, Nyx heard footsteps—loud, heavy, and fast—running behind her. They weren't dull like the sound of running on pavement, either. These were higher pitched, echoing, and metallic. It was the sound of crushing metal. Someone was running across the tops of the stalled vehicles. Nyx spun around to face the threat.

At the same time, a mass of gray fur, black claws, and yellow teeth leapt through the air. Nyx closed her eyes and flashed away on instinct. Now she was standing on the other side of the road, staring back at where she stood only a moment ago. She watched as the gray-furred creature landed on all fours in the road—it would have been right on top of her if Nyx had stayed in place. Then the monster stood up on its hind legs.

It looked, for lack of a better word, like a werewolf—or rather what Nyx imagined one would look like. It wore no clothes, but it was covered in thick, gray fur. It stood on its back two legs, but they were doubled over like an animal's, and its hands were tipped by long, dark claws that curved from the ends of its fingers like knives. It also had a tail—long and bushy like a fox's—the tip of it touching the ground, and it had high, pointed ears. Its face and snout were long and tapered, and it had yellow eyes and long, yellow teeth, bared by its snarling lips.

Nyx squared her shoulders to the monster. "Stay back!"

Kumiho growled her answer—a wordless, guttural sound from deep inside her chest. Then she charged.

Nyx punched with her right hand, and a bolt of energy shot out toward the monster. It hit Kumiho in the chest, throwing her back off her feet and sending her through the windshield of a red sedan.

For a second, Nyx thought maybe that would be enough. She could see the beast folded in half on top of itself, trapped in the front seat of the car, but then Kumiho roared—a bellowing growl from the back of her throat that shook the air. She kicked out the shattered remains of the windshield with her hind legs. Her claws tore through the thin metal of the roof, and Kumiho climbed free of the wreckage. She walked across the car's hood and dropped down to all fours, growling again, her eyes narrowing on Nyx.

At least the monster was hurt now. That was something. Nyx could see a jagged gash in Kumiho's shoulder cutting deep down to her bone —maybe deeper. Thick red blood poured from the open wound, staining the gray fur of her arm and chest a dull burgundy, and it fell freely down to the road, pooling around her front foot. If nothing else, it was enough to slow the monster down. Maybe, given enough time, it would do even more.

But then the bleeding stopped. The blood pouring from the open wound thickened. It filled the gaping cut in her shoulder like caulk, knitting the broken bone and skin back together, until all that remained was a crooked scar of pale skin, free from the heavy gray fur. Kumiho reared back on her hind legs and leapt onto the roof of another car.

Nyx closed her eyes and flashed to the other side of the road. Kumiho was behind her now. Nyx spun around and punched in the air with both of her hands, hoping to catch the monster with a double bolt in her back, but Kumiho was too fast for her. She had already turned, diving under the energy blast and lunging forward.

Nyx flashed again, back to the other side of the road. This time it made her sick—she couldn't help it. She choked back the bile rising in her throat, but there was no time for her to recover. Kumiho was running at her again. Nyx punched with her right. A thin bolt of energy shot forward and evaporated halfway to its target.

Kumiho leapt onto the hood of another car and launched herself into the air. Nyx tried to twist away, but she was too late. The curved claws raked through her side, opening three long cuts across her ribs.

Nyx spun around and fell back into the road. Her hand went to her side, and she could feel the warm, wet blood sticking to her palm. Then panic took hold. Nyx could feel herself gulping in quick and shallow breaths of air. She needed to get back on her feet. She needed to defend herself. She needed to think. *Why couldn't she think?* Both of her hands felt like they were on fire.

A deep growl reverberated from somewhere above her head, and Nyx looked up. She could see Kumiho perched on the roof of the car above her. Her yellow eyes were half-closed, and her teeth were dripping wet. She looked hungry— ready to make her kill. The monster growled again—louder this time—and jumped into the air.

Nyx closed her fists and punched out with all her strength. This time—somehow—it worked. A bolt of energy shot from each of her hands, catching the wolf square in her stomach as it fell on top of her. It sent Kumiho flying back, twisting through the air. She struck against one of the suspension cables and pinwheeled over the side of the bridge with a high-pitched yelp.

Nyx dropped her head to the pavement and pressed her hand against her ribs—a shiver of pain ran up and down her body; she reached for the contact mic around her throat. "I'm down. Nyx is down."

"Then get yourself back up!" Ellison growled over the receiver.

Another voice broke over the radio—one of the pilots. "Target has reached the tower. I repeat, target has reached the south tower."

Ellison shouted again over the receiver. "G-Force, you need to engage Yoshida! Nyx, get yourself back in the fight!"

Jeremy pushed the contact mic against his throat. "I'm working on it."

Twenty feet in front of him, the big man still stood with his arms at his sides, waiting in place, blocking the road across the bridge. Beyond him, Jeremy could see the south tower of the bridge rising into the sky. There was still time to reach Yoshida, but not if he stayed here any longer.

Jeremy clenched both of his fists. "I'm not asking you again, tough guy. Out of my way."

The big man raised his arms. "I can absorb whatever you throw."

"Yeah, you absorb. I got that much." Jeremy stepped closer. "But how do you fly?"

The man's forehead creased. "Fly?"

Jeremy raised his gravity and punched down into the road. As his fist slammed into the asphalt, Jeremy could feel the bridge ripple under him like a bobber dancing in the waves. The roadway splintered in a thousand directions, each of the cracks radiating out from the epicenter of his punch. Then it seemed like the road sagged under him. Jeremy pulled back his hand and punched again. The bridge shuddered, and he could hear the whine of twisting metal. Suddenly, the shattered asphalt caved around them, and all at once, the roadway opened like a giant sinkhole. Chunks of black asphalt, broken metal, an empty car, and the big man standing in front of him all fell straight down through the bridge, tumbling toward the water below.

Jeremy had started falling too, but as soon as the hole opened under him, he zeroed out his gravity, floated into the air, and settled back on solid ground. Then he dropped the field and took a quick breath. He looked down through the broken roadway just as the big man hit the water. Jeremy took another breath—a sigh of relief—but nothing was over. As much as he wanted it to be finished, Jeremy knew he still needed to reach Yoshida. That was the prize.

He ran forward, and as he crested the bridge, he could finally see the base of the south tower. Kaito Yoshida stood next to it, looking straight up at the orange metal, shielding his eyes from the sun.

Yoshida looked different, at least from what Jeremy expected. He still wore his hair in a high bun, but he was dressed in a light-gray suit with a white dress shirt—a change from the all-black outfit he wore in the captured video from the airport. Now, seeing him stare up at the tower, Jeremy thought he looked more like a tourist crossing the bridge than an international terrorist or an Anom assassin. Even so, there was no mistaking the man.

Jeremy stopped running and yelled out, "Yoshida!"

Yoshida didn't look, but kept his eyes fixed on the tower. "You shouldn't do that, you know. You should never yell at the person you're trying to kill. It puts you at a disadvantage."

Jeremy walked forward. "Maybe I'm not trying to kill you yet."

Yoshida laughed. "Maybe not." He looked at Jeremy. "I recognize you, though. I saw your video from Chicago. It was... impressive."

"Yeah, and I know who you are, too. Kaito Yoshida, the guy who kills other people for fun."

Yoshida turned away, looking again at the tower rising above them. "Honestly, I'm surprised we're even having this conversation. I brought Shān along specifically to deal with you. You know he absorbs kinetic energy—"

"He mentioned the absorb part," Jeremy said. "Didn't say if he could swim, though."

Yoshida looked back, and his eyebrows knit together in confusion. But as the answer dawned on him, he started to laugh again, wagging his finger at Jeremy. "That's very smart. If you can't go through the mountain, you walk around. I'm impressed again."

"Yeah, I'm a friggin' genius." Jeremy squared his shoulders. "So, let's do a quick headcount. You're up here, he's down there, and from what I hear on the radio, you got a werewolf just up the street. Where's your fourth man, Kaito? You leave him behind to watch the lair?"

"You're smart enough. Maybe not as funny as you think you are, but also reckless. I can see why the others would be afraid of you." Yoshida smiled.

"But you're not afraid of me, are you, Kaito?" Jeremy asked.

Yoshida shook his head. "No, I'm not afraid. I know the cost these powers demand of us. Even this conversation between us now— I imagine we're only talking because you need time to re-cover. Otherwise, there'd be a lot more punch-ing and kicking, I presume."

Jeremy wanted to answer—to say something like he was more than ready—but the lie would have been too obvious. Both of Jeremy's hands were still shaking from punching through the bottom of the bridge. Maybe Yoshida could see that, or maybe he couldn't. Either way, it was better for Jeremy to keep quiet.

"We're not gods," Yoshida said. "We were never meant to be omnipotent. Each one of us has our limitations, and in those limits, we find ourselves. For example," Yoshida stepped closer to the tower. "am I the kind of person who kills you where you stand, or do I use all my power to bring down this bridge instead? I doubt I have the strength to do both. And your choices are just as plain. Do you try and stop my escape, or do you hope to save these people's lives?"

Jeremy closed his fists—he knew he was out of time. "How about I choose door number three. You touch this bridge and I'll kill you."

Yoshida shook his head. "No, you won't. You can't fight against your nature." Then he pressed his hand flat against the tower, and the burnt-orange metal seemed to ooze around his fingers, bending and folding under his grip like dough. Yoshida twisted his arm, and the metal in his hand lost its shape. It pooled over his wrist, running down his forearm like rust-colored oil, falling off his elbow and splashing onto the ground. The effect traveled up the tower. Liquid-metal peeled away in heavy sheets, cascading down to the roadway.

The tower groaned above them, low and plaintive, and Jeremy could feel the bridge rock sharply to his left. It was followed by another groan—louder—turning to a high-pitched shriek. The tower was twisting over on itself. The damage was done.

Yoshida pulled his hand away and held it out to show Jeremy; it was stained bright orange from the metal. "I made my choice. Time for you to make yours."

But there was no decision to make—not with a hundred or more cars trapped on the bridge and God-only-knew how many people. Jeremy zeroed out his gravity and jumped, forcing himself higher above the road—seven hundred feet straight up into the air—until finally he was even with the massive cables running over the South Tower.

The problem before him was a simple one— the left side of the tower was compromised, and now the weight of the bridge was folding it over on itself. If the south tower fell, the weight on the cables would drag down the north tower, too, and the entire bridge would collapse into the bay.

Fortunately, the answer was just as simple. Jeremy needed to balance the weight. He needed to hold up the cables. He needed to give the people below enough time to escape.

Jeremy pushed out with both of his hands, trying to force the gravity field even farther away from his body. If he could zero out his gravity and extend the field around the cables, there was no reason they couldn't float in the air, the same as him.

Jeremy pushed out again, trying to hold back gravity with his hands, and gradually, everything around him went cold and silent. He felt like he was in the middle of nothing—no noise, no wind, no air—a perfect vacuum of space. He could feel it tugging at his face and fingers—the cold biting at his skin. A deep, throbbing pressure pounded in his ears. Jeremy closed his eyes, grit his teeth, and punched out again against the gravity field. He knew he couldn't last much longer.

Then the radio receiver crackled to life in his ear. "Target has jumped. I repeat, target has jumped off the bridge. It looks like he stepped into a waterspout—some sort of column of water."

Ellison's voice answered, "Where's G-Force?"

Jeremy opened his mouth to answer, but there was no voice—he couldn't catch enough of his breath to speak the words. The edges of his vision blurred.

The helicopter pilot answered for him. "I got your man flying over the bridge. Looks like the south tower is badly damaged. He might be the only thing holding it up."

Ellison barked over the radio, "G-Force, I order you to reengage Yoshida! Do it now!"

The pilot radioed again. "Major, I don't think you copied my last. It looks like your Anom is the only thing holding the bridge together. He —"

Ellison roared over the receiver. "Forget

about the bridge! Get to Yoshida now! He's the only thing that matters."

Jeremy pushed harder against the gravity field above the tower, both of his arms shaking and his shoulders burning under the strain. The people below needed more time—just a little more time and everyone could clear the bridge.

Jeremy's vision blurred again, the edges darkening and everything else clouding over. He knew what was happening. Jeremy opened his mouth in a final, voiceless scream, and then it was over. Everything went black, and he was falling.

Nyx was running, moving in an uneven half-gallop across the bridge. Her side felt like it was on fire—the long, jagged cuts bleeding freely—and it was hard to breathe. At least she was moving.

Suddenly, the cables on the right side of the bridge went slack, the metal wires billowing out in arcs, and the bridge itself pitched to the right. She could hear the shrill scream of twisting metal as the roadway lurched forward, rolling under her feet.

The helicopter pilot shouted over Nyx's receiver, "The Anom is falling!"

Nyx looked up at the south tower. It was bent over to the right—folded almost in half—but in the sky above the deformed metal, she could see G-Force, his unconscious body falling straight down.

Nyx closed her eyes and flashed. In the next moment, she was two hundred feet in the air, falling next to G-Force. She reached out and grabbed his arm. Then she flashed again.

Nyx opened her eyes, and she was back on the ground, kneeling in the road on the far side of the bridge. G-Force was with her, lying on his back. His eyes were still shut. He was unconscious, but alive.

Nyx pressed the contact mic against her throat. "I have G-Force. We're both safe, but he needs a medic."

Before anyone could answer, a deafening roar started behind her. It was the sound of folding steel, shattered asphalt, crushed vehicles, and desperate screams, all of them roiling together into a sickening wail—a last cry for help as the bridge fell away into the water.

CHAPTER 13

"Would you look at that." The thick-necked man pointed his stubby finger at the television screen. "They took out the whole damn bridge."

The image on the screen showed what was left of the Golden Gate Bridge. It was night in San Francisco, but the surface of the water was lit from spotlights mounted on dozens of boats. They bobbed in place on the dark water. Then the camera panned up, and the orange metal of one of the towers came into view, stabbing at a sharp angle through the soft whitecaps of the bay.

White words in a blue ticker scrolled across the bottom of the television screen: *Genetic Anomalies Destroy Golden Gate Bridge—U.S. Military Engage Terrorists at the Scene—37 Confirmed Dead—Search for Survivors Ongoing—Connection to Downed Flight 834 Still Under Investigation—*

The man with the thick neck grabbed the remote from the table and pressed the button to unmute the television; a man's voice could be heard narrating over the images of the San

Francisco Bay. "Search and rescue efforts are still under way at this late hour in San Francisco, a city reeling from what appears to be another attack by genetic anomalies.

"It's now being reported that there are thirty-seven confirmed deaths from the Golden Gate's collapse. We expect that number to rise, perhaps dramatically, throughout the night. At this hour—"

The screen went blank as the man mashed his thumb down on the power button. "Bunch of amateurs. Is that really the best you can do?" He looked over his shoulder at Gauntlet.

From the other side of the motel room, Gauntlet leaned against the water-stained wall, staring down at the television. He had been standing there, watching the news reports from San Francisco for over an hour, ever since the thick-necked man—Special Agent Morris—had summoned him from the adjoining room with a sharp, "Get in here." Before that invitation, Gauntlet had been left alone for the better part of two days, ever since he and Agent Dubov arrived from Fort Blaney.

Now Morris turned around in his chair to look at Gauntlet. "Well, what is it? Can we expect that same amateur bullshit out of you, or not?"

Gauntlet kept silent. He would let Morris wait for his answer. After all, they had done the same with him.

On the plane, Gauntlet had asked Dubov where they were going, and what they were doing once they got there, but Dubov refused to answer. Instead, after the plane landed, he ordered Gauntlet into the black windowless van waiting for them on the runway. The two of them were driven together in silence to the motel, and when they arrived, Dubov escorted Gauntlet to his room, leaving him with a single command: "Stay." Like a dog.

The motel room they gave him was sparse —bed, table, chair, and bathroom—but it was made even more so by Agent Morris removing the television and clock radio. They were kind enough to leave him a couple bottles of water, and after dinner on their first night, they thought enough to bring him a greasy cheeseburger. At lunch the next day, Morris opened the adjoining door and tossed him a room-temperature ham sandwich. The food proved to be the only distraction. Everything else was waiting, not that Gauntlet cared. He preferred the silence and the solitude. Agent Morris, on the other hand, seemed to chafe at the quiet.

"I asked you a question, and now you're ignoring me. That's not gonna stand." Morris stood up from his chair, tipping it over.

It was obvious to Gauntlet that Morris was spoiling for a fight—two days of waiting in the motel had worn the other man's nerves raw

—but that only made Gauntlet's silence more effective. Besides, if Morris really wanted a fight, Gauntlet would oblige. He turned his head, just enough to let Morris know that he was listening and watching. Then Morris's face went red.

"You're gonna say something!" Morris growled, and he started forward across the room, but before anything more could happen, the door opened and Dubov wheeled in.

"Stop it," Dubov snapped. "You're embarrassing yourself."

A woman followed behind Agent Dubov. She wore a white blazer and matching pencil skirt, and she carried a brown leather briefcase. As she came through the door, Morris lowered his arms, and Gauntlet thought he looked almost embarrassed.

"By all means, don't stop on my account." The woman set her briefcase down on the table and turned to look at the room. "After all, no one enjoys an old-fashioned pissing contest more than I do."

Morris hung his head. "No, ma'am. We're finished."

The woman arched her eyebrows. "Suit yourself." She stepped toward Gauntlet, extending her hand. "My name is Anna Jordan, COO of Reah Labs. I'm the one who asked you here. It's a pleasure."

Gauntlet kept silent.

Anna looked at him unphased; she only

dropped her hand and smiled. "A man of few words. I already knew that from your file." She sat down in the chair at the table, crossing her legs at the ankle. "Well, we should get started anyway. What's the status of your mission?"

Dubov turned his chair around to face her. "We had limited surveillance on site, but security seems as light as we thought it would be. If we're quick about it, there shouldn't be a problem."

"And extraction once you're done?" Anna turned to face Morris.

"I have men in place," Morris mumbled. "We're just waiting for you to give the order, ma'am."

"Which I suppose brings us to you." Anna folded her hands in her lap and looked at Gauntlet. "What do you know about the Knights of the Crusade?"

Gauntlet crossed his arms. "They're domestic terrorists—a would-be militia."

"Yes, they are," Anna said, "and they've taken a particular interest in Reah Labs. The Knights claim to hate all genetic anomalies, but that hasn't stopped them from claiming one among their number—a man they call the Incubus. He's proven to be... problematic." Anna reached inside her briefcase, pulling out a folder. "In your file, it states that your armor prevents us from reading your thoughts or emotions. Is that still true?"

Gauntlet nodded.

"We think this same ability will let you resist the Incubus." Anna rose from her chair. "I've brought you here to accompany agents Morris and Dubov on their mission. If the Incubus shows up and tries to stop them, I want you to kill him."

Gauntlet bristled under his helmet. "I'm not your assassin, Ms. Jordan."

"Nor do I want you to be." Anna shook her head. "Think of yourself as my insurance policy, but make no mistake, Gauntlet, if you encounter the Incubus, you'll be lucky to kill him before he does the same to you." Anna fixed the smile back on her face. "Now, if there are no other questions, I think we can get started. Agent Morris—"

Morris reached for a radio lying on top of his bed and held down the push-to-talk button. "We have authorization to begin. Roll the transport and prepare for extraction." He tossed the receiver aside. "Let's hurry up and get this over with."

Gauntlet followed Morris and Dubov out of the motel room, leaving Anna Jordan behind. As the three men stepped outside, Gauntlet could see the same windowless black van that drove them before idling in the parking lot. The side doors slid open, and a ramp lowered to the ground for Dubov. Morris climbed into the front passenger seat. Gauntlet took the seat behind the driver, and as soon as they were all loaded, the van started to move. The ride itself was shorter than Gauntlet expected. Five minutes after they left the motel, they turned right into the parking lot of a strip mall.

"Here we go," Morris said.

Gauntlet looked out the windshield at the building. If Morris meant they had arrived at a secret research facility, the strip mall certainly didn't look the part. Then again, maybe that was the whole idea. The van slowed to a crawl as they edged past the stores in the complex. Gauntlet could see that most of the shops were already darkened for the night. The only one still lit up was the second from the left. The sign above read: U.S. One Bank.

As they rolled past, Gauntlet looked inside. It seemed to him like any other bank in a strip mall, with gray walls and a row of teller windows across the back. Immediately in front of the door, the night security guard sat behind a wide desk. He wore a white buttoned shirt and a black hat. Gauntlet could see his eyes following the van as it moved past the front window of the bank. Then the van turned the corner around the side of the building.

"That was it. You ready?" Morris asked.

Gauntlet looked at Dubov. "Ready for what? It was a bank."

"Let me tell you about this *bank*," Dubov said, resting his chin on top of his hooks. "Its doors and windows are two-and-a-half-inch-thick ballistic glass. They could stop a fifty-millimeter round if they needed to. Why do you think that is? And under the security guard's desk, next to his knee, is a minigun that fires two thousand rounds a minute. Make no mistake, these men will kill us."

Morris turned around in his seat. "And that's why you're going up on the roof to kill him first. Then we can all get inside, safe and sound."

"He's just a security guard," Gauntlet said.

"No, he's a terrorist working for terrorists." Dubov folded his hooks, one on top of the other, and quietly clicked the metal. "You have your orders."

The van door opened, and Gauntlet climbed out. He jumped at the wall of the building, planted his foot on the bricks, and pivoted away, landing on top of the van. Then he jumped again, his fingers curling over the edge of the wall, and with a final push rolled himself onto the roof. He looked behind him, and the van pulled away, turning around to the back of the strip mall.

Gauntlet rose to his feet. It was darker on top of the building, away from the lights in the parking lot and the soft glow of signs hanging above the row of stores, but the Exocorium Armor was already compensating for Gauntlet's vision, funneling what little light was available directly into his eyes. Now he could see perfectly—not exactly like it was daylight, but close enough so that he wouldn't trip or stumble over any of the pipes crisscrossing in front of him.

Gauntlet picked his way across the roof until he stood over the bank. Maybe he was directly above the security guard now, but he would need to know for certain. The Exocorium Armor understood. Gauntlet's vision fogged over, and the scattered stones on the roof disappeared into a palette of blues and purples, and then three feet to his left, he saw a blob of orange and red shaped like a man—the heat signature of the guard.

Gauntlet raised his arm, and the crossbow snapped into place over his wrist. He took his aim and fired straight down, through the roof. The orange blob slumped forward. Gauntlet lowered his arm, and his vision returned to normal just as the van pulled in front of the bank.

He could hear the van doors open and close below him, followed by another sound—shattering glass. The van pulled away, and Gauntlet dropped down from the roof, landing between Morris and Dubov. He looked at the bank. The glass in the front door was completely gone now, scattered in broken shards across the sidewalk and littering the entrance of the bank.

"You said it was bulletproof," Gauntlet said.

Morris knelt down and picked up a chunk of the glass. He turned it over in his fingers, and Gauntlet watched as it frosted over. Then Morris tossed it up to Gauntlet. The shard of glass was coated in a thick layer of ice, and it was freezing cold to the touch.

Gauntlet dropped it, and as the glass hit the ground, it splintered into a dozen more pieces; he looked at Morris. "You're an anomaly, too?"

Morris winked. "You think you're the only one with tricks?" He stepped through the shattered door and called over his shoulder, "Help him inside."

Gauntlet pulled Dubov's chair over the lip of the door, and then he joined Morris standing behind the security guard's desk. The guard was bent over in his chair, his face and chest lying on top of the desk. Morris grabbed him by the shoulder and pulled him back, and his chair wheeled away from the desk. Now Gauntlet could see the Gatling-style minigun bracketed to the floor next to where the guard sat.

So, Morris and Dubov had been proven right. The man they had Gauntlet kill was much more than just a security guard. If they had walked up to the front door and the guard was still alive, he would've tried to kill them.

Morris pulled the guard's ID badge from his shirt. "All right. We're going downstairs. You wait up here."

"You mean wait here for the boogeyman," Gauntlet said.

"Whatever you want to call him," Dubov answered.

"But what are we doing here?" Gauntlet

asked.

Dubov ignored him. He raised his hook in the air and wheeled away from the security desk. Morris followed. They moved together to the steel doors of an elevator on the back wall, and Morris touched the guard's ID badge to a scanner. Then the elevator doors opened, and both men moved inside.

Morris pulled the Sig Sauer from his shoulder holster, pulled back the slide to chamber a round, and turned back to Gauntlet. "If anyone comes through those doors, you kill him. That's why you're here."

The elevator doors shut, and Gauntlet was left alone. He had understood his role in the night's proceedings even before Morris's final instructions. He was supposed to kill a guard and stand watch, but neither of those answered his question. The real reason for being here was downstairs with Morris and Dubov.

Gauntlet closed his eyes and tried to listen, straining to hear the voices from the floor below. Then it was more than just Gauntlet listening. It was also his armor. The Exocorium could *feel* the noise around him. It could detect the microvibrations bouncing through the floors of the building and translate those tremors to sound. All at once, Gauntlet could hear everything happening below him.

There was a woman's voice; she was sobbing. "I don't know. I swear I swear I don't know. You have to believe me. I don't—" Her voice was lost in a shrill scream.

Morris's voice cut in, "You're running out of time. Don't make me ask again."

The woman was still crying, but she said nothing.

"All right. You're useless, then," Morris said, and Gauntlet heard a single gunshot. The crying stopped.

"Your turn," Morris chimed.

A man's voice answered him, "But she was telling you the truth. We don't have what you're looking for. We can't help you."

"Well, for your sake, let's hope that's not true," Morris said.

Then Gauntlet had heard enough. Whatever else they were here for, the sounds coming from downstairs signaled an execution, and he couldn't allow that to happen and do nothing. He stepped to the elevator and laid his hand over the card scanner. He didn't have an ID badge like the one Morris took off the guard, but the Exo-corium armor matched the magnetic signature, and the doors slid open. He stepped inside.

When the doors opened again, Gauntlet stepped out into a room that didn't look much like a bank at all. Two long tables with black Formica tops were positioned in the center of the room, and each one held a pair of computer monitors. Gauntlet could see Dubov, sitting in his wheelchair behind the closest monitor on the left, picking away at the keyboard with both of his hooks. Farther back in the room, two doors opened off the back wall, and from what he could see, each one appeared to lead out into a separate hallway, one turning to the left and the other wrapping around to the right. On the right side of the room, another long black counter lined the wall, with a sink and coffee pot on top of it.

Everything else about the room reminded Gauntlet of the labs in Fort Blaney, with their sterile, steel walls and fluorescent lights overhead. It was all familiar to him, except what he saw on the left side of the room.

On the left, Gauntlet could see the aftermath of what he had heard above. Two bodies lay prone on the floor nearly on top of each other —a man and a woman, their dark blood pooling together under their bodies and staining their white lab coats and blue scrubs. Gauntlet looked closer at their bodies, and he could see marks on their skin over their faces and around their throats—dark, black bruises with gray at the edges and cracked open like charred wood. It was frostbite. So Morris had done more than just kill them.

Now Agent Morris stood over the bodies, and he held another man—another researcher dressed in the same lab coat and blue scrubs— by his neck. Morris held him pinned back against the wall, and with his other hand, he pressed the barrel of his Sig into the man's temple.

"Let him go," Gauntlet growled from under his helmet.

Morris turned back to face the elevator and Gauntlet. "What the hell do you think you're doing? We told you to wait upstairs."

"And now I'm here." Gauntlet stepped closer to Morris. "And I said let him go."

Morris looked back at the researcher he held against the wall. "Who are we talking about? This one here?" He poked the man in the forehead with the barrel of his Sig. "Or one of these others, 'cause it might be a little late for them."

"I'm not going to ask you again." Gauntlet closed his hands.

"Fine." Morris shrugged. "I'll let him go." Morris dropped his hand away from the man's throat and turned around to fully face the elevator and Gauntlet. Then he reached behind him with the Sig and fired twice, point blank, into the researcher's chest. The researcher jerked back into the wall, bounced off, and collapsed face down on top of the other two bodies.

Morris shot again without looking, pointing his gun down into the lifeless body. "There. I let him go. Happy?"

Gauntlet started forward.

"Ah, ah, ah!" Morris reached into his pocket and pulled out a silver remote control about the size of a cell phone. He held it out, waving the device in front of Gauntlet's face.

"You really think we'd take you out for a walk without bringing your leash?" Morris smiled. "Now personally, I think it's time you turned around and got yourself back upstairs, before I trigger that chip in your neck and pop your brainstem like it's a cherry tomato."

"You should listen to him," Dubov said, never looking up from the computer monitor. "Agent Morris doesn't believe in making idle threats."

Gauntlet didn't need the extra warning; he could hear the danger in Morris's voice for himself. He reached behind his head, running his fingers down the back of his neck until he felt the small spike at the base of his skull, like the head of a pin. Gauntlet pinched it between his fingers and flung it away, halfway to where Morris stood.

Morris laughed. "And what's that supposed to be? You expect us to believe you pulled out your own goddamn tracking chip?"

Gauntlet stepped closer to Morris. "Believe whatever you want, but if you press that button, I'll kill you."

"See that? And Dubov just warned you about making idle threats. Now we're gonna have to see for ourselves." Morris mashed his thumb down on the control panel, and a loud snap sounded from the middle of the room, like someone set off a firecracker, and a ribbon of gray smoke rose off the floor where Gauntlet had tossed the microchip.

Morris laughed. "Well, this just got a whole lot more fun, didn't it?"

He raised his gun, but Gauntlet was faster—he pushed out his arm, and the limbs of his crossbow folded into place. Gauntlet fired the bolt, and Morris turned away, covering the back of his head and the side of his face with his arm. The bolt struck the back of Morris's shoulder, but it didn't sink into the muscle like Gauntlet expected. Instead, it shattered on impact, raining down to the floor in a thousand broken pieces. Morris ran for one of the doors on the back wall. Gauntlet pulled back his arm, the crossbow reloaded, and he aimed again. He fired.

Morris careened through the open door and stuck out his hand behind him. Suddenly, a cloud of vapor filled the empty door frame, and Gauntlet could hear a sound like splintering glass. The fog dropped away, and Gauntlet could see what really happened. His arrow had hit a wall of ice and now it stuck in place like a dart in a board.

Gauntlet walked to the block of ice, reached out his hand, and ran his fingers down the smooth surface. It filled the doorway, a foot thick, clear as glass, and freezing cold. He could still see vapor rippling off its surface.

Gauntlet reached behind his back and grabbed the handle of an axe as it folded out from his armor. He brought the weapon around, over his head, and slammed it into the ice wall. The blade sank into the ice and stuck, but nothing more. There were no cracks or fissures other than the one spot where the axe struck home. Gauntlet pulled it free and tried again with the same result. It would take him hours to break through to the other side.

"Agent Morris draws heat from the air around him. He can freeze the water vapor," Dubov said from his chair.

Gauntlet started to turn to face the other man, but suddenly, heavy pressure coiled around his throat, squeezing him by his neck and cutting off his air. It felt just like someone had slipped his head through a noose, and now they were pulling the rope tight, choking him where he stood.

Gauntlet reached for his neck to rip away whatever it was, but to his surprise, it wasn't rope or wire. It felt thick and rubbery, like a garden hose covered in slime twisting around his throat. It was pulsing.

The cord jerked Gauntlet back from the door, pulling him away and nearly sending him off his feet. Then it coiled around his throat a second time, winding tighter. Gauntlet couldn't breathe. His ears burned, and his whole head felt painfully full, like someone had filled every inch of his helmet—no, his skull—with hot sand. It was difficult to think, to focus. He needed air.

He reached for the hand axe still embedded in the block of ice, but before he could grab it something heavy wrapped over his arm, holding him back. Gauntlet looked down, and he could see a long, gray tentacle with suckers on one side of it—just like an octopus—twining around his bicep and forearm, coiling over his wrist.

"Morris kills with ice. I prefer, if you pardon the expression, a more hands-on approach," Dubov whispered into Gauntlet's ear. The frail man was closer than he should've been.

Two more tentacles wrapped around both of Gauntlet's legs, and another twisted over his other arm. Gauntlet could feel the weight across his shoulders and back. Whatever it was—*whoever* it was—they were on his back. All the tentacles constricted at the same time, squeezing, and Gauntlet could feel his own pulse thrumming inside his head. He staggered back, turned, and threw himself as hard as he could against the wall.

Dubov laughed in his ear. "What are you trying to do? You think I have bones for you to break?"

Gauntlet stumbled forward. The tentacles coiled around both of his legs made it difficult to walk, fighting against him for every step, and the tentacle wrapped over his left arm tried to rip his hand away from his throat, but Gauntlet's fingers held tight in place. The little space it afforded him was the only reason he was still conscious. Gauntlet reached out with his right hand, holding onto the counter to keep himself from collapsing.

"My armor—" he choked.

"It won't save you. You can't move. You can't breathe. Soon you'll be dead." Dubov wrenched at Gauntlet's left arm again. This time he pulled it free, and Gauntlet's arm swung wildly over the counter, sending the coffee pot crashing to the ground.

Gauntlet's right leg buckled, and he fell to one knee. "The armor—" he choked again.

"Yes, your precious armor. We're going to cut it off your corpse and see what it can really do." Dubov squeezed again, constricting the tentacle wrapped around Gauntlet's throat.

Gauntlet forced himself back to his feet, pulling himself up by the counter. His vision blurred. "The armor—"

"What?" Dubov screamed in his ear. "What about your armor?"

"Conducts... electricity."

From the inside of Gauntlet's wrist, a long black dagger flipped up, spinning into place in the palm of his right hand. Dubov tried to pull back on his arm, but he was too late. Gauntlet stabbed the knife forward, jamming the blade through the outlet on the wall and deep into the electrical lines running behind it.

Suddenly, all the tentacles coiled around

Gauntlet's body constricted even tighter, the muscles activated by the electricity surging through Dubov's body. Gauntlet could hear a wild, high-pitched scream in his ear, cut off in Dubov's throat almost before it began. Gauntlet twisted the blade in the wall until finally the acrid smell of burnt skin rose around him. Then he pulled the dagger out of the socket. All the tentacles twisted around his body went limp, and Dubov slid off Gauntlet's back to the floor.

Now, for the first time, Gauntlet could turn around and see Dubov in his truest form. His hairless face with his sharp nose looked the same —except for the bright red, blistered skin cracking open and peeling from the muscle. Dubov's arms, however, were something else. Both of his hooks were gone. So were his arms. His long white sleeves were split open to his shoulders, and where his arms should have been, four charred and blistered tentacles splayed across the floor—two on each side of his body. The same was true of his legs. Dubov's pants were ripped open, and four more tentacles spread out across the tiled floor. Then Gauntlet understood what Dubov really was: an Anom hidden in plain sight.

Dubov's head lolled to the side, and he let out a whispered groan. Gauntlet reached down and grabbed the man by his shirt, pulling his head and shoulders off the ground. But as he lifted, a slather of skin stuck to the tiled floor, pulling away from Dubov's scalp. If it caused him any pain, Dubov didn't react—his nerves were already dead.

Dubov tried to smile, but the skin on his lips stuck together. "What more... can you do... to me?"

He let go, and Dubov fell back on the floor, wheezing for air. Gauntlet stood over the half-conscious man, staring down at his burned face, and there were no thoughts of pity in him. Maybe he should have felt remorse for the burned man and what he had done, but it wasn't there. Another time, Gauntlet knew, he would have felt sorry for Dubov, but not anymore. He despised the man at his feet, and the only thing he felt for him now was contempt and the satisfaction that at least, before his end, he had suffered.

Then something was wrong. Gauntlet and Dubov weren't alone in the room anymore. The Exocorium armor could feel the vibrations thumping across the floor—heavy footsteps running fast. It detected the heat-signature of another body as it crossed the threshold into the room, and then the armor was turning Gauntlet around, even before the man inside could understand what was happening.

Gauntlet's shield spiraled out from his arm and locked into place. As he finished wheeling around, he could see Morris charging across the room, pistol raised. Morris shot once, twice.

Both rounds struck against the shield and fell away.

Morris closed the gap between them, trying to shoot again. Gauntlet swung out with his left, the edge of his shield clipping the barrel of the Sig and knocking it away. He followed with a right cross, his fist aimed at the center of Morris's face.

Somehow, even off balance, Morris parried the punch. He ducked and countered with a right hook to Gauntlet's stomach and a left hook to the ribs. Searing pain ripped across Gauntlet's abdomen—more pain than he expected through his armor. He staggered sideways and threw a wild backfist with his right hand. Morris ducked easily, dancing away from the danger.

"How's that feel, huh?" Morris bounced back and forth on the balls of his feet like a boxer. "You still wanna play the hero?"

Gauntlet looked down at his armor. Across his side and spreading back towards his ribs, the red Exocorium was covered in a sheen of pale white frost. He touched it, and it felt brittle. Gauntlet closed his hand on the armor, and the Exocorium shattered under his fingers, falling away. Underneath it, he could see the exposed skin of his side and stomach. It was raw and red, like a burn, but it was only visible for a second before the rest of the Exocorium spread over the wound, filling in the gap in the armor like tar on a roof.

"That was after a couple of punches. Less than a second. Wait until I get my hands on you for real," Morris said.

Gauntlet lunged forward, feinting with his left like he would punch Morris with the edge of his shield, but at the last second he pulled back and drew the broadsword from over his shoulder, swinging it down.

Morris raised his arm to block. The sword struck Morris's arm just in front of his elbow, and it should have cut clean through. Instead, the blade shattered on contact, bits of silver raining down like confetti, and all Gauntlet held was the hilt and half of the blade.

Morris countered. He threw a right cross that landed dead center on Gauntlet's helmet, and crystals of ice overspread the Exocorium. Gauntlet staggered back, barely able to see.

"First, I'm gonna freeze your armor." Morris closed on Gauntlet again, shuffling forward with a left hook to his temple.

"Then I'm gonna freeze your skin *under* your armor." Morris threw another left hook to Gauntlet's ribs.

"Then I'll freeze the blood inside your veins 'til your dead." He grabbed Gauntlet by the throat, pushing him back against the wall, and Gauntlet could feel the cold seeping through his armor, burning against his neck.

Morris winked. "Quick and easy, sweetheart."

"Not quick enough," Gauntlet growled. He punched straight up with his left hand, catching Morris under the elbow. Gauntlet could feel the other man's joint bend and strain under the sudden pressure—and then the bones dislocated. Morris screamed.

Gauntlet wrapped his whole arm around the back of Morris's neck, reaching around to grab him by his chin. Then he pulled on his face so hard that he lifted Morris off the floor, twisting his head halfway around his body. There was a dull crunch of breaking bone. Gauntlet let go, and Morris collapsed to the floor, his head twisted at an obscene angle.

Gauntlet doubled over, leaning back against the wall as he tried to catch his breath. His throat felt like it was on fire—swollen and raw. He needed air. The Exocorium helmet split down the center and folded over his shoulders, exposing Gauntlet's head. He gulped at the fresh air, but it still wasn't enough. He stood up, raised his chin, and reached for his neck. Gauntlet could feel the brittle Exocorium under his fingers. He closed his hand around his own throat, and the armor broke away under his grip, falling to the floor. He was sure his throat looked raw and burned, but at least he could breathe.

Gauntlet closed his eyes. He needed to think. He hadn't intended to kill Morris and Dubov, but now that the deed was done, Gauntlet would need a story to explain their deaths. A bargaining chip might serve him even better.

He looked around at the carnage in the room. Morris and Dubov were obviously down here for a reason. Whatever they were after, they were willing to kill the people who worked here to get it. That meant it was valuable to Reah Labs, and that made it useful to Gauntlet. He only needed to figure out what *it* was.

Gauntlet looked at the computer monitor where Dubov had been sitting. On the screen, a gray window showed a loading bar. It was full— a hundred percent complete. Stealing information was probably a good start. Gauntlet stepped to the computer and pulled the flash drive from the side of the monitor. He held it down on his forearm, and the red Exocorium closed over it. Then he looked back at the monitor. Another program was open behind the first window, but he could only see the title: DEEP CLEAN. Gauntlet clicked over, and in the new window was a block of text. He skimmed through the words:

OXYHYDROGEN FUEL
THERMOBARIC INCINERATION
SECONDARY BLAST CHARGES
CONTAINMENT and DESTRUCTION of SITE 322

He read it over a few more times before it

clicked. It was a program to destroy the research facility. First, oxyhydrogen would flood the air, ignite, and burn up everything in the lab—paper, plastic, metal, or flesh. Secondary charges would bring the building down on top of them. For the Knights of the Crusade, it was probably a fail-safe. For Morris and Dubov, it was a way to cover their tracks. It could serve the same purpose for Gauntlet.

He looked down at the bottom of the window. Whatever password was required to initiate DEEP CLEAN, Dubov had already hacked it. All Gauntlet needed to do was point and click. He pressed the button on the screen, and red lights started flashing overhead. A five-minute countdown popped up on the monitor.

"Wait," Dubov's thin voice called from the floor.

Gauntlet ignored him.

A minute later, Gauntlet stepped out of the strip mall, walking towards the van idling in the parking lot. He climbed into the passenger seat.

The driver looked at him. "Where are the others?"

"Dead," Gauntlet answered.

The driver didn't need to hear anything more. He threw the van into gear and slammed his foot down on the gas, peeling away from the strip mall. They turned right out of the parking lot, driving in the opposite direction of the motel. Gauntlet had no idea where they were going, but the driver knew, and for now that would be enough. It meant there was a plan.

The two men rode together in silence for half an hour, turning down one dark street after another, the van rarely dropping under fifty miles per hour. Finally, they turned into an airstrip, and the van stopped next to the runway.

A small white jet sat at the end of the tarmac, lights on and engines idling. Its door was open, folded down, and at the bottom of the steps Gauntlet could see a familiar face, although it wasn't the face he was expecting. It was Agent Hayden.

Gauntlet opened his door and stepped out of the van.

Hayden smiled. "And where's Agent Morris? Agent Dubov?"

"Both dead," Gauntlet said. "They walked into an ambush."

Hayden maintained his smile. He pulled a pack of cigarettes out of his inside jacket pocket. "I see. Was it the Incubus then, or one of your more run-of-the-mill ambushes?"

Gauntlet shrugged. "It all happened downstairs. I didn't see any of it."

"But you know they're both dead?" Hayden asked.

Gauntlet didn't answer. The two men stood staring at each other, until the van pulled away from the airstrip, kicking up a cloud of dust in its wake.

Hayden turned to watch it go, it's taillights receding into the dark. Finally, he looked back at Gauntlet.

"And where are the files?"

Gauntlet shook his head. "I don't know anything about that. They told me to stand guard."

"Of course they did, and you see where that got them." Hayden looked like he was ready to laugh. "Such is the life of an Anom, I suppose." He lit the cigarette hanging from his lips. "Oh, well. You should wave goodbye to St. Louis anyway. Your stay was both short and useless. Tonight, we're flying west. Seems like our friends just can't get on without us."

Gauntlet looked to his right. Far in the distance, he could see the lights of the city. "I didn't know we were in St. Louis. No one told me."

"That's too bad. Now get on the plane." Hayden pulled the cigarette from his mouth and threw it away.

Gauntlet started up the stairs into the jet.

Hayden called after him, "You know, I couldn't track your approach to the airfield. I wonder why that is?"

Gauntlet turned around, reaching for the back of his neck. "I hit my head in the fighting. Maybe your tracking chip broke."

Hayden's smile widened. "Right. That must be it. We'll have to get you fitted for a new one back at Blaney."

Then Hayden followed Gauntlet up the stairs

and into the plane. They both took their seats, and the jet roared down the runway, climbing into the night sky and turning to the west.

CHAPTER 14

"Jeremy."

Jeremy Cross opened his eyes and knew exactly where he was standing. He was at the center of the emergency room in the University of Pennsylvania hospital. He could see the familiar beige walls and pale fluorescent lights overhead. A small huddle of doctors and nurses gathered around a patient on his left. Then in front of him, just like always, Jeremy saw his father.

Dr. Jonathan Cross stood in profile, staring straight ahead toward the waiting area of the emergency room. He smiled without looking. "Hey, bud. I guess it's been a while."

"It's been three months," Jeremy answered.

The last time they spoke was before Chicago. That's when his dad told him to walk away and leave Reah Labs behind, but Jeremy didn't listen. He stayed and fought, and almost died in Chicago, and he had been recovering from the battle ever since.

"I thought you needed space," Jonathan Cross

said. "Was I wrong?"

He wasn't. Jeremy had practically begged his dad to leave him alone the last time they spoke. Now he felt embarrassed by his own arrogance. He had dismissed his dad's warnings about Reah Labs out of hand, but it was a decision made by a child half-blind to the truth.

He wouldn't make the same mistake again. Jeremy swallowed down his feelings of guilt and shame, and forced himself to stare straight ahead at his father. Whenever he had looked away before, these visions would abruptly end, and this time, Jeremy needed answers.

"So, after three months you're back," Jeremy said. "What's changed, Dad? Is my punishment finally over?"

Jonathan shook his head. "You were never being punished, bud. I'm here because I heard about your mom and Katie. I'm so sorry, son."

"But you didn't hear about them!" Jeremy shot back. "You don't hear anything anymore, remember? You're dead!"

"Why are you yelling? Who are you angry at, son?" Jonathan kept his voice low.

Jeremy couldn't answer.

"If you want to have this conversation, I think we both need to start by being honest. Go on and ask your questions, and I'll answer the best I can," Jonathan said.

"There! Like that! You say things like that, and I don't know if it's all in my own head or if I'm going crazy or if somehow... if somehow you're not really dead."

Jonathan laughed. "You're not crazy, Jeremy. You've lived through a terrible trauma—more than one. No one needs to read your mind to know that. As for me being dead, it's not as easy as you make it sound. My body's gone, but I'm more than just a figment of your imagination, if that's what you mean."

"Are you an Anom?" Jeremy kept his eyes fixed on his dad, afraid to look away.

Jonathan nodded. "Yes, I am. Always have been."

Jeremy could feel his eyes welling with tears. "And did you know? Did you know that I was an Anom, too? Before you—before the explosion?"

"I'm your father, Jeremy. Of course, I knew." Jonathan laughed again. "I probably had this talk with you a thousand times in my own head, when I told you about your powers, but I never did it for real. I wanted you to discover what you were capable of on your own. Hell, I wanted to keep you normal for just another couple of years. That's the thing about being a parent, bud. You always think you're going to have more time."

Jeremy tried to put all these new pieces together in his head, but it was impossible to hold everything in focus at the same time. His dad was an Anom, and he was dead, but he also wasn't. He knew that Jeremy was an Anom, too, but then why would he—?

"Why did you tell me to leave?" Jeremy asked. "If you knew what I was, why did you tell me to abandon all those people?"

"You were born to help people, Jeremy. I've always loved that about you," Jonathan said. "But there are people who will see your kindness and mistake it for a weakness. There are people, like the people at Reah Labs, who will use your abilities for their own benefit, and then they'll cast you aside once they're done. You chose to stay and save those people in Chicago, and I'm proud of you for that, but my choice will always be to protect you first."

Jeremy felt a hand close over his arm. It was warm and reassuring. He turned to look, but all he could see standing next to him was the shadow of a person, her dark edges blurring and fading into nothing.

"And just like that, it looks like we're interrupted again." Jonathan Cross still looked straight ahead at the waiting room. "I think it's time you woke up, son."

Lara sat in a chair at the bedside, her hand closed over Jeremy's arm. "He feels sad... and confused... and guilty, too. I can't—" Lara shook her head. "I don't know what he's feeling right now, but he's in there."

Lara pulled back her hand. Jeremy still laid unconscious on the bed with a thin tube of oxygen laced under his nose, an IV taped to his arm, and a tangle of wires snaking out from under his gown to the various monitors.

Fifteen hours earlier, Lara was in San Francisco. She sat alone in a tiny office, focused on the single radio Ellison had left behind. She listened as the fight on the Golden Gate Bridge unfolded miles away. She heard the shouting voices and the bursts of gun-fire through the static. Then she heard the empty voice of the Blackhawk pilot—the entire bridge had collapsed into the bay. The next voice over the radio was Nyx—G-Force was down. He was stable, but un-conscious. That's when Ellison gave the order to re-treat. With one of his two Anoms out of the fight, he wouldn't risk a counterattack from Yoshida.

Within ten minutes, a Blackhawk helicopter touched down outside the hangar. Lara ran to meet it. As soon as she was on board, it lifted off, turn-ing to the south. She found herself riding with Nyx and G-Force. Nyx held a square bandage against her ribs, and every time the helicopter shook, she winced in pain. G-Force looked even worse. He was laid out across the floor of the helicopter, his eyes closed, a pulse oximeter clipped to his finger.

Lara knew they were flying to Arizona. That was always the plan if things went sideways in San Francisco. Kingman, Arizona was the closest Reah Labs training facility. They would have access to a medical unit, housing, and most importantly, a research facility to accommodate the Anoms. Lara knew it was the right choice, but it was still a three-hour flight from San Francisco. With G-Force unconscious on the floor, it felt even longer.

Lara looked over at the far wall. Nyx sat there, curled into a chair, her head leaning heavily against her arm, nodding forward as she fell asleep only to startle herself awake. Just like G-Force, Nyx was also dressed in a hospital gown, although she kept on her black cargo pants and boots. As soon as they had arrived at Kingman, she had the jagged cuts along her side cleaned and treated. They stitched her back together, but instead of going to her own room to sleep, Nyx made her way here and hadn't moved since.

Lara sat forward in her chair. "How long has it been since you've really slept?"

Nyx shook her head. "I don't know. I'm not tired."

Lara forced a smile. "He's not in any danger, Nyx. I know it must feel like Talon all over again, but it's not. The doctor said he's going to be fine. We just need to wait."

"I know what the doctor said," Nyx answered.

"I know you know." Lara folded her hands. "That's why you should go to your room. Lie down. Try to sleep. G-Force won't know if you're here or not."

"That's true," G-Force said. "Unless he wakes up and you're gone—like some kind of jerk." G-

202

Force tried to sit up in the bed, but as he rolled onto his one shoulder, he winced and fell back.

"You're awake." Lara turned to look at him, her voice rising.

Then Nyx stood up from her chair. "I should get the doctor."

Jeremy tried pushing himself up again, leaning against the inclined mattress. It was just as painful as before, but this time he didn't stop himself.

He looked at Lara. "How long was I out?"

"Less than a day. More than an hour," she said.

Jeremy rubbed his hand across his forehead. "Yeah, that feels about right."

"She was worried about you." Lara looked over her shoulder. Nyx was still standing in the open doorway of the room, her arms folded across her chest, staring out into the hallway.

Jeremy squeezed shut his eyes—the room was too bright. "What happened after I blacked out? With Yoshida and the bridge?"

"We don't have to go over that now." Lara smiled.

"Yes, we do." Jeremy already knew in his head that the bridge collapsed—not from any real memory, but he was certain it came down. It was his last real thought before the world went black. He knew it would fall the same way he knew the sun would rise in the morning. Even so, he needed to hear it for himself. He needed Lara to say it out loud and make it real—to shake it free from his dreams.

"How many were on the bridge when it fell?" Jeremy asked.

Lara shook her head. "They don't have the final number yet."

"What's the number now?"

It was Lara's turn to close her eyes. "Eighty-three. The last count I heard was eighty-three confirmed dead."

Jeremy leaned back against the bed, covering his eyes with his hands.

Lara hurried on, "But whatever the final number is, it would have been higher. That's what you need to remember. If you didn't hold up the bridge—"

"And how long was that?" Jeremy's voice hardened. "How long did I hold up the bridge?" It was the only other question that mattered, and the last one he needed to ask.

"You don't have to do this. You don't have to punish yourself like this." Lara laid her hand on top of Jeremy's arm, but as soon as she touched him, he pulled away. He wasn't going to let her read him now.

Lara took a deep breath and forced the thin smile back to her face. "They estimate about thirty seconds. You held up the bridge for thirty seconds."

Jeremy turned away to stare at the opposite wall. Thirty seconds was another failure, the same way he failed Talon—and he felt it in every muscle of his body. The eighty-three dead would be laid at his feet, too.

"How are we feeling?" a man's voice asked from the other side of the room.

Jeremy turned back to see a man wearing pale green scrubs and a white lab coat enter the room. Nyx trailed behind him as he stepped closer to the bed.

"I'm Dr. Wincott. I've been looking after you." The doctor held out his hand.

Jeremy didn't answer.

"I see your voice isn't working yet." Wincott laughed at his own joke. He arranged his stethoscope in his ears and held the end against Jeremy's chest. He listened for a couple of seconds, and then he moved the stethoscope around to Jeremy's back. "Now take a deep breath... and again." Wincott nodded and pulled the stethoscope away from his ears. "Good news—you're healthy."

Jeremy leaned back against the bed. "And what's the bad news?"

"The bad news is you're healthy." Wincott walked to the foot of the bed and pulled the chart, flipping over the first sheet of paper. "Your original blackout was caused by a lack of oxygen. The fifteen hours after that—" Wincott shrugged his shoulders. "Who knows? Whatever it was, it wasn't caused by anything physical."

Lara stood up from her chair and turned to Wincott. "We're still figuring that non-physical part out, but for now, is he okay? Medically speaking?"

Wincott cocked his head to the side, looking at Jeremy out of one eye. "Oh, yeah. I would still take it easy—see how he feels, of course —but there's nothing actually wrong with him. Medically speaking, he's fine. He might feel some aches and pains after sleeping for fifteen hours straight, but that's about it."

"When I passed out, I was ten stories up," Jeremy said. "You're telling me I don't have a single broken bone in my body? How's *that* possible?"

Wincott replaced the chart at the foot of the bed. "That's not my department. I just treat what they put in front of me."

Jeremy leaned forward, looking past the doctor so he could see Nyx. She had retreated to the far wall, standing just inside the doorway, staring down at her own feet.

"Nice catch," Jeremy said.

Nyx looked up at him. "You looked like you needed saving."

Jeremy smiled, but before he could answer again, Ellison walked into the room. The major wore a fresh uniform of gray camouflage, and as he stepped inside, he zeroed in on Dr. Wincott.

"Is the Anom cleared for duty?" Ellison asked.

Wincott scratched the top of his head. "Well, yeah, I suppose. Like I was telling Agent Mirror, there's nothing physically wrong with him—"

"Then we're debriefing in ten minutes," Ellison said. "Agent Mirror, I want you to escort our patient to the conference room. I wouldn't want him falling asleep again and missing it." Ellison turned to leave the room.

Lara started after him. "They need more time, Major. G-Force literally just woke up. Nyx hasn't slept in over a day—"

"I already have Nyx's report. She gave it to us last night. If you're asking for her to be excused from the debriefing, it's granted," Ellison said.

"That's not what I'm asking." Lara edged closed, lowering her voice. "Give him an hour. Let me talk to him—"

"He should've reported last night," Ellison said, making no effort to keep his own voice quiet.

"He was unconscious!" Nyx shouted back at Ellison. "Sorry if that was too inconvenient for you, Major!"

Ellison narrowed his eyes; he looked from Jeremy to Nyx to Lara. "I needed his information last night when it was still useful. Instead, we sat vigil while he took his beauty rest."

Lara shook her head. "You know that's not what happened—"

"I'm not done," Ellison barked over her. "There are still members of this team who insist on protecting our weakest link. It was a behavior I allowed after Chicago, and now it's cost us. It will not happen again. G-Force has ten minutes, and then he's expected in the conference room. No more excuses."

Ten minutes later, Lara pushed Jeremy's wheelchair into the conference room. Nyx followed behind them. Jeremy had wanted to walk into the room himself, but that proved more difficult than he realized. As soon as Ellison left, Dr. Wincott unhooked Jeremy's monitors and pulled his IV. Then he helped Jeremy swing his legs over the side of the bed, but as Jeremy's feet touched the ground and he shifted his weight to stand, both of his knees buckled under him. That's when Wincott called for the wheelchair.

Inside the conference room, Jeremy could see Ellison seated behind a long table; it felt identical to the setup they had at Blaney. Ellison didn't look up as they entered. Instead, he stared down at an open folder, turning over loose pages one at a time. Agent Hayden sat on Ellison's right, rocking back in his chair, indifferent, as always, to everything around him.

Behind the conference table, Jeremy could see three "Lab Coats" standing in a line, but only the man on the left was familiar—Dr. John Langer. Then Jeremy realized they must have flown him out from Blaney with Agent Hayden. In a way, it made perfect sense. Langer was the resident expert on Jeremy's power over gravity, so if something was wrong with him, Langer would be able to figure it out before anyone else.

As Jeremy caught his eye, the doctor offered a lopsided grin, and he quickly flashed a double thumbs-up. It made him look even more out of place with his colleagues.

Finally, standing at the side of the table, Jeremy could see Gauntlet. He stood with his arms folded across his chest, and the fluorescent lights of the room reflected in his armor.

Jeremy smiled. "And where have you been?"

"He can't answer that," Ellison growled without raising his eyes. "That information's been classified."

"I was in St. Louis," Gauntlet's voice rattled from under his helmet.

Hayden leaned farther back in his chair, laughing loud enough for everyone to hear him, and for the first time since they entered the room, Ellison looked up. He stared across the table at Gauntlet, and Jeremy could see the muscles working in the major's neck and jaw—straining to keep his anger from erupting.

Ellison shut the folder on top of the table and turned his attention to Jeremy. "That's not why we're here. We're here to get the final report from G-Force regarding his involvement in Operation Prodigal Son." Ellison narrowed his eyes. "Whenever you're ready."

Jeremy shifted his weight in the wheelchair. "I deployed to the south end of the Golden Gate Bridge from a Blackhawk. Then I crossed a line of hostiles and started north to engage Kaito

Yoshida. I encountered—"

"And did you engage him?" Ellison broke in.

Jeremy shook his head. "Before I could reach Yoshida, I encountered another—"

"That's not my question." Ellison reopened the folder on the table, glancing down at the top page. "I asked if you engaged Kaito Yoshida."

Jeremy started again, "After I was intercepted by one of the hostiles—"

"Did you engage with Yoshida? Yes or no?" Ellison barked.

"Yes, I engaged him," Jeremy answered.

"How did you engage him?" Ellison turned over another page in his folder.

"What do you mean, 'How did I engage him'?"

Hayden laughed, pushing himself back from the table. "He's not asking if you proposed."

Ellison looked up, fixing his eyes on Jeremy. "Did you strike him? Were you struck *by* him? Did you use a gravitational field? Did you even throw a punch?"

Jeremy sat up in his chair as he slowly realized what was happening. Ellison had called this a debriefing, but that was a lie. It was a trial, and from the smug look on the major's face, the verdict was already decided.

Jeremy glanced sideways at Lara and set his jaw. "I spoke to Kaito Yoshida."

Ellison looked down at the papers in the folder. "You spoke to him?"

"I spoke to him," Jeremy repeated. "Then he

warped the tower, and the whole bridge started
—"

"But did you ever engage Kaito Yoshida?"
Ellison asked again.

"I moved to stabilize the bridge—"

Ellison pressed his advantage. "But were you
ordered to stabilize the bridge, or were you
ordered to engage Yoshida?"

Jeremy didn't answer.

Ellison lifted the paper off the table, holding
it in front of him. He was reading now. "Did you
ignore my order to engage Kaito Yoshida?"

Silence.

"Did you attempt to physically engage with
Kaito Yoshida?" Ellison looked over the top of
his paper at Jeremy. "Did you attempt to stop
Yoshida's retreat from the bridge? Did you will-
fully disobey my direct order to reengage with
Kaito Yoshida?"

Jeremy turned away. "I don't remember what
I did. I was too busy saving people's lives."

Ellison put the paper down and closed the
folder. "Well, then I know eighty-three people
who would question your judgement."

"That's complete bullshit, and you know it!"
Nyx suddenly shouted from across the table.
"He's the only one who even got close to
Yoshida. None of us could've stopped him."

Ellison ignored her. "We function as a team,
and that team depends on a chain of command.
G-Force has repeatedly shown disregard for the

chain of command, and so it's become obvious he cannot function as a member of this team."

Nyx lowered her voice. "Don't do this, Major."

Ellison pushed the folder away from him. "Starting immediately, G-Force is suspended from operations, including all training and research. When we get back to Blaney, I'm recommending him for dismissal. We're finished here."

Jeremy laughed. "Why wait for Blaney? Dig this chip out of my neck, and I'll leave right now."

Ellison ignored him; instead, he rose to his feet. "As for the rest of you, you can wait here for my orders. Kaito Yoshida's not done with us yet. I can promise you that much."

Then Ellison and Hayden walked from the room together, and Jeremy was left in the silence.

CHAPTER 15

"Major, wait," Gauntlet called after Ellison.

Halfway down the hall, Ellison and Hayden walked side by side. They were talking together in low voices, undoubtedly plotting the next move in what they believed to be some grand scheme, but it only reminded Gauntlet of how much he hated them both.

Ellison was brash and impetuous, a man ruled by ego and emotion. He wasn't stupid—to slap him with that label would only excuse his behavior—but he was a person who spurned self-doubt, and in the process, he ignored self-reflection. His character depended on his own accomplishments, and so to question himself was the same as inviting failure. Ellison would never allow himself to take that chance. Even so, for all his faults, there was an honesty about the major that Gauntlet could appreciate. He might have been a petulant son of a bitch, but at least that was the character he showed to your face. If nothing else, it made him predictable.

Hayden, on the other hand, was something

else entirely. He was acerbic, but only from the safety of the shadows, offering his opinions and analysis as if it were guerrilla warfare. He was a counterpuncher, slipping in jabs only when the opportunity presented itself, but never willing to stand toe to toe in an honest fight. He assumed the role of a man without conviction. For Hayden, it was always a short laugh, a well-timed barb, and then silence, but Gauntlet knew that even in his silence there was calculation. It made him the opposite of Ellison—impossible to predict—and in that uncertainty there was danger. It was like playing chess in the dark.

"Major," Gauntlet called again, and both men turned around.

Hayden pulled the cigarette from his mouth. "Chasing us down to beg for your friend? I thought you had more pride."

Gauntlet ignored him. "Major Ellison."

Ellison leaned closer to Hayden, whispering, and Hayden laughed. "Whatever you want to do, Major, as long as he's wasting your time instead of mine."

Hayden turned and continued up the hallway, but Ellison walked back to where Gauntlet was standing. "If this is about G-Force, I can tell you right now that it's too late. He's already made his choices, and I've made mine. I'll stand by it, and nothing you can say is going to change that."

"G-Force isn't the one compromising this

team, Major. It's him." Gauntlet jerked his head in the direction of Hayden. "And right now, you're standing on the wrong side of things."

"What are you talking about?" Ellison growled.

Gauntlet lowered his voice. "What did he tell you about our mission in St. Louis?"

Ellison narrowed his eyes. "He told me it was another disaster. He said what should have been a routine operation cost us the lives of Agent Dubov and some other man—Morris, I think. Most importantly, he said you failed to meet any of your objectives. So, if that's your argument, maybe you should tell me again how I'm picking the wrong side, because if my choices are between your incompetence and the CIA, it would seem I'm better off—"

"The mission wasn't a failure." Gauntlet touched his forearm, pulling something away from his armor, and then he held it out to Ellison—a flash drive colored the same blood-red as the Exocorium.

"What the hell's that supposed to be?" Ellison sneered.

"It's our objective. Data files lifted from the Knights of the Crusade," Gauntlet said.

Ellison snatched the flash drive out of Gauntlet's hand. "You're withholding intelligence? I thought you were stupid before, but now I realize—"

Gauntlet grabbed Ellison by the wrist, stopping him mid-sentence. "I withheld intelligence because I know what's on that flash drive. Look at it for yourself and you'll understand."

"Let go of me!" Ellison tried to pull away.

Gauntlet held tight. "Hayden, the CIA, and Reah Labs are in this together. They have their own agenda, and it's not ours. They're playing us off each other, and we need you on our side for once."

Ellison's eyes went cold. "Let. Go." Gauntlet opened his hand, and Ellison pulled away. Then the major looked down at the flash drive, turning it over in his hand.

Finally, Ellison tucked the drive into his breast pocket. "I'll review your intelligence and relay it through the proper channels. That's what *you* should have done. As for now, you were ordered to wait in the conference room. I suggest you listen."

Ellison turned on his heels and started up the hallway again, the cadence of his boots echoing off the walls.

Gauntlet watched him retreat through the double doors at the far end of the hall. It was as much as he could've hoped for and exactly what he expected. Gauntlet turned away and stepped back into the conference room.

As he walked through the doors, G-Force spun around in his wheelchair, facing him. "So, what was that all about? You stormed out of here like you were ready—"

"We need to talk," Gauntlet growled from under his helmet.

"All right." G-Force locked the brakes on his wheelchair and pushed himself out of the seat —still not entirely himself. Gauntlet could see his arms quivering, supporting his weight as he steadied himself.

G-Force caught his breath. "Then I guess... we need to talk."

"Not here. Sit back down."

G-Force fell back in the wheelchair, and Gauntlet moved behind him, pushing him towards the door.

"Wait! Where are you going?" Mirror called after them, but they both ignored her. Instead, they moved back through the doors, out of the conference room, and turned into the hospital wing. The first room on the left was empty, and Gauntlet pushed G-Force inside, turning him around.

"So, are you gonna tell me what happened?" G-Force asked, nodding his head at Gauntlet. "You can start by telling me what happened to your sword. Not exactly the kind of thing you just lose."

"Wait," Gauntlet answered.

G-Force rolled his eyes. Gauntlet knew that showing patience would prove difficult for the younger man. It simply wasn't in his nature. G-Force was brash—maybe more like Major Ellison than he was willing to admit—and he was ruled by his emotions, speaking his mind as fast as the words could tumble out. Gauntlet knew there were advantages to be found in the recklessness of youth, but there was also danger. It was a familiar problem. Back in New York, playing chess games in the park, Dom would tell Michael that he wasn't seeing the whole board. It's why in his early games, Michael would get beat by Dom ten moves in, and he would only see it at the end. But he learned his lesson. G-Force would have to do the same.

Gauntlet raised both his arms, and the Exocorium poured off his body. It ran away from his arms and legs, dripping down his torso, pooling across the floor, and rising again, building on itself, surrounding him and G-Force in a shell of red armor just like it had done before.

Gauntlet hated this part—separating from his armor. It felt like stepping out of his own skin. It made him feel like he was less alive. Free from the armor, a violent shiver rippled across his body, and he pitched forward, catching himself against one of the red Exocorium walls before his knees could buckle him to the ground.

G-Force leaned forward. "You okay?"

Gauntlet grabbed ahold of another chair inside the Exocorium cell. He lowered himself into the seat, and then it took another moment to slow his breathing and regain his balance.

Finally, he pointed up at the red walls surrounding them. "Now we can talk in private."

G-Force looked around the closed-off space. "Anyone ever tell you you're paranoid?"

Gauntlet nodded. "Doesn't mean I'm wrong."

"So, what's this all about?" G-Force asked. "The secret meetings, and the backstory, and going off to St. Louis? What do you need me for?"

"I already told you. It's about Piper," Gauntlet said.

"That doesn't answer my—"

"They have her!" Gauntlet roared back at him, and G-Force went silent. Then, for a long moment, neither one of them spoke, until finally Gauntlet leaned forward in his chair. "We had been living together for less than a year when it happened. It was late March, but still cold. You know, the way it gets in the city..."

In his memory, Gauntlet could see himself sitting at the dining room table in their apartment, before Reah Labs or the Exocorium Armor was ever part of their lives—back when he was just Michael Reilly. He sat with his laptop opened in front of him, and in the reflection of the black screen, over his shoulder, he could see Piper looking at her own face in a mirror, turning her chin to the left and right.

Michael turned around in his chair to look at her preening. "You look great. You already know that."

Piper tucked a loose strand of hair behind her ear. "You always say I look great."

"Because you always look great." Michael stood

up, reaching into his pocket. "Here, let me take our picture."

Piper spun on her heels, reaching out her hand to push the phone away. "No. I told you a million times, no pictures. I mean it, Michael."

"Fine." He dropped the phone down on the table and watched as Piper turned back to face the mirror. "It's just, I don't have a single picture of us together. I don't have a single picture of you, anywhere. It's weird."

"Maybe it is, but that's the way I want it." Piper looked over her shoulder, a coy smile playing at the corner of her mouth. "Besides, why do you need a picture? We're together all the time anyway. You can just look at me."

Michael sank back into the dining room chair, picking up his phone. "I wanted to send a picture to Dom. Maybe if he could see you for himself, he would understand why I left."

Piper sighed. "And that's exactly why I don't want my picture taken. I don't need to be ogled by some dirty old man in the park."

Michael shook his head. "It's not like that. Dom doesn't care about how you look—"

"So why does it matter then?" Piper turned back to the mirror. "Besides, you haven't spoken to that old man in two months. You were just telling me about it last night."

"Not hearing from Dom is the problem." Michael unlocked his phone and opened his text messages, pulling up his conversation with Dom. The last text was sent February second, and it was from Michael, inviting Dom to lunch. There was no reply. "He's hurt, Piper, and I don't want that for him. Okay?"

Piper leaned in closer to the mirror. "His wallet's hurt because he lost his best player."

Michael knew it was more than that. There was always business between him and Dom—a partnership—but that was never the end of the story. It was just a chapter. Dom had lots of those. And besides, Dom was more than just Michael's business partner. He was also a teacher, guardian, and friend. The bottom line was this: Dom wanted more out of Michael than just a cut of his games. He wanted him to have the skills to earn a living. He wanted Michael to survive on his own, but now that he had gone off and done just that, somehow it felt to Michael like he'd gotten it wrong. Maybe because he left too soon. Or maybe because he left without bringing Dom with him. Whatever the reason, Michael needed to make things right. At the very least, he wanted Dom to understand.

Next to the messages, Michael saw the icon for his phone's camera. He pressed the button and flipped the camera around so it was facing him. In the mirror, over his shoulder, he could see Piper's reflection. He clicked the shutter and sent the image as a text before Piper could see him, or his own conscience could get in the way. After all, it was just a picture. Piper was being ridiculous. Suddenly, she turned around, and Michael lowered his phone and smiled.

Piper reached out for his hand. "If my picture really means that much to you, maybe I can commission a portrait or something. You know, one of those miniatures you can carry around with you all day pining over. How's that?"

"Sounds crazy," Michael said.

"Tell me about it. Almost as crazy as needing a photograph in the first place." Piper leaned over and kissed Michael on his cheek. "I'll be back for dinner. Then you can look at me all you want."

"Sounds great." He smiled.

Piper turned and walked out of the apartment, her heels clicking on the hardwood floor, but as soon as Michael heard the hallway door shut behind her, he opened the text messages on his phone. Gray letters confirmed the picture had been delivered to Dom.

He typed another message: "Hey. You working today?"

To his surprise, the answer came back quickly: "Yes. Union."

A little more than an hour later, Michael found himself walking through Union Square Park towards the chess tables. It had been at least three or four months since he had set foot in the park, but he still recognized most of the faces behind the tables—most, but not all.

There was a familiar rhythm in this section of the park. The staccato footsteps on the pavement, the softer click of the pieces moving across the boards, even the fast talk from the hustlers—

it all blended into a song Michael couldn't forget. For a second, he even thought he missed it—missed the game—but then one of those cold March winds whipped over his back, and he woke up from the dream. The game was familiar. That was all.

A voice called out from his right. "Hey, man. You look like you're a player. You wanna catch a game while you waitin' on your girl?"

Michael laughed. The man on his right wasn't much older than he was. He was sitting on a folding chair in front of a board already set up for a game, and he was wearing a light denim jacket and a brown woolen hat pulled down over his ears. He was smiling wide, too, just like a shark. It was all familiar.

The man tried again. "Hey, try your skills, my man. I'll even play you left-handed just to make it fair."

Michael laughed again, a louder, fuller laugh than it was before, but it wasn't because of the player or his banter—although the left-handed line was pretty good. Michael was laughing at himself. Had he really changed so much in the last few months that now he looked like an easy mark?

Michael looked down at his clothes. The brown shoes, designer jeans, thick sweater, and black leather jacket—the whole ensemble bought for him by Piper—certainly made him look like a man with money to lose, but back when he was hustling for Dom, he would never call out a player on his clothes alone. Saint Dom would never allow it. Dom would tell him to look a player in the eye, because the eyes *always told the story.*

Michael remembered that lesson well. One day he was sitting out with Dom, just watching the people as they walked by. The two of them must have stayed there for over an hour. Michael would try to say something, and Dom would put his hand on his arm, saying, "No, not yet, Mikey. Just watch."

Finally, the old man leaned over and whispered, "Watch their eyes. The eyes tell the story. They let you know if they're predator or prey. The predators' eyes always look hungry. You don't want those games, because they want to win even more than you do. But the other eyes—the prey—they walk around all day looking happy. Happy people don't mind losing money. Those are the games you want."

The man at the chess table called out again. "How about it, my man? I ain't got all day to keep telling you jokes."

Michael smiled. Maybe he should sit down and teach a lesson or two of his own, but before he could answer, another voice called over his shoulder.

"You don't want this game, Bobby. He'll bust you up for the next hour and talk about your mom the whole time he's doing it. Trust me."

Saint Dom stepped around Michael to stand next to the man at the chessboard—Bobby. Dom was wearing his canvas jacket and a Gatsby cap over his feathery white hair. He wore his wire-rimmed glasses balanced on top of his nose, and his thick white mustache bristled as he smelled the air.

Dom touched Bobby on the shoulder. "Let me spot

you for a break, okay?"

Bobby stood up. "All right, Dom. You got it."

Dom sat down in the chair and motioned for Michael to take the seat across from him. "It's been a while, Mikey. We thought you forgot your way to the park."

Michael knew Dom was expecting a game. He took the empty seat at the makeshift table, and the white pieces were set in front of him—common courtesy to let the suckers move first.

Michael smiled to himself. "We playing a speed game, or we playing for real?"

Dom shrugged. "You tell me, Mikey. I'll beat your ass either way."

Michael reached for the king's pawn and moved it two spaces forward. "I wanted to come by sooner. We've been busy."

Dom smiled as he countered with his queen's pawn. "That's right. You're a 'we' now. I got the picture you sent of your girl. She's pretty, and it looks like she makes you happy."

"She does. I think we're both happy." Michael moved his pawn again, capturing Dom's piece.

The old man rubbed his white whiskers and moved his king-side knight. "That's good, Mikey. Happy is good."

"Is it?"

Dom leaned back in his chair and gave a soft laugh. "What do you mean, 'Is it?'? Of course it's good." Dom raised both of his hands, motioning to his left and right. "Why do you think we're out here?

We all just wanna be happy, right?"

It was Michael's move, but instead of reaching for one of the chess pieces, his hand moved for his jacket pocket. He pulled out a white envelope and dropped it onto the center of the board.

Dom looked down at the envelope. "What's that supposed to be?"

"You told me I should never run out on a game, and I'm not," Michael said. "I'm not running out on you, Dom. That's the money you spotted me to get started. All of it. I'm paying you back like I promised."

Dom picked up the envelope and hefted it in his hand. "You mean this is her money, because I know you didn't save all this, unless you won the lottery or something."

Michael didn't answer.

Dom dropped the envelope back on the board. "You better hold on to that for me, Mikey. You never know when you might need it."

Michael picked up the envelope and held it out to the old man. "I'm trying to do the right thing by you, Dom. You're the one who taught me the rules. You're the one who said—"

"Rules?" Dom's head jerked back from the chessboard. "I was teaching you about chess, Mikey. I was teaching you how to win a game, but that envelope's not a game. That's life in your hand. There's a difference."

"You said it was the same thing," Michael countered.

Dom stood up from his chair, shaking his head and holding out both of his hands. "I'm an old man, Mikey. I say a lot of crazy shit, but you listen to me now. Life is life. That's all there is to it. Nobody can teach you the rules, because nobody knows 'em all. But you still gotta play. You understand what I'm saying? You just got to figure it out like everyone else."

Michael stood up from his chair, but Dom was already walking away, talking over his shoulder. "Why don't you come back in a couple weeks when it's warmer. We can play a real game. Maybe I'll have you play some of these kids—teach 'em a thing or two. None of them's got the game you did, Mikey—not one of 'em."

For a second, Michael thought about running after him, forcing the envelope into his hand, but he knew there was no point. Dom had made up his mind. Instead, he slipped the envelope back inside his jacket and turned for the subway.

The trip back to Piper's apartment was foggy in his memory. He remembered sitting on the subway car thinking about Dom. Thinking about his own life at the chess table and how it all felt like such a long time ago. Thinking about his new life with Piper. Happy was good—that was the proclamation by Saint Dom—but for whatever reason, Michael had his doubts.

He walked into the apartment and dropped the envelope on the dining room table. He knew how much he owed to Dom—more than just the money

—but it seemed like the old man was in no hurry to settle the debt. Michael would have to rethink his approach and figure out another way to make things right. He liked Dom, but even so, he had no interest in staying in the old man's back pocket.

Michael stepped into the living room, and suddenly, strong hands grabbed him by the arms. His right leg buckled under him, and he was forced down to his knees. Michael tried to shout, but a thick arm laced under his chin and cut off the sound in his throat.

In front of him, three large men stood dressed in tactical gear—black cargo pants, tactical vests covered in pockets, leather gloves. Each man had a pistol holstered on his hip. Michael had no doubt that a fourth man, most likely dressed as the fourth member of their barbershop quartet, stood behind him, too. The three in front looked down at Michael the same way they might regard a flattened squirrel in the road—curious enough to look at it, but too indifferent to remember. After all, the damn thing was already dead.

"You want me to zip tie his hands?" the man behind Michael asked.

The man in the center shook his head. "Can't risk it if they don't burn off. Just put him to sleep. We're almost done here anyway." As the man finished speaking, he moved to the coffee table. Michael could see a large, brushed aluminum case sitting on top of it, roughly the size of a suitcase. The man leaned over the case, reaching inside, and Michael could see him push a tangle of wires to one side. Then the other man, the one standing behind him, tightened his grip around Michael's throat, choking off his air, and the edges of Michael's vision went gray. He felt himself slipping unconscious.

All at once, the floor-to-ceiling window behind the three men shattered, falling away like freezing rain into the apartment, and a new figure launched himself into the living room, rolling across the floor and springing to his feet until he was standing in the middle of the others. This new man was tall and broad at the shoulders, wrapped in red and black armor. It was Gauntlet.

The other men all drew their weapons, and Gauntlet pulled the broadsword from over his shoulder. He swung down to his left, splaying the first man open from shoulder to hip before he could fire a shot. At the same time, a round shield unfurled from Gauntlet's left arm, spiraling into place. Gauntlet swung out with the shield, knocking the handgun away from the second man. Then he landed a front kick to the man's chest, throwing him back into the wall.

Gauntlet twisted left and dropped to his knee, dragging his sword across the third man's gut as the man fired an aimless shot over Gauntlet's head. The man fell back, clutching at his stomach, as Gauntlet rose to his feet, replacing the broadsword over his shoulder.

"Stay back!" the man behind Michael screamed, stepping back, and pulling Michael up as some kind of human shield. The vice grip around Michael's neck loosened enough so he could breathe, but he still couldn't wrench himself free. He felt something hard pressed against his temple, and in the corner of his eye he could see the dark metal of the fourth man's gun.

"I'll kill him. I swear I will," the man shouted.

Gauntlet raised his arm, and the limbs of a cross-bow snapped into place over his wrist, aimed directly at Michael and the man standing behind him.

"Where is she? The woman in the picture?" Gauntlet growled

Michael's voice croaked inside his throat. "Piper? What do you want with her? How do you know—"

The man behind him shouted again, "She's gone!" Then Michael could feel the man shift his weight; he was turning to look in a different direction. "Do it, Chris! Do it now!"

Michael looked, too. He could see movement farther back in the room behind Gauntlet. One of the men—the one who'd had his stomach slashed open—stumbled up from the floor, his hand reaching inside the metal case on the coffee table. Then everything felt like it happened at once.

Gauntlet let the crossbow bolt fly.

Michael flinched, closing his eyes, ready for the inevitable, but instead of pain—or worse—he felt the thick arm around his throat slip away as the man behind him collapsed to the floor.

Michael opened his eyes and found himself

standing face to face with the armored man. Gauntlet reached out and grabbed Michael by his forearm. Suddenly, Michael felt something cold twisting over his hand and wrist, climbing up towards his shoulder. He looked down and saw oil... or something like oil—a heavy red and black liquid, spreading over every inch of his skin, covering his arm and shoulder and creeping up to his neck.

"Wait! What are you doing? What are you—" Michael screamed.

Gauntlet jerked on his arm, and Michael stumbled toward the broken window, certain he was about to fall out of the building and land on the street below, but at the last step before the edge, he caught his balance. He wheeled back around to face the armored man, but now, the armor was gone. Standing in the apartment, Michael only saw the man—tall and dark and impossibly thin.

He mouthed the words, "Good luck."

Then everything was lost in a flash of light and a deafening roar. Michael could feel himself thrown back from the room, lifted off his feet, twisting through the air. He was falling, and everything went black.

"I woke up the next morning riding the Q train and wearing this." Michael touched his hand to the red wall surrounding them, dragging his fingers through the Exocorium like he was tracing lines in the sand. It was hard for him to be separated from the suit, but he couldn't risk putting it back on just yet. He had to finish what he had started.

"By the time I got off the train and made it back to the apartment, it looked like half the building had been blown apart, and Piper was gone."

G-Force shook his head. "What do you mean she was gone?"

"The cops recovered a body. They said it was Piper. They claimed she died in the explosion, but it wasn't her. I'm sure they already had her someplace else."

"And who was the guy wearing your armor? Where did he come from?"

"You'd have to go back in time and ask him. I searched through the debris, but they made sure his body was gone, too."

"They? Them? Same guys who faked the moon landing, right?" G-Force leaned back in the wheelchair. "You even hear yourself right now?"

Without saying another word, Michael pressed his palm flat against the red armor. The Exocorium moved under his touch. It poured over his fingers like syrup, twisting up his wrist and arm and stopping at his elbow. It felt good to have even this small bit of armor back on his body, like he could finally breathe again.

Michael pulled back his hand from the wall, and his round shield spiraled out from the armor, locking into place over his forearm. Then he turned his hand over, palm up, showing the inside of the shield to G-Force for the first time.

G-Force leaned over to get a better look, but Michael already knew what he would see there —the same thing he had been staring at for years —a stylized outline of an orchid in thin black lines etched against the blood-red metal. Then there was no need for Michael to explain anything else. That same orchid was everywhere—on lab coats and letterheads, on every door at Fort Blaney and now every door at Kingman. It was a personal brand for everything Reah Labs ever owned.

Michael rose to his feet. "They. Them. The same people who crafted this armor. They found Piper because I sent that picture to Dom—facial recognition searches; we've seen them do it before. They came for her, just like they came for you, and me, and for Nyx.

"So, you think she's an Anom," G-Force said.

"I think she knew better than to have her picture taken," Michael growled. "I think she didn't want to be found, and she was. Now they have her locked away—either at Fort Blaney or somewhere else—and I intend to find her."

G-Force turned away. "You mean if they even have her in the first place."

Michael stared down at the younger man, and grit his teeth. He knew there was nothing malicious in the comment—at least nothing intentional—but it was a barb of doubt Michael had long since exiled because any alternative would have to be worse. If Piper wasn't being held against her will, then she was already dead, and Michael refused to give that thought a foothold. Even so, if G-Force was looking for some kind of evidence or reassurance, Michael had none to give. His silence would have to be enough.

Finally, G-Force turned back. "And why do you need me for any of this?"

"Because they can't read your brain yet, which means you can still keep a secret. And because you've seen what they're capable of doing, and you have every reason to leave yourself. But mostly I need you because there's going to be a fight, and I know I can't win it alone."

G-Force looked down at his hands. "According to Ellison, I'm done as soon as we get back to Fort Blaney. That doesn't give me much time to help."

Michael nodded. "If we get back to Fort Blaney, that's all the time I'll need."

CHAPTER 16

Stuart Ellison walked quickly down the sterile hallway. In front of him, Hayden leaned against one of the walls, waiting, his arms folded across his chest. Ellison reminded himself that he still hated the man for all his arrogance and condescension—even if he could appreciate that Hayden was supremely competent at his job. Competency went a long way with Ellison. It was a rare trait worth more to the major than sheer intelligence or courage. It was the currency of trust—an assurance that, if nothing else, a job would get done.

Ellison had seen too many failures from lesser men when he knew, if he were in their place, he would have succeeded. If he possessed half the abilities of G-Force, for instance, he had no doubt the Golden Gate Bridge would still be standing. G-Force was a lesser man, incapable of doing all that was necessary for success. He compromised his duty to humor his weaker sensibilities. It was a luxury Ellison would never allow for himself, and he knew Hayden wouldn't either. At least in that regard, for all his other flaws, Hayden was an equal.

Hayden pushed himself away from the wall and fell into step next to Ellison. "So, what did your knight in shining armor want now?"

Ellison understood the obligation he was under. He had received intelligence—a flash drive—from one of his assets, and protocol demanded he share that intelligence with Hayden, but there were other considerations to weigh. To begin with, Gauntlet had barely spoken a dozen times to Ellison since they first met. That was two years ago. Now he was intentionally seeking out Ellison to share his concerns, which meant Gauntlet was desperate—or more than desperate. He was afraid.

Gauntlet made it clear that Hayden was working to preserve his own self-interests—no earth-shattering revelation there. Ellison had suspected as much from the moment he met Agent Hayden. He was a man of secrets —a manipulator aligning himself with anyone who might prove most efficient in helping him achieve his ends. That fact alone didn't make Hayden his enemy any more than it would cast him as an ally, but the contents of the flash drive could change all that. Ellison wouldn't know until he looked at the drive for himself. What's more, even if the flash drive proved to be inconsequential, if it could bring Gauntlet into Ellison's corner, a slight delay in protocol would be justified. After all, the enemy of my enemy...

Ellison forced himself to smile as he stared back at Hayden. "It was just what you suspected. He was begging to keep his friend on the team. I told him there was no chance."

Hayden smirked. "Sounds like your man's losing his edge. That's what happens when you turn a killer into a glorified nursemaid." The two men reached the elevator at the end of the hall and stepped inside. "Your team needs to wake up, Major. They need a bold new direction."

Ellison knew Hayden's assessment was spot-on. He had been saying much of the same to Colonel McCann long before Chicago. After all, it was Ellison who railed against the lack of discipline among the Anoms. Even then, they were setting themselves up for failure, and he was the only one who could see it. Everyone else was blinded by the Anoms' abilities—by the infinite possibilities offered by their genetic gifts. For Ellison, that potential could never outweigh the requisite character of a soldier. Ellison was tasked with building an army, but they handed him delinquents, all of them too self-absorbed to set aside their own interests for the good of the team. It was no surprise they failed in San Francisco again.

Even so, Ellison resented the implication against his own character—that somehow it was a failure of his leadership that set them on the wrong path. He turned to Hayden. "I can only work with what I'm given. If you think anyone else could do better with the Anoms, I can talk to Colonel McCann as soon as we—"

Hayden dropped his chin to his chest, shaking his head. "Stuart, I'm not blaming you, for Christ's sake. For the first time I'm agreeing with you. I'm saying we made a mistake when we put this team together, and I think it's time we corrected it."

"It's not that easy. Where do we find different Anoms?" Ellison asked.

Hayden smiled. "Maybe we already have some."

The elevator doors opened, and both men stepped out. They crossed to the far end of the hall and walked into a room that was supposed to be the command center at Kingman. In truth, it paled in comparison to the one at Fort Blaney. There was a large conference table at the center of the room and a computer monitor set up at each of the six seats surrounding the table, but the similarities ended there.

Blaney's command center was a state-of-the-art war room designed to monitor and respond to genetic anomalies and the threats they posed around the world. This room resembled little more than a public library computer room. A half-dozen men—slouched, unshaven, and unkempt—sat in front of the computers. Empty foil wrappers and half-crushed cans of soda littered the floor around them. It was a disgrace, but why would Ellison expect anything different? Fort Blaney was a full-fledged military operation. Kingman, Arizona wasn't.

"Have you opened a secure connection to Fort Blaney yet?" Ellison asked. He turned to face one of the computer techs, a small man with a stained green t-shirt and a beard that had overgrown his neck.

The man jumped up from his chair. "Yeah, I think so. I mean, that's what the guy on the video conference said. So yeah, I guess."

Ellison sat down in the man's empty chair. Across from him, a video of Colonel McCann played on the monitor. The colonel's voice filtered over the speakers. "Captain Reyes verified the connection was secure, Stuart. Why don't you clear that room on your end so we can talk freely?"

Ellison turned to give the order, but the computer techs were already up and moving. They filed quickly out of the room, with the bearded man in the stained shirt the last one to leave. He pulled the door closed behind him.

Ellison turned back to the monitor, and McCann was clutching his black Army mug, lifting it to his lips to take a careful drink. Ellison looked closer, and even in a day's time, he could see how the colonel had changed. The razor-thin wrinkles that had always traversed his face seemed to cut deeper than Ellison remembered, and dark, heavy bags welled under both of his eyes. For the first time since Ellison had met the colonel, he thought the old man looked frail. Ellison resented him for it.

McCann lowered his mug. "Are we alone, Major?"

"Agent Hayden's still in the room," Ellison answered.

"That's fine. Saves me from having to repeat myself." McCann reached for his head, rubbing his fingers back and forth across his brow. "Now, why don't you tell me how we screwed this one up?"

Ellison bristled, but he managed to hold his voice even. "I think that's a broad assessment, Colonel. This was an evolving threat that no one could fully understand nor anticipate. When we first arrived, I established our perimeter at San Francisco International Airport, and staged our strike team—"

"Christ, Stuart, no one cares about the damn airport. Tell me about the bridge," McCann thundered.

"Yes, sir." Ellison grit his teeth. "Once Yoshida moved to the bridge, I ordered our team to intercept him. We deployed by Blackhawk—"

"But you failed," McCann cut him off. "Why can't you just get to the damn point? You had Kaito Yoshida in the open, and you let him escape. What's worse, you let him tear down the Golden Gate Bridge in the process. Eighty-five civilians are dead, Stuart, and the number's still climbing. Eighty-five souls we were sworn to protect, so when I tell you this whole operation has been a failure, maybe you can rethink your broad-assessment bullshit excuses!"

Then it was too much for Ellison. He could endure McCann's personal criticisms—justified or not—but to aim his wrath like a broadside at the soldiers involved was more than Ellison would allow. Dedicated men fought on that bridge under Ellison's command, and each one had performed his duty admirably. None of this failure belonged to them.

Ellison raised his chin to stare back into the monitor. "With all due respect, Colonel, this failure was yours. I gave the order to take Yoshida and my men—my soldiers—did as they were told. It was your pet-project, G-Force, who failed to act. He disobeyed my direct orders to engage Yoshida. If he had only done what I said—"

"That's not how this works, Major, and you damn well know it." McCann's eyes narrowed. "You don't get to shirk the responsibility of command onto some kid when your mission goes sideways. You were given command in the field. That puts it on you. It was a CIA operation. That puts it on Hayden. As far as I'm concerned, you both have some serious questions to answer."

Agent Hayden sank into the chair next to Ellison, smiling into the monitor. "And who do you suppose is going to be asking those questions, Colonel? I'd wager it's not going to be you."

"What's that?" McCann barked.

Hayden dragged on his cigarette. "There were helicopters, soldiers, and genetic anomalies, and they were all on television again. I think one of us here is already answering to Congress for all those things. What makes you think this will be any different?"

McCann's face turned dark red. "You think you can leave me holding the bag on this? Trust me, Agent Hayden, you don't want that. You don't want me answering all the questions about to come my way. Hell, maybe I can even volunteer some information they don't know to ask me about yet." McCann drew himself up in his seat, fighting to project some air of authority. "Major Ellison, I want you and your men back at Fort Blaney as soon as possible. We can talk more —"

"We'll be back when the Anoms are cleared for travel. Not before," Hayden said.

McCann sat back in his chair silent, his jaw set.

"I'm sorry, was there something more you needed to say, Colonel?" Hayden asked.

The monitor went black as the transmission terminated from Fort Blaney. Hayden laughed and rose from his chair, walking away to the back of the room, but Ellison sat in place, staring at the blank screen. He was speechless.

"He's going to try and pin this on you. You know that," Hayden said from the back of the room.

Of course Ellison knew it. He could see that much coming before they ever left for San Francisco. The colonel was desperate, and desperate men do terrible things. The only difference now was the certainty of it all.

Ellison wanted to grab the computer monitor and smash it against a wall. He wanted to scream and curse and tell Colonel McCann exactly what he could with his lecture on command and responsibility. He wanted to wrap his hands around the old man's fat neck and squeeze until McCann's eyes bulged out of his head and his tongue rolled out of his mouth, but Ellison knew that none of that would serve—neither his men nor himself. Throwing a tantrum would only make matters worse.

McCann gave the orders, and Ellison was nothing more than an instrument in his hand. No amount of anger could change that. If McCann wanted to serve Ellison up to Congress on a silver platter to save his own career, Ellison would be obligated to go. It was the sacrifice duty demanded, and so it would happen, whether Ellison wanted it to or not.

He pushed back from the monitor, but before he could stand, a soft buzzing filled the room. Hayden reached inside his jacket pocket and pulled out a cell phone. It had never occurred to Ellison that Hayden would carry a phone with him. All cell phones were banned at Fort Blaney without exception—even Ellison and McCann were denied the privilege. If Hayden had a phone... Ellison made a mental note, despite everything else, that Hayden would need to be checked for contraband when they returned to the base.

He watched as Hayden looked down at the phone, and he saw the other man's face tighten. It was a subtle change—the skin drawing back towards his ears, and his mouth flattening— but in Ellison's experience, Hayden had never looked like that before. Something was wrong.

Hayden jammed the phone back in his pocket. "I want you to lock down the Kingman facility, Major. Keep everyone on site until I get back. Consider that an order."

Ellison rose to his feet. "What happened? Something with Yoshida?"

"If I wanted you to know the details, Stuart, I'd tell you. For now, do as I say, and keep everyone where they are." Hayden turned to leave.

"Why should I?" Ellison shouted back at him. "I don't take my orders from you!"

Hayden stopped at the door, and Ellison felt a sudden pang of regret. His anger was justified —without question—but raising his voice was a sign of weakness. Even so, there was truth to what he said. When Colonel McCann gave an order, Ellison was duty bound to carry it out. He had sworn an oath to do just that. Hayden, on the other hand, held no such claim to Ellison's loyalty. His "order" was nothing more than asking a favor, and with the condescension dripping from Hayden's voice, there was little incentive for Ellison to relent.

Hayden turned back to face the major. "You keep picking these fights with me, Stuart, but you don't need to do that. Eventually, you're going to want an ally, someone you can trust. I suggest you start with me."

It was a lie—the same lie Hayden had undoubtedly fed to Colonel McCann, but there was also a kernel of truth hiding behind Hayden's self-serving words. Ellison *did* need an ally if he was going to survive the politics of command—that much was true. It used to be the colonel, but that partnership was clearly over now. And Hayden was right on another count, too: He *could* be trusted. If nothing else, Ellison could trust in Hayden's own instinct for self-preservation. In that regard, he would never prove false. Maybe Hayden's offer held value. After all, the enemy of my enemy...

Ellison rose to his feet and stood at attention. "I'll keep the facility on lockdown, but not because of any order from you. Consider it an act of trust between us, and in return, you can tell me what this is all about when you get back."

Hayden gave a mock salute. "We'll see about that, Stuart. Maybe I will." Then he turned and left the room.

CHAPTER 17

Hayden parked on the side of the street and looked at the building. The storefront was painted neon pink, sandwiched between a dull gray building and a wrought iron fence enclosing a scrapyard. The pink store had a single bay window facing the street, but the three facets of it had been boarded over with plywood and tagged with black graffiti. Hayden could see the address over the front door, 3099 Olympic Boulevard. This was the place.

Hayden had spent the last five hours driving west from Arizona. He had only stopped once, in Barstow, for a new phone. His old phone was back in Kingman, smashed into a million pieces just outside of the town. That was the protocol.

Hayden never received messages on his cell phone—or rather, he had never received messages *before* on his cell phone. Five hours ago, he did—a single word: Aeneas.

Hayden was issued the phone from Reah Labs, and it came loaded with an advanced decryption program. Standard operating procedure was to "borrow" a local phone, place a call to the communications hub, and then use the decryption program to decode the ensuing data blast. For agents in the field, it was the safest way to communicate, but at the end of the day, it was also just a cell phone, and the first and only text message Hayden ever received was an order—a directive to drop everything and get to Los Angeles in the next twenty four hours.

If they had texted him with the name "Hector," Hayden would have ended up in Chicago. "Priam" would have sent him to Washington DC. At least Los Angeles was closer. As for the specific address in LA, he was required to have it memorized.

Hayden pulled his Sig from the glovebox and eased back the slide, checking to see that the first round was chambered in the barrel. It was. Hayden holstered the weapon under his jacket and stepped out of the car. He didn't *need* the gun—not with his other abilities—but he always felt better knowing it was there. It was another option if all else should fail.

Hayden crossed the sidewalk and reached for the door, but as his hand touched the doorknob, it pulled open on its own. Hayden laughed to himself. Sometimes the drama and secrets with Reah Labs bordered on the ridiculous. This was no exception.

Hayden stepped into the building, and the door slammed shut behind him. On instinct, he reached for his Sig under his jacket, but just as his hand closed around the contoured grip, he felt something hard press under his chin.

"Don't try it," a thin voice warned him.

Hayden's eyes trailed to his left, following the silver blade of a katana from under his chin to the hands of another man standing next to the door. This man wore fingerless black biker gloves, a leather jacket pulled over a gray hoodie, and a pair of wraparound sunglasses despite the darkness in the room.

Hayden fought back a smile. "Who's paying you six figures to stand guard, Daishō?"

The other man didn't answer, but Hayden wasn't surprised. He had worked with Daishō before as an independent contractor. The man was quiet, deliberate, and good enough for what he was—a Class Three Enhancement. In Daishō's case, that meant he could vibrate his body at harmonic frequencies, which in turn made the Samurai sword in his hands more like an electric carving knife on steroids. It all worked together to make Daishō effective at his job, if not a stunning conversationalist. In fact, Hayden tried to remember if he ever heard the man put more than two sentences together at a time.

Now Hayden gingerly touched his finger to the back of the sword, guiding it away from his neck. "Why don't you put this away before you get yourself hurt?"

A heavy hand grabbed Hayden by his shoulder. He looked to his right and saw another man standing next to him on the other side of the door. This man was tall and impossibly broad at the shoulders. He glared down at Hayden, his eyebrows knitting together over his nose.

Then Hayden couldn't hold back his smile anymore. "Wasn't sure we'd see you again after San Francisco. I thought you might be too heavy to float."

The man twisted his hand in the fabric of Hayden's jacket, pulling the Irishman up on his toes, and he cocked back his other fist ready to punch. But before anything could happen, a sharp, female voice shouted from the back of the room.

"That's enough!"

Hayden looked in the direction of the voice, and for the first time, he could see through the shadows and get a sense of the space around him. They were standing in a large, empty room. It looked like it took up the entire width of the building, and the walls, floor, and ceiling were all painted black. Two folding chairs sat in the far corner, and an overturned card table was pushed up against the left wall. Immediately across from him, in the middle of the back wall, Hayden could see an open doorway filled by a figure wearing a skirt and jacket.

"I said—" the female voice started again, but before she could finish, Hayden phased out of his physical form. His body and clothes suddenly looked like they were made of silvery mist, and he simply walked forward, slipping out of the grip of the man on his right and stepping through the folded steel of the katana under his throat. He stopped a couple of feet ahead of the others in the room and straightened his jacket as he rematerialized.

"There. Now that wasn't so difficult, was it?" Hayden smiled. "It's been a long time, Gwen."

Gwendolyn Thomas offered a polite smile—a barely-there turn at the corner of her mouth. "So it has. Thank you for getting here so quickly."

"Of course," Hayden said. "When the boss calls, you come running."

Gwen turned without an answer and started through the lit doorway behind her. Hayden followed, cursing himself under his breath.

He had always worn his apathy for the world like other men wore Armani suits, or Nike sneakers, or cheap cologne. It was both his suit of armor and his weapon of choice, but more than either of those things, it was honestly who he was. After all, why should he concern himself with others when they so often proved themselves his inferiors? Gwendolyn Thomas, however, was different. She was an equal, and the sheer effort of caring about her opinions left Hayden feeling like some other man—a person he despised. This other Hayden was clumsy, mewling, and weak. Worst of all, he was acutely aware that Gwendolyn Thomas, CEO of Reah

Labs, felt nothing more than her own apathy at his presence. Hayden considered her an equal. She saw him as an inferior, and he knew it.

As Hayden stepped into the next room, his eyes met those of Noah Kincaid, Gwen's personal bodyguard. Noah was tall, with a sharp Adam's apple jutting forward from his neck like he had swallowed a peach pit whole. Other than that, he looked like he had just rolled out of bed. He wore heavy gray sweatpants with a red hoodie, the word "Lifeguard" and a white cross printed on the front, and a pair of white earbuds were jammed deep inside both his ears.

As soon as their eyes met, Noah looked away, focusing down on the floor. "It's good to see you, too," he said.

"Good to see—" Hayden stopped himself from finishing the sentence. He was about to say something like, "Good to see you, Noah." It was a simple enough greeting, but then the other man jumped the gun and answered before Hayden could spit out the words.

Hayden tried again. "How are—"

At the same time, Noah raised his voice, drowning out Hayden's words. "I'm doing good —fine. Everything's—I'm doing—I'm doing— everything's fine."

As Noah spoke, he bobbed his head up and down with each word. Then he pulled his phone out of his pocket and swiped his thumb across the screen.

Hayden could see the other man was agitated now, and so he tried to change the subject. "I heard that you saved Ms. Thomas from—"

"He wasn't there. I mean—yeah. He was there, but that's not—he *was* there. He was there, but —" Noah started to rock his whole body back and forth, swaying like seagrass under a wave. In his other hand he clutched a small leather key-chain, rubbing his thumb in circles over the lea-ther. "We didn't see him—I didn't, but they were in the building. We didn't see him, but they were there—"

"That's enough," Gwen hissed at Hayden under her breath. She stepped closer and touched Noah's elbow, staring up into his face like she was trying to pin him with her eyes. Slowly, he stopped rocking and speaking, but he kept his head down, staring at his phone.

Gwen smiled up at him, softening her voice. "Noah, I want you to step outside and wait by the door in the other room. Is that all right?"

A wide grin broke across Noah's face, and without giving a verbal answer, he stepped out of the room, closing the door behind him.

"Good job, Hayden. You broke him," a new voice called out from across the room.

Hayden had been so absorbed with Noah and his apparent breakdown that he hadn't noticed anyone else when he stepped through the door. Now he could see the others.

Leaning against the far wall, Hayden recognized the figure of Kaito Yoshida. He was the one who had spoken. Yoshida wore a dark suit and a black t-shirt. His black hair was pulled back in a ponytail, and he offered a lopsided, half-grin.

On Yoshida's right was a tall woman wearing jeans and a white tee. Her black, pin-straight hair was swept back behind her ears, and her arched eyebrows and thin, straight mouth defied any emotion. Hayden recognized her, too, from her picture. It was the woman known as Kumiho. She was with Yoshida at the Hong Kong airport, and she was with him on the Golden Gate Bridge—and despite all evidence pointing to her early demise, she was with him now.

A shorter man stood on Yoshida's other side leaning against the back wall. He wore rectangular glasses and a gray suit, and the color of his hair was somewhere between platinum blonde and faded white. He kept his hands folded in front of him and cast his eyes around the room, never lingering on anyone for too long. Hayden thought he looked like a man trying to appear forgettable, but for all his efforts, Hayden recognized him, too. He had seen his picture boarding the same flight in Hong Kong with Yoshida and Kumiho.

Hayden squared his shoulders. "Isn't this a surprise? I didn't realize our partnership with the Ryoku included face-to-face meetings. I would've made it a point to skip this one."

Kaito laughed from across the room. "And

what makes you think you were important enough to be told in the first place? You're like her dog, Hayden. You do whatever she says." Kaito turned to look at Gwen. "How's your other pet, Gwennie? Able to get him restarted, were you?"

Gwen ignored the comment and kept her eyes on Hayden. "We've talked about this."

Hayden fished his pack of cigarettes out of his jacket pocket, shaking one loose and pulling it free with his lips. "I know we did."

"Don't even think about lighting that in here," Gwen snapped at him.

Of course she wouldn't let him smoke; Hayden pulled the cigarette from his mouth, broke it in half, and threw it away. "I know what we talked about. Okay?"

Gwen felt the need to remind him anyway. "If you talk to Noah, you need to finish your sentences. He's trying his best to answer you, but you keep changing the question. It's cruel."

"Oh, that's never stopped him before," Yoshida said. "Agent Hayden has no qualms with being cruel. Isn't that right, Ghost?"

Hayden bristled. He could accept correction when it came from Gwen—that was part of the job—but there was no reason to suffer the same slights from a pissant like Kaito Yoshida. Hayden narrowed his eyes at the other man. "You're the one who killed seventeen men and women on your way out of Blaney. You've probably slaughtered hundreds more since you've been gone, so I think we're both comfortable with our own brand of cruelty."

"Still one of the best days of my life." Yoshida beamed. "I suppose we're all just lucky you weren't there when I left. Am I right?"

"One of us was lucky. I'll agree with that much," Hayden said.

Yoshida feigned amusement with a silent laugh. He leaned over, still smiling, and whispered to the tall woman beside him, keeping his eyes on Hayden. The woman smiled, too.

Hayden wanted his cigarettes. Out of habit, he reached his hand all the way inside his pocket before he remembered Gwen's edict against smoking. Instead, he pulled it out empty and smoothed the lapels of his jacket. Then he didn't know what to do with his hands, so he rubbed the whiskers covering this throat. What he wanted to do—besides lighting up his goddamn cigarette—was to put his fist through the center of Yoshida's face.

Hayden pointed his finger at the tall woman. "What's your girlfriend doing here anyway, Kaito? Last I heard, she was supposed to be dead."

The tall woman stepped aside from Yoshida. "Not yet. Care to try?"

Before Hayden could answer, Gwen stepped between them. "She's here because she was invited. The same as you, the same as Kaito; the same as all of us."

"And he was invited, too?" Hayden pointed his finger at the other man standing by the wall. "What's his ability? The human doorstop?"

Yoshida stepped closer. "You mean Janus? Janus is the reason we're here. He had to be delivered." Yoshida looked down at his watch. "In fact, go ahead, Janus. Let's show him exactly what you can do. Open the portal."

Gwen looked down at her watch. "We were told to wait. It's still fifteen more minutes."

"We were *asked* to wait," Yoshida said, "not told. We're equal partners in this, remember? And I, for one, don't feel like waiting another fifteen minutes with our present company. Janus, open the portal."

The man in the gray suit stepped to the middle of the room. He took a slow breath and opened his arms out wide. Then he clapped his hands together, and the sharp sound echoed in the room. He stayed there, palms pressed together as if he were praying, and he closed his eyes.

Hayden leaned closer to Gwen and lowered his voice. "What's he doing?"

"Janus is a Class Four Spatial," Gwen answered, making no attempt to keep her own voice quiet, "He has an identical twin. The same DNA means the same power. Together, they can fold space between the two of them."

"It's a bridge between brothers," Yoshida

said. "Usually, they can only span a few dozen miles. We're trying for something much bigger today."

Janus, for his part, didn't seem to notice the talking. He spread his hands wide again, holding his arms out to his sides, and he opened his mouth to let out a low, resonant wail. The sound started out of him like the hollow waffling of a drone pipe, building in the air.

Then, somehow, Janus's mouth opened even wider, as if his lower jaw unhinged, and his bottom lip and teeth were sagging toward his collarbone. The lower half of his face looked like putty melting in the summer heat.

From the black void of the man's gaping throat, Hayden could see a dull purple light. Still, Janus forced open his mouth wider. His lower jaw fell to his waist, then below his knees, and finally it slapped dull and lifeless against the floor. The purple energy filled his gaping maw, and the droning noise echoed off the cinderblock walls.

All at once, the purple light emanating from Janus's mouth dimmed, obscured for the moment by a silhouette. Hayden looked closer. It was the figure of a man. He looked like he was walking out from the back of Janus' throat, getting bigger—coming closer. With his next step, he passed through the mouth of Janus, and now he was standing in the room with the others, his bare feet on the concrete floor.

The man standing in front of Hayden, framed by a purple halo of light, was old and naked. His olive skin was creased and folded by a thousand wrinkled lines, and the feathery hair atop his head and his short-cut beard were pure white. He looked, somehow, familiar.

Gwen started forward, grabbing a white bathrobe from off a chair and opening it to the naked man. He slipped his arms through the sleeves and turned, closing the robe in front of him and tying the belt around his waist. He leaned forward, holding both of Gwen's arms, kissing her first on one cheek and then the other. Hayden thought he could see the man's lips move as well, saying something close to Gwen's ear, but with the deafening wail from Janus it was impossible to hear.

The light from Janus's mouth dimmed again, and all at once, a second figure stood in the room. This woman was short, pale, and thin, with short brunette hair and dark eyes. Like the man before her, she was also naked. The woman glanced furtively around the room, looking at the others but trying not to meet anyone's eye, covering herself the best she could with her arms. Then, like before, Gwen handed the woman a robe. She quickly threw it around her shoulders, hiding herself away.

Suddenly, the noise in the room stopped. The light was gone. Janus closed his mouth and staggered back. He fell onto the floor looking only half-conscious. The woman in the robe turned around, kneeling to check on him, but the man with the white hair and beard paid him no attention.

Instead, he stepped forward into the center of the room, lifting his hands to draw in the others. "Perhaps, then, we should begin."

As he spoke, Hayden found the man in his memory, and cursed himself for not recognizing him sooner.

He was standing with Jericho Caine, leader of the Red Moon.

CHAPTER 18

Jericho Caine took the gray folding chair from the side of the room and set it down in the middle of the floor. He motioned for Kaito Yoshida and Gwendolyn Thomas to do the same. Hayden looked around the room and saw that Kaito already had one of the metal chairs in his hand. There was only one other leaning against the wall. Hayden picked it up and carried it to the middle of the room, setting it across from Caine.

Gwen sat down, crossing her legs at her ankles and smoothing out her skirt, but never looking back to acknowledge Hayden's gesture. Behind Caine, the young woman who followed him through the portal still knelt over Janus. Whether creating the portal had taken more out of him than he first bargained for, or his collapse was simply the price he was willing to pay, Hayden couldn't be sure. Janus pushed himself back against the far wall, and Hayden could see him taking slow, deliberate breaths.

Jericho Caine leaned forward in his chair. "I

thank you both for making the difficult journey to be here, but I wouldn't have called for this meeting if it were not necessary. We've reached a critical moment." Caine flipped his hand back and forth as if it were a seesaw. "Now our plans will either bear fruit, or they will wither in the field, and we must decide together how best to proceed."

Hayden felt strange standing in the same room as Jericho Caine and doing nothing. His first thought was that he should shoot the man between the eyes. After all, if Hayden were *really* a CIA operative, there might exist some moral imperative to end the terrorist's life regardless of the immediate consequences. Fortunately, Hayden was nothing more than an independent contractor, owned blood and bone by Reah Labs and loaned out to the CIA. So, if Gwendolyn Thomas wanted to take a meeting with Jericho Caine, Hayden would see that it happened.

Reah Labs insisted on maintaining their independence from the government, even if, often enough, they were so entangled with the CIA that it was impossible to tell the two of them apart. The CIA wanted access to "highly motivated" genetic anomalies, and Reah Labs wanted freedom from some of the more puritanical government oversights levied against them. The two groups found a symbiotic relationship in each other—beneficial if not always healthy.

Four years ago, this relationship resulted in

Reah Labs farming Hayden out to the CIA just as they began the final phase of Project: ATLAS. As usual, Langley was happy to sink their hooks into another Reah Labs asset. The *quid pro quo* was only fully realized two years later, when special forces deployed to Fort Blaney. Of course, none of that mattered to Hayden. He held no allegiance to the CIA, the Army, or his adopted country. His only loyalty belonged to Reah Labs. In that respect, Hayden was a free man.

Caine looked to his right at Kaito Yoshida, and slowly, everyone else in the room turned to look at Yoshida as well.

"To choose our way forward," Caine said, "we must first understand what brought us to this place—this moment of decision. Kaito, tell us why you failed in San Francisco."

Kaito laughed, but there was no sound—only a noiseless jerk of his head followed by a wide, fake smile. "I don't know what you're talking about, Jericho. My actions in San Francisco were a complete success. I brought down the Golden Gate Bridge on live TV just as we planned. It's the kind of victory you failed to deliver in Chicago. Maybe you're confusing the two of us."

Hayden may have felt no obligation to as-sassinate Jericho Caine, but Kaito Yoshida was a different story. In fact, if Gwen ever gave him leave, Hayden would welcome the opportunity to kill the man. With Yoshida, it would be personal.

The two of them first met when Hayden arrived at the Blaney Research Facility four years ago. Yoshida and Megan Reynolds—Nyx—were the only two Anoms in the program at the time. Yoshida was the older of the two, and more polished and controlled with his powers. Nyx was young and raw, but even then, Hayden could see her potential. He had no idea how long either one had been training at Blaney, but he didn't need to know. He had been sent to West Virginia with a different purpose entirely. He was there to put the finishing touches on Project: ATLAS.

Reah Labs had placed Hayden in charge of East Coast recruitment. His sole purpose was to locate suspected Anoms, test and verify their abilities in the field, and, if warranted, bring them back to Blaney for training. It had all been mind-numbingly simple until the day he was called away on assignment, and Yoshida took the opportunity to free himself from Reah's yoke. He dropped seventeen bodies on his way out the door—men and women Hayden knew and respected. So, if Hayden ever got the chance to hold him to account, he would.

Now Caine shook his head, and raised his hands, waving them in front of him. "Kaito, you sound like a schoolboy standing in front of the class, knowing he's in trouble. You pour out excuses because you're scared of what the teacher will say. Are you scared of the teacher, Kaito?"

Yoshida's smile fell away. "I think you should choose your words more carefully, Jericho."

"And now you're angry with me." Caine shrugged. "I speak as your friend, Kaito. I'm here as *more* than your friend. In all of this, I am your brother. We pledged our lives to each other—all three of us. Don't you remember?" Caine leaned forward, patting his hand on Kaito's knee. "You don't have to hide the truth from us, Kaito. San Francisco was a failure, just like Chicago was a failure before it. They both failed for the same reason."

Caine turned his eyes to Gwen, and once more, everyone in the room followed his lead.

Gwen uncrossed her ankles and lifted her chin. "Maybe Kaito's angry because of your accusations—at least the ones you're implying. If you have something similar to say to me, you can come out and say it plainly."

The old man waved his hands in front of him. "Gwendolyn—"

"The intervention in Chicago wasn't our decision," Gwen continued. "I told you that months ago when it happened. Agent Hayden advised against direct intervention, and he was overruled. What more did you want us to do? It's the price you pay when you drag in the United States military as your partner."

Caine closed his eyes. "We've already been over this. We need their military on our side."

"And I told you we don't," Gwen snapped.

Caine waved his hand in front of his face as if he were chasing away cobwebs. "Enough about the military. No more arguing about what we need and what we don't need. I didn't travel for this. I'm here because of the boy. Tell me about the one who stopped my plans in Chicago."

Gwen narrowed her eyes. "I already told you: His name is Jeremy Cross. He controls gravity. He's the reason the Willis Tower is still standing. He carved up your bronze champion like he was a paper doll."

Caine turned to face Yoshida. "And this same boy—Jeremy Cross—he was the one you faced in San Francisco? He's the one who stopped you at the bridge?"

"No one stopped me at the bridge," Yoshida growled. "That's the reason it's at the bottom of the bay."

"Stop lying to me!" Caine thundered.

Then, for the first time, Hayden could see the truth behind their partnership. For all the talk about standing together as equals, that clearly wasn't the case. Jericho Caine carried a weight that Gwendolyn Thomas and Kaito Yoshida could never match.

Caine hammered his fist down into his open hand. "I asked you to kill this boy, Jeremy Cross. He was supposed to die at your hands, Kaito, and the world was going to watch him die. So, is he dead?"

Yoshida didn't answer.

"Did the world see you kill this boy?" Caine's voice rose again. "Did they watch the boy from Chicago die on their television screens? Or did they see their hero hold up a bridge?"

Yoshida shook his head. "Jeremy Cross held up the bridge for a matter of seconds, and he saved no one. Trust me, all they saw was his failure."

"Trust you?" Caine laughed quietly as he rose to his feet and stepped behind his chair. He looked behind him at the young woman still kneeling over Janus, the one who followed him through the portal. Caine reached down his hand for the waif, and she took it, letting the old man help her to her feet. Then he brushed a strand of her dark hair behind her ear, and the woman flinched at his touch.

Even standing next to him, she kept her eyes lowered, but the way she watched Caine out of the corner of her eye reminded Hayden of a sparrow, skittering across the ground, ready to take flight at the slightest impulse. Caine didn't seem to notice—or if he noticed, he didn't care.

He turned back to Yoshida. "Perhaps you're right, Kaito. Perhaps the boy's failure was enough, but how can we know? People can see so many different things, all by looking at the same picture. How can we know what they saw: courage to hold up a bridge, or weakness to let it fall?"

Caine's question was met by silence.

The old man drew in a deep breath. "People are unpredictable. There are too many variations. How can we know what they think or what they see?" Caine lifted both of his hands and shrugged his shoulders. "The only way to understand people is by turning them back into the animals they truly are. Then instinct can take over—the small voice that screams, 'Keep me alive!' will cry out, too loud. What did the people see on their televisions? We cannot say, because they aren't yet truly afraid."

Caine led the waif forward to stand in the middle of their circle, letting the others focus their eyes on her. For her own part, the woman kept her eyes fixed on the concrete floor and stood rigid with her arms at her sides.

Caine walked back to his chair. "The people of this country must know their lives depend on our mercy. They must cry out, 'Keep us alive!' and only then will we know what to expect. To this end, I have brought you Ziada, as we agreed."

Hayden looked again at the woman. As Caine said her name, a rush of warm color filled Ziada's pale face, but she didn't look like a killer—at least not to Hayden. He tried to imagine her as some terrible angel of death brought forth to plague humanity, but the juxtaposition was only comical. She was a scared little straw of a woman, so shy that she blushed at the mention of her own name. It was almost enough to make Hayden pity her.

Caine lifted his hand, indicating the waif. "Ziada is a rare jewel even among a trove of priceless treasures. She is an anomaly who exists to amplify the powers of other anomalies. With Ziada's touch, you will be a thousand times more than what you are now. She is the reason we could travel across the world, and the reason *why* we traveled across the world. Now I give her to you, Kaito Yoshida. She belongs to you and your Ryoku."

Ziada shuffled forward in the direction of Kaito, taking her place behind his chair, standing next to Kumiho.

"You've been chosen, Kaito Yoshida," Caine continued, his voice building. "With Ziada's help, you will finally have all the power you desire, and with it, you will bring this country to its knees. But first, you're going to kill the boy Jeremy Cross. He cannot be allowed to stand in our way again."

Kaito rose from his seat. "Just tell me where he is."

Caine didn't answer. Instead, he looked straight ahead, his eyes fixing on Hayden. Then Hayden glanced quickly around the room, and to his surprise, everyone else was looking back at him, too. Apparently, he was the one they expected to answer.

Hayden looked one more time around the room. "If you're looking to kill G-Force, I left him back in Kingman. You can find him at one of our facilities. He was in bad shape, too. He might even be weak enough for Kaito to handle on his own."

"Hayden—" The sharp whisper from Gwen was meant as a warning, but it came too late.

Hayden looked back at Jericho Caine, and the other man's face darkened—his eyes folded half-shut, and his brow creased with three long lines as a flush of red rose from his neck into his face. "You insult my brother with your insolence, and so you insult us all. Perhaps it will fall to me to teach you the respect you're lacking."

Hayden wanted to laugh. He had no doubt the old man was sincere in his threat, but he wondered if Caine had the skills to follow through with it. Maybe he would invite the old man to try? He wondered what look Caine would give him then.

Instead, Hayden bit his tongue, choked back his laughter, and even managed to wipe the smug grin off his face—none of it was for Jericho Caine, but rather for the sake of Gwendolyn Thomas. He wouldn't risk embarrassing her any further.

"I apologize," Hayden managed to say through his teeth.

Caine turned away without answering and reached out with both hands for Yoshida. "Then I leave our hopes with you, Kaito. I look forward to hearing of your many successes, for they will be *our* successes as well." Caine kissed Yoshida on both sides of his face and pulled away. "And now, Ziada, if you help Janus to his feet and open the portal back home, it's time I took my leave."

CHAPTER 19

Jeremy banged his fist on the door, and the hollow clang echoed back into the room louder than he expected. For a second, there was no answer, and he thought about knocking again, but then the sharp voice of Ellison called from the other side of the door.

"Come in."

Jeremy pressed a button on the wall, and the door slid away. He stepped inside and found himself standing in a room identical to the one he had been given on the other side of Kingman's Rec Room. Just inside the door there was a narrow entryway with a closet on one side. Farther in, the room opened. A large video monitor was mounted on the left wall, and a neatly made bed covered with a heavy navy blanket was pushed against the wall on the right. The door on the back wall was closed, but Jeremy already knew it led to the bathroom, and in the middle of the floor, under the fluorescent lights above, there was a small round table with two chairs.

Major Ellison sat in one of those chairs now,

facing the video monitor. His camouflaged shirt was unbuttoned to his waist, completely untucked, and he had pushed himself back from the table, holding a glass of water balanced on his knee.

It was the most informal Jeremy had ever seen the major, and the effect, at least at first, was disorienting. Ellison looked like a man completely at ease. But what more could he hope to gain by maintaining his air of authority? Ellison had already won their battle. This was merely his victory lap.

"You wanted to see me?" Jeremy asked.

Ellison took a long drink from the glass before reaching it to the table and wiping his mouth with the back of his hand. "Yes, I did."

"Why?" Jeremy asked, "You have second thoughts about cutting me loose?"

Ellison smiled. "No."

"And why would you? You wanted me gone from the start, right?" Jeremy set his jaw.

Ellison leaned back in his chair. "I suppose this must feel terribly personal to you."

"Because it *is* personal," Jeremy shot back at him.

"Yes, it is." Ellison nodded. "But I can't understand why that's a problem. Why should my personal opinion invalidate my judgement? After all, everything I hate about you makes it clear why you're a failure. You're selfish, reckless, and petulant. Should I pretend that I like you now despite all that? Would that somehow make this all better?"

Jeremy shifted his weight from one foot to the other. "It's late, Major. If you're looking to trade insults, maybe it can wait until the morning."

"That's not why you're here." Ellison stood up, reaching for a wireless keyboard on the table. "There are other things I need you to see—certain facts you need to understand before I can let you go, and no, I'm not going to wait for the morning. I got these files from your friend, Gauntlet." Ellison tapped on the keyboard, and the video monitor changed its black screen to a picture of a man.

"You know who that is?" Ellison asked.

The man on the screen sat in front of a silver table. He had dark hair and dark eyes, and he wore a suit jacket over a white dress shirt. The top button of his shirt was left open, and he wore no tie. A glass of water sat on the table near his elbow. The man in the picture was young—younger than Jeremy ever knew him—but that didn't matter. The resemblance was unmistakable.

"I asked if you know—" Ellison started again.

"He's my father," Jeremy answered, his voice catching in his throat.

"Good. For a second, I thought you were going to play stupid." Ellison struck another key on the keyboard, and the image on the screen started to play as a video.

"Please, state your name," said a low voice off camera.

"Dr. Jonathan Fairbanks," the man in the suit answered.

"Can you tell us what you're doing here?" the voice asked.

Fairbanks pushed away from the table, twisting in his chair. "You already know why I'm here. This is a waste—"

"We need to hear it from you again. In your own words. On the video," the voice said. "Doctor, why are you—"

"I'm looking for protection from Reah Labs." Fairbanks looked straight into the camera.

"Are you afraid for your life, Doctor?"

"Yes."

Offscreen, Jeremy could hear papers shuffling over the metal table, and the voice spoke again. "All right, Doctor Fairbanks, can you go through your history at Reah Labs with us?"

Fairbanks grabbed the glass of water off the table and took a long drink. When he finished, he slid his chair forward again and folded his hands on the tabletop. "Just over seven years ago, I accepted a research position at Reah. It was my assumption at the time—an assumption that was later confirmed by my direct supervisors—that I was recruited for my research in the field of genetic manipulation. It only took weeks after they hired me when I was introduced to the phenomena of genetic anomalies."

"How did you learn about these anomalies?" the voice asked.

"At first, it was through research—the work they wanted me to build upon. Reah Labs kept an extensive library of files. Later, I learned more about the Anoms through personal experience. Reah kept several on staff mostly for security purposes, although not exclusively. They also kept some genetic anomalies as research test subjects. It was clear to me, fairly early on, that not all of these subjects were willing participants."

"Is that when you decided to leave Reah Labs?"

Fairbanks took another drink of water. "No. That never bothered me. The Anoms were necessary for my research."

"Can you go into more detail about your research? What it entailed?" the voice asked.

"I was tasked with creating an artificial genetic anomaly." Fairbanks leaned forward, looking down at his hands. "You need to understand that when we started seven years ago, we began with nothing. Reah's files on genetic manipulation were woefully inadequate. It was all classifications and understanding the mechanics of known abilities—they were concerned with the 'how.' There was nothing in their research about the 'why.' Why do genetic anomalies exist in the first place? I needed to build my research from the ground up, one brick at a time."

"And were you successful?"

Fairbanks leaned back in his chair. "I'm here, aren't I?"

"Doctor, we need you to be more specific." The voice offscreen sounded agitated. "In your research, were you able—"

"What we were attempting should have been impossible," Fairbanks continued, "but that's what they wanted. They wanted the impossible. You need to understand, life has a way of guarding itself. It resents our meddling. In the lab, if you manipulate the DNA too far, nature rejects your monster. In our case, the embryos became inviable."

"But you solved that problem?" the voice offscreen pressed.

Fairbanks smiled. "We solved it ten times over."

For a long moment, there was silence on the video. Jeremy could hear someone whispering offscreen, until finally, the voice asked, "Are you confirming that you created ten viable Anom embryos?"

Fairbanks nodded. "We did."

"Doctor," the voice continued, "if you were successful, why did you leave Reah Labs?"

Fairbanks's smile evaporated. "I left because you don't get to close Pandora's box once you've opened it. What I had done, it was already too late. I learned what Reah Labs planned to do with my research. They want to build an army."

"An army of Anoms? To what end?"

"Why does anyone want an army?" Fairbanks reached for the glass of water and finished it. "They were preparing for war, so I left. I found you instead."

"And we're glad you did." From off-camera, a hand slid a folder across the table to Fairbanks. "As you discussed with your contact, Doctor, the Knights of the Crusade are ready to give you a new identity, our complete protection, and a sizable sum of money in exchange for your research."

Fairbanks pushed the folder to the side. "My research is destroyed. I made sure of that."

Then for a long moment, Fairbanks sat staring into the camera, unblinking, and there was only silence; finally, the hand reached back across the table, gathering in the folder. "So there's nothing more for us to talk about then. We're not a charity, Doctor."

"I know exactly what you are, which is why I've brought you this." Fairbanks reached under the table, and as he sat up again, he held a large thermos in his hand.

"And what's that supposed to be?"

"It's your very own frozen Anom." Fairbanks slid the canister across the table. "You give me my new identity, you pay me my money, and you let me go. In exchange, I'll send you a new Anom every ten years—nine in total. This is number one, my down payment."

"I thought you said there were ten."

"I did, but you get nine."

There were more whispers off-camera, until the voice finally said, "One Anom every ten years? That's a long time to make us wait."

Fairbanks leaned back in his chair. "It sounds like a good reason to make sure I live a long and boring life. Do we have a deal?"

Ellison tapped his finger down on the keyboard, and the image on the monitor froze in place. At the same time, Jeremy felt off balance, as if he had spun around blindfolded, and now it took all his effort to keep on his feet. In a way, the video Ellison played was familiar—there was no doubt that Fairbanks was his father—but that recognition only made the other circumstances harder to swallow. His father was a geneticist. He worked for Reah Labs. His last name was Fairbanks?

"I asked if you knew about this?" Ellison's voice was louder than it had been before, and Jeremy gathered it wasn't the first time he was asking the question.

"Did I know about what? Which part?" Jeremy asked.

Ellison folded his hands on the table, fixing his eyes squarely on Jeremy. "Did you know about any of it?"

Jeremy's head ached. He tried to replay the conversation he just watched in his own mind, but it was difficult to keep everything in order. His dad was a man named Fairbanks. Fairbanks was running from Reah Labs. But why was he scared? Why would Reah Labs turn against him?

Jeremy pulled out the second chair at the table and sat down across from Ellison. "Major, if Reah Labs was trying to build an army, we need to know why."

Ellison laughed. "You think that's why I called you in here?" He pushed back from the table. "You think I'm worried about Reah Labs and their motives here? You're worse than Gauntlet, talking about taking sides and conspiracies."

Jeremy's face twisted. The video that Ellison had shown him just laid bare Reah Labs for the last twenty years. According to his father, the company was nothing better than a gang of genetic mercenaries. He claimed they were trying to weaponize Anoms to fight in some unrealized war. From what Jeremy could gather from his own experience, those efforts had never stopped, and somehow, despite his father's best efforts, Jeremy had allowed himself to become a part of it. Ellison and the Army were a part of it, too. If that wasn't the reason for Ellison showing him the video, then why?

"Your father was a traitor to his country," Ellison growled from across the table.

Then, suddenly, Ellison's motives were perfectly clear, and Jeremy felt his stomach drop. It wasn't enough to kick Jeremy out of Fort Blaney and Reah Labs. Ellison needed to twist the knife on his way out. He wanted Jeremy to feel it.

Ellison pointed his finger at the image frozen on the monitor. "You heard it in his own words. He sold biological weapons to a known terror group. What would you call that? Because it sounds like treason to me."

"He said he was running," Jeremy said. "He was afraid for his life."

"You heard the part where he destroyed his research?" Ellison pressed his advantage. "That included killing his own lab assistant. He shot the man in the head. It was a cold and calculated execution. That doesn't sound like a man acting out of fear. Rather like a traitor covering his tracks."

Jeremy wanted to scream back in Ellison's face, and tell him that he could go to hell with his accusations and his videos. The major was painting his dad out to be a terrorist sympathizer, or a genetic arms dealer, or both. Nothing could be further from the truth. His dad wore his integrity as if it were a suit of armor, and he carried his own moral compass in his back pocket. Ellison had to be lying, but as Jeremy looked up at the monitor and saw his father grinning for the camera, his own doubts killed the denial in his throat.

Instead, he turned away from the screen. "What is it you really want here, Major?"

"I already told you, we want answers."

"I don't have any. I don't know about any of this." Jeremy could feel his pulse thrumming in his temples like tack hammers beating on either side of his skull. He desperately wanted to end the conversation and leave.

"Let's start with the embryos?" Ellison leaned forward in his chair. "Where are they now? How did your father access them?"

"Why would I know that?" Jeremy stood up.

Ellison laughed. "Because he's your father. Why do you think we recruited you in the first place? It's time you finally gave us some answers."

Jeremy shook his head. "That's not true. This was never just about my dad."

Ellison was ready to answer again, but before he could start, the door to the bathroom opened. Framed in a cloud of steam, Lara stepped into the room, her bare feet padding silently across the tiled floor. She wore a long, white robe cinched at the waist, her hair was wrapped under a white towel balanced on top of her head, and her face and neck still glistened from the shower. She took two steps into the room, still tying the belt around her, when she looked up. Her eyes found Jeremy first.

He watched her face transform in that moment. She started with her eyes watching her own fingers tie a knot, and then she was staring at him, her mouth open, her skin flushed, as if she was the one who somehow made the mistake. Finally, her eyes fell on Ellison and her jaw tightened.

"What the hell are you doing?" she hissed at him from across the room.

Ellison answered without taking his eyes off Jeremy. "You're just in time, dear. I was asking G-Force some of the questions we prepared—the ones about his father."

Lara turned on her heels for the bathroom and slammed the door behind her. Ellison flinched at the sharp sound, but he refused to look back over his shoulder.

Jeremy forced a smile. "That go the way you planned it?"

"I don't know. She's still here isn't she?" The corner of Ellison's lip edged into a leer. "I know what you think about her—what you hope for the two of you—but you're wrong. As far as Mirror's concerned, you're nothing more than her assignment."

Jeremy's back straightened as Ellison's last barb found its mark. Even if he could ignore the major's other words, Jeremy had realized that last truth for himself, and there was no armor against truth. Ellison was right. At the end of the day, Lara was still here, and she was still with him.

Jeremy looked away at the video monitor. "I don't know anything about my dad or the embryos. Is there anything else?"

Ellison leaned back in his chair. "Not to-night. The rest can wait for morning. You're dis-missed."

CHAPTER 20

Jeremy laid on his bed for hours, eyes shut, waiting. When he left Ellison's room, he had stormed back to his own quarters, kicked off his boots, and collapsed on top of his bed in a heap. He wasn't tired. There were still too many raw emotions for that, like the doubt that grew in his brain like algae, clouding and coloring his thoughts, or the absolute anger rippling through his whole body.

He was angry at Ellison. It had taken all of Jeremy's self-restraint not to punch his fist through the Major's smug teeth. Their whole interview—from the video of his dad to Ellison dragging out his questions just long enough so that Jeremy would have to see Lara step out of the shower—it was designed to grind Jeremy into the dirt. It was cruel, and vindictive, and effective.

There were other targets for his anger, too. He was angry at Lara, even if she had done nothing to earn it. She certainly never made him any promises about their relationship, but what did that matter? There was still the deception

—careful omissions on her part, if not outright lies. She let Jeremy think they were closer than what they really were. Now he knew the truth. Lara's job required her to find answers, and so everything about their friendship—and Jeremy's own infatuation—only proved a means to an end.

Then there was his own dad, or the man Jeremy thought was his dad; the man Ellison identified as Jonathan Fairbanks. How could he have worked for Reah Labs? How could he sell himself and his research to the Knights of the Crusade? Jeremy needed answers—an honest conversation with his father—but that required sleep, and sleep wouldn't come. Instead, Jeremy lay on his back, waiting for the morning.

All at once, a red light flooded the room, and the piercing screech of a siren split through Jeremy's ears. He rolled out of the bed. The siren blasted again, and somehow it felt even louder this time, the shrill noise shaking through his skull. Jeremy looked at the clock on the video monitor. It read: 0438. He pulled on both of his boots, and without tying either one, he ran for the door. Thankfully, it slid open.

If nothing else, it was quieter in the main Rec Room. The siren's wail was deadened and trapped behind the closed doors of the other rooms. Here, the only thing out of place were the sweeping red lights mounted to the walls, the same crimson strobes you would see on an ambulance—just enough of a disturbance to get your attention.

Jeremy looked over and saw Gauntlet already standing in front of his own door, wrapped in his red and black Exocorium armor, the metal helmet sealed over his face. Gauntlet's arms were folded across his chest, and for just a moment, Jeremy wondered if he hadn't been standing guard like that all night.

"You order the wakeup call?" Jeremy yelled at him.

The sirens grew louder as the door on Jeremy's left slid open; Nyx stepped out into the Rec Room. "What the hell's going on?"

At almost the same time, across the room, another door opened, and John Langer stumbled out. His hair was wild atop his head, and he was still pulling his arm through the sleeve of his white lab coat.

"What's happening?" Langer asked, his fingers moving to his green flannel shirt, unbuttoning and rebuttoning the same two buttons at his chest. "Are we under attack? What is it?"

Across from them, Ellison's door slid open, and the major stalked out into the Rec Room. "We don't know yet, Doctor, but that's what I intend to find out."

Ellison wore his gray camouflage and his Beretta pistol was holstered on his hip. As he walked into the room, he was still carefully rolling the sleeves of his uniform. Lara stepped out behind him, walking toward John Langer. She wore her navy skirt with a white blouse, and her dark blonde hair was twisted up on top of her head. She was still trying to look like herself without acknowledging that just a minute ago, she woke up in the major's bed to sirens blaring all around her.

Ellison finished with his sleeves and looked up. "I received a call that a pair of SUVs breached our outer perimeter. They're five miles out and moving toward our front door. Nyx and Gauntlet, you're both coming with me to see exactly what they want. The rest of you should secure yourselves in this room. Nobody comes in or out without my authorization."

Jeremy raised his hand. "You said Gauntlet and Nyx, but I should come, too. Just in case—"

"In case of what?" Ellison growled. "In case the rest of us fail?" Ellison shook his head. "You don't get it. Our team is better off without you. Let that sink into your thick skull. We have a better chance *without* you. The last thing I need is to bring you along and get us all killed."

Jeremy could understand the major's mistake even as he was making it. Ellison was willing to gamble with all their lives to satisfy his ego. He wanted to answer this new threat on his own—to prove his team was capable without Jeremy Cross—but he was also underestimating the danger. Jeremy had faced down Kaito Yoshida on the Golden Gate Bridge. He knew the devastation the man was capable of, and it was more than Gauntlet or Nyx could handle on their own. If Yoshida was coming for them now...

"Don't do this." Jeremy lowered his voice. "Let me help you."

"He's right," Nyx said, stepping closer to Jeremy. "You can kick him out of the program and exile him from Blaney. That's your right, but G-Force is part of this team. He's earned the right to go up there with us."

Ellison narrowed his eyes at Nyx. "And if I refuse, then what? You stay down here with him? Are you refusing my orders?"

Nyx shook her head. "No, sir, I'm not. I'll go where you send me, but if there's going to be a fight, I'd rather we fight to win."

Ellison turned away and started for the door. "That's precisely what I'm doing. Nyx and Gauntlet, you're both with me. The rest of you stay here and secure the room."

"Secure it yourself, Major! I'm going out there." Jeremy started after him. "Unless you can figure out a way to stop me."

Ellison wheeled around, his face scarlet. He was ready to scream something back at Jeremy, but Lara stepped between the two of them. She wrapped her hand around Jeremy's arm, pulling him back.

"Stop it! Both of you!" Lara turned her back

on Ellison, positioning herself directly in front of Jeremy. "Let them go. Let them handle this. If they need you, they can always call. You're right here."

But Jeremy didn't move. The major didn't move, either. He stood on the other side of Lara, unflinching, his face and neck still bright red. Lara reached up and put her hand on top of Jeremy's shoulder—maybe holding him back, but more likely trying to read his emotions—trying to predict how far he would let this go.

"She's right, G." Langer's voice cracked from somewhere behind Jeremy. "I mean, it's like backup, right? They can call in the cavalry or something. That's a thing they do, right? Just chill here, man."

Lara looked up at Jeremy. "I'm asking you, please, don't do this."

Then Jeremy realized both of his hands were balled up into fists at his sides. His teeth were clenched, and his shoulders and arms shivered as if he were cold. He wanted this fight—he wanted to knock Ellison's head clean off his shoulders—and the only thing stopping him was Lara.

Jeremy caught his breath and looked past Ellison at the others. Gauntlet stood by the door with his arms folded across his chest, unchanged from the moment this all started. Whatever should happen outside, whether Jeremy was part of the fight or not, Gauntlet was ready. Nyx stood beside him, defiant, her hands resting on her hips, but as Jeremy caught her eye, she shook her head—an almost imperceptible movement of her chin—and even without the words, Jeremy knew she was right. They could only afford to be in one fight at a time, and right now, Major Ellison was the least of their concerns.

Jeremy opened his hands. "Then it looks like I'll be here if you need me."

Ellison turned his back on him. "Trust me, we won't."

The major started for the door, and Nyx and Gauntlet trailed after him.

CHAPTER 21

The ride up the elevator was quiet. Neither Gauntlet nor Nyx spoke a word, and Ellison was grateful. If nothing else, they could appreciate the weight of the moment. As the elevator doors opened, Ellison pulled back the charging handle on his M4 and stepped into the hallway. Sergeant Stevenson and five of his men, all of them arrayed in full tactical gear, stood waiting.

Stevenson smiled. "What's the good word, Major?"

Ellison could appreciate a man like Stevenson. He was singular and focused—a professional soldier.

Ellison nodded at the double doors in front of them. "Two SUV's approaching fast. If they breach the gate, we'll put 'em down. I want you and your men flanking left and right. No one fires unless I give the order."

Stevenson fit his helmet over his head, buckling the chin strap. "Sounds easy enough. And what about your freak-force? What are they supposed to be doing?"

Ellison bristled at the comment, but he understood Stevenson's distaste for the Anoms. In the major's experience, soldiers always functioned best when the individual could be subverted for the unit. Anoms like Gauntlet and Nyx were outliers from that model—the antithesis of conformity. Their entire purpose was to *be* exceptional. That's why, as much as Colonel McCann and Agent Hayden were desperate to integrate the Anoms into combat, Ellison knew it would never work. They would always be "the others," and in the crucible of combat, that made them a liability.

That decision to deploy the Anoms, however, was above Ellison's paygrade, and it was certainly beyond the scope of someone like Sergeant Stephenson. Maybe Ellison had given the sergeant too much credit. A *real* soldier would adapt, overcome, and limit the failings of his team, not shine a spotlight on their weaknesses, driving doubt into the minds of his men before taking the field of battle. It was a mistake by Stevenson, and Ellison would need to correct him. But not now.

"The Anoms are here to do the same thing we are," Ellison answered. "They're going to defend this facility at all costs. Follow your orders, and they'll do the same."

Stevenson nodded. "I hope so, Major."

Ellison raised his rifle to his shoulder. "Take

up your positions."

The soldiers in the hallway burst outside through the double doors, fanning out left and right into the gray-filtered light of the early morning. Ellison followed them. Outside of the main building, there was little to see. A chain-link fence topped with barbed wire circled the facility a hundred yards away from where they stood. In front of that, a pair of tiny guardhouses were positioned on either side of the main gate. Two men—Reah Labs security—waited on the left and right sides of the gate outside the fence, their rifles raised to their shoulders and trained on the empty road.

A pair of black SUVs raced around a hill into sight. They sped up the dirt road toward the facility, plumes of gray dust trailing behind them, until they reached the gate and stopped short, side by side in the road.

Ellison touched the contact mic at his throat. "Sentry One, order them out of their vehicles."

Across the distance, Ellison could hear the first guard scream, "Get out of your vehicles! Now!"

To Ellison's surprise, two of the doors opened —one from the car on the left and the other on the right. It felt like a mistake. Ellison tried to think through what was happening—to give the aggressors the benefit of the doubt—but it only

made him surer of his first instinct. There was
no tactical advantage to starting a fight so early,
especially on the other side of the perimeter
fence. If *he* were leading the charge into Kingman, he would have rushed the gate and split
his forces once they were inside the fence line.
Ellison would have relied on speed and surprise
to achieve his objective. This move smacked of
amateurism.

Ellison pressed his contact mic again. "Order
them out of the vehicles."

The guard screamed again, "I said get out of
your cars!"

From the car on the right, a man lumbered
out of the open door, gaining his feet and rising to his full height. He slammed the door shut
behind him and straightened his jacket. Even at
this distance, the man appeared to be massive,
and impossibly broad at the shoulders. Ellison
recognized him at once. He was the Ryoku from
the bridge, the one Yoshida had called Shān. The
man took a step in the direction of the first sentry.

"Keep him back," Ellison said into his mic.

"Stay where you are!" the guard yelled. "The
rest of you, get out!"

On the left, a new figure emerged from the
other SUV—just as tall as Shān, but somehow
lean and lithe, her body covered in thick gray fur.
She had a pointed face, like a wolf, and when she
snarled, Ellison could see her yellow teeth. The

major knew her name, too. Kumiho.

The second guard yelled, "We said stay where you—"

Before the guard could finish, Kumiho lunged at him, and the man's voice was lost in a burst of gunfire. It came too late. Kumiho was already on top of him, pinning him to the ground. The guard tried to scream—a wild cry that was choked off in his throat as Kumiho snapped her jaws down on his face.

"Major Ellison?" Stevenson's voice was taut next to him.

Ellison touched his contact mic. "Hold your positions. Do not fire. I repeat, do not fire!"

The guard on the right pulled the trigger of his M4 anyway, unloading his magazine into the center of Shān's chest. Nothing happened. Shān stood exactly where he was before, unharmed. The guard dropped out the empty magazine and reached for another on his belt, but before he could load it, Shān grabbed him by his throat, lifting him into the air and throwing him back against the wall of the guardhouse.

Even at a hundred yards, Ellison could hear the dull crack of the man slamming against the cinder block building. As the guard collapsed into the dirt, it looked as if his whole body had broken and splintered in on itself.

"Major?" Stevenson raised his voice again.

Ellison pressed his mic. "Do not fire. We need to know if Kaito Yoshida is in one of those SUV's.

I repeat, do not engage until our target is confirmed."

The rest of the doors on the two SUVs kicked open, and three more men jumped out. Each carried a submachine gun tucked under his arm, and they took up firing positions outside the fence line. Ellison couldn't care less about them. Any man carrying a gun was nothing more than a nameless thug. Meanwhile, the major was flanked on either side by special forces. If the situation deteriorated into a firefight, Ellison was confident he would win.

The three thugs were followed by a fourth man, whom Ellison didn't recognize. He moved slower than the others, and he stayed close to the SUV. The man looked at ease standing on the other side of the chain-link fence, and Ellison realized his attitude could only be affected through experience. He wore a black leather baseball jacket, a pair of wraparound sunglasses, and in his hand, he carried a sword.

Ellison pressed his contact mic against his throat. "Target the hostiles with guns first. We'll come back for the others if they clear the fence."

From the back of the SUV on the right, a new figure stepped out into the morning light. She was young and pale, with short, dark hair. Ellison had never seen her before, either; she wasn't with Yoshida on his flight from Hong Kong, and she wasn't with him on the Golden Gate Bridge— but unlike the man with the sword, who looked comfortable standing in front of half a dozen soldiers holding machine guns, the woman appeared nervous. She stood next to the open door of the SUV, her eyes fixed on the ground and one of her arms crossed over her body, clutching her other arm as it hung limp at her side.

Finally, Kaito Yoshida emerged from the SUV. He wore a pair of gray slacks, black shoes, and a plain black t-shirt. His dark hair was pulled back in a neat ponytail, and he looked, at least to Ellison, like a man without a care in the world. As he climbed out of the SUV, he looked directly above him at the brightening sky, letting himself close his eyes and breathe deep from the desert air, savoring the moment. Yoshida slammed the door shut behind him, and he started forward, smiling.

"Major Ellison, target is confirmed." Stevenson's voice was urgent now, but Ellison knew there was still time.

"Let him get closer," Ellison said.

Yoshida walked by the man with the sword, slapping his hand down on the man's shoulder as he stepped around him, as if they were old friends. He walked past the other men, too, the ones holding their guns tight against their shoulders. Yoshida stepped in front of both SUVs, moving forward alone, until finally he stood directly in front of the chain-link fence.

"Sir?" Stevenson begged.

Ellison ignored him.

Yoshida reached out with both hands for the gate, wrapping his fingers through the chain links of the fence, and for a second, Ellison thought he intended to climb over. Then the metal fence wavered in the morning light. It looked to Ellison as if he were watching the fence through the heatwaves of a distant mirage. The dull silver twisted in Yoshida's hands, spreading and drooping between his fingers like over-stretched putty, dripping out of his fingers, but even as the metal transformed to liquid, it changed again, evaporating away into the desert air like steam.

Yoshida smiled. "I promise you, I only came here to talk. Let's not make this any uglier than it needs to be."

Ellison touched his contact mic and whispered, "Let me try to draw them in." Then he raised his voice and called out, "You killed two of our men, Yoshida! You don't get to talk here."

Yoshida narrowed his eyes. "I wasn't speaking to you." Then he turned to face Gauntlet and Nyx standing on Ellison's right. "It's good you see you both again. Gauntlet, it's been a long time. I only wish the circumstances could be different."

"And he wishes you were dead," Nyx shouted back, answering on Gauntlet's behalf. "I guess we're all living with disappointment today."

Yoshida laughed. "Same old Nyx. Kumiho told me she met you on the bridge. She said you were tougher than she expected for someone so tiny."

"That's funny. I haven't given her a second thought," Nyx said.

Yoshida ignored her, still smiling. "But Gauntlet, you were missing from San Francisco. Instead, you sent a boy who can hold up bridges. Where is he now? I hope I didn't break him."

Then Ellison had heard enough. He pulled back the charging handle on his M4, letting it snap into place. "Your friend from the bridge is waiting inside. Why don't you send the rest of your gang away, and I'll take you to see him right now? How's that sound?"

"Is he really inside there?" Yoshida's smile fell away. "That's everything I needed to hear."

Suddenly, Yoshida raised both of his hands over his head, and the waif moved behind him. She laid her hands over his shoulders and bowed her head to her chest. Then Yoshida looked up at the sky. He spread his fingers wide as if he were straining to reach for something, and he screamed—a low growl like an animal ready to strike—as he clenched his fists, pulled down with his arms, and the sky above them went dark.

"Take him!" Ellison pressed his hand to his throat, but he knew it was already too late. There was a flash of electricity, and he could feel his stomach twist over like he was going to be sick, but it didn't matter. He was going to die regardless. Ellison squeezed shut his eyes and pulled the trigger of his M4, screaming over the percussion of gunfire.

"Major! Major, stop!" Nyx shouted in Ellison's ear, her voice so close that it sounded like it was coming from inside his own head.

Ellison let go of the trigger and opened his eyes. No one stood in front of him anymore. Yoshida and the Ryoku were gone. So were the chain link fence, the two SUVs, and the guard-houses. Ellison was standing somewhere else entirely. He looked left and right. Stevenson and the other soldiers were gone, too. Ellison was left alone with Gauntlet and Nyx, standing in the brown-green shrubs of the Arizona desert, staring at a range of hills on the distant horizon.

Ellison lowered his rifle. "Where are we?"

Before Nyx or Gauntlet could answer, the ground rolled under Ellison's feet—a soft swell like a wave. Then he heard the explosion behind him. It was a single, resonant boom that was somehow too dull, like a low thunderclap filling the air.

Ellison turned back to look. Far in the distance, he could see a pillar of pale gray smoke climbing into the cloudless sky.

Ellison looked down at Nyx. She stood between him and Gauntlet, one of her hands holding onto the wrist of the armored Anom, her other twisted in Ellison's sleeve.

"What did you do?" Ellison asked her.

"I saved our lives." Nyx jerked her head in the direction of the smoke. "I saved us from that."

Ellison looked back at the plume rising in the desert, and he realized it was centered over the Kingman facility. Then, through the dissipating smoke, he could see a black spire standing at least a hundred feet tall above the horizon, and he understood what had happened. Somehow, Kaito had dropped a mountain of stone out of thin air, and when it landed on top of Kingman, the effect was no different than a bomb.

All at once, Ellison couldn't hold back the bile in his stomach anymore. He doubled over and spit across the ground.

CHAPTER 22

Jeremy felt it all at once—the ground shaking under his feet, the roar of sound obliterating the air, and the ceiling and walls pancaking down on top of him. The Kingman facility was being crushed like a tin can.

Without thinking, he tackled Lara to the ground and raised his gravity. Then he felt the weight of Kingman crashing down on top of him. It landed across his back and shoulders, like someone had hit him with a two-by-four when he wasn't looking. Jeremy's arms and legs buckled.

Lara was pinned under him, their bodies pressed together, and Jeremy could see the panic in her face. She was still alive—for now—but if Jeremy dropped any lower under the weight, they would both be crushed. Suddenly, the noise roaring above them stopped. Whatever force caused the building to collapse on top of them had ceased. Only the weight and pressure remained. Lara wedged her hands between their two bodies, lifting her fingers to touch Jeremy on either side of his face. The panic in her eyes was gone.

She looked at Jeremy. "I know what you're feeling, but we can get out of this. Raise your gravity a little more."

Jeremy pushed back against the weight on top of him, trying to lift himself off the floor —fighting to get his hands and knees under his body. But it was no use. He closed his eyes, clenched his jaw, and tried again. Then Jeremy could feel the weight shift above him. Maybe he bought them another inch or two to breathe, but he could still barely move. They were both going to die.

"Jeremy!" Lara shouted from under him, and her voice sounded far away, like she was stand-ing in another room, calling through a locked door. Jeremy could feel her body shifting under him, wrestling herself free, and all at once, there was space between his chest and the floor— enough room to take a full breath, if he dared. Jeremy drew his knees under his body, and he tried to push up with his legs, too. He wanted to fill the empty space around him with the gravity field, but his arms started to shake, and he knew it wouldn't last much longer.

"Jeremy!" a hand touched his arm. He looked to his left, and Lara was kneeling next to him. "There's a pocket of space just over there in the stairwell," she said. "It looks stable. You can make it."

Jeremy looked past Lara, and he could see it, too. Through a gap in the rubble, only a couple of yards away, there was an open space lit by the amber glow of emergency lights. It wasn't much bigger than a closet, but it was big enough for both of them. Jeremy nodded and started to inch to his left.

Then a new voice—weak—coughed from his right, "Wait. G, wait."

Jeremy looked in the direction of the voice to see John Langer lying flat on his back only a couple feet away from him. The doctor was staring up at the concrete floor hovering inches above his head, and his round face was ashen and scraped. Jeremy could see a splatter of blood staining the lapel of his white lab coat. Then he looked closer, and Jeremy felt his stomach turn. Both of Langer's legs disappeared above his knees, lost under a block of concrete.

Langer choked again, "Help me, G."

Jeremy pulled back to his right toward Langer. If he could reach the doctor's hand, he could drag him out, too. They could all make it to the stairwell before the gravity field dropped, and if they could stop Langer's bleeding, there was still a chance for all three of them.

Lara's hand closed over Jeremy's arm. "You can't." She shook her head. "You can't save him."

Jeremy tried to push up against the ceiling. If he could create more space around them, Lara could reach the doctor, and Jeremy would hold up the building while she dragged him to the stairwell. But the concrete above him wouldn't move. Jeremy pushed up again, and both his arms trembled violently. He looked back at Langer, and the edges of his vision blurred like water. He just needed to reach Langer's hand and pull him free.

Lara still held onto Jeremy's arm. "Even if you could reach him, there's no time. Your strength's giving out. You know that."

"Don't. Please. G-Force, please." Langer's voice wavered.

Jeremy blinked, trying to force the gray clouds at the edges of his vision to go away. He knew he could reach Langer. He could save him, or at least he could try—but he also knew that Lara was right. If he moved to get to the doctor, he would fail. Lara pulled gently on his arm, and Jermey slid his hand to the left, away from Langer. He knew it was almost over.

"We go on three," Lara said, her breath pressing against Jeremy's ear as she wrapped both of her hands around his arm.

"Help me!" Langer cried out, his voice louder than it had been before, but Jeremy couldn't see the doctor anymore. The gray fog closed over his eyes. It was all darkness now. Jeremy tried to arch his back—tried to push up against the concrete—tried to give them all more time.

"One," Lara counted.

"Help me!" Langer's voice broke from far away, and Jeremy knew the man was sobbing, "Please—please, don't do this!"

Jeremy's arms buckled under him, and he couldn't feel his hands any more pressing against the floor. Everything was going numb.

"Two," Lara said, louder.

"Please, God!" Langer cried out. "Please, don't do this. Please, don't do this."

Jeremy opened his mouth and screamed, and all the strength that was left inside him found a voice—a terrible cry of surrender.

"Three!" Lara shouted.

Jeremy's arm jerked to his left. His body followed. He could feel himself rolling away, turning over on top of something soft and pliant, pulled over and around Lara's body. A shallow *boom* filled the space around them, and the rest of the ceiling collapsed. Coarse dust filtered down into the open space of the stairwell, settling on top of Jeremy's clammy face and hands. At first, he could feel it sticking to his skin, but then even his sense of touch felt like it blurred, and all Jeremy knew was silence, and stillness, and darkness—and Lara lying under him, her body rising and falling as she drew in each breath.

They stayed that way for what felt like hours. Jeremy wasn't asleep, but he was trapped in the space between—lost in the half-world between thoughts and dreams usually reserved for the University of Pennsylvania emergency room and his father. Only now, there were no familiar walls, or floors, or his father standing motionless in front of him. There was only a soft darkness, like he was floating underwater at night. He was glad. For now, this was better. Then, suddenly, the darkness burned away in a brilliant light. Jeremy rolled over and lunged forward, grabbing at his chest. He couldn't breathe.

"You're all right. You're okay," Lara said, and her voice was close.

Jeremy fell forward onto his hands and knees, gulping at the air.

"Jeremy, you're okay," Lara said again.

Jeremy turned over, pushing himself back against the wall. Everything about him hurt. His arms, legs, and back all felt weak and torn, like his strength had been bled away. His ears buzzed and his vision was still blurry.

Lara sat across from him. Jeremy could see a scrape of red visible below her hairline, and a layer of thin gray dust coated her face, but otherwise she seemed to be all right. She even smiled.

Jeremy knew they were lucky that Lara had found this space when she did—a stable pocket she called it. It was more like a miracle—a single chance for life in the twisted steel and concrete around them. She probably only found it thanks to the amber emergency lights shining above them. The space left in the stairwell was just tall enough for them to stand, but not wide enough to lie down. Jeremy had seen enough movies to know it was only a temporary stay of execution. They needed water, food, and oxygen to survive. Eventually, they would miss one of the three, but for now the space alone was enough. At least it gave them time.

Jeremy closed his eyes and tried to think. "How long... how long was I out?"

"A few seconds. Maybe a minute," Lara said.

Jeremy shook his head. The answer didn't feel right. He could've sworn he was unconscious for half the day. Jeremy looked off to his side, trying to get his bearings. Filling the doorway into the stairwell, he could see blocks of concrete sealing them inside.

Lara edged closer, putting her hand down on his arm. "It's not your fault—with John. It was my decision to leave him."

Jeremy shook his head. "I could've done more."

"If you had done anything more, we would all be dead. I saw John's injuries. Both of his legs were gone. He would've bled out as soon as you moved him. He was already dead."

Jeremy closed his eyes and leaned his head back against the wall.

For a long time, they sat together in silence. Lara reached for Jeremy's hand, and her touch was warm and familiar. It was almost enough to make him forget the orchestrated manipulations of the last three months—the way Lara nurtured his infatuation when there was never really a chance. He wanted to be grateful they were at least trapped together, but then he would remember her stepping out into Ellison's room, wrapped in her towel—

"I never wanted you to see me like that," Lara said quietly.

Jeremy shifted his weight against the wall, pulling away his hand. "I don't want to talk about it."

"But there are things I need to say," Lara answered. "Things I need you to hear even though you won't understand. I've made a thousand choices to get myself here, Jeremy, and they're choices I don't regret."

"So why are you telling me now?" Jeremy snapped, and there was more anger in his voice than he'd intended.

Lara looked around her. "I'm telling you because we're trapped here, and I don't want to meet my end feeling guilty or ashamed. I've wasted too much time on that already." She pulled her legs up to her chest, hugging her knees. "In my earliest memory, I was already ten years old. I was making cookies with my gran. That's not normal, Jeremy. Why is that where *my* life begins?" Lara turned away, and Jeremy could hear her voice cracking; she rubbed at her eyes. "I've spent my whole life living through other people. You don't know what that's like. To touch someone and literally see all their thoughts? To live through their memories? It killed whatever decent person I might have been." Lara shook her head. "So I make my choices to survive, and I don't expect you to understand that, but you can't blame me for it, either."

"What makes you think I don't understand?" Jeremy moved across the stairwell to the opposite wall, trying to look Lara in the eye. "You've suffered because of your abilities. We all have that in common."

Lara turned back, smiling through her tears. "You can't understand because you don't live in the same world as I do. You have this perfect idea of who I am—who you want me to be—but I'm not her, and I'm never going to be her."

Jeremy wanted to deny it, but he could see Lara again in his memory, standing in Ellison's room with that look of betrayal etched on her face. Then all his emotions from the previous night came flooding back unbidden—his anger, embarrassment, and grief—and there was nothing he could say. Lara was right.

She leaned her head back against the wall. "There are things I love about you, Jeremy— your kindness and your courage—and there are things I hate, like the way you act like an asshole when you don't get your way." Lara smiled again. "Maybe if we had met somewhere else, and you weren't you, and I wasn't me, I could've loved you the way you wanted me to." She paused.

JASON R. JAMES

"But we don't live in that world, either. What you want between us is never going to happen. I won't let it."

Jeremy turned away. Now it was his turn to swallow his pain and gather himself—to hold it together and listen to what Lara had to say. He already knew she was telling him the truth, but that didn't make it easier.

Lara took Jeremy's hand again. "I knew that after Chicago," she said. "I should've told you then, and let you make your peace with it, but it was easier to stay quiet. It was selfish and easier to let you hope. That's the only thing I'm sorry for."

Jeremy set his jaw. "So, we're never going to happen, but you'll keep sleeping with Ellison?"

"I'll keep sleeping with Ellison because love will never be a part of it with him." Lara smiled. "And you can keep thinking I'm a whore."

"I don't." Jeremy sat up straighter against the wall. "I wouldn't. I think of you the same."

Lara looked down at Jeremy's hand held in her own. "We both know that's not true."

"No, it's not." Jeremy shook his head. "But I'll work at making it true. I promise I will." Lara looked away and let go of Jeremy's hand, but he wasn't finished. "And you deserve better than Stuart Ellison. I don't need to love you to tell you that. You deserve a hell of a lot more than him, and I can promise you that, too."

Lara looked straight up at the stairs above

them, refusing to look Jeremy in the eye. "And when do we ever get what we deserve?"

Before Jeremy could answer, a flash of purple light filled the pocket of space around them. As it faded, he could see Nyx kneeling on the ground between him and Lara. She blinked her eyes, trying to see through the shadows of the stairwell, until finally, she settled on Jeremy.

Then a broad smile broke over Nyx's face. "Just where we left you."

"You're alive!" Lara screamed, lunging forward and wrapping her arms around Nyx's back before the other woman could turn and see what was happening. It knocked them both off balance, and they pitched forward into Jeremy.

Nyx raised her eyebrows, choking from Lara's arm wrapped around her neck. "I am. So are you." She pried Lara's arms open and ducked out of the hug. "We weren't expecting that." Nyx looked around the stairwell again.

"How did you find us?" Jeremy asked.

Nyx smiled. "Turns out that microchip in the back of your neck is actually good for something. That's how we knew you were still alive. Sorry, Mirror. We just assumed the worst for everyone else..."

Jeremy ran his fingers up the back of his neck, feeling for his scar.

"But that doesn't explain how you got here," Lara said. "You couldn't see us. How could you teleport down here if you couldn't see us?"

Then even in the shadows, Jeremy could see Nyx's face redden; she rubbed her shoulder. "Once we knew G-Force was alive and where he was, I had Gauntlet stand off at the same distance to give me a visual cue of how far I had to jump. We got the direction from Ellison's tracking device…" Nyx shrugged. "Then I closed my eyes and just did it because it needed to be done. I wasn't leaving him behind."

"So, Gauntlet and Ellison are alive, too. Who else?" Jeremy asked.

Nyx shook her head but didn't answer.

Jeremy felt his stomach tighten. "What happened up there?"

"I'll have to show you." Nyx grabbed Jeremy and Lara by their arms. Then she closed her eyes, and all at once, the stairwell around them was lost in a brilliant flash of light.

CHAPTER 23

Lara felt her stomach twist over and turn to water. She reached out to steady herself, but instead of her hand touching the solid floor of the stairwell, it slid across the coarse dirt of the Arizona desert. Lara opened her eyes and looked up.

Above her, she could see the cloudless sky, but cutting across her field of vision, like a dark scar against the field of blue, there was something else—a black tower of obsidian stone rising above the earth.

Lara scrambled to her feet and staggered back from the stone tower. She looked around her and saw Gauntlet and Ellison standing not far away, but there was no one else in sight. Then she saw the perimeter fence of Kingman circling behind them and broken cinderblocks littering the ground, and she realized exactly where she was standing. Lara looked back at the tower, and it all made sense. The obsidian spire stood directly over the main building of Kingman—or rather where the main building should have been if it hadn't been crushed and destroyed. Lara looked again at the monolith rising over the desert. With a thousand sheer facets, it reminded her of the dark windows on the Willis Tower in Chicago. Then she imagined *that* building dropping from a thousand feet in the air so it could obliterate everything in its path.

"We should be dead," she whispered.

"Mirror!" Ellison stepped closer, and Lara could hear the relief in his voice. He wore his gray camouflage fatigues and looked, for the most part, unscathed. He held his M4 rifle in one hand, and in his other, Lara could see a silver remote control about the size of a cellphone.

"We didn't know—" Ellison stopped himself and tucked the silver control into his left breast pocket. "We thought G-Force might have survived because of his gravity."

Lara forced a smile. "Then I'm lucky we stayed together."

G-Force stood next to her, still staring up at the tower and shielding his eyes with his hands. "Who did this?"

"It was Yoshida," Gauntlet answered, his voice rattling behind his helmet.

Lara looked at the tower again and laughed. "There's no way. Kaito's powerful, but he's never been capable of anything like this—"

"It was Yoshida. I watched him do it," Ellison said, and Lara felt her teeth tighten at the interruption. Ellison didn't seem to notice. Instead, he pointed back toward the opening in the fence. "Yoshida stood right there, and some woman we've never seen before laid her hands on his shoulders like she was praying for him. Then he pulled this down on top of us out of thin air."

Lara stared back at Ellison. "You're saying Kaito has a Resonance?"

G-Force shook his head. "What's that? What's a Resonance?"

Lara looked at G-Force before turning back to Ellison. "A Resonance is an Anom who can magnify the powers of other Anoms. They're rare— incredibly rare—but if that's what this woman really is, it could explain all of this." Lara looked up at the stone spire. "The only question is where did Kaito find her? If she wasn't on the plane with him..."

"It doesn't matter where he got her," G-Force said. "If she's helping Yoshida, then we need to stop them both. Where are they now?"

"That's not our concern," Ellison growled, "and I won't allow you to put the rest of us in jeopardy so you can play hero again. We follow the protocol here, which means securing our perimeter, reestablishing communications with Fort Blaney, and waiting for orders from Colonel McCann."

G-Force laughed. "If we do any of that, Major, then it's already too late." He looked at Ellison. "Your boy Kaito Yoshida is out there dropping mountains on top of buildings now. He's not going to sit around and wait for us to regroup. So, where would he go?"

"Vegas," Nyx answered, and everyone turned to look at her.

"You don't know that!" Ellison barked.

"Yes, I do!" Nyx shouted back at him. "I know it because I know Kai. He's learned a new trick, and now he wants to show it off. That means going someplace popular and public—somewhere he can do the most damage. Las Vegas is the closest place that fits the bill."

It all made sense. Lara thought about the attack on the Golden Gate Bridge, and how bringing down the plane from Hong Kong hadn't been enough to satisfy Yoshida's brand of terror. He needed the audience—it was almost as important as the collateral damage itself—and few places could offer the same visuals as Las Vegas.

G-Force smiled. "If we're going to Vegas, we're gonna need a car."

"That's enough!" Ellison suddenly roared, and Lara flinched at the ferocity in his voice. The major stepped closer to G-Force. "I'm still in command here, and I gave you my orders. I want you to secure this perimeter—"

"Secure it from what, Major?" G-Force threw open his hands, turning in place, taking in the whole of the desert. "From Yoshida? He's gone! He thinks we're all dead. Otherwise, he'd still be here!"

"G-Force is right," Lara said, and her voice

was low. "If we have a chance at stopping Kaito, we can't just stay here and do nothing."

"I gave you my orders!" Ellison fixed his eyes on Lara, but she could hear the break in his voice. Maybe no one else noticed it, but for Lara, it was enough. Stuart Ellison draped himself in his own authority, but now that he was being challenged, the veneer was cracking.

"We're not staying here, Major." G-Force squared his shoulders to Ellison. "Nyx thinks Yoshida is headed for Las Vegas, so that's where I'm going, too. You can stay behind if you want and secure your perimeter yourself, or you can come with us and help. That's your choice. The only thing you can't do is stop us."

"You want to make that bet?" Ellison reached inside his breast pocket and pulled out the silver controller, waving it in front of G-Force's face. "You know what this is for?"

Out of the corner of her eye, Lara could see Jeremy run his hand up the back of his neck, feeling for the thin scar left from his tracking chip. There was no doubt he understood Ellison's threat—they all did—and it made Lara's blood run cold.

"That's right. Maybe you should reconsider your boasts," Ellison sneered, "or try telling me again what I can and cannot do."

Lara turned to look fully at Jeremy. She could see his hands clenched down at his sides, and the tension held in his jaw and near his eyes. She didn't need her powers to feel the anger burning through him, or to sense the gravity field building in every ounce of his muscle. He was a man ready for a fight.

Jeremy raised his chin. "I told you what I'm doing, and you're not going to threaten me again."

"No." Ellison's smile curdled on his face. "No more threats."

Suddenly, Lara darted between the two men, grabbing Ellison by the arm and looking up into his face. "Stuart, don't do this!"

She had never touched Ellison before while wearing her locket. That restraint had always been her choice. The locket allowed her to remember what she saw in others—their memories and secrets. It was a burden she never wanted to bear for Stuart Ellison, because for Lara, ignorance was truly bliss.

Of course, the inverse was equally as true —knowledge only brought suffering. She had no doubt that reading Ellison now would reveal something dark and unforgivable inside of him, just like it did with everyone else she ever touched—and that knowledge would make their perfect arrangement impossible. And what then? A return to the nightmares and countless sleepless nights, and the slow descent into madness? Nothing was worth that price to Lara, but she was also tired of doing nothing—of closing her eyes and allowing Ellison's cruelty. She deserved better. They all did.

As her hand fell over Ellison's arm, Lara could feel the major's rage slamming against her body like she had run into a brick wall. Then the anger darkened and burned under her skin, infected by Ellison's own arrogance and the unshakeable belief that he could bend the world to meet his expectations.

A light flashed behind Lara's eyes, and all at once she could see herself standing in Ellison's room at the Citadel. She was a senior, dressed in Ellison's school uniform. Her hands went cold at the memory of the underclassmen and the way Ellison reviled them for their disobedience and immaturity. Then she found herself smiling, remembering the pleasure Ellison found in nursing small fantasies of revenge against each and every one of them.

Another flash of memory, and Lara saw herself standing in the woods in Ellison's place, staring back at G-Force, clutching the Beretta in her hand. It felt like sharp needles stabbing through both of her eyes, and she could remember fearing for her life in that moment and hating the man across from her. G-Force had all the gifts in the world, but he would never be her equal. He lacked the discipline and courage, and he always would.

Then another one of Ellison's memories crashed over her. Lara was standing in a room with Hayden and McCann, and Hayden was confessing to the murders of Emily Cross and Kate Marino. He had killed them in their sleep, making it look like a heart attack and an overdose. Lara could feel butterflies in her stomach—elation at the thought of telling G-Force everyone he loved was dead. The arrogant prick deserved it.

Lara shook her head, trying to chase Ellison's memory away, but then another thought crowded into her mind. She could see herself standing in the infirmary, wearing the major's gray camouflage, and she was looking at herself —at Lara.

The other Lara raised her chin. "Yes, sir."

Then Lara answered with Ellison's own voice, "That's better," and she could feel the electricity dancing over her skin. The other woman was a prize, and with her obedience, she was claimed. Lara savored the goosebumps running over her arms, and she lingered in the pride, jealousy, and adoration, but those feelings only belonged to Ellison. She was nothing more than his prize to be treasured.

Lara closed her eyes, trying to refocus. She couldn't stay here in this memory of herself or lose her purpose to the sudden nausea rising in her gut. She needed answers.

Lara opened her eyes again, and now she saw herself standing in front of G-Force; she was still dressed as Ellison, but she was waving the silver tracking device in Jeremy's face and shouting,

"You know what this is for?"

All the anger and arrogance she felt before still burned under her skin. Lara could taste it rising in her throat like bile; she despised the boy standing in front of her. But now another emotion squeezed at her heart, choking the rage from her lungs. She was terrified. She could feel a hundred doubts tightening around her ribs like someone was constricting her with a belt, and suddenly, she couldn't breathe. What if this one mistake cost her the future she had orchestrated so perfectly? What if this momentary outburst spoiled everything else that was supposed to follow? What if this was the end of her career —her life? Whatever satisfaction killing G-Force could bring her now, it was too big of a risk and a price that Ellison would never pay.

Lara closed her eyes again and slid her hand off Ellison's arm. "He's not going to stop us. We can leave whenever we want."

"Stop *us*?" Ellison looked down at her. "You're not going to be that stupid, are you?"

Lara shook her head. "I was stupid before, Stuart. That's why I needed to know what you would really do." She looked down at Ellison's arm, then back into his face. The major was turning red.

"He's too afraid to stop us." Lara raised her voice so everyone else could hear. "He doesn't want to ruin his future if Hayden or Reah Labs disapproves."

Ellison narrowed his eyes. "I can still change my mind."

Lara gave a curt smile and leaned forward, putting her hands down on Ellison's shoulders; she whispered, "You can change your mind, and I can tell G-Force what really happened to Emily Cross and Kate Marino." She kissed Ellison softly on the cheek. "You think you could press that button and kill him before he rips you in half?"

Ellison pulled away. "You can't run away from this. There are going to be consequences."

Lara still held her smile. "You're a small man, Stuart, trapped by the rules you make for yourself. You're cruel and you're a coward. The worst of it is, you're too stupid to realize any of that, but I'm not—not anymore." She turned to face the others. "There's a maintenance garage to the south, far enough away that it should still be standing. We can find a car or van there to get us to Las Vegas. The major won't stand in our way."

Lara walked away to the south, and Gauntlet, Nyx, and G-Force followed close behind her, until Ellison stood alone. Slowly, he lowered his hand—the one holding the detonator—and he let it fall to the ground. Lara had been right. There was nothing he could do to stop them.

CHAPTER 24

The ring from the telephone jerked Hayden out of a dead sleep. He fumbled across the bed, slapping his hand at the nightstand until finally his fingers landed on the receiver.

"Hello?" he exhaled into the phone.

"Mr. Hayden," a voice answered, "Ms. Thomas would like to see you in her suite."

"I'll be right there," Hayden said, hoping to sound more awake than he was.

"Perfect. Ms. Thomas is waiting for you in the —" Hayden hung up before she could finish. He already knew where Gwen was waiting.

Hayden threw off the bedsheets and forced himself to sit up, swinging both of his legs down to the floor. He reached for the digital clock on the nightstand. It was seven thirty in the morning—not an unreasonable hour to be awake, but still earlier than Hayden would have preferred.

He stood up and looked over the room. If nothing else, it was considerably nicer than the room he rented in Morgantown. His room at the Peninsula had a flat-screen television, a lush king-sized bed, a leather lounge chair, a desk, a free wireless network, and Hayden's worn suit hanging in the closet. Of all those amenities, the only one shared with Morgantown was the closet for the suit, but even the quality of the hangers at the Peninsula made it a poor comparison.

Hayden stumbled over the plush carpet into the bathroom. When he left Arizona, he'd given no thought to spending the night in Los Angeles, so now he was left staring at his whiskered face in the mirror. On the counter in front of him, he could see the complimentary soap, shampoo, and conditioner, but there was no complimentary razor, shaving cream, comb, deodorant, toothbrush, or toothpaste. A small placard on the counter offered additional toiletries available at the front desk, but Hayden knew that would take too long. Instead, he gargled with some water, rubbed a wet bar of soap under his armpits, and dressed in his wrinkled suit. That would have to do for now.

After their meeting with Kaito Yoshida and Jericho Caine, Gwen arranged for a car to meet them on Olympic Boulevard. It was a black Mercedes. Hayden didn't recognize the driver, and he wasn't sure if the man was a real employee of Reah Labs, or more than likely, one of Gwen's mind-controlled drones.

The car stopped in front of the boarded-up shop

on Olympic, and Noah opened the rear passenger door for Gwen, helping her inside, and taking his own place in the front of the car. Hayden walked around to the rear driver-side door. As he sat down inside, he asked Gwen what he should do about the car he had driven from Arizona.

"Leave it," she said.

The rest of their car ride passed in silence. They reached the Peninsula hotel just after midnight.

As Gwen, Hayden, and Noah crossed the lobby toward the front desk, the man stationed behind the marble counter forced a smile. "Good evening and welcome to the—"

"I need a suite," Gwen interrupted, staring down at the clerk. Then, glancing over her shoulder at Hayden, she added, "And I suppose a second room as well. Please."

The clerk looked down at his monitor, typing into his keyboard. "Yes, that's a suite and an additional room... I'm sorry, ma'am, but all of our suites appear to be occupied at this time. I might be able to arrange for two adjoining rooms."

"No, I don't want an adjoining room. I didn't ask you for an adjoining room. I'd like to have a suite." Gwen closed her eyes, her patience already at its end. From the other side of the counter, Hayden could see the young clerk go taut, undoubtedly bracing himself for the tantrum that was about to follow. Hayden smiled at the boy, wondering how often he was berated by the rich and famous.

"Yes, ma'am," the clerk's voice cracked as he

punched more keys on his keyboard. "I've found two rooms on the third floor. I think—"

Gwen opened her eyes. "The Green Suite. You can give me that one. The couple you have staying there are leaving—tonight. They're packing their things now. You should send someone to help them."

The clerk stifled a nervous laugh. "Ma'am, I'm sorry but I don't—"

Gwen ignored him. "Your staff is going to help them pack. They will change the linens and clean the room. It shouldn't be more than an hour."

The young man typed into his computer and shook his head. "I can assure you, ma'am, all the suites at the Peninsula are reserved—"

Suddenly, the clerk's face changed. His eyes glazed over, and the tension he was holding in his jaw slipped away. He stood straighter, with both of his arms dropping to his sides, and when he spoke again, his voice was dull and lifeless. Apparently, Gwen's patience was at its end.

"The Green Suite," the young clerk droned. "Is there anything else I can do for you?"

Gwen smiled at the boy. "Yes. You can bring me a chamomile tea. Warm, not hot. Thank you, Brett."

Hayden laughed and turned away from the counter. "That's beautiful, truly, but why do you bother thanking him when you put the words in his mouth? You might as well thank yourself for making the effort."

Gwen turned around, and her thin smile was gone. "Mr. Hayden, it seems as if your own room is already waiting. Third floor. Brett will give you your key." Gwen nodded her head at the clerk behind the counter. *"I'll call for you when I'm ready in the morning."*

Hayden looked back at the clerk, and the young man was holding out a keycard over the counter. Hayden laughed quietly again. He had always liked Gwen. He appreciated her edge and how quickly she could cut him down to size. He had been trying to strike up some friendly banter with her, but she was having none of it. Honestly, he expected nothing less.

Hayden took the keycard from the clerk and started for the elevators. Gwen and Noah walked off in the opposite direction, toward a sofa in the lobby.

That was seven hours ago. Now, it was morning, and Hayden found himself standing in front of the door to Gwen's suite feeling more unsure of himself than he would have liked. Last night he was too tired to care about any of Gwen's judgements or her opinions. In the cold light of day, his views were considerably different. Maybe it would have been better to shower and make Gwen wait the extra five minutes.

Hayden raised his fist to knock on the door. He hesitated, looked down at the creased lapel of his jacket, and was ready to turn back and start all over, but then the door pulled open and Noah was standing on the other side.

Hayden thought about offering up some clever quip—something about Noah replacing

Lerch from *The Addams Family*—but he remembered Gwen's injunction against starting to speak and failing to finish, so he decided against it. Instead, he bit his tongue and smiled. Noah kept silent as well, nodding his head and motioning Hayden into the room.

Inside the suite, Hayden could see the extravagant living room with its two deep-gray upholstered sofas, a large fireplace, and in the corner, a baby grand piano. The walls of the suite were pale green, and the floor was covered by an intricate area rug showing a scene of birds and cherry blossoms. The rug was almost large enough to hide the entire parquet floor. The only thing missing was Gwen, herself. Maybe Hayden would have to talk to Noah, after all.

He looked behind him, and saw Noah standing inside the foyer, guarding the single door leading out into the hallway. He was staring down at his iPod, intently nodding his head in rhythmic bobs up and down with the music. On second thought, Hayden decided it would be better to keep silent and wait.

"Mr. Hayden," a soft voice sang out from the living room.

Hayden looked back over his shoulder, and walking around the corner, her high heels clicking on the wooden floor, he could see Anna Jordan. Anna was tall, with long red hair framing her face and pale green eyes—a striking woman on the outside, but so painfully ordinary in every other regard.

Anna smiled and pulled her leather-bound portfolio closer to her chest. "Would you care to join me in the dining room, Mr. Hayden? Ms. Thomas will be with us shortly."

Hayden nodded. "Of course I will."

He followed Anna into the next room, where a long table lined with wooden-backed chairs was arranged beneath a crystal chandelier. The table itself was covered by an off-white table-cloth, and on top, Hayden could see a pair of wire baskets overflowing with breads and rolls. Three small jars of jam were arranged at the center of the table, and at one end, waiting at the head of the table, a single brown egg sat perched in an egg cup.

Hayden pulled out the chair at the other end of the table and took his seat, lounging to one side against the arm of the chair. Anna moved to the sideboard on the far wall.

She looked back at Hayden. "We have coffee, water, or bloody marys, if you prefer."

"Don't be silly, Anna." Gwen's voice called over Hayden's shoulder as she stepped into the room. "I'm sure Mr. Hayden would never spoil perfectly good alcohol with something as healthy as tomato juice."

Hayden half-stood up from his chair, a hollow gesture he never intended to complete. Once Gwen walked by him, he folded back into his chair and opened his napkin.

"Oh, she's right about that," Hayden said. "I think I'll have the coffee, and if you want to spoil that with some alcohol, you can pour in as much as you'd like."

Anna carried a cup and saucer to the table and placed it in front of him; she smiled. "No Irish coffee this morning. Sorry, Mr. Hayden."

She returned to the sideboard and carried another cup of coffee in one hand and a bloody mary in the other to Gwen at the head of the table, but Gwen didn't look up to acknowledge her. Instead, she stared across the length of the table at Hayden.

Anna retreated to the sideboard and returned again, this time carrying a pitcher of ice water and a goblet. She filled the glass, placed it in front of Gwen, and stepped back from the table. Finally, Gwen lowered her eyes from Hayden, looking over her own place-setting, checking to see that everything was arranged exactly as she wanted it. She touched her fingertips to the silverware on either side of the egg cup, smiling.

"Thank you, Anna," Gwen said. "I think that's everything. If you would excuse us?"

"Of course." Anna crossed to the double doors, pulling them shut behind her, and then Hayden and Gwendolyn Thomas were left alone.

Hayden tried to remember another time when the two of them were alone in the same room together. They had certainly spoken in private before. Hayden remembered a handful of times when he was called into Gwen's darkened penthouse office to provide her with confidential reports on various Reah Lab projects, but Noah had always been in those meetings, too —not as a part of the conversation, but rather skulking in some shadowed corner of the room. His absence made this morning a first, and Hayden didn't know if he should be the one to speak first or if he should wait. Rather than decide, he reached for his coffee instead, drinking deeply and spying on Gwen over the ceramic rim of the mug.

For her part, Gwen seemed to ignore Hayden completely. Her eyes were fixed on the brown egg waiting for her in the silver egg cup. She reached for the butter knife on her right-hand side and tapped it sharply into the side of the egg, peeling the shell off the top.

Then, reaching for her spoon, she looked up at Hayden. "I assume you have questions about our meeting yesterday?"

Hayden lowered his mug but kept quiet. It was an invitation to confidence, but he doubted he could take Gwen's words at face value. There was always another agenda with the woman, and if Hayden thought this breakfast was any different, he would only prove himself a fool.

He reached across the table for one of the wire baskets. "I don't want you to think I have any illusions about holding the moral high ground here, Ms. Thomas. I know what I've done and what it is you pay me to do... and it's not asking questions."

Gwen set her spoon delicately back on the table and drank from her water goblet; as she lowered the glass, she smiled. "Of all your many qualities, Mr. Hayden, the one I appreciate most is your discretion. But our meeting yesterday was something else... let's call it exceptional. I would understand if you were confused, and, if I can say it plainly, I'd rather you ask your questions now than have to suffer through your misconceptions later."

Even now, in her vulnerability, Gwen had a talent for making him feel small. It was a gift Hayden couldn't help but admire... and hate. Here she was, inviting his questions, but at the same time, she was also making him feel like an idiot for even asking.

Hayden forced a smile. "Let's start with an easy one, then. You can tell me why we're doing this.'"

Gwen reached for the teaspoon again. "You mean why are we partnering with known terrorists? I'm afraid that answer is painfully obvious, Mr. Hayden. We're doing this to collect power and influence in our world."

"And how is that?" Hayden leaned back in his chair.

"By maximizing our leverage." Gwen sipped her bloody mary and dabbed her mouth with her napkin. "Presently, our company boasts a healthy supply of a very limited resource. What do you think will happen if the Ryoku or the Red Moon succeed in attacking America with genetic anomalies as their weapon of choice? Can't you just imagine our country's demand for an answer—*every* country's demand for an answer? We'll be able to name our price, and if American history has taught us anything, it's that money is the same as power. We'll be able to shape the course of international relations for the next hundred years."

"So, we get money and power out of this deal." Hayden nodded. "What are we offering in return?"

"We're offering them a stage to advance their agendas—nothing more." Gwen laughed to herself. "Honestly, it all sounds silly when you try to explain it out loud. Kaito Yoshida, for instance, cares about securing his legacy. He wants to be loved, and feared, and celebrated, or God-only-knows what else. If he thinks attacking America can make that happen for him, I say let him try. As for Jericho Caine, he wants freedom for his people, or he's fighting to save the holy land, or he's fighting for whatever other insanity he mutters about in those God-awful videos he puts out twice a month. Why does it even matter? They're both ideologues, Mr. Hayden, and I don't overly concern myself with either one."

Hayden looked at the bottom of his empty

mug. "That's fair enough. So, I've got one last question, if you'll humor me?"

Gwen smiled—a thin and biting look—and Hayden could see his time was almost up. He continued anyway. "If these Anoms are just a way of turning a profit, why did we send Kaito into the desert to murder our own people? Isn't that the same as burning money?"

Gwen picked up her own cup and sipped her coffee. "Our people at Kingman were getting in the way. I already told you, we need Yoshida or Caine to *succeed*. Besides, that's why we have a second team already in place. Isn't that right, Mr. Hayden?"

"Oh, we have a second team," Hayden said. "Not sure I'd call them 'in place' yet, but they certainly have potential."

"Then I trust they'll be ready when we need them." Gwen carefully placed her cup down on her saucer. "It does, however, bring us to a more pressing concern. It seems that Colonel McCann has also become a problem. I think it's time we arrange for a permanent solution."

This was more familiar ground for Hayden. He could see that Gwen's vulnerability was at its end, and there would be no more questions that might mistake the two of them for equals. Gwen was ready to give her orders, and Hayden knew better than to question her.

"Colonel McCann is an old man," Hayden said. "I'm sure his heart won't last much longer."

Gwen steepled her fingers. "Not this time, I'm afraid. For Colonel McCann I'd like our answer to be something more, for lack of a better word, obvious."

Hayden smiled. "I can do that, too, if you prefer. I'm good at obvious."

Gwen reached for her bloody mary. "You know, if there were a second quality I admired in you, Mr. Hayden, it would be your directness. And yes, I would, in fact, prefer it that way."

"Ms. Thomas?" Anna Jordan cracked open the door and called into the dining room. "I'm sorry to interrupt you, ma'am, but there's something on the news you should see."

Gwen rose from her chair, blotted her napkin across her lips, and followed Anna out of the room. Hayden trailed after them. In the sitting room, the flat-screen television was on and the sound was muted. On the screen, Hayden could see a video of a man dressed in all black taken from some distance away. The man was standing in the middle of a city's intersection. Then the camera focused in tighter on the man's face, and Hayden could recognize Kaito Yoshida. He stood with his arms out to his sides, and he was turning a slow circle in the middle of the intersection. A chyron scrolling across the bottom of the screen read: *Breaking News—Genetic Anomalies Attack Las Vegas!*

Gwen reached for the television remote and turned on the sound; the voice of the anchor picked up mid-sentence. "—twenty minutes ago. Las Vegas police appear to have set up a perimeter approximately a hundred yards beyond these stone towers that have formed—or fallen —in the middle of the city streets."

The camera pulled back, and in each of the four roads radiating out from the intersection, maybe a hundred yards away from where Yoshida stood, Hayden could see a black onyx mountain wedged between the high-rise buildings, blocking the roads.

The voice coming over the television continued, "City officials are asking everyone to avoid the intersection of Flamingo Road and Las Vegas Boulevard, and, if you are already in the area, police advise you to shelter in place immediately.

"Once again, if you're just joining us, an unidentified man has created four stone towers at the intersection of Flamingo Road and Las Vegas Boulevard, completely blocking both roads. There are several individuals who appear to be trapped within the confines of this intersection. We don't know if they're being used as hostages, or quite possibly they are accomplices to the man responsible. We are asking everyone—"

"That's terrible," Gwen said as the television blinked off. With the remote still in her hand, she turned back to Hayden. "So, we've chartered a plane to fly you back to West Virginia. I expect the matters we discussed to be resolved within the week. Anna, do you have Mr. Hayden's new phone?"

Anna held out a cell phone. "Of course, Ms. Thomas."

Hayden took the phone and tucked it inside his jacket pocket. Then he followed Gwen into the foyer of the suite. Noah still stood beside the front door, leaning against the wall and staring down at his iPod. Gwen stepped to Noah's side and touched his elbow. The other man quickly looked up, smiling a sheepish grin, and Hayden suddenly realized Noah had been ignoring them on purpose—playing one of his juvenile games. How else could you surprise a man who sees the future?

Gwen leaned closer and whispered in Noah's ear. Whatever she said, he must have heard it over his music, because he walked away into the living room. Hayden considered offering some parting comment about Gwen trusting her life to a child, but as Noah left, he thought better of it.

Instead, he pulled open the door and stepped into the hallway. "I guess that's it. I have my orders."

"A car will meet you out front in thirty minutes," Gwen said. "I suggest you use that time to clean yourself up. I'll have Anna send fresh clothes to your room."

"Don't bother yourself." Hayden fished his cigarettes out of his jacket pocket. "I'm taking a private car to get into a private plane, right? No one there to impress but myself."

"So, it would seem." Gwen feigned a smile.

Hayden shook free one of the cigarettes and used his lips to pull it out from the pack. "I do have one last question, though, if you don't mind my asking."

"Oh, Mr. Hayden, I think the time for asking your questions is over." Gwen turned back into the suite, closing the door behind her.

CHAPTER 25

The blue-gray tops of the Vegas casinos rose in the distance, peeking above the brown walls lining either side of the Nevada highway.

Inside the SUV, a reporter's voice droned over the radio, "It now looks like Las Vegas police are moving back. They're pulling their perimeter back another hundred yards from the intersection. Once again, if you're just joining us, we can confirm that Kaito Yoshida, the genetic anomaly believed to be responsible for the collapse of the Golden Gate Bridge, is surrounded by police at the intersection of Las Vegas Boulevard and Flamingo Road. Police and first responders are waiting—"

"Turn it off," Gauntlet growled from the passenger seat of the SUV.

From the driver's seat, Lara pressed the knob on the center console, killing power to the radio. "I guess you were right." She glanced over her shoulder at Nyx. "This is the place."

"Wish it wasn't," Nyx said.

Lara changed lanes to her right, curling the

SUV up exit twelve A. "I'm not sure how close we can get. Police are diverting traffic."

"Do the best you can." Nyx leaned forward in her seat, looking out the windshield. "I'll take us the rest of the way."

"Or you don't have to go at all." Lara twisted her hands over the steering wheel, tightening her grip. "I can keep driving."

Jeremy shook his head from the seat behind her. "What are you talking about? Of course we're going. That's why we're here."

Lara drew in her breath. "But it doesn't have to be. As far as I'm concerned, when we left Kingman, we left everything with it. Reah Labs. The Army. That's all behind us now. There's no reason this has to be our fight."

Jeremy leaned back in his seat. "No. We didn't run just to run. We're gonna end this."

"How?" Lara raised her voice, slamming her palms down against the steering wheel. "Seriously, how? Kaito just dropped a mountain on top of us! How do you think this is going to end?"

No one answered.

Lara fixed her eyes straight ahead on the road. "Kaito Yoshida's a killer. We trained him, and I'm telling you right now, he's better at this than you. He's better than all of you put together. And that's just Kaito by himself. Only he's not by himself, is he?" Lara's question hung in the air. "Is he?" she shouted again.

The SUV slowed to a crawl, funneled into

a single line of cars edging forward, and for a long time, no one spoke. Out of the driver's side window, Jeremy could see an abandoned street leading into the heart of the Las Vegas Strip. It was empty except for the blue police barricades, a dozen cop cars all with their lights flashing in the morning sun, and a small army of police officers huddled behind them. Farther out, rising from the middle of the street, a dark stone spire sat wedged between the buildings. Jeremy knew Kaito Yoshida waited on the other side.

Finally, Gauntlet turned around in his seat, trying to look at Lara, Nyx, and Jeremy all at the same time. Then his helmet split down the middle and peeled away from his face.

"Mirror's right," Gauntlet said, and he pressed his lips together, weighing his words. "Yoshida has every advantage here. It's too late to change that now. So, we need to go after the king. If we all attack Yoshida at the same time—ignore everything else around us—we still have a chance."

"No, we don't." Lara slammed on the brakes, and the sudden stop rocked them all forward against their seatbelts. She put the SUV in park and turned around in her seat to face the others. "I've spent my whole life just surviving—*barely* surviving—and now I'm finally ready to have a life, and you want me to throw that away. You can't ask me to do that."

Jeremy shook his head. "We're not, but we

JASON R. JAMES

can't just walk away, either."

Nyx folded her arms. "What did you think was going to happen here, Mirror?"

"I don't know!" Lara raised her eyebrows. "But I didn't drive for an hour and a half to watch you all die!"

Then one of the drivers behind them laid on their horn, and through the front windshield, Jeremy could see a uniformed cop walking towards the SUV; the officer waved his hand in a quick circle, yelling, "Let's go! You can't stop here!"

Lara ignored the cop and looked at the others. "This is what I know: Right now, everyone in this car is free to do whatever we want. We can literally go anywhere, but if you get out of this car and face Kaito, that all changes. We have this one chance, and so I'm begging you, please don't do this."

Nyx edged forward in her seat. "But you can't ask us that, either. Kai's not going to stop at Vegas. You know that. More people are going to die."

"But it's not our responsibility anymore!" Lara shouted. "Why does it matter where he stops?"

"It matters to me." Jeremy answered; he looked at Gauntlet and Nyx. "And it matters to them. It matters when we can do something to stop it."

"But I can't!" Lara's voice wavered. "I can't

fight, or control gravity, or swing a sword. I can't help any of you, and I can't just sit here and watch."

"Then you need to go." Jeremy focused on her eyes. "And let us take care of it."

The police officer reached the driver's side window and rapped his knuckles against the glass. "Ma'am, you can't stop here. You need to keep moving."

Nyx looked past the cop out the window. "No time for goodbyes. Sorry, Mirror." She grabbed Gauntlet and Jeremy by their wrists, and in a flash of light, they were gone.

In the next instant, Jeremy blinked his eyes against the sun. He could feel the sharp pang of nausea in his gut, and he knew Nyx had flashed Gauntlet and him out of the car. The three of them stood together in the middle of the street —a modern-day canyon lined with palm trees, glass-plated casinos, and dazzling neon lights, but it was also painfully quiet, bereft of all that same life that made the city possible. A dark spire rose in front of them in the middle of the street, cutting against the hazy blue sky.

Jeremy turned around. Behind him, he could see a dozen officers waving their arms, shouting orders for Jeremy, Nyx, and Gauntlet to get back behind the line. Even farther back in the intersection, he could see the white SUV with Lara behind the wheel. She pulled the car forward until finally, she was lost behind the corner of a building, and Jeremy knew she was really gone.

He turned back to Gauntlet, tapping his knuckles against the other man's chest. "Looks like you better buckle your chinstrap."

Gauntlet seemed to understand. The metal pauldrons rose off his shoulders, folding around his head, reforming his helmet. Then the three of them started up the street toward the spire.

"About my plan..." Gauntlet's heavy voice rattled behind his helmet. "You know it won't work."

Jeremy stopped walking. "What do you mean it won't work?"

Nyx stopped walking, too. She stood next to Jeremy. Gauntlet managed another couple of steps up the road, moving closer to the spire, but finally, he turned back to face the others.

"We can't all attack Yoshida and ignore everything else," Gauntlet said. "If we do that, Yoshida's men will collapse on top of us, and we end up just as dead. We need someone to stay back and draw out his lieutenants. We need someone to hold them off while the other two face Yoshida."

"That's the opposite of everything you just said in the car!" Nyx screamed. "It's the opposite of the plan! Why wouldn't you just make *this* the plan from the beginning?"

Gauntlet shook his head. "Because I didn't want to fight about it in the car."

Jeremy laughed. "Great! Let me guess who

plays the bait."

"Not who you think," Gauntlet said. "Not with your powers. You're the only one of the three of us who stands a chance against Yoshida. Nyx is how you get there. That leaves me as the bait."

Before either Jeremy or Nyx could answer, a new sound started in front of them. It was like a sharp thundercrack splitting the air, followed by a low rumble. They all looked, and the black spire in front of them seemed to disintegrate. It fell away in thick sheets of dark water, cascading into the street below and rising again as heavy fog.

"No more time for debate," Nyx whispered, and Jeremy squared his shoulders for whatever came next. Then, through the cloud, he could see three shadows advancing toward them. They walked side by side, and as they stepped out of the fog, Jeremy recognized the man in the middle. It was the Anom he'd fought on the bridge.

"The big one there is Shān," Jeremy said, keeping his voice just low enough for Gauntlet and Nyx to hear him. "He has an ability that cancels out kinetic force, so punches and kicks don't do anything. You're better off saving your strength. It's like hitting a wall."

"And Kumiho's on his left." Nyx nodded her head in that direction. "I think she can heal herself through her blood, so if you actually kill her, you're just going to have to kill her again."

The seven-foot tall beast with bristling gray fur, yellow teeth, and dark claws walked next to Shān on his left. With every step she took, Kumiho's thin, pointed face turned from one side to the other, sniffing at the air, and even at this distance, Jeremy could hear the wet champing of her jaws.

"That's two," Gauntlet said, "and the third is just some guy with a sword."

On Shān's other side, a smaller man walked with him. He wore a leather baseball jacket, a pair of wraparound sunglasses, and a samurai's katana sheathed at his side. Other than the sword, at least this man looked normal. For a second, Jeremy though Gauntlet could be right —maybe this third man was just some guy carrying a sword—but he also realized the mistake of underestimating him. If he was walking alongside Shān and Kumiho, he was there for a reason.

Suddenly, the three Ryoku broke into a sprint, running down the street together, but after three steps, Kumiho outpaced the other two. She lunged ahead of the others, running on all fours like a true animal, racing across the asphalt.

Jeremy closed his fists and raised his gravity. "I gotta tell you, Gauntlet, this new plan of yours sucks!"

"I agree." Gauntlet raised his arm to his chest, and his round shield spun out from his armor, locking into place with a metallic *shink* over his hand and arm. Then he ran forward to meet the Ryoku.

Jeremy cursed under his breath and started after him, but he only managed half a step before Nyx's hand close over his wrist. There was a flash of energy, and when Jeremy opened his eyes again, he was staring at an empty street and the intersection ahead where Yoshida stood waiting.

From somewhere far behind him, a wordless roar echoed into the air. Jeremy spun back around. The three Ryoku lieutenants were closing in on Gauntlet.

CHAPTER 26

In a flash of light, Nyx and G-Force were gone, teleported a hundred yards beyond the fight and far away from Yoshida's lieutenants. It was better this way. Without Nyx or G-Force at his side, Gauntlet could fight with abandon. There would be no hesitation or worrying about the others —no guarding against their inevitable mistakes. This fight was his alone, and Gauntlet was always better alone.

The three Ryoku ran at him with the beast —the one called Kumiho—outpacing the other two. Gauntlet raised his arm, and the crossbow mounted to his wrist unfolded into place. He fired. The bolt struck Kumiho's shoulder, and as it hit, she lost her footing, tumbling across the road.

Gauntlet spun to his left, and a black dagger flipped out from his armored bracer, locking into the palm of his hand. Gauntlet finished his spin and threw the blade at the man with the sword and sunglasses. The dagger should have buried itself in the man's chest, but before it could find its mark, the man drew his katana, knocking the dagger aside. Then there was no time for Gauntlet to try again. The man in the middle of the pack, Shān, was already bearing down on top of him, only three steps away from tackling him into the street.

Gauntlet reached behind his back, drawing out his hand axe and swinging it down for the center of Shān's head. The other man raised his arm to block, but Gauntlet knew it wouldn't matter. The blade of the axe would cleave through Shān's arm and bury itself in the middle of his skull—only that didn't happen. The axe struck against Shān's arm and stopped in place. It felt as if Gauntlet had swung the blade down into a blacksmith's anvil. There was no cut, no blood—only the man standing in front of him, smiling.

Gauntlet pulled back, ready to try again— ready to swing even harder this time—but before he could, Shān punched out with his fist, connecting under Gauntlet's solar plexus. The impact was heavy and sharp, a much harder punch than it should have been through the Exocorium armor, and Gauntlet felt the weight shudder through his body, stealing his wind and staggering him back.

He raised his shield, ready to block the next attack, only Shān didn't follow. There was no second punch ready behind the first. Instead, the massive Ryoku held his ground, waiting. So,

Gauntlet obliged. He spun the axe over his head, starting forward, feinting high and dropping the blade low to aim at Shān's ribs, but even as he swung, Gauntlet felt another threat start from his right. The Exocorium armor turned his head just in time to see Kumiho launch herself into the air.

Gauntlet threw up his arm, catching the beast under her under jaw and somehow holding her back, but as she slammed into him, the impact sent both of them off their feet to the ground. Kumiho's weight pinned Gauntlet to the pavement, and all he could see was her yellow teeth snapping above his face and a tangle of gray fur. Gauntlet's right arm pushed against Kumiho's throat, but his strength was failing. He could feel her sharp claws digging against his ribs—not enough to tear through his armor, but he could feel the weight and impact of every blow. She slashed again into his side, and the sharp pain stole his breath for a second time. One of his ribs dislocated.

Gauntlet grit his teeth and swung up with his shield, punching the edge of the blocker into Kumhio's side, hoping to return the favor. She didn't move. He punched again at her ribs, and then he swung the shield into the back of her head. Finally, she pulled away, howling in pain. It was enough space for Gauntlet to draw in his legs. He kicked up at Kumiho's waist, sending her tumbling overhead as he scrambled back to his feet and swung down with his axe. Kumiho twisted herself around and raised her arm to block, but this time, the axe cut clean through her flesh and bone.

Kumiho shrieked—wild and wordless—throwing back her head as her maw gaped wide. Blood poured from the ragged end of her arm, spilling across the street, and as she tried to regain her feet, she fell sideways against a parked car.

Gauntlet stepped closer to her, raising his axe above his head, ready to swing down and finish what he started, but all at once, Kumiho's screaming stopped. So did the blood pouring out of her arm. Instead, pushing out of the jagged end of Kumiho's severed arm, Gauntlet could see a new hand. The skin looked pale and hairless, but it was fully grown and almost identical to the one she lost. Kumiho opened and closed her new hand, staring down at the curved black claws gracing the end of each fingertip.

Gauntlet tightened his grip around the handle of his axe. He could still see his crossbow bolt lodged deep in Kumiho's shoulder, only its black fletching visible against her gray fur, but if she still knew it was there—if she felt it at all—there was no indication, and just like with her arm, there was no more blood, either. The wound had closed completely around the arrow.

Nyx had told him that Kumiho could heal herself through her blood. Apparently, she could grow back limbs, too. Gauntlet would need to carve away a much bigger piece—a wound so severe that it would kill her—and he would have to do it without letting her bleed and heal.

Gauntlet raised his axe, ready to charge again, but before he could start, the Exocorium armor heard footsteps racing behind him. Then Gauntlet could feel the wind displacing at his back, and the armor was dropping him to his knee. He turned to look just as the katana swung clear above his head.

It was the third man with the sunglasses; he pivoted back to his right, swinging his sword low for Gauntlet's waist. Gauntlet jumped away from the blade, and then he saw an opening of his own. The other man had overextended himself, and now he was off-balance. Gauntlet swung down, aiming his axe at the man's chest, but Sunglasses turned it aside, parrying the axe with a quick swipe of his katana. Gauntlet swung again. Sunglasses parried and countered. Then he darted forward.

Gauntlet tried to twist his body away from the sword again, but this time he was too slow. Sunglasses dragged the blade through Gauntlet's side, and now Gauntlet could feel the searing pain open deep across his abdomen. He was cut. In his mind, he knew it should have been impossible—the Exocorium Armor had stopped bullets before—but now he reached across his body, and he could feel it just under his ribs: a warm, wet gash carved through his side.

Gauntlet pushed his hand against the wound, and he could feel the Exocorium closing under his fingertips, reforming across the tear in his armor, and even more importantly, filling the cut in his side, stanching the blood as a new wave of pain rippled through his body.

Gauntlet pulled back his hand, looking down at his blood-stained fingers. "Why don't you try that again?"

The man with the katana spun the sword in a quick circle in front of him, and then behind his back, and forward again, the blade whipping around in a flash of silver, before he finished with the katana held high. "When I try it again, you'll be dead."

"Not if you're dead first." Gauntlet raised his axe.

Suddenly, a heavy, barreling weight crashed against Gauntlet's back, and a pair of thick arms wrapped around his chest, engulfing him in a bearhug. It was Shān. Gauntlet staggered forward under the unexpected weight, and Shān's arms closed tighter around his chest, squeezing the air out of his lungs. Gauntlet threw his head straight back, slamming his helmet into the face of the other man, but nothing happened. Shān didn't move, and his grip remained tight.

Gauntlet's vision blurred. He reached behind him, over his shoulder, grabbing Shān by the back of his head. Then he pitched forward, dipping his shoulder, and using his own momentum to throw Shān over his back. The bigger man tumbled head over heels, rolling across the asphalt in a perfect somersault—surprisingly nimble for a man his size—and then he sprang back to his feet.

Gauntlet held out his arm, and the crossbow on his wrist unfolded into place. He fired a bolt aimed at the center of Shān's chest, but when it struck, the arrow clattered away to the ground.

Gauntlet aimed again, this time at Shān's face, but an ungodly roar stopped him from firing. He wheeled around to see Kumiho charging at him, running on all fours. He shot the bolt at her instead, and it sank into her shoulder. This time, Kumiho didn't break stride. Gauntlet shot again. The bolt hit her in the abdomen, but she still sprinted forward. He shot again. The third bolt found her eye, and Kumiho pitched forward across the ground.

Gauntlet raised up his axe and started after her. He would take off Kumiho's head—see if she was powerful enough to survive that—but with his first step, the Exocorium could feel someone else attacking from his left. Gauntlet turned and swung his axe down at this new threat. The man with the sword ducked under Gauntlet's blade and swung up with his katana, slicing across Gauntlet's chest and cutting another long gash through the blood-red armor

Gauntlet staggered back, the searing pain from the katana blinding him—robbing him of all thought—until finally, the Exocorium closed over the wound. Then Gauntlet wanted to counter. He wanted to chase after the man with the sunglasses and bury his axe in the back of his skull, but that's what Sunglasses wanted, too—a half-crazed Gauntlet charging head-first into his katana. It was a trap, and Gauntlet was better than that.

Instead, he raised his axe and shield, ready to defend himself against the next attack from the katana. If the smaller man wanted to dart in and take his shot, Gauntlet would let him, but he would also make him pay for it. Sunglasses was quick, but if Gauntlet held his ground—if he forced the other man to trade blow for blow in close combat where Gauntlet's own strength would be an advantage—he would win.

The smaller man stood back, his sword raised next to his ear. He was waiting, too. *Waiting for what?* Then Gauntlet heard the low growl from his right side. He turned, and Kumiho was back on her feet. Thick blood stained her gray fur from the last volley of arrows, but any bleeding had already stopped. He could see the pale skin where her wounds had closed around the arrows buried deep in her body. Even Kumiho's eye had regrown around the bolt lodged in her skull.

He would have to answer her attack first. Kumiho was savage, relentless, but he was the smarter fighter. If he could keep her at a distance, cause enough damage with his crossbow and close in to finish her off with his axe, maybe he could still win. *But why wasn't she attacking either?*

Gauntlet's armor could feel the third man's presence behind him. He turned around to see Shān walking slowly forward, closing the distance between them, as the big man cracked his knuckles and rolled his neck from side to side.

Finally, Gauntlet realized the truth. He was better than all of them one-on-one, but not together. He would never be able to finish one before the others could intervene. All his skill and strength, his intelligence and experience meant nothing. They had the numbers, and that would be enough. Gauntlet would lose this fight.

All at once, his anger found voice in a single, wordless scream.

CHAPTER 27

Jeremy and Nyx walked down the street side by side. In front of them, standing in the middle of the intersection, they could see Kaito Yoshida. He wore a dark shirt under a black suit, and his long hair was pulled back in a ponytail. He stood with both of his arms outstretched to his sides, staring back at them, waiting.

Behind Yoshida, sitting in the road, a woman with short hair pulled her knees up to her chest, and Jeremy remembered the Resonance described by Lara—the Anom who could magnify other Anoms. Now, she looked away from Yoshida, keeping her eyes fixed down on the road, hugging her knees even tighter, and Jeremy had the distinct impression that she was scared. He almost felt sorry for her. If she was really the Resonance, Jeremy thought, maybe she wasn't the danger they all imagined.

Then Yoshida yelled from the intersection, "It's good to see you again—both of you! I wasn't sure I'd have the pleasure."

Nyx reached down and grabbed Jeremy by his wrist. She kept her eyes fixed straight ahead, but her voice was low, meant only for Jeremy. "Once we start, we don't let up. We do whatever it takes. Promise me."

"I promise," Jeremy said.

Nyx tightened her grip around Jeremy's wrist. "I'm going to flash us to the other side of the intersection, so that we're behind them. As soon as we hit, you go after Yoshida. Don't give him room to breathe. I'll try to flash the Resonance away. If he reaches for her—"

A loud scream broke through the air behind them, wordless and desperate. Nyx wheeled around, and Jeremy turned, too. A hundred yards away they could see Gauntlet standing in the street, an axe brandished in one hand and his shield held in the other. He was surrounded by Yoshida's lieutenants.

"He's not going to make it much longer." Nyx dropped her hand from Jeremy's wrist. "Look at him. He knows it."

Jeremy looked at Gauntlet, and he could see it, too. The armored knight stood his ground, his axe still raised, but something in Gauntlet's shoulders, the way they angled down from his body, gave him the look of a man resigned to his fate. Jeremy knew the odds were always against them, but human nature delights in denial. Now, seeing it play out in front of his eyes, there was no escaping the truth.

Jeremy grabbed Nyx by the hand. "You're right. He's not going to make it unless you help him."

Nyx shook her head. "If we ignore Yoshida, we're all dead anyway. He'll pick us off one at a time."

"We're not ignoring him," Jeremy hissed under his breath. "I'll go after the king. You save Gauntlet."

Nyx pulled away her hand. "You can't go up against Yoshida alone! We're just trading one problem for another."

"I know that." Jeremy looked at Nyx, meeting her eye. "So, you save Gauntlet first, and then both of you save me. That's our plan. That's the new plan. Fight with me, not for me, remember? We can still do this."

Nyx hesitated. For a second, it looked like she was ready to argue again. But then she closed her eyes, and in a flash of light, she was gone. Jeremy was left alone.

Yoshida laughed from the intersection. "And just like that, we're down to one. I wish I could tell you I was surprised, but that's Nyx. She was never much of a killer—always lacked the stomach for it—and now her weakness is going to cost you your life."

"Then you don't know anything about her." Jeremy squared his shoulders to Yoshida. "You don't know who she is, or what she's capable of doing. Maybe you did, once, but that's not her anymore." Jeremy started forward, balling up his fists. "As for costing my life, last I checked I'm still here. You brought down a bridge, and I'm still alive. You dropped a mountain on me, and I'm still alive!"

Yoshida offered a thin smile. "You're still alive for now."

Then Jeremy broke forward in a sprint. Yoshida still stood a hundred feet away, and Jeremy's only chance was to close the distance between them before Yoshida could make good on his threat. He only managed three steps.

Yoshida punched out with his fist. At the same time, a cylinder of stone formed in front of Jeremy's face. It looked like a Greek column flipped on its side, cut from onyx. The stone shot forward through the air, moving at the same velocity as Yoshida's fist. Jeremy spun away to his left, and the stone missed him, falling to the ground and crushing the pavement under it as it landed.

Yoshida punched again. Another cylinder of black stone shot forward, just as wide as the first. Jeremy darted to his right, stumbling. Yoshida hammered his fist straight down through the air, and another pillar of stone dropped from above. Jeremy dove forward, rolling across the street just before the piledriver slammed into the asphalt behind him.

Jeremy was only ten feet closer to Yoshida than he was before, and he had almost died three times.

He scrambled back to his feet and started forward again. Yoshida threw a left hook. A cylinder of stone swung out from Jeremy's right, and there was no time to dodge. He raised his right arm, covering the back of his head, turning away and raising his gravity as the battering ram crashed against his side. The impact was sudden, sharp, and heavy, and the stone exploded in a thousand fragments of shrapnel. Jeremy staggered to his left.

Yoshida kicked out with his leg, and the black asphalt of the street rippled forward, rising up on itself and surging forward like a wave racing to meet the shore, until it crested six feet high. Jeremy zeroed out his gravity and jumped over it. The wave crashed under him with chunks of stone and tar spraying across the street like bullets.

Jeremy fell back to the ground, and Yoshida punched again, this time throwing an overhand right. Another column of stone cut down through the air. Jeremy dodged to his right, twisting his body out of the way and losing his balance for a second time.

Then Yoshida dropped to his knees, sweeping both of his hands over the pavement. Suddenly, the ground gave way under Jeremy's feet like it was made from sugar glass—like he had broken through the ice, and now he was sinking into a river of tar. The liquid asphalt closed around him, swirling over Jeremy's waist and chest. There was time for one last breath, and then his head dipped under the surface, and the darkness closed over him entirely.

CHAPTER 28

Nyx opened her eyes. Only second ago, she had been standing next to G-Force, ready to face off with Kaito Yoshida. Now she stood back-to-back with Gauntlet, a hundred yards away from where she started. And just like Gauntlet, she found herself surrounded.

Nyx could see Kumiho standing to her left. She was hunched over at the shoulders, her gray fur bristling and her body as taut as a bowstring. She was waiting, but it wouldn't last. Kumiho only needed the opportunity, and she would charge, relying on her ferocity, her teeth, and the panic and chaos of the moment.

On Nyx's right, Shān took the opposite tact. He wasn't waiting for anyone. The massive Anom was ambling forward like a glacier, slow and unstoppable. So he would be the one to start the fight, and why not? The man couldn't be hurt. He would create the opportunity Kumiho was waiting for, and then, in the aftermath, Shān would finish off whatever was left of Nyx and

Gauntlet.

Nyx forced herself to take a breath. Shān and Kumiho were each formidable on their own, but working in tandem, it would be worse, and now they were joined by a third. Somewhere, on the other side of Gauntlet, there was a man with a sword—one more threat lying in wait, as if getting killed by Shān and Kumiho wasn't enough. She knew Gauntlet wouldn't survive on his own, but now, standing with him, she doubted their odds were any better.

"This wasn't the plan," Gauntlet growled behind her.

"Plans change," Nyx countered, and suddenly, hearing the words out loud, changing plans didn't sound like such a bad idea. Why should she wait on Shān and Kumiho? Nyx could start this fight herself.

Without warning, Nyx punched with her fist to the left, and from the edge of her hand, a bolt of energy crackled through the air. It was aimed at Kumiho, and it struck home in the center of the monster's chest, staggering her back. Then all the waiting was over. Kumiho lunged forward on all fours, racing at Nyx in a full sprint.

"Wolf on your right!" Nyx yelled over her shoulder as she twisted around Gauntlet's side, firing another bolt of energy blindly at the man with the sword. It didn't matter for now if she hit him or not. She just needed to hold him back and buy more time. If they could fight the Ryoku one at a time, they had a chance.

From behind her, Gauntlet spun on his heels, throwing his hand axe across the distance at Kumiho. It sank deep into the monster's shoulder. Then Kumiho reared up on her hind legs. Gauntlet raised his arm, and three quick bolts sang out from his crossbow, two of them hitting Kumiho's abdomen, the third burying itself under her throat. Nyx looked over her shoulder, and she could see the fletching of the arrows sticking out from Kumiho's fur. Gauntlet shot again. Another crossbow bolt struck Kumiho in the center of the chest, and she pitched forward, thrashing across the ground.

"That's not enough to stop her!" Nyx yelled.

"She's stopped for now," Gauntlet growled back under his helmet.

Nyx punched again in the direction of the swordsman, hoping it was enough to hold him back. She thought about firing off an energy bolt at Kumiho, too, but there was no time. Out of the corner of her eye, she saw that Shān had closed the distance between them. He stood over Gauntlet and Nyx with both of his fists raised above his head like a pair of sledgehammers, ready to pummel down into their skulls.

Gauntlet started to turn and raise his shield, but somehow, Nyx was even faster. She reached behind her, and as her fingers brushed against Gauntlet's armor, she flashed them both away. Now they were standing on the opposite side of Shān, and they watched as he swung his fists down through the empty air—through the exact space where they had both been standing only a moment ago.

"Guy with the sword!" Nyx yelled. It was the only instruction she could manage as she jumped onto Shān's back, wrapping her arms around the bigger man's throat. Then she flashed again, and they were gone.

Nyx squeezed shut her eyes. She had intended to teleport Shān three thousand feet straight into the air, and she didn't need to see now to know that it had worked. The air racing over her face and roaring in her ears was enough. That and the falling. If Shān could survive this, he deserved it.

"I'm sorry!" Nyx screamed in his ear, but she had no way of knowing if he heard her or not. She pushed herself away from the falling man and flashed again.

In the same instant, Nyx was back on the ground where she started, only now she was lying flat on her back in the middle of the road. On her left, Kumiho still writhed across the ground with thick, dark blood oozing from the arrow wounds in her chest. On Nyx's other side, she could see Gauntlet squaring off against the man with the sword. For a second, neither one of them advanced. Gauntlet stood his ground, his shield covering one of his arms and a hand axe raised in the other. Then the man with the sword attacked. He lanced forward, swinging his katana left and right, faster than Nyx thought possible, the silver blade lost in a cloud of steel.

Gauntlet stepped back, deflected a blow with his shield, and turned another aside with his axe—but he was still too slow. The man with the sword lunged to his left, dropped to his knee, and dragged his blade across Gauntlet's thigh, opening a long cut through the armor. Gauntlet's leg buckled, even as the other man rose to his feet. He circled behind Gauntlet's back, his katana poised over his head, eyeing Gauntlet's neck, and Nyx realized the armor alone wouldn't be enough to stop him.

She rolled onto her side, grit her teeth, and punched out with her hand. A bolt of energy shot through the air, hitting the other man in the ribs and sending him sideways into the street. Then, she was exhausted. She fell back, her hands on top of her chest, and she was sucking in air like she had just finished a race.

"Where did you go?" Gauntlet asked, rising to his feet as the armor closed over the cut in his leg.

Nyx couldn't catch enough of her breath to answer. Both of her arms ached from her shoulders to her hands, and from inside her chest, her lungs felt like they were on fire. She needed to stand up. She needed to get her legs under her and clear her head.

Nyx rolled onto her side. "Here. Help me up."

Gauntlet reached down for her arm, but suddenly, from behind him, a human body crashed face down into the street, splintering the asphalt as it hit. The sound of the impact was louder and somehow sharper than it should have been for a falling body. It was enough to make Gauntlet flinch.

Nyx raised herself up to assess the damage. Ten feet behind Gauntlet, she could see Shān lying in the broken street. From the height that he fell, his body should have been transformed into a messy puddle on the asphalt, but it wasn't. Shān's body was still perfectly intact. There wasn't even blood on the street. Then Nyx watched him stir, slowly pushing himself up onto all fours.

Gauntlet reached down, pulling Nyx to her feet. "Looks like that wasn't enough to stop him, either. Any more change of plans?"

"I'm working on it," Nyx said.

A new sound stopped her from saying more. It was a rolling, guttural growl. Nyx turned her head, and from behind her, she could see Kumiho standing back on her feet. Every muscle in the monster's lean frame tightened, and Nyx thought she looked somehow even wilder than before, as if the last of her conscious thought was finally lost to baser instinct. Kumiho snarled and snapped her jaws, and another growl rattled deep in her throat.

"Wolf!" Nyx shouted.

Gauntlet wheeled around, raised his arm, and shot another crossbow bolt at Kumiho. It found its mark in her shoulder, and she roared in response, her anger reverberating against the empty street—but it didn't stop her. She started forward. Gauntlet shot again. The crossbow bolt sank into her hip.

"That won't work," Nyx cried out. "The more she bleeds... "

"...the stronger she gets," Gauntlet finished. "So we stop the bleeding." Gauntlet shot again. The arrow hit Kumiho in her ribs, but it didn't matter. She still didn't slow down. Another step and she would be on them both.

Nyx grabbed Gauntlet by his outstretched arm. If she could gather enough of her strength, she could flash them away like she had done before with Shān—

Kumiho was too fast. She crouched in front of them, ready to leap into the air, and there was nothing Nyx could do to stop it.

All at once, Gauntlet opened his hand, and Kumiho pitched forward. Her body hit the street, and she was heavy, still, and lifeless, as if all her animus had been drained at once. Nyx looked down at the monstrous form lying dead at her feet. Kumiho laid stretched out on her back, and for the first time, Nyx could see the full extent of the damage inflicted by Gauntlet. The crossbow bolts he shot into her body had somehow expanded—all of them—each arrow hollowing out into a concave shell so that Ku-miho looked like a dozen black craters were ripping open her muscles and fur. Still, even with all that damage, something about her body looked wrong. Something was missing. Nyx looked again and realized there was no blood pouring from these fresh wounds. The bolts tearing open Kumiho's body had also filled her severed veins, stanching the blood in her vessels before it could heal her.

"So, is that *your* new plan?" Nyx asked.

Gauntlet lowered his arm. "The bolts are made from the same material as my amor. It lets me stop my own bleeding when I need it, and so I thought I could do the same—move!" Gauntlet suddenly roared from behind his helmet.

Nyx tried to turn and look, but Gauntlet's hand had already closed over her arm, pulling her away. The unexpected force and change of direction lifted Nyx off her feet, and as she stum-bled backwards, she could see Gauntlet step for-ward, taking her place, raising his shield up to his chest. In the next moment, the man with the sword crashed into him, stabbing forward with his katana. The blade pierced clean through the shield and sank down to its hilt. Nyx could see the blood-stained sword jutting through Gaunt-let's back as both men fell over in the street.

The other man—the one with the sunglasses —scrambled up first, standing over Gauntlet, and Nyx could see the doubt in his face. He wasn't sure if their fight was really over, but Gauntlet stayed on his back, motionless, the katana pinning his shield to his chest.

The man with the sunglasses looked at Nyx, and then she could see any of his lingering doubts melt away. He reached down to rip his sword free from Gauntlet's body—to start after her and finish his day's work—but now, as the man pulled back on his sword, the katana held firmly in place. Nyx looked closer at the blade, and she could see the black metal from Gauntlet's shield closing around the steel sword, oozing over the silver katana like heavy sap from a fresh cut tree. The man with the sunglasses put his foot down on Gauntlet's shield, standing on top of him as he tried to wrench his sword free again, but it didn't move.

Then, from the ground, Gauntlet raised his other arm. The crossbow locked into place on his wrist. The other man had just enough time to look down when Gauntlet fired. The bolt struck between the man's eyes, disappearing completely inside his skull. For a second, the man with the sunglasses seemed to keep his feet under him, but it was only an illusion. All at once, the man's legs went limp, and he collapsed under his own weight like a marionette without its strings.

Nyx started forward. "You're not dead."

Gauntlet coughed, rolling onto his shoulder. "You sound surprised."

JASON R. JAMES

Nyx took another step closer, but suddenly, from behind Gauntlet, she could see Shān rise to his feet. The massive Anom staggered back, unsteady, but then he lurched forward, closing in on Nyx and Gauntlet with his anvil-like hands balled up over his head.

Nyx squared her shoulders and glanced down at Gauntlet. "You stay where you are and keep quiet."

Gauntlet tried to push himself up with one arm. "That's not gonna happen—"

"I said stay down!" she screamed again as she punched out with both of her hands. Two bolts of energy exploded from her fists, landing against the center of Shān's chest, but it didn't affect the other man at all. She doubted he even felt it. Shān advanced another step closer, and Nyx looked down at her feet where Gauntlet still laid prostrate. If nothing else, she had to draw Shān away from him. She had to give Gauntlet a chance.

Nyx closed her eyes and flashed to the other side of where Shān was standing. She punched again with her left and right in quick succession. Two more bolts crashed against Shān's back. It was enough to get his attention. He turned around to face her.

Nyx retreated three quick steps. "You don't have to do this. We don't need to kill each other. I can let you walk away."

Shān advanced, and Nyx punched again with

her left. Another energy bolt glanced off his arm, but it hardly mattered now. He was moving faster. Nyx took another three steps back, trying to get away from him, but there was no more room to retreat. Her back slammed against the trunk of a palm tree rising from the median in the road.

All at once, Shān was on top of her, his thick hands closing around her neck, and Nyx could feel her feet jerk off the ground. He was holding her in the air by the throat against the palm tree. She choked, but there was no sound. Her mouth opened and closed as she desperately tried to fill her lungs with air.

Nyx reached up, curling her fingers around Shān's wrists, trying to pry his hands apart, but it was no use. Then she closed her eyes, and even through the darkness, she could see a flash of light. All at once, the hands holding her by the throat let go, and Nyx fell to the ground. She opened her eyes to see Shān still standing in front of her. Nyx had only flashed three feet away, but it was three feet straight back to the other side of the palm tree. She had taken Shān with her. Now the palm tree rose through Shān's stomach and chest, the rest of its trunk continuing into the air through the back of his shoulder blades.

Nyx staggered away from him. She could see streams of dark red dripping down the trunk of the palm tree, and then Shān's eyes went wide as he finally understood what was happening. He opened his mouth to cry out, but there was no sound.

"I'm sorry," Nyx said.

Shān's eyes rolled back, his knees buckled under him, and he sank lower down the trunk of the tree, still upright as if he were kneeling in prayer.

Nyx took another step back. Then another, her eyes fixed on the dead man in front of her. She wanted to take it all back—to think of some other way to escape—but she had panicked, and now it was done. She took another step back and felt the smooth glass of the building behind her press against her shoulders. There was nowhere else to go.

Nyx let herself slide down the side of the building until finally she sat on the sidewalk, her head leaning against the glass behind her, and her eyes never leaving Shān.

CHAPTER 29

Trapped underground, the darkness around Jeremy was consuming. It filled the gaps and seeped into the crevices so completely that he felt claustrophobic and lost at the same time—a single man adrift at sea.

He had tried to stop Yoshida. Jeremy had spent all his strength to reach the man and throw a single punch to end him, but he never got close. Kaito Yoshida was toying with him from the start.

Jeremy could feel his lungs go tight—burning inside him—desperate for air. He needed to breathe, or he needed to resign himself to the darkness and what waited beyond. *Maybe he should.* After all, if this was really his end, it would be better than some. It would be better than what happened to his dad, or all those people who died on the bridge, or to John Langer. It would be his choice, and his alone—but Jeremy knew that was a lie, too. Choices aren't endings.

Whatever he chose now, the consequences

would ripple out like waves racing beyond his reach, and they would crash over Gauntlet and Nyx. Those two would pay the price, along with a thousand others. They would each fall like dominoes in a chain. It would be easier to believe the lie, but it was too late. Jeremy had his answer. The choice was his, but he was never alone.

Jeremy closed his hands. He could feel his gravity rising and the earth and stone pressing in tighter around his arms and legs, his face and skin. There was a low, building noise all around him—a deep, guttural growl like heavy tires pacing over a gravel road—but Jeremy didn't stop.

The burning inside his chest spread out to his fingers. It coursed up his neck and into his face, but he ignored it. He raised his gravity even more, and his whole body screamed for escape until finally, Jeremy couldn't take it anymore.

He reversed the gravitational field, pushing everything away in a sudden explosion of negative energy. The dirt, stone, and asphalt around his body erupted in a thousand directions at once, and the low rumble he heard before broke like thunder, shaking the ground and air and every fiber of Jeremy's body. Above him, he could see the pale blue of Nevada's cloudless sky, and under his feet, Jeremy could see the yellow ochre of the desert curving around him in a shallow crater. He was free.

Jeremy rose off the ground, floating into the air—rising to the level of the street—his lungs still on fire. Then he dropped the gravitational field, his feet touched the ground, and the hot Las Vegas air swirled around him, filling the vacuum. Finally, he could breathe.

Across from him, Kaito Yoshida clapped his hands. "Well done! That's the third time you've kept yourself alive. You're making a habit out of this."

Jeremy didn't answer—he couldn't trust himself to speak. The strength it took to escape Yoshida's pit was more than he anticipated, and it was all Jeremy could do not to collapse in the street. If his voice wavered or broke—if Yoshida realized how badly he was hurt—Jeremy would be dead for sure.

"Where are all those jokes I enjoyed so much on the bridge?" Yoshida laughed. "Or maybe you already realized how this ends." Yoshida stepped forward, and as he planted his foot, his left knee buckled—not enough to make him fall, but it was enough for Jeremy. Yoshida was weakened, too. Kaito straightened, and a thin smile crossed his face. "I've been holding back—you know that. But that's all over now. I'm going to kill you quick and painless this time."

He was lying. Yoshida was never holding back—not on the bridge, not in Kingman, and not here. Jeremy had taken three of his best shots, and he was still standing. If Yoshida could kill him on a whim—if he had the strength to even try it—they wouldn't be talking. Yoshida needed to buy himself more time, and Jeremy just needed to call his bluff.

He closed his fists and started forward, raising his gravity. "You want me dead, Yoshida? Then do it already."

Yoshida didn't answer, but Jeremy could see the truth written in the other man's face—he saw the panic in his eyes. There was nothing Yoshida could do to stop him. Ten more feet and Jeremy would end it.

Somehow, Yoshida was still faster. He reached down and wrapped his fingers through the dark hair of the waif sitting at his feet. She screamed, and Yoshida ripped her to her feet, closing his other hand around her throat, holding her in front of him as a human shield.

"That's far enough!" Yoshida roared, and Jeremy could hear the anger in the other man's voice and the fear laced under it.

Jeremy stopped, still standing ten feet away from Yoshida, but it could have been a mile. He had gone after the king, just like they had planned, but now with the Resonance in his hands, Yoshida had changed the game. Whatever happened next, there was nothing Jeremy could do. He had made his play and lost.

The woman standing between them found her voice through bitter sobs. "Please, Kaito, don't do this!"

"Let her go," Jeremy said.

Yoshida ignored them both, the thin smile spreading again across his face. "Do you know what she is? Do you have any idea what I'm capable of because of her?"

The waif shook in his hands. "Kaito, don't."

"You remember the mountain I dropped on you and your friends this morning?" Yoshida asked. "Can you imagine four of those falling around us here?"

Then for the first time, Jeremy took his eyes off Yoshida. He let himself look at the buildings around them—glittering casinos, each one filled with people—and he understood. The collapse of the Golden Gate Bridge had been a symbol of Yoshida's power, but it wasn't enough to sate him. If he could deliver on his boast now, thousands more would die, and Jeremy would be helpless to stop it.

He looked up at the sky and saw the news helicopters circling above them. Nyx had said Yoshida wanted a show. He would get it. His genocide would be aired around the world, and Kaito Yoshida would make himself the most feared Anom on the planet.

Jeremy looked back at Yoshida and shook his head. "If you do this, I'll kill you."

Yoshida laughed. "You said something like that before in San Francisco."

"No more bullshit!" Jeremy shouted back at

him, "You can either destroy Las Vegas, or you can stop me. You won't have the strength to do both—not even with her."

Suddenly, Jeremy saw a blinding light out of the corner of his eye, and he could feel someone standing behind him. He looked over his shoulder and saw Nyx and Gauntlet. They were both alive, and they were both here. Jeremy started to smile, but all at once, that sense of relief soured in his stomach. He turned back to Yoshida.

Across from him, Kaito Yoshida pulled the waif closer to his body, pushing his hand under her chin. "It seems like you've made my choice for me. Let's find out how much strength I really have!"

Yoshida reached his other hand straight into the air, grabbing at the sky, and the waif began to scream—low and feral—an elongated wail that started from deep inside her. It was more than pain. It was power birthing power. Jeremy could see the woman's white teeth covered in a sheen of pink blood. It fell onto her lower lip and ran from the corners of her mouth, streams of red trailing down to her chin, falling from her eyes like tears and staining her face. Still she screamed louder. She was dying.

Then another sound started. It was a crackling hiss, vibrating in Jeremy's ears and cutting through the center of his chest. He looked up and saw four shadows in the cloudless sky—four towers of black stone in free fall—and there was nowhere to go, and nothing he could do.

The first spire crashed into the Bellagio behind him. The casino exploded in a cloud of gray dust, and the sharp hiss of the falling tower turned into a roar of sound as debris plumed into the air, cascading in every direction. The ground under Jeremy's feet shuddered and rolled, pitching him off balance.

He needed to get his bearings. If he could reach the next tower before it hit, then maybe he could knock it off course, but there was no time. The second tower fell to earth, landing on top of Caesars, obliterating the casino into shrapnel, dust, and sound. Then the third and fourth towers fell, slamming into the earth like dark javelins cast down by invisible gods. As the ground rocked under him, Jeremy fell into the road. The cloud of concrete and glass closed over him, turning the sky to night.

Jeremy rolled onto his back, and punched out with both of his hands, zeroing out his gravity. He pushed against the air around him—the same air around Nyx, and Gauntlet, and even Yoshida —and as the gray silt from the explosions fell back to the earth, it filtered over and around the shield of negative gravity. Jeremy's pulse thrummed in his ear as he pushed against the air, and he could feel the stillness around them—the absolute quiet—even in the middle of the chaos.

Then, Jeremy heard laughing. It was broken by a sharp cough but followed with another thin trill—a sound of satisfied delight—and it turned Jeremy's stomach. He dropped his hands, and the gravity field fell away as he pushed himself up from the ground.

Across from him, Jeremy could see Kaito Yoshida still lying on his back in the road with his arms folded over his chest. Next to Yoshida, the waif was curled up on her side, hugging her legs. She was still alive, but blood dripped from her mouth, pooling on the ground under her face, and her eyes were closed. Honestly, Jeremy didn't care if she was alive or not. She had played her part, and there was nothing else for her to do now. She wasn't the one who needed to answer. Jeremy stepped closer and stood over Yoshida.

Yoshida stopped laughing as he met Jeremy's eyes. "I didn't know if it would work." Yoshida coughed again. "Even up to the very end, I wasn't sure. Then it did. Did you see it?"

Jeremy didn't answer. Instead, he closed his hands, and the gravity field swirled around both of his fists.

"There's no going back," Yoshida said. "Not after this. We changed the world today."

Jeremy raised the gravity field even more, and both of his hands felt cold and heavy, as if he were holding steel dipped in ice—like they were separate from the rest of his body.

Yoshida coughed. "What now? Are you going to drag me back to West Virginia? Or are you still going to kill me like you promised?" Yoshida smiled. "I told you on the bridge, Jeremy, you can't fight against your nature. You're just like Nyx. You're not a killer."

"Not yet." Jeremy dropped to his knee, punched down with his hand, and raised his gravity even more. Then, even through the distance and the cold, he could feel everything. He could feel Yoshida's bones splinter under his hand, and the warm blood spray over his fist and his forearm, until finally, Jeremy felt the dull heaviness of the road connecting with his hand on the other side of Yoshida's skull. It was a quick end. Jeremy couldn't say if it was painless.

He rose to his feet and opened his hand. It was wet and crimson, and bits of hair and bone stuck to his skin. He looked down at Yoshida. Where the man's face should have been, there was a mangle of blood, teeth, and cartilage, the skin torn and caved in toward the center of his skull. Jeremy retched.

"I'm sorry," the waif said next to him, her voice little more than a whisper.

Jeremy turned to look at her. She was lying on her back now, her eyes open, staring at the cloudless sky, and a thin line of blood trickled from the corner of her mouth. Gauntlet stepped over her. He held out his arm, and the crossbow mounted to his wrist folded into place.

Jeremy tried to speak, but his voice caught in his throat. "Wait."

A crossbow bolt shot down into the chest

385

of the waif. Then a second. Jeremy flinched, but that was all he could offer. The woman on the ground blinked twice, slowly, as if she were trying to wake up from a dream, and a low breath of air passed over her lips.

"What are you doing?" Nyx suddenly screamed from behind them, her voice curdling in the air. "Why?"

Jeremy turned to look back at her, and Gauntlet did the same. Nyx was on her feet, both of her arms folded around her stomach and her face twisted.

Jeremy looked back at the two bodies lying in the road, and then he realized the question didn't matter. Nyx had already answered it for herself, and it was an accusation against them both. It was rage given voice. What they had done was murder, and it was indefensible.

"They couldn't live," Gauntlet growled. "And you know that."

Nyx turned away from Jeremy and Gauntlet. Whatever more she wanted to say—if there were words at all—they were lost on the wind. Instead, she started up the street alone, holding her stomach and shaking her head. Beyond her, Jeremy could see the flashing lights of emergency vehicles, their shadowed outlines just visible through the fading cloud of gray dust, and he could hear the wail of sirens filling the desert air.

Jeremy stepped closer to Gauntlet. "This might be our best chance. If we let them take us into custody and send us back to Fort Blaney, I'm done. I won't be able to help you. If you want to escape and look for Piper, we can both leave, right now, and we would never see Reah Labs again."

"And we would both regret it," Gauntlet's voice rattled from behind his helmet. "That's not what I want. I'm not running out on this game. I mean to finish it."

Then Gauntlet started after Nyx, walking in the direction of the lights and sirens, and Jeremy followed after him.

CHAPTER 30

Stuart Ellison stepped out of the helicopter, ducking his head to stay clear of the rotor blades. Agent Hayden followed him, shielding his eyes with one hand from the dust and grit kicked up by the helicopter's downwash. They quickly walked off the helipad, and Ellison looked back over his shoulder. He could see the glossy black exterior of the helicopter contrasted sharply with the white leather seats inside, and painted on its rear panel was a stylized orchid in white—Reah Labs' company logo. It all made him uncomfortable.

Ellison thrived on the olive drabs and navy grays, the stripped-down utility of the military, but the Reah Labs' helicopter was an extravagance. It was a projection of the company's wealth and power, and so just like any other extravagance, Ellison resented it.

"Would you stop moping, Stuart?" Hayden chided next to him. "None of us wants to be here, but it doesn't do any good to wear it around on your face."

It had been a short flight from Kingman, Arizona to Las Vegas, Nevada—less than thirty minutes from the time the helicopter touched down in the desert and Hayden ordered Ellison inside to when they were circling over the Vegas strip, surveying the devastation wrought across the city.

Ellison looked out his window. Below him, he could see the four stone towers rising above the city's skyline, each twice as big as the monolith Yoshida had dropped on top of Kingman. He could also see hundreds of flashing red and blue lights, filling the Vegas streets, radiating out from the four spires. Whatever chaos and urgency were raging below them, at ten thousand feet in the air, Ellison understood the finality of it all. The die had already been cast, and Yoshida had won.

"I should've stayed behind in Arizona and coordinated the rescue efforts. This fight is already over." Ellison leaned back in his chair as the helicopter banked away from the Vegas strip.

"You're right," Hayden said over the helicopter's radio. "And I should've been on a private jet heading back to Fort Blaney, but then your Anoms went off on their own and blew up a casino in Las Vegas, so here we are."

Across from the helipad, Ellison could see a black SUV with tinted windows. Hayden and Ellison approached it together, and Hayden opened the rear door.

"Get in, Stuart," Hayden said. Ellison did as he was told, sliding into the gray leather seat.

The contrast between the sunlight outside of the car and the shaded interior of the SUV was stark, but even half-blinded, Ellison realized he wasn't sitting alone. He blinked his eyes, and slowly, the woman next to him came into focus. She wore a navy-blue blazer and skirt, and her hair was twisted into a tight bun at the back of her head.

She smiled, extending her hand. "Major Ellison, it's nice to finally meet you. My name is Anna Jordan. I'm the chief operating officer for Reah Labs."

Ellison looked down at her hand but left it hanging in the air without taking it; instead, he shifted his weight in his seat. "What am I doing here, Ms. Jordan?"

Hayden climbed into the front seat, closing the door behind him, and the SUV pulled forward, turning onto the access road leading into the city.

In the back seat, Anna dropped her hand but kept her smile. "I imagine you already have some idea of what it is you're doing here, Major."

Ellison kept silent. There was no advantage to giving away his private thoughts so early in the interview. For now, it was better to listen and learn all he could.

Anna pressed on, "I have to tell you, it's nice to finally put a face with a name. I've been reading your status reports for some time, now. We were all relieved you weren't hurt in the Kingman incident."

"The Kingman Incident?" Ellison chafed. "Is that what we're calling it?"

He already knew the woman across from him was lying. Ellison had worked with Reah Labs long enough to understand their paranoia and just how much they valued information. If Anna Jordan was really the chief operating officer for the company, it was impossible this was the first time she was seeing Ellison's face. No doubt they had his picture stored away in a personnel file, but the lie itself didn't matter. Ellison was more concerned with the reasoning behind it. Anna Jordan was trying her best to put him at ease, and that meant she needed him for something. That knowledge gave Ellison an advantage.

He sat back against the leather seat. "Kingman, Arizona was more than an incident. It was a massacre. Forty-two men and women are dead or missing. Those were my men—good soldiers."

Anna folded her hands into her lap. "It was a tragedy for everyone involved, Major, not just your men. Kaito Yoshida was a problem of our own creation, and he should have been resolved long before today. That failure belongs to us, and that's why Reah Labs is coordinating our search-and-rescue efforts with local authorities and the Arizona National Guard as we speak. I can assure you, Major, we're doing everything in our power to save lives at Kingman."

Maybe Anna Jordan was still lying to him, but if nothing else, at least Reah Labs understood the magnitude of their own mistake. It cost Ellison dearly, but if the company was willing to take responsibility for those lives lost, it was more than most would be willing to offer. Even so, Ellison wouldn't make this any easier on them.

He pressed his advantage. "I appreciate your efforts, Miss Jordan, but it doesn't get us one step closer to explaining my presence here. I should be back in Arizona leading the search-and-rescue effort."

Anna twisted around in her seat to better face Ellison, and her smile was gone. "There were other tragedies besides Kingman today, Major. You saw what happened here. It was *your* team of Anoms that went missing from Arizona. It was *your* team that was part of this disaster. For all we know, *your* team may have caused it. Are you still unsure why you're here?"

And there it was. She was more than happy to have Reah Labs take responsibility for Kingman, because Kingman was nothing compared to the devastation in Las Vegas, and they were laying Vegas at *his* feet.

"I ordered them to stand down!" Ellison roared, his face turning scarlet. "They disobeyed my direct orders and went AWOL. So, if you're looking for a scapegoat, Miss Jordan—"

"No one's blaming you." Anna reached out with her hand, laying it on top of Ellison's arm. "I already told you, we have *all* of your reports. In fact, there are pages and pages warning us that this is exactly what would happen. You were very clear when you said your team was not prepared for real-world operations."

"And you ignored every word," Ellison growled.

Anna shook her head. "Another mistake, but you need to understand that we had just as many reports assuring us of the contrary. Colonel McCann insisted his Anoms were ready for combat. I can only assume that's why he deployed them to San Francisco over your objections."

Ellison laughed. "If that's what you think happened, you're dumber than I thought. Hayden and I are the ones who sent the Anoms—"

Hayden turned around sharply in his seat, staring back at Ellison. "You're not listening, Stuart. Let the woman finish."

Anna continued, her voice slow and deliberate. "When you received credible intelligence of Kaito Yoshida traveling to America, Colonel McCann is the one who ordered you to intercept the target over your strenuous objections. No doubt, he was trying to make amends for his previous mistakes in the Battle of Chicago."

Anna reached inside her purse, pulling out a folded paper.

"What's that?" Ellison asked.

"It's your last report from Fort Blaney, submitted immediately before the events in San Francisco." Anna held out the paper to Ellison. "I took the liberty of printing it out to help you remember."

Ellison opened the report and read:

Report: 2236

Subject: ANOM Deployment

Colonel McCann has ordered ANOM TEAM ALPHA to intercept known hostile KAITO YOSHIDA and associates. Once again, I have objected as our team is not prepared for active combat or real-world operations. Colonel McCann continues to ignore those objections. I am left with no choice but to recommend Colonel McCann be removed from the ANOM project and relieved of his command.

Ellison stared down at the paper. "I never wrote any of this."

"That doesn't make it any less true, does it?" Anna took the report out of his hand. "After all, you were the only one telling us not to use the Anoms in active combat. That should count for something, don't you think?"

Ellison hesitated. "If I go along with what's written here, I'm not sure you fully understand the implications."

Anna forced a smile. "I think we understand the implications better than you do, Major, but our country demands someone take responsibility. It was true after Chicago, and it will be true again after Las Vegas. We need to give them someone to excoriate and burn in effigy."

The notion of sacrificing McCann was familiar ground, retread in Ellison's private thoughts countless times over. It came down to the simple fact that the colonel was no longer fit for command, and as much as that felt like a betrayal, the truth was inescapable. McCann's failures had been written on the wall ever since Chicago, and now they were floating in a cloud of smoke and debris over Las Vegas. Even so, Ellison had a responsibility to his men.

"What about Fort Blaney and the men who serve there?" he asked.

Anna turned to look out her window. "The program at Fort Blaney needs to continue, now more than ever. I think we both know Kaito Yoshida won't be the last genetic threat we have to face. That's why we're recommending you for a promotion, Major. We want *you* to take command of Fort Blaney. Reah Labs will secure a new team of Anoms, and this time they'll be hand-picked by you and Agent Hayden. We'll give you all the resources you need to train them as you see fit. Something like Las Vegas won't be allowed to happen again."

Then Ellison knew she was right. Blaney was far too valuable to abandon. If genetic anomalies were truly the future of modern warfare, the Anom training program needed to continue, and Ellison's obligation was clear. He would pay the price leadership demanded of him—even if that price was Colonel McCann.

He reached inside the breast pocket of his uniform and pulled out a thumb drive, holding it out to Agent Hayden. "Then I think you need to see this."

Hayden looked down at the token, his thin lips curling into a smile. "And what have you got there, Stuart?"

"They're computer files stolen from the Knights of the Crusade. Gauntlet gave them to me."

Hayden plucked the flash drive out of Ellison's hand. "And how long have you had this?"

"It doesn't matter," Ellison answered. "As of today, there are no more secrets between us. There can be no more rivalries. If I assume command of Fort Blaney, we need to move forward on the same page. That's the only way this works."

Hayden turned the flash drive over in his hand. "In that case, I think we're going to work out just fine, *Colonel* Ellison. Just fine, indeed."

Ellison sat back against his leather seat. He stared out the windshield of the SUV, smiling as gray smoke filled the Las Vegas sky.

EPILOGUE

"We're five minutes out."

Ethan ignored the man speaking from the front seat of the town car. Five minutes away or five hours, it didn't matter. Ethan was ready now. He was always ready.

Instead of saying as much, he leaned forward to look up through the moonroof of the car. High above the road, Ethan could see the tops of the palm trees lining the street, passing overhead in hypnotic rhythm. He reached inside his jacket pocket and pulled out a small notebook and silver pen. He leafed through the first dozen pages —all covered in words, figures, arrows crossing the page, and bullet points scribbled into the margins—until finally he found a fresh canvas. He quickly jotted down the note: *Palm trees; beautiful?*

Then Ethan glanced over at the man sitting next to him in the back seat of the car. Shane was decidedly *not* beautiful. He wore dark cargo pants, a pair of black combat boots, and a bulletproof vest marked with the word "POLICE" in block letters. It was the closest thing they had to a uniform.

The man in the front seat, Greg, wore the same style pants, the same style boots, and the same bulletproof vest. Both men wore Kevlar helmets and smoke-gray tactical goggles, and they both carried identical MP5 submachine guns strapped across their chests. They may as well have been twins. They were equally disciplined, equally focused, and even the same age—both of them, at least, in their thirties.

Ethan was none of those things, nor did he care to be. They had tried to make him wear the same uniform—once. He refused, and then they never tried again. Instead, he wore whatever he wanted. Today that meant his black suit, white button up, and a razor-thin black necktie. He combed his dark hair straight back from his forehead and finished his look with a pair of all-white Jordans.

His bodyguards still insisted he wear a bulletproof vest, and after some lengthy negotiations, Ethan finally relented as long as he could wear the armor under his suit. Even so, he found the vest uncomfortable. Now he reached up for his collar, trying to pull the Kevlar down away from his throat.

"Less than five minutes, sir," Greg said again from the front seat of the car.

Ethan looked out the window. "I heard you the first time, Greg. You're not a goddamn alarm clock."

"Yes, sir," Greg answered.

"And you both got spiked before we left? I don't want to have to kill one of you," Ethan said.

"Yes, sir," Greg and Shane answered in unison.

Next to Ethan, Shane checked his MP5 again, pulling back the charging handle. Ethan always found it curious watching his bodyguards prepare themselves as they neared their destination. It was like they didn't know what to expect when they first stepped into the car. Five minutes away, and suddenly they clutched their guns tighter as if they were talismans. Maybe it was force of habit. They were afraid the first time they went into combat and still managed to survive, so why not be afraid again?

The town car pulled off the road into the driveway in front of the hotel and slowed to a gradual stop. A man wearing a blue shirt, gray vest, and gray hat approached the rear passenger door. Ethan didn't wait for him. He opened the door himself and climbed out into the California sun. Greg and Shane both followed.

The man in the vest touched his hand to the bill of his cap. "Welcome to the Peninsula, sir."

Ethan was well aware of the strange image they cast to the public eye—his lithe frame, dressed in a suit, flanked on either side by paramilitary bodyguards holding machine guns. At least, to the doorman's credit, he didn't ask the obvious questions: *Who are you? What do you want? Why are you here?* Instead, he stood silently holding open the car door. Ethan could appreciate his restraint.

Inside the hotel, the lobby of the Peninsula was a temple of white marble, punctuated by deep-set leather chairs and dark, mahogany doors. Ethan approached the front desk as Shane and Greg both circled the lobby.

A man in a white jacket and black bowtie stood waiting for Ethan on the other side of the counter, a warm smile stenciled on his face. "Hello, sir, and welcome to the Peninsula. How may I help you?"

Ethan drummed his fingers down on the marble counter. "I need access to one of your rooms. Look up the name Gwendolyn Thomas."

The clerk's smile never faltered. "Sir, I'm afraid I can't do that. We respect the privacy of all our guests—"

"You can do whatever I say." Ethan reached inside his jacket pocket and pulled out a folded slip of paper, slapping it down on the countertop. It was a warrant—or rather it was a forgery of a warrant so close to the real thing that the hotel clerk, his manager, or the judge whose signature they faked on it would never know the difference.

The clerk reached for the paper and started to read.

"You take as long as you need with that. It's

not like we're in a hurry." Ethan turned his back on the hotel clerk, looking around the lobby, counting the patrons.

On the left side of the room, he saw three guests—an older man and woman sitting across from each other on the couches, talking quietly and drinking their coffee. Farther back, there was another man in a dark suit, sitting in a high-backed chair reading a newspaper. On Ethan's right, he counted two more people—a man in a vest standing behind a bar in the lounge, and the lone patron, a balding slob in a blue blazer nursing a tumbler of ice. The clerk at the front desk made six in total. That was good news. There were fewer people than he expected.

Finally, the clerk looked up from the warrant. "Very well, sir. What was that name again?"

Ethan snatched up the paper and slipped it inside his jacket pocket. "Gwendolyn Thomas. I need her room number and a key."

"Yes, sir." The clerk looked down at his monitor and started typing—

The change in him was sudden—quick enough that it took Ethan by surprise. One moment, the clerk was typing a name into his computer. The next, he was leveling a Glock at Ethan's head. One more breath—another fraction of a second—and he might've actually pulled the trigger, but he wasn't fast enough. As quick as it all started, the clerk froze in place, his finger curled around the Glock's trigger, only now he stood like a statue, unmoving, his gun still several degrees away from coming to bear on the center of Ethan's skull.

Ethan raised his voice, "Clear the room!"

Shane and Greg tucked their MP5's into their shoulders and fanned out to either side of the lobby. The doorman outside in the gray vest was the next to attack them. He came barreling through the glass doors screaming like a wild man with both of his arms raised above his head, running at Shane as if he were some kind of possessed linebacker. Shane answered with two quick rounds from the MP5, dropping the doorman to the marble floor. Then more gunfire erupted from Ethan's left—from Greg. In its own way, the noise was reassuring. It was one less thing for Ethan to worry about.

He turned his attention back to the clerk behind the counter. Across from Ethan, the man still stood in place, unflinching, the Glock raised only halfway to its target. Ethan reached for the gun, and the clerk didn't resist him. Ethan pushed the grip out of the clerk's hand, but the other man's index finger was still curled inside the trigger guard. That was all Ethan needed now, to accidentally shoot himself while taking the clerk's gun away. It would be better not to take the chance. Ethan turned the gun sharply to the right, pointing the barrel away from him, until he heard a soft pop—the sound of the clerk's finger dislocating. The other man didn't react. He didn't scream out in pain. He didn't even blink his eyes.

Ethan pulled the Glock free of the clerk's mangled finger and stepped behind the front desk. He looked down at the computer monitor and saw the name *GWENDOLYN THOMAS* at the top of the screen, along with her room number and what appeared to be an itemized copy of her bill.

Ethan reached for a blank key card stacked on top of the desk. He slipped it into the scanner, clicked the button on the monitor, and synced the information to the key. Then he looked at the gold nameplate pinned to the clerk's lapel.

"That's a good day's work, Brett. I appreciate all your help." Ethan jammed the barrel of the Glock under the clerk's jaw and pulled the trigger. Brett fell straight down in a pile, as if he were a ragdoll dropped by a careless child. Ethan looked down at the body, slumped and folded on top of itself, and at the burgundy blood pooling over the white marble flooring. Then he saw his own shoes. Slashes of red stained the white leather, and the rubber soles looked like they were dyed a soft pink from standing in the blood. He would need a new pair when this was all over.

Ethan stepped over the clerk's body, and back around the front desk. In the lobby, Shane and Greg stood back-to-back, their weapons trained in either direction.

"Lobby's all clear, sir!" Shane barked.

"Good. Deploy to the stairwells." Ethan pointed with the barrel of the Glock to the left and right. "I'll take the elevator, and we'll meet in her room."

Shane and Greg stalked off in opposite directions, moving across the lobby as if they were clearing mudbrick houses in some nameless village, their weapons raised to their shoulders, sweeping left and right with every step.

Ethan watched them go, both men hunching forward, leaning into their weapons, and he wondered how effective that posture truly was. *He* never walked around like that—ever—and he was still alive. Maybe it was another tradition they were too afraid to break. Maybe the tradition itself was the only real benefit. Ethan considered pulling out his notebook and scribbling down his thoughts, but there was no time. He would have to remember it for later.

Instead, he walked to the bank of elevators just beyond the lobby, slipped the keycard into the scanner, and pressed the up button. A soft, electronic chime signaled the elevator's arrival. Ethan stepped in front of the gold-plated doors, waiting, but as they pulled apart, a young man dressed in a white jacket dove at him out of the elevator. Ethan stepped aside, and the other man froze in place, halfway into his lunge, completely off-balance. His own weight and momentum took care of the rest. He fell face down against the marble floor with a dull thud. Ethan stepped over him into the elevator. Then he turned around and raised the Glock, firing three quick rounds into the back of the fallen man.

It was a short ride up the elevator. When the doors opened again, Ethan stepped out into an empty hallway. He turned to his left, and the first room on the right side was marked *Green Suite*. If Gwendolyn Thomas was still in the hotel, this is where she would be. He slipped the keycard into the scanner and opened the door.

Even before he saw her, Ethan could hear the woman scream. There was a flash of gray in front of his eyes, but then all at once, she froze in place, and only a small woman with dark curls stood in front of the open door. She wore a pale gray dress with a white apron cinched around her waist, and in her right hand, raised above her head, she held a serrated steak knife. It was aimed at Ethan's chest.

"Sir?" Greg's voice came from the open doorway behind him. "Do we have her?"

Ethan turned around to see the other man standing in the hallway. Greg was breathing heavily, his MP5 held down by his waist, a splatter of blood smeared across his face and neck.

"She's not here, Greg. We wouldn't be fighting maids and bellhops if she were." Ethan hammered his fist against the doorjamb. "Where's Shane?"

Greg shook his head. "No answer on his radio."

"Then he's already dead. I guess you're lucky she ran away to the left instead of the right." Ethan turned back to face the maid still frozen in the room. "I want you to keep the hallway clear. I'll only be another minute."

"Yes, sir," Greg answered, raising his weapon to his shoulder.

Ethan reached for one of the maid's dark curls that had fallen in front of her eyes, gently tucking it behind her ear. "I'm sure you have so many questions." He smiled at the frozen woman. "Questions like, 'Why can't I move?' or, 'Why can't I call out for help?' The short answer, I'm afraid, is me. The longer answer involves the chemistry inside your brain, but we don't have to dwell on that now." Ethan reached for another strand of hair, moving it out of the woman's face. "People say the experience can be terrifying. That's why I'm explaining it to you, so you don't have to be afraid."

Ethan stepped back, reached into his pocket, and pulled out a jackknife. He pushed up with his thumb, and the blade flipped open, locking into place. In the quiet of the room, he could hear the woman's breath quicken.

"I wonder if she's still in there with you." Ethan stepped closer, whispering in the woman's ear. "Is she still rattling around inside your head, telling you what to do, or did she toss you aside like she does with all the others? I hope not. Otherwise, this might be cruel."

Ethan put his hand behind the woman's neck and dragged his knife across her throat. She made no reaction—no last, desperate gulp for air. Instead, she stood perfectly still as a sheet of red poured from her neck, turning her gray uniform wet with blood. Finally, her eyes rolled back, and she collapsed to the floor.

Ethan stepped away and loosened his necktie, pulling it free. He used it to wipe the sheen of blood off his knife, and then he carefully folded the blade back into place, tucking it inside his pocket. He dropped the dirty tie to the floor.

"Call someone to clean this up. We're leaving," Ethan said.

"Yes, sir," Greg answered.

Ethan walked out of the room, turning down the hallway towards the elevators.

Greg lifted his radio, looking back into the suite at the body. "Location clear. One man down in the west stairwell. Clean-up needed. Incubus is on the move."

ACKNOWLEDGE-
MENTS

I want to thank my amazing wife Vanessa and our two children, Aidan and Fiona, for their unending support as I've chased my dream of writing.

I also stand indebted to an incredible group of "Beta Readers" who have patiently critiqued my writing, and buoyed my spirits along the way: Vanessa, Michael and Nan, Courtney and Doug, Whitney and Joe, Matt and Sarah, Jeff and Jackie, Jeff and Kara, George and Shannon, Ryan and Karen, Eleasa, Mike Shaw, and Michael "Mourgus" Morgan. I truly believe none of my writing success would be possible without your help. I am grateful beyond measure.

I am particulary thankful to the dedicated members of the Pitman Writers' Guild who have challenged me as a writer, and helped me become better at my craft, and to Michael Morgan, for troubleshooting my failing PC when I was afraid all hope was lost.

Once again, I am thankful to Liam Carnahan and his team at Invisible Ink Editing for fixing my mistakes, and to Andrea Vraciu for designing another brilliant cover, and a worthy successor to her artwork for ANOM: Awakening.

For more information about my writing and future installments
in the ANOM series, please check out my website at:

www.jasonrjames.com

Made in the USA
Las Vegas, NV
19 September 2021